To Treasure an Heiress

Books by Roseanna M. White

LADIES OF THE MANOR

The Lost Heiress
The Reluctant Duchess
A Lady Unrivaled

SHADOWS OVER ENGLAND

A Name Unknown
A Song Unheard
An Hour Unspent

THE CODEBREAKERS

The Number of Love
On Wings of Devotion
A Portrait of Loyalty

Dreams of Savannah

THE SECRETS OF THE ISLES

The Nature of a Lady
To Treasure an Heiress

TREASURE

AN

HEIRESS

ROSEANNA M. WHITE

BETHANYHOUSE

a division of Baker Publishing Group
Minneapolis, Minnesota

© 2022 by Roseanna M. White

Published by Bethany House Publishers
11400 Hampshire Avenue South
Minneapolis, Minnesota 55438
www.bethanyhouse.com

Bethany House Publishers is a division of
Baker Publishing Group, Grand Rapids, Michigan

Printed in the United States of America

Library of Congress Cataloging-in-Publication Data
Names: White, Roseanna M., author.
Title: To treasure an heiress / Roseanna M. White.
Description: Minneapolis, Minnesota : Bethany House Publishers, a division of
    Baker Publishing Group, [2022] | Series: The secrets of the isles ; 2
Identifiers: LCCN 2021032983 | ISBN 9780764237195 (paperback) | ISBN
    9780764239892 (casebound) | ISBN 9781493436101 (ebook)
Subjects: GSAFD: Adventure fiction. | Love stories. | LCGFT: Christian fiction.
Classification: LCC PS3623.H578785 T62 2022 | DDC 823/.92—dc23
LC record available at https://lccn.loc.gov/2021032983

Scripture quotations are from the King James Version of the Bible.

This is a work of historical reconstruction; the appearances of certain historical figures are therefore inevitable. All other characters, however, are products of the author's imagination, and any resemblance to actual persons, living or dead, is coincidental.

Cover design by Jennifer Parker
Cover photography by Todd Hafermann Photography, Inc

Author is represented by The Steve Laube Agency.

Baker Publishing Group publications use paper produced from sustainable forestry practices and post-consumer waste whenever possible.

To Jennifer Malone Stump,
who ran through childhood with me,
created stories with me,
and found adventure with me in the least likely places.
We never dug up any pirate gold,
but we found treasures untold in our imaginations.

The Isles of Scilly

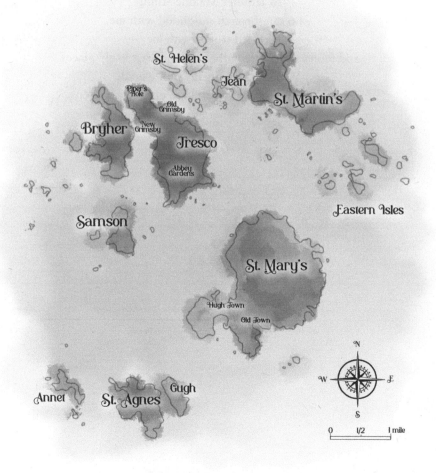

St. Helen's

Tean

St. Martin's

Piper's
Hole

Old
Grimsby

Bryher   New
Grimsby

Tresco

Abbey
Gardens

Eastern Isles

Samson

St. Mary's

Hugh Town

Old Town

N
W   E
S

0   1/2   1 mile

Annet   St. Agnes   Gugh

Cornwall due East 28 miles >

Prologue

P rince . . . or pirate? Rupert felt like neither as he stood on the bluff, the sea beckoning him, the wind whirling about him, and the most beautiful woman in all the world pressed against his chest, her cheeks damp with tears. He hadn't expected this when he came to the Isles of Scilly after being exiled from England for his service to the Crown. He'd expected brothers-in-arms. Compatriots. Soldiers.

"Briallen." Her name whispered from his lips like a blessing, just as she had whispered into his life, into his heart. Only an island lass—that's what society would say, were it here to say it. And his family . . . He could only imagine what his family would think of her. His father, German prince Frederick V. His mother, daughter of James VI of Scotland and I of England. They would look on his precious primrose and see only a thorny vine trying to ensnare him.

She was anything but that. She was his wings. She was his soul. She was his heart. The only person in all his one and thirty years to make him crave home and hearth above the next battle, the next adventure. The only person in all his one and thirty years to make him think it mattered not whether he ever had a palace or an estate or a relative on a throne—that he would live on this bare rock of an island all his days, no luxuries beyond his next breath, if he could live there with her.

He pressed a kiss to the lips he had memorized with his own. "I love you."

"And I you." Her fingers smoothed back a lock of his hair that the wind had torn free, her gaze following its path as she tucked it back into the binding at the nape of his neck. Her lips pressed tight together.

She wouldn't ask him to stay, he knew she wouldn't. But she must be thinking it, even as he was.

His own glance darted to the shore, the water, his ship at the ready there in deeper waters, a rowboat waiting to take him to it. They must sail, and soon. Mucknell had already bidden farewell to his own wife, and neither the tide nor the pirate admiral would wait for any man—even if that man *was* a prince. "I could stay. What do the courts of Portugal or the waters of the Caribbean have that Tresco does not?"

Briallen breathed a laugh and rested her head against his chest. "Wealth and treasure and enemies of the Crown for you to rout, that's what." Her hand pressed there, just above his heart. "You cannot stay, my love. There is nothing for you here."

"There is you. You are everything." Sweet words he had never imagined himself saying—or meaning, at any rate. His whole life, it seemed, had been war. Even as a child he'd trained for it. As only a child, he'd found it. One and thirty, but already he'd been fighting seventeen years. What room did such a life have for love? "Come with me, then."

He'd asked it before. But as before, she shook her head. "To the courts in Portugal? And leave my parents to face the winter on their own? You know I cannot. Perhaps, had we more time to plan for them . . . but I cannot leave them." His darling pulled away a few inches, tilting her head back so she could look him in the eye. "I will be here when you return for me. I will wait a thousand years if I must."

8

A smile teased his lips. It was likely to be two years, at least, before he could return. The waters around the Isles of Scilly had grown too risky for the pirate fleet, what with Cromwell setting so many of his own hirelings to patrol for them. If he meant to work for the uncle who was king, the cousin who would next rule, he must go. Find richer waters to prowl. Do his part to restore England to its rightful heir.

But *must* held little allure compared to this need to stay with his young bride. His parents would say he shouldn't have married her. His uncle, his cousin would say the same. They'd say he'd ruined his own future hopes by lashing himself to an island lass. If he *did* take her with him to Portugal, it would be pure misery for her.

He'd give it all up and more for her. But it was his sworn duty now to provide for her. And to do that, he must go. There was no living to be earned here on Tresco, not anymore. He sighed, pressed one more kiss to her lips, and reached for the bag at his feet. "I have something for you."

"Rupert." How could her voice be at once chiding and touched? "You've already given me more than I could have ever dreamed."

"Well, you will have to learn to dream bigger." Grinning, he pulled out the trinket box he'd long carried with him. Before, it had held cuff links and medallions and buckles and other assorted whatnot. Now, it held all the coins of silver and gold he could scrounge together. He pressed it into her hands. "'Tisn't much. But enough, I pray, to see you through until I return with a crown or two for that ivory brow of yours."

She laughed but didn't lift the lid. She merely traced a finger over his crest, engraved in the wood and leafed in gold. "I will treasure it."

"Nay—*use* it." He leaned down, put his mouth at her ear. Too many sailors loitered on the shore, and one never knew when the wind might snatch one's words and deliver them to another's ear. "If it is not enough, if something happens to me, if you need more . . . inside you will also find a key to fortune enough to set you up for life."

9

She would know exactly what he meant. But her eyes flashed not with greed but with a stony determination. "Nay. I'll not be stealing from Mucknell after all he has done for you, dearovim."

And this was why he loved her. "Only if your survival depends upon it. I would sooner you be a thief than a corpse."

"And I would sooner die of hunger and fly into the arms of my Savior than feast like a queen in the company of the devil." The fire in her eyes flamed down again, turned to a merry twinkle. "But perhaps that is too hard for you to understand, *Rupert le diable*."

He made a show of wincing at the nickname he had earned by the age of three, given to him by his tutors. Rupert the Devil. Yes, he had been a little terror. And, pray God, he still was, to his family's enemies. But not to her.

A shout came up from the beach, along with the frantic waving of his first mate's arm.

Briallen surged forward, pressed a fierce kiss to his lips, and then leapt away, the box clutched to her chest. "Go. Now, before I forget why you must."

He nodded, pivoted, and started down the sandy path toward his ship, his men, and his only hope of a fortune worthy of her. But he had to pause at the bottom and look up once more.

She stood there on the hillock, the wind whipping her dark hair into a storm of onyx, the sky a startling blue behind her, the box still held tight against her chest. He would picture her just so every day. An image to carry with him. He would imagine her standing just like this every morn, every night, with every tide. Waiting for him.

He hastened away, so that he could hasten back to her side. It may be a year, or two, or three, but he would come back to Tresco again. And he would take his princess with him, wherever next he went.

1

11 JULY 1906
SAMSON, ISLES OF SCILLY

Beth Tremayne crept silently through the creaking doorway of the abandoned cottage as the first strokes of dawn painted the sky over the islands. This had been home for most of the summer—this leaking, moldering hovel that hadn't been in use for half a century. She'd come through that door with the dawn dozens of times, crawled into that corner to steal a few hours of sleep, keeping one ear always alert to the sound of anyone coming her way. Once or twice she'd had to make a quick getaway.

No more. She stood here today not in the trousers she'd pilfered a decade ago when her brother outgrew them, but in her usual day dress. Rather than a desperation not to be seen, she had to get home to Tresco before the others awoke, so that no one would know she was gone. She couldn't frighten them again. She couldn't—not with her grandmother only back on her feet a few days.

Guilt didn't just pierce at the thought of the unknown ailment that had felled Mamm-wynn just feet from this door a week ago—it pummeled her. Mamm-wynn, precious Mamm-wynn, one of the only people she had left in the world. Injured not by the heartless,

11

greedy snakes from whom Beth had thought she had to keep them safe, but by her own aging body, her own endless worry.

Beth had done it to her. Not the reprobate Lorne or the cold-blooded Scofields. *Her.*

She stirred herself and hurried to the corner of the cottage, pried up the rotting board. Last week, when she saw Oliver's letter telling her that Mamm-wynn was unconscious, she hadn't bothered to pause for such trifles as her supplies—she'd simply run to the sloop she'd hidden away and sailed home. But she couldn't risk anyone else finding these things. No other island lads needed to get caught up in this business. And if the other treasure hunters found her maps, her notes . . .

No, that wouldn't do at all.

The board gave way under her hands, and inside the cubby it covered, she found exactly what she'd left there a week ago. The map she'd drawn herself and marked with the locations she'd searched. A few of the letters from the pirate John Mucknell to his wife that she'd copied and made notes on. A book from her grandfather's library that told of all the old, abandoned sites around the isles— prime locations, in her view, for a pirate to have stashed his cache.

A warm summer breeze whispered through the door she'd left open, reminding her to hurry. Beth shoved the lot of it into the satchel she'd brought for that purpose and hurried back out of the cottage, down the hill to where the *Naiad* was anchored—plain as day, there for anyone to see if they looked.

She checked the sun rather than her watch. Just peeking its head above the horizon. Her brother would be stirring soon, ready to take part in the weekly gig race around Tresco. She had to hurry.

The winds were favoring her this morning, though, and she soon had the *Naiad* under tack and gliding through the familiar waters, back to its home in the quay on Tresco. No one else was there when she returned, praise God. The fishermen were out already, the racers not yet arrived. She dropped anchor and secured her sloop, dashing back up the path toward home. Housewives might be up, stirring

12

fires and clattering about for their morning tea, but only in their own kitchens. No one was out on the streets to call a hello. No one to wonder where she'd been this time.

No one to chastise her yet again for always craving a taste of Elsewhere, for seeking adventure when she ought to be tucked snug in her bed, content where she was. Or—the one she was awaiting with dread—lecturing her about *still* chasing Mucknell's treasure when it had already cost the Tremayne family so much. Oliver would no doubt deliver that speech any day. The only reason he hadn't already was because he was distracted with his new fiancée.

God bless Libby Sinclair.

She could hear Mrs. Dawe humming in the kitchen when Beth slipped in through the garden door, but she tiptoed by, up the back stairs, and made it to her bedroom without running into Oliver or his guests. *His*, not hers. If it were up to her, she'd toss the lords out on their ears.

Well, she had no argument in particular with Libby's brother, Lord Telford. Except that he was inexplicably friends with that greedy, thieving buffoon, Lord Sheridan.

Her fingers tightened around the strap of her satchel. Lord Insufferable Sheridan would probably snatch it all from her if he saw it. Paw through it. Exclaim over each and every article—*her* search, *her* clues, *her* finds.

But it wasn't just hers anymore. She'd drawn Oliver and their cousin Mabena into it without meaning to—and Mabena had brought her employer, Libby, here. That part, at least, was good. But the fact that *everyone* now knew about Mucknell's treasure . . .

Well, they thought they did. They knew about the silverware they'd dug up together last week. But they seemed to think that was the only piece of the hoard she'd had a lead on.

She knew better—and so did the Scofields, the family she'd thought could be trusted with it all, given that her best friend was the daughter of said family. But they'd betrayed her.

For a moment she stared at her bed, which still felt too soft to her after weeks of sleeping on the ground. Then she shook herself. She had work to do, and only a few minutes in which she could do it. With silent efficiency, she fished the key to her desk drawer from its hiding place in the heel of her shoe, opened it, and slid these missing pieces into her collection of research, then stashed the weatherworn satchel out of sight.

But she hesitated before closing and locking the drawer again, her fingers hovering over the book that rested on top of her stack. *Treasure Island*. It had been her best friend during the first part of her hunt—and then the missing piece that had bothered her endlessly. She snatched it out, grabbed a few sheets of clean paper and a pencil, and then locked everything away again.

Ollie was up, whistling his way down the corridor. She gave him time to exit before following his invisible footprints downstairs, out the door. He'd have aimed himself straight down the village streets, toward the water and his teammates. Beth turned instead to the bluff, where she could see the racers go by. She chose a spot that would afford her the best view, the same spot where Morgan, their elder brother, had always watched the races.

She settled herself to the ground and ran her fingers over her book.

All right, not *her* book. It was Oliver's—not that her brother had so much as picked it up in a decade. Still, she felt guilty for all the pencil markings she'd put in the margins and crowded between the lines in the last few months. Not guilty enough that she stopped doing it . . . but enough that she'd placed an order for a new one for him. It ought to be arriving any day.

And it wasn't as though she'd set out to ruin it. She'd borrowed it from his shelves simply because *Treasure Island* seemed a rather apropos read when she realized she was on her own treasure hunt, here on her own island. She'd had it with her when she sat in this very spot to read the post that had come for her from her friends the Scofields in London. A letter that had been full of information on what she ought to be looking for, and how she ought to get them

14

more information. She'd needed somewhere to write it all down. Somewhere that wouldn't cause Ollie or Mamm-wynn to bat an eye at her—which they would certainly do if she carried a thick letter about with her.

And poor *Treasure Island* had been a ready conspirator.

She smiled a bit as she opened the book and drew out the blank paper she'd just tucked in a few minutes before. From her pocket she pulled the pencil. For a moment she stared at the mocking stretch of white, and then she screwed her mouth up and started writing.

Once upon a time, in the islands called Scilly, lived a girl called Elizabeth, who everyone called Beth. Brought up on the sea and the granite and the isles, Beth sought adventure above all. And she found it. First, by exploring every rock and rill of her island home. And then, when the call of romance grew loud in her ears, she turned her sights toward the mainland. But no true love awaited her there, and so home she came once more.

Then, one day, this island lass found a treasure map hidden away in her grandfather's house, which had once been the home of a pirate king. "Could it be?" said she. "The long-lost treasure of Mucknell the Menace?" Knowing not whether she should dare to hope, she remembered her dearest friend from her year at school—sweet Emily, whose father was of great renown. "A trustee is he," thought Beth to herself, "of the greatest museum in all the land. If it be true, he will know, and if false, he shall advise."

And so off she sent her map to grand old London Town, where the earl of renown declared, "By Jove! Follow this map, dear girl, and it'll lead you to the pirate's hoard! And anything you find, you may send my way. For I have a friend who will pay you well."

Visions of Seasons swimming in her head, fair Beth set out to unlock the secrets of the map. But wanting to keep her family from thinking her foolish, she convinced her brother, Good Vicar Oliver, to let her spend the summer on the next island over, so in secrecy she might search.

Little did she know that this friend of the earl was none other than the Nefarious Marquess of SheriDoom. And when he heard

15

that pirate treasure could be found in the isles, he sent his hench-
man with vile intent. Lorne was the henchman's name, and black
was his soul.

Now, Beth had spent her whole life long learning every secret of
her island home. Quickly she gathered every clue to be found, which
lit a fuse of envy in evil Lorne. "I must," said he, "find the secrets
too." And so he hired an innocent lad to aid him.

But when the lad realized how dark was Lorne's heart, he cried,
"Nay!" and tried to break free, receiving as a reward a hero's death
at the hand of a villain true.

She pulled her pencil from the page, squeezing her eyes shut.
Poor Johnnie. He'd deserved so much more than what he'd gotten.
He'd deserved a future, a wife, a brood of children to run over the
islands just as he had once done. Not a blow to the head in Piper's
Hole and a mother who would mourn him the rest of her days.

Beth sniffed and opened her eyes again, staring at the page. It
was rubbish. She'd never let another soul look at it.

But she had to get it down. Tell Johnnie's tale, and her own
stupid part in it. Sucking in a breath, she bent over the page again.

Devastated by the downfall of her young friend, fair Beth knew what
to do when a threat landed on her own rented doorstep: "Tread with
care, O Lady Fair, or yours will be the next to pay."

Frightened for the good vicar her brother and their aging
grandmother, Beth made the only decision she could. To her sloop
she flew, with supplies to see her through, and off to another isle
she sailed. Using the secrets she'd learned of her home, she hid
her boat and herself during every day, and by night she sailed
and searched.

But what Beth couldn't know was that her cousin came home
while she was away, bringing with her another lady called—

No, the rhythm of that was all wrong. Beth gnawed on her lip
and crossed out the last line.

16

But while Beth hid away, home came her cousin, alarmed at the cessation of letters. And in her care was another lady so fair, also called Elizabeth, it seemed. Into Beth's rented cottage the two soon settled . . . and into Beth's sad troubles they stumbled. For the wicked son of the earl mistook one for the other when he came to check on her finds. "The treasure," he demanded of this second Elizabeth, "or soon you will pay. For SheriDoom demands his prize."

So, the unwitting Elizabeth stepped into Beth's shoes . . . and into good Oliver's heart. While they strove to solve the mystery, they soon fell in love, bringing hope from the ashes of tragedy.

But their cousin was struck, and their grandfather too, and their grandmother dear fell ill in shock. So, home Beth flew to those she loved best, only to discover that even that refuge had been compromised.

For the Nefarious SheriDoom had descended upon the isles. He had stolen fair Beth's most prized possession already and now threatened to steal any treasure she found. For no amount of pirate gold could satiate his greed, and no price was too steep for his seeking.

Together, the friends soon followed the map to a castle of crumbling stone. Down they dug, in search of the silver that the earl of renown said they'd find. And there, in a crate of splintering wood, branded with the crest of the pirate king, did it lie. Silver—not nuggets nor bars nor doubloons, but fashioned as knives, forks, and spoons. With "Elizabeth" etched into every piece—the gift, one time, for a queen.

But the wicked earl's son and the vile henchman Lorne had put their evil heads together by now. They captured Beth's cousin, along with her beau, and soon came for Beth as well. But it was Elizabeth they found and mistook her again and swept her away to a cave. Only by the grace of the good God above, and the foresight of Beth's valiant grand-dame, were this lady fair and the good vicar able to triumph over the vicious Lorne.

In shackles that fellow was soon marched away—but the tale was far from complete. For the wicked son of the earl got away, and SheriDoom hunkered to wait. "We'll find the rest," he threatened and boomed, "and then to my coffers it goes."

*Fair Beth swore it wouldn't but swore it in silence. For she
knew that wisdom said, "Wait." There was clearly more treasure
waiting to be found, treasure that would bring the hunters to her
door. And only one way to fend them all off: she must be the first to
discover it.*

Motion caught her eye, and she looked up, watching the two
five-man gigs race by on their outbound leg of the race. She watched
them until they were out of sight and then looked back to her paper.
And heaved a sigh. Ridiculous, of course. She'd known it would be.
Everything she tried to write down was.

She folded the papers and shoved them back into *Treasure Island*,
then flipped through the familiar typed pages, to the last note she'd
scrawled in the margin before she'd accidentally dropped the tome
in her harried flight from St. Mary's Island nearly two months ago.

Thieves will end up with empty pockets.

She'd scratched the words onto the page in a rage, which had
boiled down to a low fury while she was hunkering out of sight on
Samson for six weeks, trying to find the long-lost pirate treasure
without putting Ollie or Mamm-wynn at risk. Living on her wits,
her fishing skills, and the store of necessities she'd taken with her
to the abandoned cottages. That fury had flared up again, though,
when she came back to Tresco a week ago.

When she saw, in her own house, the man behind the thievery.
Guest of her brother. Unapologetic and arrogant and obstinately
refusing to see reason when she told him point-blank that the trinket
box the Scofields had sold to him had not been theirs to sell. And
she had not given them permission. It was stolen goods, nothing
more. But the irritating man wouldn't listen.

"Well now. This is quite a vista, isn't it? I daresay I wouldn't grow
tired of that view. Or, well . . . I suppose I might. Any view can grow
old after time enough. Don't you think?"

Her shoulders went tight as springs at the very voice she least
wanted to hear, but she didn't give Lord Arrogance Personified

Sheridan the pleasure of seeing her reaction. Nor did she dignify his observation with a reply.

Even if it *was* the very thing she'd thought herself countless times. She loved the islands. They'd always been home. But they weren't *all*. There was so much more world out there, just begging to be seen. Explored. Discovered.

Why could her brother never understand that?

Her silence didn't seem to shout to Lord Sheridan that he ought to keep on meandering, unfortunately. He crouched down beside her, his gaze on the water but his presence so very *there* that she couldn't help but scowl at him.

This was all his fault. All of it. Not, of course, that she'd found those letters from the islands' most famous pirate in the foundation of her grandfather's cottage. But he was the one who promised the Scofields he'd buy anything they found. He was the one who threw so much money at them that they thought they ought to start a bidding war with some other antiquities hound with more money than sense. He was the one—blast him—who had offered such a ridiculous sum for her most prized heirloom that the Scofields sold it to him without even asking her first.

She'd have it back. She would. It was the last thing her mother had given her—a gift for her seventeenth birthday, just a week before her mother's death. He'd had no right to buy it. It wasn't for sale, it oughtn't to have been sold. It was stolen goods, and if she thought she had a hope of winning in a court of law against a family as powerful and connected as Lord Scofield's, she'd sue them, and him, for its return.

But an island miss, a vicar's sister, a girl with nothing more to her family name than a small estate on the Cornwall mainland, wouldn't stand a chance against an earl and a marquess.

Besides. The Earl of Scofield may be a money-grubbing thief, but his daughter was one of her dearest friends.

As for the Marquess of Sheridan . . . he'd made himself comfortable on her bluff, just as he had in her home, and reclined back on his elbows as if he hadn't a care in the world. As if his cutthroat determination to collect antiquities hadn't very nearly gotten her killed once already. As if he had some right to be here still, "helping" search for more of Mucknell's treasure. As if he had a claim to it.

"Remarkable, really." He nodded to the sea.

She blinked, not certain what conversation he'd been having in his head while she flayed him in her own, but she knew that his observation didn't directly follow his thought about growing tired of vistas. "What is?" She mentally slapped herself for asking. In their weeklong acquaintance, she'd already learned that it took nothing more than a single word to get Lord Sheridan talking.

So why in the world couldn't she keep her stupid mouth from giving him those single words?

"The color of the water. It looks nearly Caribbean, doesn't it?" His lips twitched up. "Were I Libby—Lady Elizabeth, I mean—I'd wonder why. Some . . . what's-it-called or such in the water? Micro . . . things. Or minerals. Maybe you care for such things too?"

He glanced over at her with a lift of his auburn brows.

She made a point of looking away, toward the waters. Had she met him some other way, in some other place, perhaps she'd think him handsome. If he weren't a low-down, mean-spirited, dirty rotten thief. "No. Oliver has always been the one to ask such questions." A memory cartwheeled through her mind, pulling a smile to her lips despite the company. "My mother always marveled at how the three of us were so different. She said that Morgan would be eternally grateful for the beauty of the water, as if it were a special gift from God to him. Oliver would wonder why it was so blue, and I . . ."

Blast. She hadn't meant to talk to him. She *never* meant to talk to him. So why had she ended up doing just that each and every day since she came home?

"And you?"

She sighed. "I would wonder where the water could take me."

20

He chuckled. Probably thinking her a stupid girl, full of dreams that would never come true.

But no. His chuckle wasn't cruel, and she wasn't so unfair as to pretend it was. It was empathetic. As was his smile. "That *is* the thing about it. I think, anyway. The going, I mean. Or rather, that it's a veritable portal to anywhere in the world."

Beth closed the book in her lap and watched the waves roll in. "It is the thing, indeed."

He nodded, stretched out his long legs, and crossed them at the ankles. "Do you miss him?"

She drew in a long breath. No question about which "him" he meant. Morgan had been gone for only two years—finally snatched by one of the ailments that had plagued him since he was a lad— but she felt the ache of it daily, just as she felt the gaping hole of their parents, who had died only a year earlier. "He never missed a Wednesday morning race. He could never participate—he was too weak. But he'd always be right here in this spot, no matter how ill he was. If he couldn't walk down, he'd ask Mr. Dawe to wheel him in his chair. He had to cheer on Ollie." She breathed a laugh and shook her head. "In a lot of ways, Morgan lived through us."

His nod was simple. Sincere. "And still does."

Double blast. That was the sort of observation that made it very hard to remember that she didn't like him one bit.

"Do you ever race?" He nodded to the point, around which the rowers had still not appeared. "Or—well, I suppose I don't know if you could. If they'd let you, I mean. That is—girls. Are they allowed?"

She chuckled at the thought of pulling at the oars, sandwiched between her brother and his best friend, Enyon Thorne. Or even funnier, in the opposing boat with Casek Wearne—the giant of a headmaster who had long been Oliver's rival and was now betrothed to their cousin Mabena.

Leave for a few weeks, and the strangest things could happen.

Who'd have ever thought tempestuous Mabena would end up with him?

But then, who'd have thought that while she was away, her brother would fall in love too?

She shook her head. "It's never come up. Not to say it won't at some point, I'm certain. But for now, none of us girls have any desire to get in the middle of that. Far more fun to watch, and then to take our gigs out later without all that male competitiveness."

"But you watch from here? I think—didn't Lady Elizabeth say something about the beach?"

Lady Elizabeth—the girl whose finger now bore Mother's ring. Apparently one of the reasons she'd been happy to come to the Scillies with Mabena was to escape a marriage to the very gentleman beside Beth now, which Lord Telford—Sheridan's best friend—was trying to arrange. *That* motivation Beth could well imagine.

She sneaked another look at his lordship. Handsome enough, yes. But he was a blithering dunderhead, so obsessed with his archaeological and historical pursuits that he didn't care who he stepped on to get his hands on his next prize. It served him right to have his would-be fiancée snatched from his grasp by Beth's brother.

And just to poke at him, she ignored the question about why she preferred to watch from the bluff versus the beach and said, "Speaking of Libby. I expect you're quite fond of her."

"Oh. Ah." He cleared his throat, but it did nothing to keep a blush from staining his neck. "She's . . . well, a fine young lady. To be certain. And your brother! They make a fine pair. Wish them every happiness. And more."

He didn't exactly sound heartbroken. More's the pity. "More than every happiness? Wouldn't that then get into things that are *not* happiness? Rather rude of you."

The man didn't seem to know when he was being insulted. He laughed and sat back up. "You know what I mean."

"Do I?" She traced a finger along the engraving on the cover, with its gold leaf spelling out the letters. $T - R - E - A - S - U - R - E$.

22

"For all I know, you wish them ill. After all, Lord Telford brought you here to convince her to marry you, didn't he? And from what I'm told, you were game."

"Well. Somewhat. That is—willing, I suppose, at the time." He shrugged and lifted a hand to shield his eyes from the morning sun. "She's a nice girl. Deserves a husband who will respect her. Indulge her . . . unique interests."

The fact that she would spend the entire day after the gig race in the botanical gardens, he meant, studying and drawing each specimen she could find, and then adding the Latin names to them when she joined Mamm-wynn for tea. With Oliver's help, of course. He'd been tending the exotic plants in the Abbey Gardens alongside the official gardener, Mr. Menna, for years. "And you really don't mind that husband being my brother instead of you?"

Because she was none too certain they should trust him as Ollie had so quickly done. He might *seem* affable enough, but they oughtn't to forget that he'd employed two different men to hunt for any artifacts they could find related to Mucknell and one of his associates, Prince Rupert of the Rhine, knowing well how fierce the competition could become. No, not just knowing it—*counting* on it. Hoping for it. He had *deliberately* pitted two artifact hunters against each other.

Johnnie Rosedew had died because of this man's drive to possess what wasn't his.

His lordship could say all he wanted that he'd never sanctioned such actions. Just as he could say he'd make no attempt to hold Libby to the engagement her brother had tried to arrange. But saying things didn't make them so.

Yet he looked utterly sincere—and charmingly self-deprecating too—when he said, "Actually . . . I'm a bit relieved. She's terrifying sometimes—Libby. When any wildlife is at stake. You may have noticed? Lectured me for an hour last Christmas about some moss my digs had upended. Or lichen? Maybe it was a fern."

Another snort of laughter snuck its way from her throat. Libby would no doubt remember exactly which specimen had been in danger. "I can't say as I find it particularly terrifying, though I've certainly noticed the tendency. But then, we all tend to be rather protective of our plants around here." She swept out a hand to encompass the islands at large. "Without the flower industry, the Scillies would still be poverty-stricken, as we were centuries ago."

His gaze followed the circle of her hand and then landed back on her. "Mm. So rich in history though. I'm hoping to explore while I'm here. The Druid cairns, I mean. Not just for Mucknell and Rupert. They're everywhere, aren't they? The stones?"

"You can hardly take a walk without stumbling over one." Her fingers twitched on the cover of the book. Druids weren't her particular interest right now, nor were cairns or standing stones or anything else so ancient. She wanted to explore history only two-and-a-half centuries past—but she still thought Mucknell may have used some of the more ancient sites for his own hiding places, and it wouldn't do to have Sheridan stumbling across them. "My grandfather will take you about, if you wish. And tell you any tale you'd like about them. Some may even be true." Tas-gwyn could be trusted to steer his lordship wherever Beth asked him to.

When Sheridan grinned, she could nearly believe he was just an oblivious, coddled lord who really hadn't meant any ill. "There's always a kernel, right? Of truth, I mean. In every legend and all the lore."

"Well. Depending on your definition of *kernel*." Tas-gwyn Gibson's tales were far more imagination than anything, much of the time, and all the more entertaining for his embellishments. Her favorite pastime as a girl—other than exploring the islands—was curling up in his lap and listening to story after story. He would take her away with those tales, without ever leaving his house.

And when Tas-gwyn wasn't there to regale her, Mother had been the one to pull her close and whisper her favorite stories. So many times had Beth snuggled close and said, "Tell me of the pirate and the princess!"

And no matter how many times she'd told it before, her mother would smile, smooth a hand over Beth's hair, and settle in for the telling. *"Once there lived, and once there was, a beautiful maiden at the edge of the world. She made her home here on the islands, where the sea surrounded them day and night, bringing them life and bringing them death. And one day, it brought her a prince. . . ."*

She flipped open the cover of *Treasure Island* again, barely able to stop from reaching for the nub of a pencil in her pocket. So many times had she tried to write down that story. Too many to count. But it was never right. She could never capture the cadence of her mother's voice, the way she would drop it to a whisper in one moment and then imitate the crashing of a wave in the next. She kept trying though, over and again, through the years.

Maybe it was the blank page's fault that the words were never right. Maybe if she wrote it here first, as she'd done the silly little fairy tale she'd made up to catalogue the items she was searching for evidence of . . .

"Oh, is that *the* copy of *Treasure Island*? The one you made the notations in?" A hand appeared in her line of vision, reaching for the book.

She snatched it away, holding it out of reach. Instinct, mostly. And a sound one. She scowled at him. "*My* copy, yes." No point in quibbling about whether it technically still belonged to her brother. "And there are no notations of any interest to you."

Lord Sheridan didn't look the slightest bit abashed, though he at least put his hand back where it belonged. "Libby made it sound so intriguing."

Beth still fought back a wave of embarrassment every time she thought of her brother's new fiancée having studied her notes. Reading each and every one. Using them, if unwittingly, to take on Beth's role in the treasure hunt.

Those words had never been meant for anyone else's eyes. And they still weren't. "They are hardly intriguing. Idle musings, nothing more."

His brows lifted. "Then why not show me?"

As if he had to ask. "Because the last time I 'showed' something to someone even remotely associated with you, it was stolen from me. I've learned my lesson. You're a thief, Lord Sheridan, and I don't mean to let you touch anything else I hold dear."

2

Theodore Howe, Marquess of Sheridan, had been called many things by many females in his twenty-six years of life. A bore. An eccentric. A foozler—which he remembered solely because it had taken him a week to puzzle out what that one meant, and which he could hardly argue with once he puzzled it. He *did* tend to be clumsy when taken by surprise.

But no one had ever called him a thief before. It probably shouldn't amuse him. But really. Never in his life had he—or would he—resort to thievery. He paid good money for each and every artifact that he hadn't dug up with his own hands. Not to mention funding a good many ventures that had netted him absolutely nothing.

He'd parted with a hundred pounds sterling for that trinket box she was no doubt talking about—no trifling amount. That was as much as he paid Ainsley in an entire year. A hundred pounds! And he knew for a fact Lord Scofield had sent the money to her. "I didn't realize. That thieves paid for the items they procured, I mean."

She glared at him, turning her eyes into two lovely slits of . . . what? He had yet to decide exactly what color they were. Dark, but not brown. Not quite blue either. Well, perhaps slate blue. Blue-grey. Or, in this particular light, simply grey. Though *grey* sounded far too dull a word to describe the lovely circles that spat fury at him more often than not in the last seven days.

Even so. She was without question the most beautiful woman he'd ever set eyes on, and the moment she'd bowled into him a week ago, he'd been sunk.

Pewter?

Or lead. As in, the lead shot of a weapon ready to blow him out of the water. See, even now she was hissing like a lit fuse, sparks showering from her whatever-color eyes.

She scrambled to her feet, no doubt so that she could tower over him. "You may not have known at the time that it was stolen property, but you do now. I don't care if it *is* the crest of Prince Rupert on the lid, that does not entitle you to it. The box is *mine*. Give. It. Back."

Usually, he would have let her tower. Seemed a bit unfair, really, to push himself up and then tower over *her*—she was a petite thing. He must have a good ten inches on her. And if he were to put his arms around her, he had a feeling she'd fit rather perfectly in their circle.

Not that he was oblivious enough to give that one a try. Instead, he stood solely so that he could make a show of turning out his pockets. As if she'd thought he had the trinket box on him right that moment. He gave her enough space that he wouldn't seem quite so towering.

And so that none of those sparks would catch him on fire. One never knew when the metaphorical might take on substance.

She let out a rather adorable huff of aggravation. "I realize it's in . . . wherever you come from. But you could at least promise its return."

He *could*. But he didn't. "The Lake District." He smiled and put his pockets back to rights, leaving his hands in them. "My home, I mean. The wherever that I come from. Rather lovely, really. Not *this* lovely, but a fine home base. We call it—"

"I really don't care what you call your enormous estate with its

28

ancestral halls, Lord Sheridan." She hugged *Treasure Island* to her chest and made a show of facing the water again.

Well, that was a shame. He half intended to use it as a bargaining tool to win her attention. It had worked for that Darcy chap in the Austen novel his sisters read aloud at least once a year, after all. Elizabeth Bennet herself had said so. Perhaps partly in jest, but he'd detected a kernel of truth in her statement. Perhaps Elizabeth Tremayne could be similarly persuaded. "Pemberley."

It at least brought her face turning his way again, shedding its sun-bright light upon him. Though she was frowning. Was that a step up or down from scowling? "Your estate bears the same name as the one from *Pride and Prejudice?*"

"Well, no." He looked out over the water, well able to imagine pirate ships just there. Had Prince Rupert stood on this very spot, even? A thrill ran through him at the thought. Sheridan wasn't exactly a *direct* descendant of the prince, but close enough that he'd claim it. How many people really had a pirate prince in their lineage, after all? "It's called Sheridan Castle. But my sisters claim it's based on it. Pemberley, I mean. On Sheridan Castle. Not the other way round. Utter rot, probably, but Millicent's convinced of it."

"Millicent?"

"My sister. The younger one. That is, of the two of them. Both older than me. Eldest is Abbie." She'd like them. Everyone liked Millicent—who *never* went by Millie—and Abbie—who *never* went by Abigail. Well, perhaps there were a *few* exceptions. Like when people didn't care for his sisters' tendency to take control of a situation. Invited or not. But Beth would like them. Perhaps. And they would like her too. They never met a new person that they didn't deem an instant friend. Well, unless it was one they deemed an instant adversary.

Not that he knew how he'd ever lure Beth Tremayne to the Lake District to see his home and meet his sisters anyway. Maybe she had an aunt and uncle she could tour with, like Elizabeth Bennet. If they were casting him in the Mr. Darcy role.

29

Which they weren't. He wasn't nearly so gruff. And he liked dancing quite well. Though Darcy did have the right opinion about a fine set of eyes.

He could probably lure her there with the promise of her trinket box's return, though. Take her on a tour of the grounds. And then . . . what? *"All of this could be yours for the low price of your hand in marriage!"*

His lips twitched. Abbie would test him for a fever if she knew he was plotting how to propose to a girl he'd just met a week ago. Who had yet to look at him as something other than a half-villain.

Though that was better than viewing him as a nuisance, which was how Libby had always seen him, and he'd been ready to let Telford talk him into formally proposing to *her*.

He'd never really minded annoying Libby, though, he had to admit. Beth, on the other hand . . . "I've probably ruined the solitude you were after. Sorry about that." Sort of. He edged back a step. "As I told your brother last week, feel free to tell me to go away if I'm bothering you."

Her frown grew a bit more perplexed. "That would be a bit rude, don't you think?"

"Not at all." He chuckled and stepped closer again when a bit of movement caught his eye on the water. "I'm not easily offended. Is that them?"

Beth spun, lifting a hand to shield her eyes, and nodded. "Oh, and it looks like Team Tremayne is in the lead. Come on, Ollie!"

She hadn't immediately told him to leave. That was something. Progress. At this rate, she'd be Lady Sheridan in a decade, at the most. "Are they the same each week? The teams, I mean?"

"More or less." She went up on her toes, though it surely afforded her no better view. What would she do if he hoisted her up? Probably sock him in the nose. "There are alternates. And it used to be our fathers leading the teams, not Oliver and Casek. But the rivalry between the Tremaynes and the Wearnes has been going on for so

30

long that they were the natural lines for drawing teams when the races started."

Sheridan had never had a rival. It would keep life interesting. Perhaps he should invest in one sometime, just for the experience. Maybe he could convince Telford to act the part, though he had no idea what they'd be competing for.

His chest went tight. Hopefully not over Beth. Telly hadn't shown any signs of real attraction toward her, and Sheridan had been watching for it. He knew how his best friend behaved when he found a girl intriguing, after all. And though Sheridan thought Beth's sunlight-spun hair and not-blue-not-grey eyes utterly captivating, Telford hadn't been sneaking any glances.

The tightness eased, though its momentary appearance should probably convince him that he didn't, in fact, have any desire for a rival. And come to think of it, he *did* have a few semi-rivals in the world of antiquities—or had, back in his Viking hunting days—and it really hadn't been any fun at all. Far better to steer clear of them. Perhaps he'd tell Oliver so. A bit of friendly advice.

"Is our lad in the lead?"

Sheridan spun around at the intrusion of a new voice, though its tone was one that brought a smile to his lips. The Tremayne grandmother was coming their way, her shoulders encased in a shawl and her eyes bright. She was ninety if she was a day. A bit more perhaps, even. And when he and Telford had arrived in the Scillies last week, she'd been confined to her bed, unconscious, with some mysterious ailment that had made Oliver Tremayne fear it could be her end and the news of which had brought Beth out of hiding.

But today she looked right as rain. She'd tire easily, if the pattern of the past two days held, but she was awake and lucid and looked steady enough on her feet. Even so, the Abbie in his head gave him a prod, so he jumped forward to offer her an arm for support.

Beth surged too, though not as quickly as he did. "Mamm-wynn! You shouldn't be out in the cool air."

31

"Oh, nonsense, Beth." Mrs. Tremayne smiled at her grand-daughter even as she let Sheridan bring her hand to a steadying rest on his forearm. "A little fresh air will do me good."

Beth was apparently not ready to relent. "Does Mrs. Dawe know you're out here?"

The lady chuckled and patted his arm. "She does. I told her I was going to find our pirate prince." She winked up at him.

He grinned right back. He'd heard the Tremaynes muttering a bit about their grandmother getting lost in her mind, confusing present with past—and even, it seemed, with the future. But just now he saw nothing but a teasing glint in her eyes. When she'd heard that he'd come here chasing stories of *the* pirate prince, she'd taken to calling him that. A joke that in his mind proved hers wasn't so scattered. At least not always. "Careful, lady fair, or I may snatch you away and run off to the Caribbean with you."

She laughed in delight—a sound as whimsical as the dainty silver bells Millicent had hung in the rose garden for any fairies who came wandering by—and leaned into him. "Oh, this one's charming. You're going to stay awhile, aren't you, my lord?"

"The rest of the summer, at least." It was how long Libby's holi-day cottage on St. Mary's had been let for, and there was no prying her away from it. And no prying Telford away from his sister's side, now that she had a young man stealing kisses from her. And, by extension, no prying Sheridan away either.

Not that he always went where Telford did. Well, he did. Most of the time, other than when he was on a dig and couldn't convince Telly to join him. But only if it suited him. It just happened that their wants usually aligned. Especially in this case—he'd been want-ing to come to the Isles of Scilly for years and intended to explore them fully before he left again. "And you may call me Sheridan, Mrs. Tremayne. Or even Theo, if you prefer."

"Theo?" It was Beth who asked, which gave him a fine excuse for looking her way again. The sunlight was playing with her hair in a way that made him a bit jealous.

He made a point of blinking at the question. "That would be my name. Given one. Well, Theodore. Millicent and Abbie call me Theo." They were the only ones in the world who did—he'd inherited the title of Sheridan when he was only four, so the rest of creation had been calling him by that for his entire memory, and it was how he'd come to think of himself. But Mrs. Tremayne certainly deserved the honor of using his first name if she'd like to. Especially if he could finagle her granddaughter down the aisle.

There was a tack—*Your grandmother loves me, you see, so you should too. Won't you marry me for her sake?*

Mrs. Tremayne tugged him toward the bluff and the view of the two gigs speeding across the waters. "I would be delighted. And you must call me Mamm-wynn."

Beth sighed.

Sheridan grinned. "Excellent. I've never had a mamm-wynn."

"Well, of course not. You're not Cornish. Too much a wanderer to be any one thing, aren't you?" Mamm-wynn squinted at the boats. "Come on, Ollie! Pull! Oh dear, I do think Casek's lads are going to overtake them."

A wanderer. He'd done a fair amount of it, true. Though not as much as he still planned to do. There hadn't been time enough yet, between school and university—he'd only managed a trip or two a year. He kept trying to convince Telford to join him on an expedition, but his friend's feet were firmly planted on Telford land, for the most part. So, Sheridan's sisters were still his usual companions when he traveled. Well, and Ainsley, much to his valet's occasional dismay.

Sheridan looked back to the water, where the second gig was indeed overtaking the first as they slid out of sight around the point of land. "Can't win them all, I suppose."

Beth was actually smiling. Not at him, of course—each of the times he'd seen that breathtaking turn of her lips, it had been directed at someone else—but it still made his pulse scatter and pound. "You'd think they believe they could, to hear the teams boast of their prowess."

33

Mamm-wynn chuckled. "I wonder what wager your grandfather is about to lose. A fruit pie this week, do you think? Or scones from the Polmers' bakery?"

Sheridan found it highly amusing that the locals put wagers on the gig races, and that said wagers were nothing but an excuse to gather and eat and drink together. Who was buying may change from week to week, but the outcome was always the same. The participants would be at the pub or the bakery together, sharing a pint or a pie or a cream scone come Wednesday evening.

It rather made him mourn the fact that he had no such community at home. Oh, there were all the clubs in London at which he'd more or less inherited a membership. But it wasn't the same.

He should spearhead something like this at the village abutting his estate. Not that they could have gig races. But there must be something else they could do. Something that involved pastries as rewards.

"Well. Perhaps Ollie and crew will catch them up again." Beth turned away from the sea and tucked her book under her arm. "I imagine we'll know soon enough. In the meantime, we had better get you back inside, Mamm-wynn." She held out a hand toward her grandmother.

The lady took it and squeezed but didn't let go of Sheridan's arm. No, she just tugged Beth closer to them.

He knew he liked the matriarch.

It wasn't a long walk from the bluff to the house, but it was a lovely one. From here they had a perfect view of the quaint Tremayne home—much larger than its neighbors but dwarfed by the Abbey, whose roof he could just make out in the distance and which was the only proper manor to be found on the islands. That would be where the Lord Proprietor lived. Some Dorrien-Smith or another, if he recalled correctly. Telford had been rather rude about pointing out how small this stone cottage was, but only because he was trying to needle Oliver at first. Had to make sure he wasn't just after the Telford wealth with his interest in Libby, after all. In truth, Sheridan knew his friend found the place every bit as enchanting as he did.

34

As they approached the house, the housekeeper and cook, Mrs. Dawe, stepped out of the kitchen door, wiping her hands on her apron and smiling at them. "Who was in the lead?"

"Hard to say," Mamm-wynn said in reply. "Ollie at first, but Casek looked as though he was overtaking them. I told you we ought to have gone down to the beach if we wanted to know who'd won before they get home."

"A bit of a walk for you yet." Beth gave her grandmother a concerned look. It was easy to see her love for the woman, and her fear.

"Oh, bah. I told you, dearover, I'm back to normal."

"Mamm-wynn—"

"Don't waste your breath arguing with her." Mrs. Dawe pushed the door open for them and held it so they could pass. "We'll just keep an eye on her. Won't we, madame?"

Mrs. Tremayne sniffed. "You all are worse than jailers. Well, my pirate prince will help me sneak away now and then, won't you, dearovim?"

Oh bother. To endear himself to her, or to Beth, who was shooting daggers at him with her eyes again? He put on his best pirate drawl. "The moment their backs are turned, we'll be on our way to Port Royal."

Mamm-wynn rewarded him with a laugh. And greater wonder, Beth very nearly smiled at him, even if she also shook her head.

Mrs. Dawe shut the door behind them. "I believe your man just returned, my lord, with the newspaper you like. We can have it delivered with the others, you know, while you're here. Ainsley needn't run to Old Grimsby every morning after it."

He'd already suggested as much. But Ainsley had just given him that look. "He likes the walk in the morning."

Beth shot him a dubious glance. The kind that said she found it easier to believe that Sheridan was simply an ogre of an employer who demanded his servants inconvenience themselves for his whims, even when it was completely avoidable.

She'd obviously never gotten *that look* from Ainsley.

35

Well. Much as he'd like to defend himself, he suspected it would be a waste of breath. Especially since she was already making for the stairs, up which he had no reason to follow with his arguments. His room, the sole guest chamber, was downstairs. Telford had been put in the room once belonging to Morgan Tremayne. And their valets had at first been crammed together in the basic servants' quarters, until the Dawes had offered Ainsley a room with them next door.

He helped Mamm-wynn settle into her chair at the breakfast table and, when he didn't see the newspaper already set out for him, strode toward his room.

Ainsley was within, a shoe in each hand and a look of utter bafflement on his face when Sheridan entered. "How did you manage this? I just cleaned them last night."

"Oh." He'd heard tales of menservants who didn't, in fact, question their employer's every outing and greet soiled shoes with questions better suited to a nursemaid. But then, Ainsley was a decade his senior . . . and had been hired by Sheridan's sisters when he was fourteen to play governess as much as valet, he suspected. "I went for a walk with Telly last night. Couldn't sleep."

Ainsley just looked at him. And blinked.

"Well, it was a fine night. And I thought a bit of fresh air may . . ."

Ainsley didn't even look back up at him. Just reached for the cloth bag he used to transport soiled items to his own quarters, where he kept his brushes. His every movement a rebuke. Sheridan huffed out a breath. It was absolutely not fair that his valet was so dratted put together all the time, while Sheridan was at constant loose ends. Ainsley's hair, raven with a few strands of silver threading through it—dignified—was always perfectly pomaded. His face, just beginning to line—in a dignified way, of course—was always perfectly composed. His bearing—utter, confounded dignity—was always smooth and confident.

Sheridan spotted the newspaper on the chest of drawers and swiped it up. "Well, you needn't lecture me. Isn't as though *you* don't enjoy your walks."

"You ought to enjoy my walks too, since I spend the whole of them lifting you in prayer before the Lord. Heaven knows what scrapes you'd get into if I didn't."

Sheridan turned back to the open door. Still, he couldn't help the grin. He *did* in fact appreciate the prayers—but if ever he said so, Ainsley might keel over in shock. "You're an absolute Puritan, Ainsley."

"Just don't let the lady calling you a pirate give you any ideas. I don't know if I can pray you out of trouble if you go stealing from passing ships."

How did he even know that Mrs. Tremayne . . . ? Never mind. Sheridan chuckled. "Only one way to find out, as they say."

He stepped into the hall before his valet could lob a shoe at him. Not that he'd ever done such a thing—terribly undignified as it would be—but the chap was full of surprises.

Newspaper in hand, he aimed for the breakfast room. He'd eat, he'd read, he'd hear who won the race. Perhaps by then Telford would have roused himself, though he'd still be a good hour away from exchanging so much as a good morning with anyone. And then they could plan their day.

Because they had a real pirate prince and his admiral to hunt up information on. And he would muddy every shoe he had with him in the quest if he must.

3

Though Senara Dawe offered a smile for old Mr. Cardy, it felt tighter than when Josephine had tried to squeeze into her little sister's dress last year. She was grateful for the boat ride from St. Mary's to Tresco—truly—but she still couldn't quite believe she was home. That it had come to this. That somehow, in the course of a week, the life she'd built for herself so carefully had unraveled. That she had no position. No employment. No little Josephine and Rose and Paulette filling her days and making her smile.

But it had started long before a week ago, hadn't it? It had started years ago, when she first met Rory Smithfield. Or a year ago, when she let him kiss her. It had started when she put her hopes for their future above her day-to-day life with the girls.

Her throat went tight. She loved the Clifford children—she *did*. But they weren't hers. Was it so terrible to want a life of her own? A husband, her own babies?

Habit had her reaching up and touching the pendant secreted away under her dress. It had always been a reminder to chase her dreams, her hopes. A symbol of family, which meant more to her than anything, the last gift from her paternal grandmother before she passed into eternity. She could still hear her voice as she let the necklace pool in Senara's hand. *"Family,"* she'd whispered. *"Family is the key to every happiness, Senara girl. Never forget that."*

Family. All she'd ever wanted.

And she'd have it. Soon. They'd only had a minute together in the flurry and fury of her dismissal, but Rory had whispered that he'd find her. Told her to go home, and that he'd soon follow. She wasn't certain how he meant to escape the responsibilities of his own employment, but she'd been thinking for weeks that he had something in the works. He'd been so mysterious about it all . . . but that was probably because he didn't want anyone else to overhear and report back to Mr. Griffith about it.

She dropped her hand from the pendant and forced her mind back to the here and now. He'd come for her soon. They'd marry, right here on Tresco. Ollie could officiate—a thought that made her lips twitch up. A few weeks, perhaps another month, and she'd be Mrs. Rory Smithfield. The shame of being sacked after being discovered in his arms would wash away. It would *all* wash away, like so much sand in the face of an ocean. There would just be the future, bright and shining.

Funny how little that promise did to make the sting of today go away. Mr. Cardy didn't turn to her yet—not given the holiday-goers he was tipping his hat to. And waiting for a tip from. Two young ladies, one an actual lady and the other her maid, given the uniform. They had been largely quiet on the half-hour trip, which had suited Senara fine. She'd not paid them any particular attention, beyond noting that the redheaded lady wore a dress in the height of fashion and kept her wide brim shading her ivory complexion at all times—which must be a constant chore, if she meant to avoid the freckles that paired so easily with the hair. The lady reached now into her handbag and pulled out a few coins that she dropped with an absent smile into Mr. Cardy's palm. And then she was on her way to wherever she meant to go—likely the Abbey Gardens—her maid trailing along behind like a puppy.

Senara and Mr. Cardy both breathed a bit easier with them gone and turned back to his little boat. And her trunk, still sitting like a barnacle inside it, and heavy as an anchor. At the quay in St. Mary's, there had been a stevedore on hand to load it. Here, on the other hand . . .

Mr. Cardy pursed his lips. "I'll fetch Alfie to carry this up for you, aye?"

She certainly wasn't going to ask Mr. Cardy to try to heft it. "Or I'll send Tas down."

But Mr. Cardy was shaking his head. "Your ol' tas wouldn't have an easier time of it than I would. Nah, we'll leave it to younger backs. Alfie can manage it, and he'll be home with the day's catch in an hour or so. Soon enough?"

"Soon enough. Thank you, Mr. C." She reached out to grip his hand and gave it a squeeze. "It's good to see you. Give my regards to your wife and tell her I'll be round soon to see what new books she has in her shop."

"Oh! She has one that Beth ordered, now as you mention it. Just came in last night. Would you let her know?"

"Of course." Senara smiled at the very mention of Beth—though usually she preferred her tales more fanciful than books were wont to deliver, ones told with a voice instead of neat type across a page. Though perhaps Beth had outgrown that favoritism. She would, after all, be . . . what, nineteen now? No, twenty.

Senara pressed a hand to her cheek and turned toward the road, carpetbag in hand. How had so much time sped by? Ten years since the islands had been home. Ten years since she answered the Cliffords' advert for a governess, armed with references from two Mrs. Tremaynes. Ten years since she set out to chase her dreams. It was with Beth and Ollie and Morgan she'd learned how much she loved tending children's minds and spirits and bodies.

But she'd thought it would do her good to get away from Tresco for a while. Meet families other than the few that made their home in the Scillies.

Squaring her shoulders, she set out for home—though at a pace slow enough to give the lady with the ginger hair a good head start. Thankfully, she had set out at a good clip and seemed to know where she was going. She was soon out of sight.

Senara let out a breath and switched her bag to her other hand. She'd last walked this path at Christmas—the Cliffords had spent the holiday with other family and so could spare her for five days. Not so long ago, but summer certainly painted the islands in different colors than did winter. No low, heavy skies threatening rain at every hour. No fields lying dormant, all the flowers sleeping, holding their breath until the Scillies' early spring came to stir them. No cold, biting wind ready to gnaw at one's very bones.

Christmas. She'd spent it dreaming of Rory, imagining what he was doing. He'd gone to visit family too, his letters had said. But not at home as usual. They'd all gathered with his cousin at his employer's.

By next Christmas, they'd be wed. Perhaps even have a child on the way. Where would they spend it? Here? With his mum? Or perhaps they'd return to the castle Rory's cousin was employed at—she'd get to see for herself all the ridiculous artifacts in it that had filled his stories.

"Senara Dawe? Is that you, girl?"

She turned her head at the familiar voice, smiling at old Mrs. Gillis. Decade gone or no, she was just the same as she'd always been. "It is, Mrs. G. Home for a visit with Mam and Tas." Not a visit like any she'd made before, but if it ended with a wedding, that would override any other misgivings they had about her protracted stay.

"Oh, won't they be thrilled! You're a good girl, Senara. Always have been." Mrs. Gillis fell into step beside her, and Senara slowed her pace still more to match.

A good girl. Her insides prickled as Lord Clifford's parting words to her scalded her mind anew. But she was no worse than any of the high-and-mighty guests who came for house parties, was she? She hadn't tumbled into Rory's arms just for the diversion, as lords were wont to do. She *loved* him. And she'd soon be his wife, so it would all be excused. Besides, at thirty-one, she wasn't a *girl* anymore.

She kept her smile in place for Mrs. G. "Well, thank you. How's everyone been?"

Mrs. Gillis sighed. "Everyone was right shaken by poor Johnnie Rosedew's accident. Your mam wrote to you of it, I trust?"

Senara nodded, the mere mention bringing a sting of tears. The Johnnie she remembered was just a mite of six, mischievous as any island lad, and sweet as honey. She'd only seen him a handful of times in the years since—not enough to dislodge that picture. "I can't believe he's gone. He slipped in the cave, she said? Hit his head?"

"That's right. A crying shame, that. To be cut down in his youth as he was, and for no good reason." With a shake of her head, Mrs. Gillis let out one more long breath and then visibly perked up. "Oh, but you mayn't have heard the *good* news yet, though you'll learn it soon as you get home, no doubt. Young Ollie's got himself engaged!"

Ollie, engaged? She'd barely wrapped her mind around the fact that he was the vicar now in place of his uncle—though even as a lad, he'd shown the markings of one. Her eyes went wide. "To whom?"

"Oh, a sweet young lady who came for a holiday on St. Mary's— Mabena Moon's employer, before she officially resigned last week. She and Casek Wearne have taken up now, too, believe it or not. Lady Elizabeth Sinclair, sister of the Earl of Telford. You'll meet her dreckly, I imagine. She'll be in the Abbey Gardens right now but will take lunch with Oliver and Mrs. Tremayne."

A lady? That was surprising—the Tremaynes tended to avoid the titled class as a rule, given the disdain with which society had always greeted their family. And . . . "Wait—Mabena too? With a Wearne?" How was that possible? Last she'd known, Mabena had flown from the islands after the other Wearne twin broke her heart, and she'd sworn never to return.

The woman's eyes sparkled at her. "And have you found no young man yet to start your own family with? You can't tend others' children forever, as I keep trying to tell you."

Senara squeezed her bag's handle and worked to control her smile. It wouldn't do to tell Mrs. G about Rory and his whispered promises before telling her own parents. "There may be someone I fancy, but I've no announcement just yet."

Mrs. G beamed at her. "Well, don't dally too long, dearover. I'd like to see it, and I've only so many years left, you know. Though in the meantime, we've weddings enough to enjoy the planning of. At the race this morning, we were all trying to talk our lady into having hers and Ollie's in the Abbey Gardens. She took right to the idea, too, though that brother of hers may insist on something on the mainland."

It took her a moment to even realize that "our lady" was the girl Oliver had claimed. She summoned a chuckle. "Keeping high company, are we?"

"Swimming in it! Our lady has been here all summer, and now we've her brother here—and his friend. Lord Sheridan." Mrs. Gillis laughed. "High company and handsome too. Want to snag yourself a lord, Senara girl?"

She chuckled. "No lords for me. I try to steer clear of them."

"Well, you'll have a time of that. They're both staying with the Tremaynes. There were no more places to let, you see."

"Oh." Her stomach tied itself up into a few dozen sailing knots—slip, hitch, and mariners, all rolled into one. She hadn't counted on having to share space with strangers in these next few weeks. But visiting lords meant visiting valets, which meant Mam's kitchen wouldn't be the oasis of peace she'd hoped for. How was she to soothe away that prickling inside with a bunch of people she didn't know always about, forcing her to keep on a mask of politeness?

Worse still—what if they were acquaintances of the Cliffords and somehow learned that she'd been sacked for moral turpitude? There'd be no hiding it then. Her parents would hear, and she'd have to face the disappointment in their eyes. The accusation. The condemnation.

She forced the cheer to stay fixed to her face and voice. "Well, then Mam ought to be glad for an extra set of hands."

"I imagine so. Well, here's my gate. Good to see you home again, Senara. How long this time? A week? Or a fortnight, perhaps?"

She'd already worked out how to tell it to her parents. But it didn't seem quite right to say it first to a neighbor, before they knew. So, she kept her smile vague. "I'm not entirely certain yet."

Mrs. Gillis snorted a laugh and lifted the latch to her gate. "Oh, to have the leisure to change your mind at a moment's notice, aye? No doubt your employers will send you a wire and expect you at their beck and call by next morning."

It had happened before. It wouldn't this time, but the precedent allowed her to let the comment stand on its own two feet. She lifted a hand and kept walking. "Have a lovely day, Mrs. G."

It was too much to ask, of course, that she see no other familiar faces on the remaining couple minutes of her walk. There were is-landers out about their tasks everywhere, and they all lifted a shout and a hand to welcome her home. She smiled and returned each greeting, until her lips felt stretched thin and her ragged emotions were pounding at her chest like a prisoner.

She smelled home before she saw it. Baking bread and a myriad of blooms—that was what greeted a visitor approaching the Tremayne door. She breathed it in and let it beat back the war within her. Let her gaze take in the profusion of colors rioting around the fence, the trellis, the door. Some were chosen by her father, some by Mrs. Tremayne, others by Oliver. The only harmony here was the true, natural kind—notes in abundance, all shouting out for attention at the top of their lungs but kept in order by the same hands that had planted them with love.

As if her thoughts had summoned him, her father rounded the corner of the house, trowel in hand. He was a bit more stooped than he'd once been, and he moved more slowly. She knew very well that Oliver kept taking over more and more of the garden chores to relieve Tas's aching back. But never so much that he felt useless. She'd thanked him for that, at Christmas. And he'd taken her elbow in that way he always did that made him such a natural vicar, looked directly into her eyes, and promised her that he loved her parents as he did his own family and would never suffer they be injured by either too much work or lack of it.

A good boy, Oliver Tremayne. Or, now, a fine man. She was proud to see what he'd grown into.

"Tas!"

At her call, her father stopped. He straightened, dropped the trowel, widened his eyes, and opened his arms. "Senara!"

He laughed, and so did she as she let her bag fall to the ground and raced into his embrace. His arms closed around her, hugging her tight. And he smelled, too, of bread and flowers and home, with a bit of earth thrown into the mix.

He was still laughing when he pulled away, sending his eyes over her from head to toe, as he always did when she came home. Cataloguing each feature as he did his plants. Black hair, still pulled back in a neat chignon. Tall frame, still sturdy and more square than curved. Good hands, still ready to correct posture or give comfort, whichever was needed. He'd see in a glance that she was the same Senara she'd always been.

And hopefully he wouldn't look deep enough in her eyes to see anything more just yet. She kept her smile in place as a shield. "Surprise! I thought it would be fun to pay a visit, as I found myself in possession of the time. I hear we have guests? That Mam could use the extra hands?"

He planted a kiss on her forehead before nodding. "Lords Telford and Sheridan are here, along with their valets. Collins, Lord Telford's man, is up at the house, so we've taken Sheridan's man, Ainsley, into the spare room at our place. Though don't worry—your room is still free, as always. Ready and waiting for you. And here you are! We didn't dare hope to see you again until Michaelmas."

Ainsley. Why did that sound familiar? The lord's name didn't, so it couldn't be that they'd been guests together at Cliffenwelle. What, then?

Her mind was too tired from the long journey and the whirlwind preceding it to sort it out.

But never mind. Whoever this Ainsley was, he wasn't going to ruin the first moments with her parents. She refocused on what Tas had said. "I didn't dare hope it either, hence why I didn't say anything." She backtracked for her bag. "Is Mam in the kitchen, then? I'll say hello and then take my things home and tidy myself up. I've been traveling forever."

Tas was still smiling, but a bit of worry darkened his eyes. "You stayed in Penzance last night, I hope."

Because to be here at this time of day, she would have had to come on the first ferry. And to make the first ferry, she'd either have had to stay in Penzance the night before or, as she'd actually done, be on a train all night that chugged into the station in the morning.

She forced a grin. "And waste time I could be spending with you? No, I haven't stopped. I just slept on the train."

He shook his head. "You haven't stopped since you left Northumberland? Gracious, dearover. We aren't that interesting. You oughtn't to have been quite so eager to get here."

She laughed and continued on the path toward the back of the house, so that he wouldn't see in her eyes that they hadn't been her reason for hurrying.

Whatever chore he'd been about apparently forgotten, Tas followed her back around the house. "Still can't believe you're home. First Mabena Moon came back, and now here you are, without warning. It's like all our chicks are flying back to the coop at once. We'll have a fine time at the pub tonight, toasting the winning team. You'll have to join us, if you're up for it."

She loved joining her parents and neighbors at the heart of the village—in general. Just now, it sounded utterly exhausting. "Perhaps if I manage some rest this afternoon. Who won today?"

"Wearne." He laughed. "Which means Old Man Gibson owes everyone some ginger fairings. He was on his way to Polmers' last I heard. You likely passed him on the water."

Likely, though she hadn't honestly been paying much attention. She'd simply sat in the bow with her face turned into the wind and up to the sun, wondering how she'd come back here like this, with no prospects other than waiting for Rory to come for her. "Well, it's been ages since I had decent fairings. Incentive."

A clatter sounded from behind the door that stood open to receive the fresh breeze, and a moment later her mother filled the space, eyes wide in disbelief. "Senara? I heard your voice but thought I must be imagining it!"

"Mam." This time Tas caught her bag before she could drop it to the ground again. Which meant her arms were free to come around her mother and give her a mighty squeeze.

Unlike Tas, she didn't carry the scent of flowers and earth along with the bread. No, Mam's essence was cinnamon and vanilla and yeast and all things delicious. Smelling that familiar smell again brought too many feelings crowding into Senara's throat. "I've missed you." It was all she could manage to whisper.

And even that was too much, apparently. Mam pulled back, hands clasping her shoulders and all-seeing eyes drilling straight into her. "What's the matter, then? Your health?"

"I'm quite well." And why, when she was a woman grown, did her mother's concern make her come unraveled? Her smile shook in the corners, and her nose burned with the press of tears. Best to get it out. Get it done, so they could address it and move on to what mattered. "But I've lost my position."

"What?" Both her parents shouted it in unison, with matching incredulity.

Senara squeezed her eyes shut. Seeing their outrage was too much. It made those prickles inside turn to outright jabs of conscience. "You remember my mentioning Rory?"

"Aye." Mam touched a finger to Senara's chin that meant *Look at me.* She was helpless to do anything but obey and found her mother's gaze as she'd expected it to be. Encouraging but wary and accepting nothing less than the truth. "Valet to Lord Clifford's cousin. You've been sweet on him for years."

Senara gave one quick nod. "He's sweet on me too. We were talking in the stable the other night and someone reported it to his lordship, who assumed the worst. He sacked me immediately."

Fury burned in Mam's eyes. "And Lord Clifford didn't give you a chance to defend yourself? After all your years of loyal service?"

Heat stung Senara's cheeks. What his lordship had believed had been his own eyes. Yes, someone had clearly tattled to his lordship. But a rumor wouldn't have been enough to get her dismissed. Her own actions accomplished that. A truth she couldn't pull to her lips, not with her parents looking at her like that. So ready to defend her. To believe the best.

She shrugged.

Mam huffed. "Let's get you resting up, then. Give me just a moment to move the pot off the heat and I'll see you home."

"Oh, Mam, you needn't—"

"Who said anything about need?" Mam spun away, her mission set.

Tas chuckled from behind Senara. "You know better than to argue." He slung an arm around her shoulders, gave her another squeeze, pressed another kiss to the top of her head. "Glad you're home, my girl, and not sorry you're staying awhile this time. As long as you need. Forever's fine with us."

Her smile felt small and sad on her lips. This wasn't how she'd ever meant to come home. Not with shame and disgrace trailing her and her only hope of redemption resting on Rory showing up soon, before her parents thought to ask more questions.

"There." Mam bustled their way again, smile in place. "I just took in the tea things for the ladies, so I can steal away for a few minutes."

"Mrs. Tremayne and Beth? Or is Oliver's young lady here? Mrs. G mentioned her." Senara stood on tiptoe to peer around her mother—not that she could see through all the walls between the kitchen and drawing room, but she had to admit to some curiosity, even given her exhaustion.

"Lady Elizabeth, yes. And Lady Emily just knocked a minute ago too—Beth's friend from finishing school, you'll recall. They both have rooms on St. Mary's."

She had vague recollections of Beth telling tales about her dearest friend from school, but she'd never paid particular attention to them. And the presence of a stranger who wasn't about to marry into the family was enough to temper her curiosity. She turned with Mam toward the kitchen door. "How lovely for Beth."

"Well. Not as lovely as one might think—but you don't need that story quite yet. Get settled and rested, dearover, and we'll tell you all about everything later."

Everything? What could possibly be going on that would make Beth's friend being here not a happy occasion?

"Senara?"

"Coming." She turned with her parents toward the garden.

They chattered a bit as they walked, but nothing that required her attention. And it took only a minute to pass through the side gate connecting the Tremaynes' spacious garden to their small one, and then they were at her own back door.

The moment they stepped inside, a too-familiar sound met her ears and scratched its way down her back. The sound of a coarse fabric brush going to work.

Which meant that Ainsley the valet was here, right now. Perhaps when she met him she'd be able to place why the name sounded familiar.

"Ah, right." As if reading her mind, Tas bustled up the stairs ahead of her. "We'll have to make quick introductions. Ainsley! You'll never guess it. Senara's come home!"

She felt her brow furrow even as she followed her father up. How long had this fellow been here? Tas called out to him as though he were an old friend—an old friend who'd been told all about their daughter and how rarely she made it back to Tresco.

The brushing sound stopped, and the floor creaked. By the time their trio made it to the top of the stairs, the door to the guest room had been opened and a dark-clad man stepped into the corridor.

He looked a few years older than she was. Handsome, as valets who traveled with their employers generally were. His voice, when he said, "How lovely for you all!" sounded smooth and deep and sincere.

But he didn't look at all familiar. No, that wasn't *quite* true—there was something about his eyes . . . or the shape of his mouth? She shook it off, despite how she hated not being able to place a name, and pasted on a tired smile. "How do you do?"

"Very well, thank you. And you?"

"Likewise." Or at the very least, she *would* be well. Everything would be well. Because she was home now, and Rory would come soon.

The disgrace would soon be far behind her.

4

Beth followed the crook of her grandmother's finger away from the dining room after luncheon. She'd been trained to follow that crook since she was old enough to toddle—and she'd learned, too, over the years, what each expression on Adelle Tremayne's face meant. This one, a placid smile paired with the sparking eyes, meant it was time to have a conversation.

In her own defense, Beth had tried a dozen times over the last week to have an earnest conversation with her grandmother. But each time she'd found Mamm-wynn alone and slid to a seat beside her, each time she'd opened her mouth, Mamm-wynn had stayed her with a request for this or that. Or with a question. Or, two days ago, with a clear, serious, "Not yet, Elizabeth Grace. You're not ready yet."

Not yet. It wasn't the first time in her life that she'd been set to offer an apology and Mamm-wynn hadn't allowed it. Because her grandmother was wise enough to know that Beth would say the words that needed saying without necessarily meaning them.

But she'd thought she *had* meant it, the very moment she saw that note Ollie had left her a week ago, telling her Mamm-wynn had fallen ill. She'd been sorry. Sorry all her efforts hadn't done what she'd hoped. Sorry, so very sorry, that the people she loved best had been so worried. Sorry they were paying the price for her actions. So why, then, wouldn't Mamm-wynn let her say so two days ago? She'd been racking her brain and examining every facet of her heart to try to see whatever it was that her grandmother had seen. And she'd come up empty.

Sunshine greeted them as they stepped out into the back garden, and birds trilled their greeting. Beth expected Mamm-wynn to move to one of the chairs by the table, but instead she meandered toward the roses climbing up a trellis. Beth kept pace beside her and stole a sidelong glance at the family matriarch. "Am I allowed to apologize yet?"

The corners of Mamm-wynn's lips curved up, but only slightly. She kept her gaze on the roses. "Have you determined *why* you need to be apologizing?"

A huff slipped its way from Beth's lips. She might as well be five years old again. "For worrying you and Ollie. For going off alone without telling anyone. For bringing all this trouble down on our heads."

When her grandmother had first opened her eyes again after that terrifying bout of whatever-it-was that left her unconscious for days, they'd looked clouded. Vague. Pained. That had cleared, yes, but there'd still been something worrisome in them. Something . . . distant. Not rooted to the here and now.

But in the present, her gaze cut through her just like it always had, twin blue arrows. And her voice had nothing tremulous about it either. "Try again, Elizabeth Grace."

Beth sighed and lifted her arms. "I don't know, but whatever it is, I'm sorry for it. I promise you I am. And I also promise I'll not do it again."

Mamm-wynn chuckled as she reached out to touch one of the silky petals of a rose. "You don't know what it was, but you'll not do it again?"

She'd always hated having to apologize. She was no good at it— well, she was better than her cousin Mabena, who just refused to do

ROSEANNA M. WHITE

it altogether, but when compared to Oliver and Morgan, she was all
stumbles and new frustration. "Won't you just tell me?"

"You're the one who must do the telling." Mamm-wynn looked
over at her again and this time held her gaze. "And you know exactly
what I mean. This isn't over, is it? That silverware hiding in your
grandfather Gibson's foundation—is that all the treasure for which
dear Emily's family will be searching?"

Beth's throat went dry and tight. Leave it to Mamm-wynn to
somehow know the one thing Beth had still been hiding. The one
thing she didn't want to share with everyone else quite yet. "Unlikely."

Mamm-wynn's delicate white brows arched. "Why, then, have
you said nothing more to your brother and the others?"

Though Beth didn't dare to look away, she'd have liked to. Her
back went stiff. *It's mine*, she wanted to say. *My search. My work.*
Sharing had never been a strength of hers—but for good reason.
Growing up the youngest and the only girl meant her ideas were constantly dismissed by her two brothers. This, though . . . she'd poured
too much of herself into it. Too much time, too much energy. She'd
taken such huge risks, spent so many hours on it. If the others saw
it all and dismissed it or called it inconsequential or incomplete . . .

But that wouldn't be what Mamm-wynn was concerned with.
Not the treasure hunt, not the stacks of notes and books hiding even
now in her desk drawer. No, she'd be concerned with the relationships Beth had injured with her secrecy—and the ones that may be
injured still more if she didn't rectify it.

Another huff puffed out. But the frustration melted into regret
in the next second. "I shouldn't have kept it all from you and Ollie.
I was selfish. And then afraid—so afraid."

"There now, dearover." Mamm-wynn rested a hand on Beth's
cheek. Her knuckles had knotted over the years, and her skin was
soft and wrinkled. But she cupped Beth's cheek in just the way she'd
always done. "You're forgiven."

"Am I?" It made her chest go even tighter. "Even by Ollie?"

53

Her grandmother gave her a small smile. "I daresay his frustration with you has been greatly tempered by the fact that your poor choices led him to his dear Libby. But perhaps you ought to ask him, just to make sure. After."

"After?" But she knew what Mamm-wynn meant. After she came clean to the others and confessed that it was unlikely the Scofields would let this rest. Because they knew, as she did, that there were still many more clues to be followed. Many more pieces of treasure to try to find.

Her shoulders sagged, but only for a second. Then she mustered a smile and squared them again. "All right. I'll go and tell them now, shall I?"

Mamm-wynn's eyes twinkled. "You always were my favorite."

Exactly what she needed to make her laugh—given that Mamm-wynn said that to *all* of them—and shake off the uncertainty. She leaned over to kiss her grandmother's cheek. "I love you, Mamm-wynn. You can't know how glad I am that you're back on your feet."

"Well, I certainly can't be leaving you all yet—you need me far too much." She winked, grinned. "I had a good talk with the Lord about it, and I think He agrees."

Beth prayed He did. She and Ollie had said good-bye to so many family members in the last few years—she couldn't bear doing it again. Not yet. Not now.

Drawing in one more rose-fragrant breath, Beth turned to the house and marched toward it, then followed the voices still coming from the dining room. For a moment, she just stood there and watched them—this unexpected collection of people brought together because of her. She'd thought she was on a solitary adventure. How had it ended up so crowded?

Beth sighed. And cleared her throat, forcing a smile. "Mamm-wynn and I agreed that it was time I tell you all of . . . of everything else I've found."

Her brother's brows knit together as he looked up at her. "Everything *else*?"

She winced at the way he said it. "You don't really think one crate of silverware is Mucknell's entire haul, do you?"

Oliver opened his mouth, clearly ready to say that he had, but Lord Sheridan sprang to his feet first. "Obviously not! That is . . . well, I know *I'm* still here because there must be more."

Bully.

She kept her gaze on Ollie, watching the emotions that flowed over his face like a current. His expression settled on determination. Or perhaps resignation. "Well. If there is more, we should see it."

"Ah!" Sheridan sprang away from the table, eyes ablaze. "Excellent. I mean, do you need any help?"

What he *meant* was that he wanted to get his grubby paws on all her research, all her finds, all her weeks—months—of work. She sent him a scowl that he probably wouldn't even notice through the haze of his own excitement. "I have everything in my room, so . . ." The idiot man was starting around the table, as if he meant to vault up the stairs and grab it all. "So, *no*. You're not stepping foot in there, as my brother and everyone else with a shred of sensibility will guarantee."

He didn't slow. "Library! I'll clear the tables!"

She might have muttered a phrase that she'd learned from the girls at finishing school. And it might have made Emily giggle even as Libby frowned in confusion. And it also might have made her brother clear his throat and rise with that vicar cloak around his shoulders.

She rolled her eyes and turned to the door, but she couldn't convince her shoulders not to bunch up or her fingers not to curl into her palms. Perhaps Mamm-wynn was right that she *must* share, but that didn't make it any easier to do so.

Libby must have noted it. She reached out to put a calming hand on Oliver's arm, her face all compassion. "We don't have to go over it all if you don't want. Do we, Oliver? There's no need to hunt for more of Mucknell's treasure. We've found the silver, and that's all anyone was searching for, wasn't it? Why not let it rest?"

"What?" Lord Incorrigible was back in the doorway, horror on his face. "You can't—she mustn't—Telly, tell her."

Beth turned her head, along with everyone else, toward Lord Telford, Libby's brother. He hadn't said much through the meal, but that was no great surprise. He was utterly silent upon rising, never seemed to say a word until eleven, and was still largely quiet at midday. Though by afternoon he had a sarcastic rejoinder for every observation.

Beth quite liked him.

And Sheridan's oddities never ruffled him in the least. "Certainly. Libby, it's like this." He leaned forward, hand waving along with his words. "Sher is obsessed and won't give us a moment's peace until either we find every last coin of Mucknell's treasure or he's convinced that what remains can't be found by someone else."

Yes, she really quite liked Lord Telford.

Sheridan huffed. "Thanks, chum."

Telford grinned at him. "I am, as always, at your disposal."

And sarcastic or not, he was right. Even more to the point, they had reason to think that Emily's brother, Nigel, might be every bit as obsessed and considerably more cutthroat about it, so . . . "I need just a moment to gather it all."

"I'll help you." Libby moved to her side, a bit of apology now in her eyes.

Beth couldn't help but smile at her. She was a strange girl in some ways, this lady who kept her hair in a braid and wore the same style blouse and simple skirt that any islander would—other than at dinner, when she donned a gown, on those evenings when she joined them here. But it hadn't taken long to see why she'd captivated Oliver so quickly. She had a keen mind and a heart even keener to know and be known.

Libby loved Oliver. She loved Mamm-wynn. She loved the Scillies. And so Beth would welcome her to the family with open arms. "I appreciate it."

She darted a look to Emily to see if she wanted to tag along, too, which was all it took for her friend to scurry after them. Not surprising. Emily never liked being left alone with gentlemen. She'd flush crimson in about two seconds and forget she knew how to speak English. Funny, since she was bright and buoyant in the company of other girls, or even mixed company.

At the top of the stairs, Beth turned into her room, her eyes moving straightaway to the wall of shelves with its bare spot. For the last three years, that was where her trinket box had sat, proudly displayed in the place of honor. As a girl, she'd admired it endlessly on her mother's dressing table. She'd traced a finger over its crest, imagining the prince whose symbol it was. He would be tall, she'd decided, with hair as black as any Cornishman's. Handsome—obviously—with the sort of roguish charm that always sounded so intoxicating in a story, and which would be considerably less so in reality. And, of course, he would be a regular swashbuckler. That, after all, was part of the story.

Once there lived, and once there was, a beautiful maiden at the edge of the world. She made her home here on the islands, where the sea surrounded them day and night, bringing them life and bringing them death. And one day, it brought her a prince.

But he was more than just a prince, exiled here when his family's crown was stolen. He wasn't satisfied to sit and wait while his fortunes were restored. He had inside a drive to be the one to restore them. And so, this prince took to the seas, where he could wage war on his enemies and take back his family's lost treasure.

And he took to the Scillies, where an island girl waged war on his heart.

Not just a prince, but a pirate. She ought to have pieced together long ago that it was Prince Rupert her mother was talking about, the legendary pirate prince. He was a regular character in Tas-gwyn's tales—but then, that was the problem. Her grandfather had so exaggerated Prince Rupert's exploits, frequently turning him into a cursed figure, a magical one, a mythical one, that she'd forgotten he was *real*. Real and once vibrant and breathing and capable of falling in love with a girl who could never, except in a fairy tale, be accepted by his family.

They would have had, then, the typical dilemma—to defy family and risk losing everything he had to his name and marry her, or to indulge the yearning and defy their morals but save *his* reputation at the cost of hers.

In Mother's story, they married. What else would she tell her? But ever since the Scofields had verified that the crest on that box did indeed belong to Prince Rupert of the Rhine, she'd begun to wonder. That he'd given it to a local lass was likely. That he'd loved her was a reasonable explanation for the action. That he'd married her was as farfetched as Tas-gwyn's tales of walking skeletons.

And now who knew if she'd ever even see the box again? Unless she sneaked away to the Lake District and stole it from Sheridan's blasted castle.

Her lips tugged up. Come to think of it, that sounded like quite an adventure.

"Oh no. What are you grinning about?" Emily leaned close to Libby. "That grin is always a sign of trouble. She led me into all sorts of mischief when she grinned like that at school."

Beth laughed and turned to her desk and its locked drawer. "Relax, Em. I'm only deciding if I should break into Sheridan Castle and steal back my trinket box."

Emily's eye twitched. "*Only*, she says. *Relax*, she says."

Libby, at least, laughed. "I've been to Sheridan Castle. I can tell you the best way in. Though fair warning, it's a veritable museum, with all the artifacts he has. You could well get lost for a month trying to find one little box amidst all his ridiculous antiquities."

Emily turned a horrified look on Libby. "Now you've done it. She'll be gone again by morning."

"Don't tempt me." Beth toed off her shoe, which earned her raised brows from both her companions. At least until she pried away the heel and slid out the small key to her desk drawer.

58

Then they added dropped jaws to the look.

Beth sighed. "What? There's a thief in my house. I'm not taking any chances, nor do I trust him not to sneak in here looking for more Prince Rupert memorabilia when I'm not at home."

Emily looked dubious. "If you honestly believe he's so nefarious, why would a flimsy desk lock stop him?"

"I don't imagine it would *stop* him. But it may slow him until someone catches him at it." She turned to Libby—their resident Sheridan expert. "He doesn't know how to pick a lock, does he?"

Libby blinked. "Not that he's boasted of. Though really, I don't think he's quite as bad as all that, Beth. He's annoying, but he's *not* nefarious."

Funny. Beth didn't find him annoying—she simply didn't trust him even a morsel. Because he was a selfish, greedy, thieving cad. "He stole my trinket box."

Emily sighed. "That was my father. Though I'm certain he'd misunderstood your intentions."

She could excuse that opinion, given that Emily was his daughter. For her own part, Beth was happy to wash her hands of every Scofield but the one before her now.

Lord Scofield had been out only for his own profit—he and Emily's older brother both. She'd not yet met the younger Scofield, Nigel, but only because he'd mistaken Libby for her. Poor Libby. She'd received both the threats and the violence meant for Beth.

But even so. She crouched down to insert the key into the drawer's lock—which wasn't as flimsy as one might think. Morgan, when he was well enough, had enjoyed tinkering with such things. He'd not only fitted it with a stouter lock than it had come with, he'd also reinforced the drawer.

Well, granted, that was after he and Oliver had broken the old one in search of a diary, which she didn't even keep. Typical brothers. But he'd paid his penance with the fortifications. Unlike some other people she knew, whose sins went unrepented.

"Your family wouldn't have had that *misunderstanding* if Lord

More-Money-than-Sense hadn't offered them such a ridiculous sum for anything linked to Prince Rupert. Perhaps your father let his enthusiasm for a sale get ahead of his reason"—though she doubted it had been anything but intentional—"but Sheridan was still at the root of it."

Beth yanked the drawer out and pulled a stack of letters from within, holding it up for whoever wanted to take it. Someone did, so she followed it with another.

With the addition of what she'd added that morning, the drawer was crammed full. Letters from Mucknell to his wife, letters from his wife back to him—presumably from some point before his final voyage to the Caribbean, given that he must have brought them home with him again and stowed them there. Copies she'd made of the map that had led them to the queen's silverware Mucknell had stolen from a ship called the *Canary*. Books she'd borrowed from their library or her grandfather's, with helpful pages marked. Reams of notes she'd taken on other books she couldn't borrow indefinitely. Lists of every ship Mucknell's pirate fleet had reputedly struck and the cargoes they'd supposedly carried, when the Scofields had been able to dig them up for her in London.

It was rather fortunate that so many of the ships had been East Indiamen. The Company had kept meticulous records.

"Gracious." Emily took a stack of those manifests from her hands. "Did Father send you all of this? I had no idea it was so much. He must have had someone . . ."

At the way her voice trailed off, Beth looked up to find her friend staring into empty space, a frown marring her brow. "Had someone what?"

Emily blinked, pulled out a smile that looked about as authentic as the copy of the *Venus de Milo* Beth had attempted when she was ten, and cleared her throat. "Nothing, I'm sure. I only meant that he wouldn't have spent the days in the archives that fetching all this would have required. But he would have simply hired a clerk to do it. That's all."

If that was all, it wouldn't have given Emily such pause. Pursing her lips, Beth pulled out the last of her research, pushed the drawer closed, and stood. Rather than try to get her shoe back on without the help of her now-full hands, she toed the second one off too. "Which means someone else has a list of all the ships Mucknell took. For that matter, these aren't the originals, which means someone made the copies. Someone knows everything I know."

Emily hugged her stack of materials to her chest. "Well, of course. And I always assumed Father kept a record of everything he sent you—he's that sort. So naturally Nigel would have it all, but he's never been one to fuss over papers. I suppose I just had the thought . . . well, whoever else they have interested in this—the American. If perhaps he were as resourceful as Lord Sheridan has proven himself, willing to hire someone else to determine what we've learned . . ."

"If that someone finds the clerk who did this work," Libby filled in, "then he could access it all as well. If it were someone whose loyalty could be bought, not your family members themselves."

Emily nodded.

Beth let out a loud exhale and stomped to the door. "Just in case we hadn't enough players involved already, I suppose." She flashed a smile at them over her shoulder to let them know she didn't begrudge *their* involvement—much—and led the way back into the corridor and down the stairs.

And truly, she did appreciate having friends surrounding her. Without a doubt, this quest had grown too large and dangerous for her alone. Still, it had been rather grand in the spring when it was her own private mission. Just her own wits, her own sense of adventure, her own intimate knowledge of every nook and cranny of the islands, earned through two decades of bold—and occasionally foolhardy—exploration. Her own victory when she found another piece to the puzzle. Her own disappointment when she ran into a dead end. No one else there to cluck their tongue or scowl at her.

Or to all but leap upon her with their demands and expectations the moment she entered a room, as Sheridan did when she dared to step foot in the library. "Let me help," he said with his lips as he snatched a few books and papers from the top of her pile. *Let me see everything you've worked so hard to find*, he said with his overeager claws.

Had she another set of hands, she would have grabbed the things right back. "Bar the windows, Ollie. Don't let him make off with *these* things."

She was a bit surprised when Sheridan turned to meet that little barb rather than letting it roll off him. "I believe," he said with half a smile, "that of the two of us—well, *I'm* not the one with a habit of vanishing. Am I?"

"Touché." Oliver had moved forward, too, to relieve Libby of her burden. And to linger there at her side. But he smiled. Actually smiled at a reference to Beth's disappearance, which she knew well had caused him no end of grief and worry.

He'd forgiven her, just as Mamm-wynn had said he had. Beth had to blink a few rapid times to clear the unexpected relief of it from her eyes. Worrying him had been the last thing she'd wanted to do.

No, not true. Seeing him hurt, or Mamm-wynn, had been the last thing she wanted. She'd gone into hiding to avoid it, after Johnnie Rosedew was killed and her own life threatened by one of the thugs Sheridan had hired. She hadn't known how else to keep them safe.

But she hadn't. The danger had still found them. Tas-gwyn and Mabena had both been clubbed over the head. Mamm-wynn had suffered an episode that had left her unconscious. Oliver had been shot—though only grazed, praise God.

"Oof," Emily grunted, walking into Beth's back while she stood there in a daze of forgiveness.

"Sorry!" Beth took a large step forward to catch her balance and hurried to the table to get out of the way. Not soon enough, though, as evidenced by thuds of books and notebooks hitting the floor. She winced, hoping both that Emily was all right and that nothing she'd dropped was damaged or their order lost.

But the books looked fine, and none of the loose sheets had been in Emily's charge. Libby and Oliver were already helping to pick it all up, and Telford strode that direction too. Beth decided she could best serve the cause by staying out of the way and laying what remained in her arms out on the table. She moved to its far side to do so, leaving the nearer one open to her friends.

Sheridan had already spread out the things he'd liberated from her and was poring over them. "Ships' manifests, yes?"

"Mm." As if he couldn't tell that easily enough.

He ran a finger down one of the columns. "From the ships . . . must be what Mucknell took, then?"

Was it even a question? "Clearly."

"All East Indiamen."

"Hence the mark of the Company in the corner of each sheet." She crossed her arms over her chest. Was he really talking to her, or just to himself?

He flipped through the stack of manifests, brows hiking upward. "Quite a career he made of it, didn't he? I say. All these in—well now. How long was he prowling these waters? Must have been . . ." He looked upward, lips moving as he presumably performed some sort of calculation.

Beth rolled her eyes and turned back to the others. He didn't need her input. And if she were being honest with herself, she didn't much like watching anyone else thumb through the documents she'd paid such a high price for.

But it wasn't just her—she had to keep reminding herself of that. They'd *all* paid a high price.

Well, most of them. So far as she could tell, Lord Sheridan had gotten off quite easily thus far. Come out ahead, in fact.

Oliver moved to her side, sliding his stack onto the table but also leaning closer to her. His hair, as dark a brown as his eyes, brushed his collar. Always in need of a trim.

He looked so much like Mother. The dark Cornish hair, the deep Cornish eyes. Sometimes it hurt to look at him. But the good kind of hurt that made her never want to look away.

He glanced over the table as the others put down their pieces. He'd be noting what she already knew. That it was so much to go through. So much to have gathered. So much of her time spent on this when she'd lied to him and said she was after a holiday. She turned her back on it all and rested against one of the chairs.

He bumped his shoulder into hers. "I know how hard it is for you. To let us all see it."

Her breath eased out in a whoosh, and she let herself lean into him. The others were all facing the table now, but she stayed facing away, toward the window. "I suppose you'll say I should have invited you in from the start."

His laugh was quiet. Just theirs. "Part of me wants to. But if you had, then Benna wouldn't have brought Libby here. So, all in all, I wouldn't change your choices."

For a moment—just one—she let her head rest on his shoulder. "I never meant for anyone to get hurt."

"I know." A beat of silence and then, "That's a lot of adventure on that table, isn't it? And to think it was all from right here on our own little islands."

Her shoulders went tense again. Not at what he said, but at what he didn't. What he'd be thinking, what he had said so many times before. In his mind, the Scillies held everything anyone could ever need. And here was the proof, gathered by her own hands, that even the adventure she craved could be found here. That she had no reason to look anywhere else for it. No reason ever to stretch her wings. To leave the islands.

Oliver sighed. "Beth . . . for what it's worth, I don't believe Sheridan ever meant anyone to get hurt either. Go a little easier on him, will you? He's our guest."

"He's *your* guest. I—" She cut herself off when a figure passed by the open window. "Senara!"

5

Mrs. Dawe had said she'd arrived home this morning, but Beth had scarcely believed it.

Still didn't, even when Senara paused at the greeting and walked back to the window with a smile. "Little Beth, still hanging out of windows when she ought to be studying."

She hadn't been hanging out of it—but she did so now, with a laugh. "Silly Senara, always after me to mind my manners when she ought to be having fun." Oh, how good it was to see her. When she was little, she'd always wanted to be just like Senara. So pretty, with that Cornish dark hair Beth had wished *she* had inherited from Mother instead of Mamm-wynn's fair coloring. So smart, so beloved by everyone. And *older*, which was what Beth had wanted most at the age of ten.

The really interesting things in the stories only ever seemed to happen to older girls.

She'd been convinced when Senara left to be a governess that she'd come home married to her employer, like any proper Jane Eyre would do. Except that her employer was quite married already, and his wife was no madwoman locked in an attic and soon to die. And, Senara being as she was, she'd been far too focused on raising

65

the Clifford children all these years to pause to find a likely hero elsewhere.

Beth smiled. "I can't believe you're home! How long? A week? Don't rush off again before we have the chance to spend some time together." Which could be tricky to find, given the collection of people behind her who she wasn't about to allow to take over her treasure hunt.

Senara's glance moved past her into the room, then settled on Beth again. Her eyes were a strange sort of quiet, absent the dancing spark of light usually in them. "I won't be rushing off."

No? That was rather odd.

"Ah!"

Beth's head swiveled back around to see what Sheridan was exclaiming over *now*. He had a packet of letters in his hand, that was all. She turned back to the out of doors.

Senara gave her a tight smile. "Methinks the lady had better attend her guests for now. But we'll catch up, Beth. I'll tell you all about how I lost my position."

"You *what*?" But that was unfathomable. There was no better governess to be found in all the world, and Senara loved the Clifford girls like her own. How could she possibly have been sacked?

Senara's glance darted into the room again. "Later. If not tonight, then tomorrow. I promise."

Beth frowned, but she could do little else than mutter, "All right." Something was clearly amiss with her old friend. But now was clearly not the time to discover what.

Senara gave her another tight smile, lifted a hand, and strode away. Beth turned slowly back to the room again.

Oliver was taking charge, as Oliver always did, in that quiet way that tricked you into thinking he was serving you, not commanding you. Assigning each of them something to read, making it sound like a suggestion based on each's preference. And the others accepted their assignments with smiles and enthusiasm.

Beth let herself grin. It was always amusing to watch him do such things with others. It was a bit less so when she was the one he was subtly bossing, and she didn't even realize it until she was halfway through whatever he'd got her doing. There were a lot of half-finished projects lurking around the islands as a result.

"And Sheridan, if you . . ." Oliver trailed off as he turned to Lord Sheridan, who had somehow made himself comfortable in one of the hard little desk chairs and was already through two letters, it looked like. Oliver just nodded and turned to Beth. "Are you going to supervise us?"

Stand there like an imbecile, he meant. Do nothing while the others learned something new. She fidgeted at the very suggestion. But what was left for her? She already knew the material, and his divvying up hadn't left a portion for her anyway.

She ought to have jumped out that window—it was ground floor, it wouldn't have mattered—and joined Senara.

Or . . . there were still those empty margins of *Treasure Island* beckoning to her and the story she now believed to be about Prince Rupert begging to be put to paper. "No, I have another task waiting. Excuse me just a moment."

She had to dash back up to her room to fetch the book, which she'd stashed inside a hatbox that morning, but she was back again in a flash, pencil in hand. Leaving the table to the others, Beth folded herself into one of the comfortable reading chairs in the corner of the room, tucking her shoeless feet up under her and using her knees to shield the book from her brother's sight. If he saw her writing in his book before she'd presented him with his new copy, he might just toss her out of a window that was *not* on the ground floor. Her seated position was terribly unladylike, but just now, Beth didn't care.

Blame it on the month spent in hiding on Samson. The wind and rain and days of unending quiet had taken some of her finish off, she suspected. Returned her, as she could imagine Libby saying, to a state closer to nature.

To how she could imagine that island girl from centuries gone by being. She would have had to be beautiful, to catch a prince's eye. But not the kind of beauty he could find in the courts of Europe. A wild beauty. Untamed. Like Mabena, maybe—heaven knew half the lads on Tresco had been in love with her growing up. She glanced up, expecting to see her cousin there, but then grinned at her absence. Benna had declared the Tremayne house far too crowded with society—and she had a point. Another few days and Beth might escape to her aunt and uncle's house too . . . though she still couldn't imagine darkening the door of the Wearnes', which was where Mabena had been spending much of her time.

Or maybe the island girl had been like Senara, with that quieter strength that had always said, *"You can shake me, storms, but I am made of Tresco granite. I'll not budge."*

Beth scrawled a few paragraphs into the margins, trying to remember each and every word as Mother had said them. Scrawled them lightly, so that if she remembered something differently later, she and a rubber eraser could put it easily to rights.

And he took to the Scillies, where an island girl waged war on his heart.

She paused a moment. If this *was* Prince Rupert, then her imaginings hadn't been so far off. She'd dug up a bit of history about him when she realized her box bore his crest and found a book that had prints of paintings of him, along with descriptions. He was indeed tall—standing at six feet, four inches. His hair, long enough to be fashionable in the seventeenth century, had been black as night. In the painting, he'd worn it curled, but that's not how it would have been on his ship. He'd have had it tied back, revealing the sharp lines of his face. And in place of the regalia from the artwork, he'd have been in serviceable clothes, captain's clothes. Pirate's clothes.

When he first stepped foot on Tresco, would the girl have even realized he was more than the average buccaneer? Had he told her, or waited until he knew she loved him for himself, not just his title? These were the questions Mother's story had never delved into.

Beth's pencil hovered over the paper. She wanted to get it down exactly as it had been told her. But perhaps she'd write another version later too. One with her own imaginings thrown in.

For now, Mother's version.

As a storm blew itself out in the Scillies, the prince sought shelter with a local family. They were island stock, born and bred. Island stock, half-starved and double-stubborn. But gracious to strangers, and they took him in. Offered him what food they had, a bed to rest in. They had two daughters, this fine family. One married already and to another island gone—one at home still, and learning to keep it. The prince took one look at her upon crossing the threshold and fell deep into the throes of love.

"That's quite a look. Of question, I mean. On your face."

She flicked her glance to the side, where the voice had come from. And down. Where, inexplicably, Lord Sheridan had settled himself onto the floor beside her chair. He was spreading the letters out before him in a semicircle. Perhaps the table hadn't offered room enough?

Still. She never would have thought to find the marquess in such a position. It was disarming. Which was probably what convinced her tongue to loosen. "Do you believe in love at first sight?"

The stack of letters still in his fingers fell to the floor. Luckily only three inches. "Oh, ah. Well." He drew in a breath and angled a look up at her. "Do you?"

She shrugged. "I want to. And it's part of the story about Prince Rupert and his island miss. It's part of so many old stories. But the real-life love stories I know—my grandparents, my parents, Mabena and Casek, those two . . ." She nodded to where Oliver and Libby had their heads together at the table. "That sort of love, the kind that goes so deep, takes time to dig in. Perhaps not much. But more than a glance."

Sheridan nodded, too, looking as though he was actually contemplating the question. "Perhaps *love* isn't the word, then. For that first strike, I mean. Infatuation. Attraction. Though, too—there could be a knowing. Yes? The thought, from the first glance, that this is the one for me. Perhaps the deep love has to dig in over time. Chisel itself in. To one's heart, that is. Or rather, chisel the heart into its shape. But sometimes lightning does strike."

She nodded. He had a point. "And lightning can do in a heartbeat what it would take a chisel forever to accomplish." Perhaps it was silly to try to put logic to something as defiant as love at first sight. Perhaps it was silly to hope there *was* an explanation for it.

He smiled at her. "Just so."

He was related, if distantly, to the prince. Did they share any features? Perhaps later she'd hold that print of the painting up to him and compare. She had a feeling he'd be game for the experiment. Perhaps Prince Rupert's smile had been like his. Earnest and bright, its light deceitfully simple.

The island miss would have had no idea what secrets and intrigues he was hiding behind that innocent-looking smile.

She put pencil to margin again.

Though he knew he should not, the prince tended that love and nurtured it, seeking to win his lady's heart against all logic. But the girl resisted his wooing words. She had no use for a pirate—and less of one for a prince. But as the days and weeks wore on, her heart grew ever warmer toward him. It was not his sweet words that won her. It was not the gifts he pressed into her hands. It was the honor and respect he gave to her parents, the recognition that in order to give to him, they went without. A sacrifice he was determined to repay.

At last, she had to admit that her heart was his. But alas, she was nearly too late! For the prince must sail off soon, in search of the treasure to restore his kingdom. One night but a week before he was set to sail, she confessed her love under the light of a full moon. And the prince, in a rapture, fell to one knee, begging her to become his bride then and there.

It was foolish—for what king would accept an island miss as his daughter? But love demanded nothing less than this. And so they found the island priest and they had an island wedding, and for one blissful week, they were simply an island man with his island wife.

But then came the day when the prince must sail again. He clasped his bride to his chest and kissed her farewell, half hoping she would beg him to stay. But our new princess knew that her island, beloved but bare, was no kingdom for her love. She knew he must leave her for a while. Strong as the granite, brave as the wind, she bade him Godspeed.

And into her hands he pressed one last gift.

Beth paused again, a smile playing over her lips. This had always been her favorite part of the story. When Mother got to this part, Beth would bounce up and down, the wonder of it too great to hold inside. *"The box!"* she'd cry. *"The box!"* And she'd run from wherever she was to her mother's room, grab the trinket box from the dressing table, and run back to her laughing mama with the treasure clasped to her chest.

A wooden box, once filled with naught but a prince's trinkets. Filled now with a prince's treasure. Not that she opened it then to see. Nay, in that moment, the only treasure she cared for was the love in his eyes. She needed nothing more, she said to him. But he bade her take what he had to give, to care for herself while he was gone. And he promised that the box held the key to her future, and that he would return to her as fast as sea and sail allowed.

"The key to your future."

Beth jumped a bit at Sheridan's mumble, looked over. Fully expecting to find that he had risen to his knees and was peering over at what she'd just written. She wouldn't put it past him.

But he still sat cross-legged on the floor, hunched over the letters.

Beth closed *Treasure Island* over her pencil. "What was that?"

Sheridan tapped a finger to a page. And then to another. And another. "A phrase. Keeps reappearing. Mucknell to his wife, over and again. Much like—there's the one at the end. That we've already sorted. The 'look to the birds' bit that helped us know how to read

71

the map to the silverware, but this . . . you've noticed it?" He looked up, green eyes like twin flames of excitement.

Beth shook her head, her pulse skyrocketing half in anticipation and half in dread. Had she really missed a vital clue after all the times she'd read through those letters? Or was he just reading into it something that wasn't really there? "What does it say?"

He turned back to the old pages. "This first one—they're still in order—he says, 'I know you disapprove, my love, but this is the key to your future.' And then in this one." He picked up another page. "'I know sometimes it must seem that the key to your future is just out of reach.' And then here again . . ." He replaced that page and reached for a third. "'I am sorry it has been so long that I've been away. But remember that I've left you with the key to your future.' Is it me? Or does that sound like a *thing*?"

"It does, yes." And she'd noticed that during her own readings, too, and assumed he was referring to something he'd entrusted to her care that she could sell, or even an action she could take. But now her own words, Mother's words, were still fresh in her mind, and she had to wonder if it was that straightforward. "That's odd, though."

"What?"

She reopened the book and stared at her scribbles. "In this story my mother used to tell about the pirate prince, there's the same phrase." She looked up again and saw that the others were listening now too—except for Lord Telford, who'd taken the chair in the opposite corner and sat with a book open, eyes intent on it, and a finger resting at his mouth. Libby's cat, which Beth hadn't even realized was in the house today, was curled up on his shoulder.

"Really." Now Sheridan did push to his knees and try to look over her shoulder at the book.

And now she let him, even indicating the line. "But this is the prince—Prince Rupert—to his island bride."

"Prince Rupert didn't marry," he muttered, eyes already on her writing. "Kept a string of mistresses."

She'd read the history books just as he had. Though she had to admit the statement sounded a bit different when it was spoken by a man two inches away instead of in neat, orderly black text on a page.

Princes and brides and mistresses. Illegitimate offspring that he at least acknowledged and left his estate to. It didn't seem quite proper to discuss it with a marquess hanging over her chair.

But it was the story. "Perhaps he had those mistresses because he *did* marry, but he left her here in the Scillies. He never came back for her, but he must have acknowledged the vow enough that he didn't do something as low as take a second wife and pretend the first didn't exist."

Sheridan frowned. "Certainly the same phrase. What are the chances that both Prince Rupert and Admiral Mucknell spoke to their wives about 'the key to their future'?"

From his place at the table, Oliver cleared his throat. Apology was etched on his face. "Not to put a damper on whatever it is you're thinking, but I don't recall that part of Mother's story about the prince. I daresay it's far more likely that Beth has put it in *because* she's read all those letters so many times. She must have picked up on the phrase without realizing it and inserted it into her account."

Her shoulders went stiff as boulders. "I did not."

"It's not an accusation, Beth. We all do such things without knowing it."

Her brother's attempt to mollify her only made her that much more certain. "You didn't hear the story as many times as I did. She told it the same each and every time, word for word, and I'm telling you that this phrase was in there."

Libby looked from Beth to Oliver, clearly not enjoying the argument. "Perhaps it was. But even if so, it can't be anything but an interesting coincidence, can it? It's still just a story your mother told you."

Beth shook her head with energy enough that a flying curl caught on Sheridan's jacket and she had to smooth it back to her own head. "She heard it from her mother, and her grandmother before that. I daresay she took the words straight from their mouths, just as I've done."

"It isn't far-fetched." Sheridan rested his arms on the chair, not seeming to notice how he crowded her. "Oral traditions are—well, rather sacred really. Often preserved with more care, even. Than written accounts, I mean. It's quite possible that this story as Beth has written it is exactly, word for word, what was first told, oh, centuries ago. Two and a half, perhaps."

Miss Tremayne, he ought to be calling her. Were they in London, he'd never have dreamed of using her nickname so freely.

But they were on the islands, where *everyone* called her Beth. And at the moment, she nearly liked him, so she let it slide. "Exactly. Which means it's no coincidence. It means that Mucknell and Rupert both used the phrase to their wives before they left together for the Caribbean."

"*Might* have." Oliver's apology had turned into a stubbornness of his own. "Though I find it unlikely that it means anything, even if they did."

"Why?" Sheridan, finally, rocked back down to his heels. "That other phrase in the letters was the clue, wasn't it? To the silver-ware, that is. The map. Why not think this is the same? A clue that will lead us . . . somewhere?" He turned his hopeful gaze to Beth. "Where though?"

Where indeed? That was the question. Beth tapped a finger to her lips. "I think we can assume this key to their future is some sort of money or treasure that Mucknell secreted away as a form of security."

Oliver snorted. "Quite an assumption. We don't even know there *is* more of Mucknell's treasure."

"Take it back!" Sheridan looked ready to challenge her brother to a duel for such a statement. "You think the Scillies' most famous pirate would—that one crate of silver was all?"

"All he captured and kept? No." Oliver slid a look to Libby. Perhaps for support. Or perhaps just because he was *always* sneaking looks at Libby. "All that he didn't spend or trade or return to the Prince of Wales, whom he was supposed to be turning it over to? Perhaps."

"Even if that's true, our point now is what Mr. Scofield believes." Libby's fingers had woven with Oliver's again. That seemed to happen as often as the looks they were always sneaking. "Do they have copies of these letters?"

Beth shook her head. "Not all of them, anyway. I sent transcriptions of two. The one dated the twelfth of October 1649, and the one from the first of February of the previous year."

Sheridan plucked the two from his semicircle, eyes flying over them. "I don't think . . . no. The phrase isn't in these."

"Which means that Nigel Scofield knows nothing about it, which means it oughtn't be where we direct our attention." Oliver said it so decisively, as if it were the last word that needed to be said on the matter.

Beth tossed *Treasure Island* to the floor just to hear its hollow thud when it smacked down. "Are we trying only to stop Nigel Scofield, or are we trying to find Mucknell's treasure?"

"Stop Scofield." From Oliver and Libby, Telford and Emily—though Em said, "Stop Nigel," naturally.

"Find the treasure," Sheridan shouted at the same time. Louder than the others. But singly.

Beth wished she had another something handy to toss down too. Of all the people to be her ally in this, why did it have to be *him*? "Well. You all can focus on what Em's brother knows, then. Lord Sheridan and I will find the rest of the treasure by ourselves."

From his chair, Telford snorted. "Right. Just like that. How long have you both been looking already?"

You know, come to think of it, she didn't really like Libby's brother after all.

"He's right, Beth." The apology was back in Oliver's voice, though it was flinty this time. "Even if there *were* more treasure, and even if this phrase in the letters and Mother's story *were* a clue, and even if finding it *were* at all our priority, we'd still have no idea where to look."

She pushed to her feet, scooping the book up with her on her way. Just in case she needed to throw it again. "*You* may not have ideas where to look. *I* have plenty of them." She pivoted Sheridan's way and found he'd stood too. "What do you say, my lord? Do you want to go exploring with me tomorrow?"

He may be a selfish, greedy thief, but at least he knew how to play co-conspirator. Sheridan grinned. "Name the time."

6

Y ou're mad."
This pronouncement, delivered by Ainsley with his usual calm demeanor, was inspired by the fog billowing its way through Old Grimsby.

Well, to be fair, it wasn't the fog that had Sheridan's valet calling down indictments of insanity. It was the fact that, despite it, Sheridan was still reaching for his hat. "Beth said she can navigate through it without a problem."

"I don't doubt that she said so." Before a normal outing, Ainsley would be holding out the pair of shoes he'd prefer Sheridan wear, insisting he take off the clean ones he'd designated as house shoes. Just now, he stood there with arms crossed and hands decidedly, accusingly empty. "The fact that you believe her, and are willing to stake your life on it, is what makes you mad."

"Thanks for spelling it out." He looked down at his own shoes. He'd worn this pair outside before, hadn't he? They'd be fine for hiking over whatever outlying island Beth was about to haul him to.

Or perhaps those brown ones there would be better. Those soles had more grip, didn't they? Though none of them were right. "Why on earth didn't you pack my boots?"

Were he anyone but Ainsley, Ainsley would have rolled his eyes.

"I didn't realize you'd be undergoing any archaeological digs. This was supposed to be a quick trip to bring Lady Elizabeth home."

Sheridan tried on that too-long blink, though he suspected he didn't pull it off quite so well. "Have you met me?"

It won him a breath of a laugh. "I have. Which is why I *did*." And like a magician worthy of Merlin himself, he opened the wardrobe, moved aside something or another, and produced Sheridan's favorite pair of sturdy leather boots.

He seized them with glee. "You're getting a raise."

"Mm. I would settle for you rethinking this morning's outing. It's too dangerous."

"Hardly. She knows these islands inside out." Sheridan sat on the chair beside the wardrobe so he could take off his house shoes and put his feet in their happier home.

"And locals who know it just as well nevertheless end up caught out and losing their lives far too often." His face a mask of sobriety and sorrow, Ainsley held out a hand for the rejected pair of footwear.

Sheridan handed them over and tugged on the first boot. "Bully. The shoes, I mean. Not you. Although now that I mention it . . ."

Ainsley shook his head. "The Tremaynes' parents died on these seas. And they were hardly the first victims of a capricious current."

"I'll say a prayer to the sea gods." He tied the first boot's strings.

Ainsley said nothing. Just *breathed*.

Sheridan sighed. He really was a bully. "A joke. I'm not a heathen. Abbie and Millicent wouldn't stand for it." He might not be quite as vocally devout as his sisters—or his valet, for that matter—but he was far from a pagan. Which Ainsley ought to have known, given the daily reading of Scripture they always had as a group whenever they were on a dig, in which Sheridan took part with no complaint. And he barely even fidgeted at home anymore when Millicent held morning prayers with all the staff. He enjoyed learning about the Druids and ancient Britons, true, but that was only because they'd left such interesting artifacts behind that he enjoyed puzzling out—

standing stones and burial cairns and the like. He didn't actually believe as they had.

He put on the second boot. Tied it. Stood. And blustered out another sigh at Ainsley's continued silence. "Look, Ains, I appreciate your concern. Truly, I do. But Beth Tremayne has asked me to join her, and I'm not about to let her go alone, which she would. Gentlemanly, right?"

Ainsley cocked his head and blinked. Again. Though this time he spoke too. "You like her."

Sheridan's neck went hot. Blasted complexion. "Of course I do. She's a fine young lady." Adventurous. Spirited. Intelligent. Tempestuous. And beautiful too. "Much like Lady Elizabeth and Lady Emily. I like them all."

"Somehow I doubt you'd be beside Lady Elizabeth in this fog if she was insisting upon a search for some flora or fauna."

Sheridan's face screwed up at the very thought. "You have a point. All right then, I admit it. It's the treasure hunt too. And nearly all the islands have cairns. I've been wanting to explore some of them, and the fog will keep other tourists away."

"That *should* be what it is. But it's not all, is it?" Ainsley folded his arms over his chest and shook his head. "You *like* her."

It wasn't the proper word for it. Though the ones he'd listed last night when she'd about given him an apoplexy, asking his opinion on love at first sight, didn't seem right either. Infatuation sounded so . . . juvenile. Attraction—true, but far too simple. There were scads of beautiful girls in the world, after all. And it wasn't as though Telly—who usually had fine taste in women—reacted to her as Sheridan had. So it had to be more than pleasing features and neither-blue-nor-grey eyes.

Maybe it was that *knowing* he'd tossed out just to see if she denied the possibility of it. An instant recognition.

"My lord. No."

No? How was *he* to know if Sheridan's soul had recognized its perfect match or not? Though come to think of it, how was he to read his mind either, to know that's what he'd been debating? "I beg your pardon?"

"It isn't a good idea to direct your attentions that way."

Not a mind reader, but a decent Sheridan reader nonetheless. Not that he had any right to dictate Sheridan's choice in a wife, as he did his choice in shoes.

Though, blast it, he didn't look dictatorial, just concerned. "You're a marquess. You own the largest estate in the Lake District. You can trace your lineage back to King James the First."

"I know my pedigree, Harry."

Ainsley winced. So far as Sheridan had been able to ferret out, no one in all the world called Henry Ainsley *Harry*. Which was why he saved it for these moments when he most needed to poke at the chap.

Still, his valet decided to have his say. "The Tremaynes are a landed family, and I realize there will soon be an alliance between them and the Telfords. But they are not your peers in any sense of the word, and you know very well your sisters would not approve."

Wouldn't they? Sheridan had been reaching once again for his hat but paused. It had never occurred to him that they'd look at her family connections instead of herself. They were always so quick to make friends, both of them. Why wouldn't they take to her as they did everyone else?

But he'd never introduced anyone else as a possible future marchioness and sister-in-law. Well, other than Libby, but she was obviously a fine match, from the society point of view.

But the Tremaynes *were* a fine family. Perfectly respectable. And if they dared say anything in opposition, he'd just liken her to Elizabeth Bennet and pray they wouldn't point out that Mr. Darcy had no title he had to live up to.

"Relax, Ainsley. I haven't proposed." Though last night he'd added another stupid way of doing so to his growing list of them. *So, Beth, you said you wanted to believe in love at first sight? Well, you've made a believer out of me. It's only fair, then, that you marry me.*

He swiped his hat off the table and left the room before his valet could dispense any more advice, spoken or silent. Marched directly to the front door, where he was to meet Beth. And frowned out the window.

The fog was thick as wool. It really *was* pure madness to try to sail in it.

"Ready?" But there his lady was, a smile on her face and flinty determination in her eyes. She was dressed more like Libby than her own usual choices, a cardigan of green topping her blouse and doing lovely things to her face.

"Ah." He cleared his throat. "If you are. Though if you'd rather wait for the fog to clear . . ."

Beth waved that away and pulled open the door. Fog billowed in around her. "If we wait, Oliver will talk me out of going."

Sheridan snorted a laugh. "I don't believe you."

She smiled, then stepped out into the cloud. "All right, he'll *try*. And having to be stubborn before breakfast always ruins my day."

"Noted."

He followed her voice into the mist and softly closed the door behind him. He could make out Beth easily enough, being only a step away, and maybe, possibly, the trellis beyond her. But past the gate, the world ceased to exist.

Blast it, Ainsley was right. Utter madness.

Beth hooked her arm through his. So now there was nothing he could do but go along.

She led him through what he presumed was the village, though it was more hulking, shifting shadows than buildings. The streets were still quiet, whereas he'd normally have expected a bit of activity by now. But the fishermen would already be out, he supposed, and the land-run businesses not yet open.

And he didn't exactly mind the sensation of being utterly alone with her, their own little island in a world of clouds. It seemed wrong to shatter the stillness with words, so he held his silence as they followed the road down toward the quay. He knew that Beth

81

had her own sloop, smaller than the *Adelle*, in which her brother had ferried them all about. He'd yet to see it, and he'd certainly never been invited aboard.

The fog was no less wooly at the shore, but the sounds of the sea broke the silence. Which must mean he could do the same. "Have you always sailed?"

She grinned up at him, her fair curls darkened to gold by the mist. "Always. For a Scillonian, sailing is like riding a horse on the mainland. We all learn it, along with swimming. It's our only way of connecting the islands, and none of them are large enough to be entirely self-sufficient. The water is our road."

Like he'd said yesterday morning. Look at them, in agreement about so much. How could they be anything but soul mates? "So, your sloop is like a pony? Every child gets one when they turn five?"

She laughed outright at that—a victory he knew he'd won by taking her side yesterday afternoon. It wasn't the fairy bells of her grandmother's laugh, but full-throated and warm. "I'd been manning the *Adelle* since I was big enough to hang onto a line, but I was thirteen when I got my own. I think most people thought my parents were spoiling me by giving it to me, but Uncle Jeremiah is a shipwright. He crafted matching sloops for Mabena and me. Her *Mermaid*. And my *Naiad*. She's the loveliest sloop ever to sail round the archipelago."

He had to wonder if the names would earn the same silence from Ainsley that his joke about sea gods had. "I can't wait to meet her. How will I know if she likes me?"

Another laugh punctuated her tug toward a particular mast. "If she doesn't toss you into the drink."

"Ah. Just like all the girls, then." He waited for the rest of the boat to take shape through the fog, hoping it was as lovely as she claimed, so that he could agree with her some more.

He needn't have worried. Even draped with mist, Jeremiah Moon's expert craftsmanship was on display. Elegant lines, streamline shape, smooth wood polished to a shine. "Does your uncle export any of his masterpieces? I have a lake." And a boathouse already full of things to put on it. But none so lovely as this.

She quirked a brow at him. "For the right price."

"So I assumed. Craftsmen rarely part with their work for the *wrong* price." And he rarely tried to haggle them down. He knew full well he was better off than most people—his ancestors had been a boring lot, making wise investments, never gambling it all away, not even purchasing expensive houses in out-of-the-way towns for keeping mistresses in. He couldn't squander his inheritance even if he tried.

A few minutes later, they were aboard the *Naiad*, Beth had unfurled the sails, and they were tacking into the breeze. And the fog. "Not that I doubt you. But let's call me curious. You've no instruments. No vision to speak of just now. How do you know where you're going?"

She pulled a watch from her pocket and held it up like it was some sort of answer. "With this and my lead line, I can tell how fast I'm going. I've a compass in my other pocket to give me my direction. What more could I need?"

He could think of a few dozen things. A hot cup of tea currently topping the list. Wasn't this part of the country supposed to be warmer than the rest? It certainly didn't feel like it just now, with the fog biting at his fingers. He folded them under his opposite arms. "Are you going to tell me yet where we're going?"

She'd refused last night, though he liked to think it was to spite the others and not because she didn't trust him. Wishful thinking, but what was life without a few wishes?

She considered it for a long moment first. "Gugh."

"Gugh. Rhymes with Hugh and holding hands with St. Agnes."

Those lovely golden brows quirked up at him again.

He decided to take it as a compliment on his clever mnemonics. "Not how you learned all the islands' names?"

"Can't say that it is. Why did you bother learning them at all?"

Now she sounded like Telly, who hadn't much appreciated his

83

mnemonics either as Sheridan chanted them over and again on the train to Penzance. "Because I'm here. What's the point of coming to a place if you don't learn about it? It's half the fun."

He couldn't tell by the way she regarded him if she agreed with that or not. But she tilted her head in a way that had her braid spilling over her shoulder, and the fog curled around her, and he was fairly certain she was the naiad after whom her sloop was named, all magic and myth. "So, what did you learn about Gugh already? Aside from the fact that it rhymes with Hugh."

"And is holding hands with St. Agnes. Don't forget that part." He grinned and turned his face toward what he suspected might be the sun, though he couldn't be entirely certain. A slightly lighter part of the sky, anyway. "I admit, I'm charmed by all these tombolos connecting your islands. This one's only visible at low tide, correct?"

"That's right." She hummed out a sigh. "I sometimes wonder what Scilly was like in the Roman days, before the sea rose, when it was all one big island."

"Nearly tropical—or so I've read. All of England, that is. Or much of it. They grew orange trees here, you know."

"Really?" She fished her compass out of her other pocket and held it out to him. "I have a feeling you know how to use this."

He kept his own in *his* pocket at all times. But no point in digging it out if hers was unearthed already. "Looks exactly like mine." And it was still warm from her body heat too. *You should marry me, Beth, so our compasses can be friends.*

He cleared his throat. "Otherwise—back to Gugh. There's the Old Man as the primary interest. Standing stone from the Bronze Age, most likely. And a cairn that Bonsor excavated a few years ago. Quite a chap—I heard him lecture in London last year. Not about Gugh. An excavation in Spain. Even so, it was fascinating stuff. Did you meet him while he was here?"

Her lips twitched. "I might have."

He'd only known her a week, but he knew mischief when it twitched. "What did you do?"

84

"A few of us children might have played a bit of a prank, that's all. We snuck into Obadiah's Barrow one night and buried a few surprises for him."

"No!" He didn't know whether to be amused or horrified. "You interfered with a sanctioned archaeological dig?"

She chuckled. "I wouldn't call it *interfering*. It was only chicken bones and a few beads. Didn't fool him for a moment, much to our dismay. Which was considerable, when he then found us watching him from Kittern Hill and put two and two together. The lecture we received was certainly far less fascinating than the one you heard in London."

He laughed, though he commiserated with poor Mr. Bonsor. "What did you find, then? Not *then*, at his dig. But to bring us to Gugh now."

Her amusement banked itself into flintiness again. And the sun was definitely elbowing its way through the fog. A glint of it danced on her braid. "A line from those letters of Mucknell to his wife—the first one that had the line you found about her future. He also said, '*The old man can tell you the way.*' And, as you just pointed out, the standing stone on Gugh is called the Old Man."

"Interesting. I'd assumed he meant the literal old man he'd mentioned in the previous line. And the way to the weaver's he said he found, whose cloth she would like. But of course it would be hidden behind something so mundane, if it were a clue to the treasure."

"Exactly so. Heading?"

He checked the compass. "South-southeast, dead on."

She adjusted the rudder just a bit. "I feel a bit of sympathy for poor Elizabeth Mucknell, I confess. She was clearly either dead set against using any of the plunder he took or terrible at deciphering his hidden messages and codes. She certainly never collected any of his treasure."

"Prince Rupert was known for it, though. Working with codes, I mean. Did you know he was rather famous for his ability to break ciphers?"

She shook her head and actually looked at him as though he was more than either a dunderhead or eccentric. That was progress. Worth two years off his estimate, certainly. Eight years, at this new rate, and he could convince her to be his marchioness. "I knew he was a scientist in later years. A founding member of the Royal Society."

"Ah. Yes. The 'philosophic warrior,' they called him. Invented weapons, methods of dyeing granite, quadrants, a new brass." He very nearly went off on a tangent about the so-dubbed Rupertinoe naval gun and the Prince Rupert cube, but he caught himself. Best not let her eyes glaze over and remind her of yesterday's frustration with him. *Focus, old boy. Mucknell. Treasure. Pirate.* "But ciphers too. So, if he came across any of Mucknell's attempts . . ."

Beth's hand gripped the tiller more tightly. "Then he could well have cracked them. He'd know where some of his earlier loot was buried. Which means what? Could he have already looted the loot?"

Sheridan opened his mouth to assure her that the prince would have no reason to steal from his comrade-in-arms, the man who taught him all he needed to know about pirating.

Then the irony of it struck him—he'd taught him *pirating*, for heaven's sake—and he had to shrug. "Any mention of it in your mother's story? You didn't finish writing it out yesterday."

She shook her head. "According to the story, the prince never returned to the islands. His bride died alone."

"That's terrible." He meant it. It was one of the things he hated about the old tales—they so often ended in death and tragedy and betrayal. Abbie always went on about King Arthur, when she wasn't rereading Jane Austen, and he'd never understood why—except that Telly was all rapt attention when she did, which urged her on. What was so alluring about a man cuckolded by his own best friend and the woman he loved?

"But it would mean the treasure is still there. And it must be worth finding if both Mucknell and Rupert were trying to direct their wives to it."

"That's the spirit."

86

She smiled. At him. Again. This was real, true progress. Maybe eight years was conservative. If he could make her forget the trinket box, he might talk her down the aisle in a mere six years.

She had him take the tiller a moment later while she did something with the lead line and her watch, demanding her compass back too. He had only the vaguest idea what she was about and didn't ask for details. So long as she didn't wreck them into a sandbar, he was quite happy to let her remain the expert here.

And she seemed happy enough with the course. She took the tiller back and then asked him to tell her more about Prince Rupert. Which, really, was like paying him a compliment, if one squinted just right. She was acknowledging that he knew something she didn't. And wanted to.

Five years. And, perhaps, a half. Because he'd likely bore her to tears by the time they landed at Gugh.

She kept asking questions, though, so he kept regaling her with all the research he'd uncovered on his ancestor. His early life in the courts of Bohemia, where his father briefly—disastrously—reigned as king, The Hague, and King Charles here in England. His military career, which was well documented and far longer than it should have been. Who in their right mind sent their fourteen-year-old son to war?

But he'd made a reputation for himself during the Civil Wars—both first and second—and fought in Germany and France when England ran out of battles to offer him. He didn't return here until 1660—ten years after he sailed with Mucknell to Portugal and then the Caribbean.

He showed an interest in art. Science. Mathematics. A true Renaissance man.

The fog thinned as they sailed, though it didn't dissipate altogether. He could make out the hulking outline of St. Agnes as they approached, and the smaller outline of Gugh beside it.

Tide was in, so the tombolo connecting the two would be underwater. Between that and the fog, they ought to have the island to themselves.

This may be madness, but there was a method to it.

"So, what's your family connection to him? If he never married—so far as history knows," she added with a half-smile, "then what's he doing in a marquess's lineage?"

"Ah. Well, he's certainly the most interesting character in it. I come from the dullest family in all of England, I think. But his daughter, Ruperta—illegitimate but recognized—married Emanuel Howe. Who isn't my direct ancestor, but he's occupying a branch in the family tree. Same surname, you'll notice."

Her half-smile had vanished. And a thunderstorm flashed in her eyes.

That was it—their color. The blue-grey of a storm cloud low on the horizon.

"You mean to tell me you don't even have any blood in common with the prince, yet you think having the same last name as his daughter's husband gives you a right to my trinket box?"

Well, bother. This was a bit of a setback. Even ten years was looking rather optimistic just now. "Well, I—that is. I never said I had a *right* to it. As in, some law of inheritance. But I think I may fairly be called the foremost expert on Prince Rupert at present, and so naturally . . . I've quite a collection. A few surviving Prince Rupert's Drops—those teardrop-shaped glass canisters that explode when—"

"I don't care about his blighted weapons!" She yanked hard on the tiller, and he had a suspicion it wasn't because she suddenly remembered a sandbar.

The *Naiad* responded with a quick turn into a wave, which obeyed what was clearly Beth's command that it spray him from head to toe with a refreshing dose of the North Atlantic.

He may die of cold if the sun didn't soon bully its way into the sky, but he was determined not to be tossed fully in the drink and clung tightly to his seat. "That wasn't very nice."

"You know what isn't nice?"

"Something about keeping trinket boxes one paid good money

for, I suspect." They were nearing the smaller of the islands, at least. He only had to cling to the bench for dear life for another minute or two.

Then all he'd have to worry about was her leaving without him and stranding him there.

Well. Tide would go out and he could walk to St. Agnes if it came to that. They liked tourists there. The guidebook said so.

"You are an insufferable prig."

"But I'm an insufferable prig who believes your hunch about Mucknell and thinks you're right to continue the search." He gave her a smile that felt weak even to him. "No? Not enough right now?"

And her scowl was back. "Why should I bother? You'll just run off with it and leave me empty-handed even if we *do* find something."

"Actually, I was imagining a fifty-fifty split. To the devil with the others since they don't believe us. It's all ours, I say. Eh?"

Then marry me, and you can call it all yours.

"So, you're a cheat as well as a thief."

Perhaps it was time to take a lesson from Ainsley. He buttoned his lips and decided silence may be his best friend right now.

If only he'd adopted that tack a minute sooner.

7

Beth checked her watch. Gauged the density of the fog. Tapped her foot. And decided that if she meant to explore Gugh before other tourists braved the weather and ruined the solitude, it might require leaving Sheridan behind.

If only her parents hadn't ingrained basic manners into her. "What are you even looking at?"

They'd anchored on the far side of Gugh, in the hopes that none of the locals from St. Agnes would spot her sloop. And though she was familiar enough with the island that she could have started her search anywhere, it had seemed logical to begin at Kittern Hill, since that's where the Old Man stood. Which had apparently been a mistake. Sheridan had aimed himself directly toward the burial cairn of Obadiah's Barrow and the nearby standing stone instead of the path leading away from them and had been poking about under some gorse for at *least* five minutes already.

She'd entertained herself at first by hunting up something to take to Mamm-wynn—a tradition of hers since she was a child. Today she'd selected a pretty little stone in shades of pink and grey, which was now nestled in her pocket. And, that task ticked off, she was ready to begin. Sheridan, on the other hand . . .

"I think—yes, I'm quite certain. Pottery shard. Could be part of a cremation urn."

She could understand his fascination with that in general, and may have even been intrigued, if it weren't Sheridan poking at it. When they were supposed to be hunting pirate treasure. "We're not here for the cairns or the menhir. He just points the way, remember?"

No reaction.

"The line from the letter?" Beth continued. "This is our starting point, not our destination."

"Just give me a moment."

That was what he'd said five minutes ago.

She growled. The sun was making earnest progress now, and they didn't have that much time. "You know what? Take your time. You'll be able to find me easily enough. The island's not big enough to get lost on."

"Right behind you."

She'd probably have to pry him away in an hour when she was ready to set off for Tresco again.

Well, that was fine by her. She didn't need the company of Lord Know-It-All anyway, even if he *did* have fascinating knowledge about Prince Rupert of the Rhine.

She reached into her pocket and pulled out the copy of the letter she'd made last night. There it was, the line that had brought them here.

I meant to tell you before I left, Lizza, but I found a good weaver for you on St. Agnes. Stumbled upon her cottage and her wares that evening I was there. The old man at the crest of the hill can tell you the way.

Evening. Which meant that the sun would be in the western sky, and the Old Man's shadow would be pointing east.

Away from St. Agnes. Certainly not toward any weaver's cottage. There were no cottages on Gugh, nor ruins of them, had there been some in Mucknell's day. The only evidence of civilization here was what Sheridan was still poking through.

91

So then, to the east. She set out across the heather, blazing her own path since there weren't any to speak of otherwise. Most of the tourists were only interested in the Druid sites, or they'd wander the coast. Few struck out through the heath and bracken.

Within a few minutes, she was down the opposite side of the hill, out of sight of Sheridan and St. Agnes even without the help of the fog. She could have tended toward the southeast, back toward where the *Naiad* bobbed, but she let her feet veer northeast instead, following the natural slope of the land.

Perhaps Mucknell had done the same. Let granite and gravity decide his path.

Though where he could have buried anything on this side of the island she wasn't certain. Bedrock was just below the surface, under the thin layer of soil and ground cover that flourished here as it did on the other isles. Ample cover for shrews and feral cats—not prime for burying anything of significant size.

But there were cairns on the western side of the isle. What if there was another over here, unrecorded? It could happen. New cairns were being unearthed in the Scillies all the time.

Well, not *all* the time. But occasionally. It had happened in her lifetime, anyway. So it was at least possible that the archaeologists who had explored Gugh before had missed some sign of one, buried under the flora that Libby would find more interesting than what it hid.

And if the Druids could dig a cairn here, surely a pirate could dig a hole of his own. Perhaps even *at* a cairn.

That sent a shiver up her spine. She had been the one to lead that little foray into Obadiah's Barrow six years ago, but it hadn't seemed quite as fun when she was crawling inside with her beads and dinner scraps and realized there were human bones in there. People. People who had lived and loved and died right there on the islands, before they sank into the sea. Before Christianity ever took root. Before there was a proper England to claim the islands as her own.

A cairn wouldn't be her choice if she were burying something new.

92

But then, she wasn't a pirate. Mucknell didn't strike her as the sort of man to get squeamish over the idea of a few skeletons, given his propensity for making more of them whenever someone crossed him.

A gust of wind blew fog into her face and then whipped past her. She let her feet drift to a halt and closed her eyes.

Oliver felt closest to God in a garden, he said, where tending the flowers reminded him of how God tended His children.

Beth felt closest to Him out here. Where the wind could tear across the hillocks without anything man-made in its way, where there was nothing but heather and seagrass and sand and water before her. Where she was keenly aware of how big He was. How untamed. How humanity was just a scratch in the earth, their marks so quickly covered over by His nature.

And yet He loved them with a ferocity as wild as that wind. As deep as that sea.

She'd had a lot of time with no one but the Lord for company in the last little while, and before she found that note Ollie left her, telling her Mamm-wynn could well be dying, she'd fancied herself closer to Him than she'd ever been.

It hadn't taken her long to slip right back into old habits, though, had it? Bickering with Oliver, throwing books to the floor in anger. Snapping at Sheridan.

He deserved it. But pointing it out constantly probably wasn't the best example of the grace of Christ.

"I'll do better, Lord," she whispered into the wind. "Though you'll have to help me. Because that man . . ."

A shearwater cried from somewhere overhead, and it sounded like heavenly laughter to her ears. "Yes, I know. I falter even as I ask for help. It's a good thing you're more patient than I am, Father."

She opened her eyes again, adding a silent plea that He show her where she ought to look. And frowned at a shape playing hide-and-seek with the fog to the north. A mast? That was certainly what it looked like, but she didn't know who else would be fool enough to be out in this.

Curiosity pulled her that direction, though another cloudbank drifted in a minute later, thicker than any she'd sailed them through that morning. Had there been a trail, she'd likely have lost it, given that she couldn't see more than a foot in front of her. She certainly had no hope of seeing if the boat out there had an owner nearby. She could run right into someone and not know it until—

"Oh!" She hadn't expected to *actually* run into someone the moment she thought of it, but she very nearly stumbled directly into an immobile figure blocking her way. "Excuse me. I couldn't see you."

And how ridiculous was it to run headlong into someone when she wasn't even on a path, and when there were acres of emptiness all about her?

It was a man, she realized, when vague impressions clarified into a well-made cardigan and trousers and a head topped by the flat cap favored by any fellow who spent more than a day fighting the wind for his fedora.

A *young* man, she saw when he pivoted, hands lifting, ready to steady her.

Not that she'd fallen, nor had any intention to. She took a step back, tilting her head a bit to allow a view of his face.

It was quite a face. Well-chiseled cheekbones, snapping green eyes, a patrician nose. Handsome. The sort of handsome that she'd always imagined for the prince in Mother's story. She could almost imagine him in buccaneer's garb, his hair long and tied at the nape, a sword and a blunderbuss both strapped to his side.

His eyes met hers, and her stomach went tight. It was the story, or the fog, or the arrangement of his features. She knew that.

Still, the question she'd asked Sheridan last night flitted through her mind. *Do you believe in love at first sight?*

The stranger flashed her a smile that sparked and smoldered. "Well now. What is so fair a lady doing out on so foul a morning?"

His accent branded him an incomer—a man of education. A gentleman. A tourist. And a charming one, at that.

She couldn't help her smile. "Looking for a pirate prince."

His grin said he could be persuaded to take on the role. "What a coincidence. I was looking for a princess." He took a step to the side, proffered an arm. "Shall we search together? It may keep us from stumbling into each other."

"How gallant." She tucked her hand against his arm, almost wishing she wore her lacy gloves and one of her lovely day dresses. Or that she'd done her hair up properly.

But no, this better suited the fairy tale. Visiting gentleman, common island girl. He most likely was no prince, but she'd forgive it. "Are you staying here or just visiting for the day?" Her eyes moved again to the mast she'd spotted on the water.

The fog had cleared a bit in that direction, fickle as it was. Revealing that it was no little sloop like the *Naiad* anchored there. It was a small yacht, its every sleek line screaming wealth.

"Just a day trip. I never pass up the chance for a bit of exploration. Sailed over last night."

He must have been anchored there all night, then. A visitor wouldn't have dared to sail such a craft through the shallows in this fog. "And how are you liking our island chain?"

"Well." He angled a charming smile down at her. "I confess I'd been thinking it a bit dull. But I may have to revise my opinion. I didn't realize it boasted such lovely locals. Do you live on St. Agnes?"

He wasn't the first tourist to offer her a piece of flattery. But he was the first she wanted to believe meant it. Even so, she wasn't about to spill her life story. "No. Just a day trip." She offered a cheeky smile instead of more information.

It earned her a chuckle. "A lady of mystery, I see. Seems appropriate for a pretty girl who materialized from the fog. You probably live in a fairy cave somewhere. There are a few of those in the Scillies, aren't there?"

"Two, both dubbed Piper's Hole—one on Tresco and one on St. Mary's. Said to have earned their names because you could hear the fairies piping in their depths." She leaned a little closer and put a bit of Tas-gwyn's inflection into her words. "And legend has it that the two caves are connected. That a dog who got lost in one emerged four days later from the other, half his fur rubbed off from the tight passages he squeezed through—but they're big enough for a fairy, of that there's no doubt. So one never knows when a troublesome little beastie might steal a sweet cooling on a windowsill in Hugh Town and leave it as a gift at a house in Grimsby."

And when the fairies were too lazy for such mischief, Beth and Mabena had helped them out a time or two, just to get the talk going in the pubs that week.

His eyes danced. "And how many sweets have you stolen? Or is that beneath a fairy princess? Because certainly that's what you are."

Laughter tickled her throat. "You've found me out."

"I knew it. No mortal could possibly have eyes that color, or a face so enchanting."

And he had a tongue of pure silver. She wasn't fool enough to take it seriously, but she was human enough to enjoy it. "Inherited from my grandmother, who all of Cornwall knows is the fairy queen."

"She, then, is Titania. Which makes you . . . ?"

"Oh no, good sir. A fairy mustn't tell you her name. There is power in it. Learn my name and you could hold me captive with it."

Her companion lifted his brows. "I thought that was only true of Rumpelstiltskin."

But it was such an interesting element that Tas-gwyn had borrowed it for countless stories, whenever a magical creature waltzed into his scene. "Who obviously had fay blood. So why should you doubt the same rules apply to a distant cousin?"

"Ah. Foolish me. Though now I'm even more intrigued. All I must do is learn your name and I can hold you at my side forever?"

Gracious. It hadn't sounded so flirtatious when it had come into her head. Though she couldn't quite decide if she wanted to parry it or keep it going a bit longer. She opted for a tilt of her own brows. "You can't expect me to reveal all the secrets, good sir. That would be foolish of me. And Titania's granddaughter is no fool."

"I'd never think you are." They'd meandered their way out of the heather, to the edge of the sand. "I'll simply have to guess, then. Let's see." He turned a bit to face her, screwing up his face in thought. "Peaseblossom?"

He knew his Shakespeare, she'd grant him that. "That's Grandmama's servant, not her granddaughter." Or so said the Bard in *A Midsummer Night's Dream*.

"Of course. My apologies. Ah, I know. Rhiannon."

She drew away a step in mock irritation. "I am Cornish, sir, not Welsh."

"More apologies." He swept his cap from his hair, revealing hair that was not Prince Rupert's black, but rather a deep red. He wiped the mist from his face and put the cap back on again. "Then you must be Morgan le Fay."

She sobered instantly. *Morgan.* In their house, it wasn't the name of a sorceress of Arthurian legend. It was her brother. And hearing it fall from unknowing lips brought a flood of loss into her soul.

Here she was, flirting with a stranger and hunting pirate treasure, and Morgan was gone. Having never done most of the things he'd helped her dream of doing. Contenting himself, year after year, with tales of her adventures, when he never had the strength to find his own. It was so unfair. Why had God made him with a body that constantly betrayed him but paired it with a spirit that had so much to give? Why had his flesh withered away when his soul still had so much life left in it? She'd spent hours curled up beside him, exaggerating the mischief she'd found. Telling him of all the new places she'd explored.

Would she ever stop missing him?

Her companion's smile turned to a frown. "I haven't guessed it, have I? Is that the look of a fairy now bound to a mortal man?"

She had to blink to clear the past from her eyes. She managed a smile, but she knew it was dimmer than before. "No, I'm afraid not."

"Then—"

"Beth? Where are you? Who are you talking to?"

She spun around, just able to make out Sheridan tramping through

97

the heather at the top of the hill. She briefly considered letting him meander by, but he'd clearly heard her. The fog had probably carried their voices to him, which made her cheeks warm. It had only been a silly conversation, innocent flirtation, but still. The thought of him having heard it made a strange something wiggle its way through her chest.

He spotted them in the same moment that she turned, and he started down the hill.

Her stranger muttered something blistering enough that her head snapped his way again. He'd taken a step back, and his gaze was locked on Sheridan's approaching form.

Sheridan shouted the same phrase and broke into a run. "Scofield? Get away from her! Beth!"

Scofield? *Nigel.* The red hair, the handsome face—probably all the more pleasing to her eye because she realized now that it was familiar. She'd never met him, but he and Emily looked enough alike that she ought to have realized straightaway who he was.

Had he known who she was? Been waiting for her?

Those questions and thoughts flew through her head in the two seconds it took for Sheridan to launch himself toward Scofield. And for Scofield to knock him from the air with a kick she'd not have thought possible, much less ever expect to see performed. She staggered back a step, out of range of flying limbs. She might have shouted—probably something inane like "Stop!"—but her voice was lost to the grunts and moans.

Sheridan recovered quickly and leapt to his feet again, fists raised. His boxer's stance was confident enough that she was able to catch a breath and remember that he and Telford had been chatting the other evening about their regular matches at some club or another in London.

But Scofield settled into a very different stance. Knees bent at a different angle, arms held out at shoulder height instead of raised to protect his face. He was no boxer. She just didn't know what he *was*.

"I have no argument with you, Lord Sheridan," he said, voice as

98

smooth as it had been while he was flirting with her. "You've always got on just fine with my father, haven't you? No need for that to end here, between us. We're after the same things."

Sheridan glanced her way, but only for a quarter of a second. Gauging her reaction? "Hardly. I don't condone violence in my searches. You encouraged it. It's because of you and Lorne that the lad is dead." He lunged, swung.

Scofield ducked the punch. "*You're* the one who hired Lorne. Can't blame me for pooling our resources, can you?"

"I certainly can when it leads to the sort of underhanded dealing you've cooked up! Who's the American you've brought in?" He took another swing.

This time Scofield blocked it with a quick jab of his arm. Pushed, knocking Sheridan off balance. Shoved his palm into the marquess's nose with a sickening crack. "Ah, I see. You're just upset that you've some competition for the artifacts. Afraid of a little bidding war, my lord?"

Blood was streaming from Sheridan's nose, which only seemed to infuriate him. "You—" He lunged again.

Scofield's legs flew up, out, around. How on earth did he move like that? She should probably do something. Try to throw herself onto him, tackle him to the ground. But she couldn't anticipate where he'd be in the next second, or if Sheridan would get up and be where she threw herself instead.

So, she did the next best thing and put herself between the brawling men and the yacht. And sure enough, a moment later, Sheridan was sprawled flat on the beach and Scofield had spun and begun to run straight toward his yacht. Straight at her.

He cursed again and skidded around her, nearly wiping them both out in the process. His arm ended up around her waist and he spun her with him, probably in an effort to keep his balance and transfer his momentum, but it felt ridiculously like the times her father had swept her in a circle with a throaty laugh.

Different though. So very different.

So why was Scofield laughing? "Beth. Ought to have guessed. Well, I know your name now, darling. Does that mean you're mine?"

A cross between a yell and a moan sounded from behind them.

Scofield spun her away, and when she tried to latch hold of him— arms, clothes, anything—he jumped out of her reach with another laugh. "I *do* feel the same, my love. Next time."

Of all the . . . If she had any idea what a good retort to that would be, she would have delivered it. But he was running again, and then splashing into the surf toward his yacht.

She could catch him. But then what? He must have four stone on her. She'd have no hope of stopping him, not with those moves of his.

She spun back to Sheridan instead. He was pushing himself onto his hands and knees, but with such obvious effort that she could only imagine his condition. Blood stained the sand under his face. "My lord! Are you all right?" She fell to the beach beside him, sliding an arm around his torso to help him straighten.

Or trying to. He shook her off, though the effort knocked him onto his side again. Then he scalded her with a look of pure betrayal. "Shouldn't you be running off at his side?"

"What?" She'd been reaching for him again, but that froze her arms in their stretch. "Why in the world would you say that?"

"I *heard* you." Blood was still dripping from his nose. Fury was still dripping from his eyes. But he pushed to his feet and staggered a few steps toward the waterline.

Scofield had already hauled himself onto the yacht and weighed anchor, and the sound of an engine—foreign and strange in these waters—roared through the fog. He'd be gone in moments.

"I didn't know who he was! I've never met him. If you recall, last week I was digging up silverware with *you* when he abducted Libby and Ollie and Telford. He thought she was me."

"As if that excuses it."

"Well, *yes*. It does." It wasn't as though she'd give his handsome face another thought now that she knew who he was. That he was linked, at least in part, to Johnnie's death—though it was Lorne who had killed him.

Lorne . . . who had been hired not by Scofield but by Sheridan. She planted her fists on her hips. "And are you really any better than he is? You *say* you don't condone violence. But you knew Lorne's reputation. You admitted it was why you had him searching for Rupert in the Caribbean."

Apparently deciding against plunging into the surf after him, Sheridan spun back to her, only wobbling a bit. "I may have known he was single-minded and determined, but I didn't know he was *violent*. And *I*, as you just pointed out, didn't abduct anyone and hold them hostage until silver was exchanged."

"Because you didn't *have* to. You were the one digging up the silver. And what have you been arguing ever since? That *you* ought to be the one to take possession of it. That the blasted British *Museum* oughtn't to be trusted because there's a Scofield on the board, but that *you* can be. You're nothing but a selfish, greedy—"

"And *you* are nothing but a . . . a weak-willed female ready to simper at any handsome face that comes with a yacht and a promise to take you away."

"How dare you." Her hands curled into fists, and all thoughts of exploring the island blew away with the wind that was finally making earnest progress at clearing the fog. She wasn't going to spend a single second that she didn't have to with this man. And to prove it, she stomped southward along the shore.

"Where are you going? Off to rendezvous with your prince?"

"Imbecile." She pivoted back to face him but didn't stop moving, even if it required walking backward. "I'm going home. And I ought to leave you here to insult someone else's common sense and integrity."

"So you can find some other criminal to flirt with, you mean." He was stomping after her. And he looked awful. His clothes were stained with his blood, and though he was digging even now in his pocket for a handkerchief, it couldn't possibly clean him up with any success. The best it could do was catch the red still dripping from his swollen nose. Bruises were forming already under both his eyes.

He needed ice or a compress or something. She should probably take him to St. Agnes and its little pharmacy.

But just now, she didn't much care if he had a broken nose and two black eyes. She frankly didn't care if he had to swim back to Tresco—though he could simply toss some money at someone and have them ferry him anywhere he wanted. She didn't care *what* he did.

She was going home, where at least she could escape his company in the privacy of her own room.

8

There was something comforting about sitting in the kitchen more familiar to her than any other room on Tresco, shelling peas. The snap of a pod. The plunk of plump spheres into a wooden bowl worn smooth by the decades. The scent of crisp green life stinging her nose. The slant of late-morning sun through the window, brightening the world.

Senara had done this very thing in this very spot more times in her youth than she could count. And any time she'd visited during the summer months when fresh peas were to be found. It was rhythmic. Soothing. Solace.

Peas made excellent company.

As did Mam, who hummed an old ballad as she mixed up the batter for a cake she'd serve with tea in a few hours. Last night, Senara had joined them at the pub, laughing and listening to Old Man Gibson tell stories as everyone enjoyed the ginger fairings he'd brought over from Polmers' on St. Mary's. It had been an evening to remind her of who she was, of where she came from. To forget for a few hours *why* she was home.

A soprano voice joined in with the hum, coming from the doorway.

Senara looked up as Mrs. Tremayne entered the kitchen, her voice a bit more tremulous than it used to be, but no less sweet.

"With a good sword and a trusty shield
A faithful heart and true
King James's men shall understand
What Cornish men can do
And have they fixed the where and when?
And shall Trelawny die?
Here's twenty thousand Cornish men
Will know the reason why."

The Tremayne matriarch was clearly as comfortable in this kitchen as Senara was, despite belonging more properly in the other areas of the house. Mamm-wynn snatched a few peas from the half-filled bowl with a wink, slipped them into her mouth, and rested her gnarled hand on Senara's shoulder.

She'd been too many years without her own grandmother. But she'd always had Beth and Oliver's to claim when she needed one.

Mamm-wynn gave her shoulder a soft squeeze. "I do love it when you come for a visit, Senara. How are the girls?"

Her throat went tight, and she had to clear it before she could answer. "Quite well when I left them."

Not even teary-eyed at her departure, because they'd not been told she was leaving. It had all happened too fast. When she'd tucked them into their beds with their favorite story, all had been well. By the next morning, she was on a train bound south, not given the chance to tell them good-bye.

"You've always had such a way with little ones, dearover. We always knew Morgan and Ollie and Beth were in good hands when you were about." She chuckled and looked toward the main part of the house. "Sometimes I think Beth could still use you. If you're here long enough, perhaps you'll do her some good. My rosefinch still tends to fly away first and consider consequences later."

104

Would she still be Beth if she didn't? Senara chuckled and reached up to cover the beloved arthritic fingers with her own. "Shall I play lady's maid to her while I'm here? As an excuse to be around to rein her in?"

"Would you?" She padded over to the door and peered out through the open top half. "I haven't even seen her this morning."

"Master Oliver was mumbling at breakfast about her sailing through the fog to Gugh with Lord Sheridan." Mam poured the batter in a buttered pan, careful to scrape all but a single swipe from the bowl.

She'd save that swipe for Senara—or whoever else lingered nearby with a ready finger to sample it.

"Ah. And Libby, Mabena, and Emily are back on St. Mary's. I think I shall go and see if I can win a few words from Bram, then." Mamm-wynn's eyes twinkled as she turned back around. "Always a challenge before luncheon, I've found."

Senara cracked another pea pod. Plunk, plunk, plunk. "Bram?"

"Lord Telford," Mam supplied.

"Libby's brother," Mrs. Tremayne added.

Senara nodded. She'd spotted both young lords in the garden last evening but had walked the other way rather than draw near enough to have to explain her presence to them. She'd been introduced to gentlemen here and there over the years, but always as *"Miss Dawe, our governess."* Words that served as a clear boundary, a clear explanation. Words that proved her respectable, honest, educated, and off-limits to anything but a cursory greeting if their paths crossed elsewhere.

She didn't have that buffer anymore. That identity. Here, she wasn't Miss Dawe, governess. She was just Senara. The housekeeper's daughter. Sheller of peas and borrower of grandmothers.

It wouldn't be enough to fill out the rest of her life. But until Rory came and made her Mrs. Smithfield, that was all she had.

And what if he didn't come? Her fingers stilled on the next pod as the fear she'd tried so hard to hold at bay swept over her. What if he decided she wasn't worth the loss of his position? What if it turned out she'd given up everything for nothing?

Warm, gentle fingers touched her cheek and brought her face back up from her bowl, in which direction it had dipped. Mrs. Tremayne looked deep into her eyes for a long, quiet moment. And then she whispered, "Sweet Senara. You are precious. Beloved by God. Cherished by us."

Tears stung her eyes. How did she always know just the thing to say? "Thank you, Mamm-wynn."

The lady leaned over and pressed paper-soft lips to her forehead, then walked away with another pat on her shoulder.

Mam let out a long breath after a longer moment. "I daresay Beth really could use your steadying hand."

Senara sniffed, blinked away the emotion she wasn't ready to be tangled up in, and forced a smile to her lips. Her hand didn't feel particularly steadying just now—but *she* could use Beth's unbridled vigor. "Well. I plan to spend plenty of time with her anyway."

Low laughter from outside interrupted, and a moment later, Henry Ainsley and Nicholas Collins—Lord Telford's valet—let themselves into the kitchen with smiles and easy greetings. She and her parents had taken supper with them last night, along with Thomasina Briggs, Lady Emily's maid, before they'd ventured to the pub. It had been rather crowded at the kitchen table, which had meant much laughter and joking and camaraderie. The sort she'd heard from the kitchens at Cliffenwelle but had never been a part of. Her place, even for meals, had been the nursery. On those rare occasions that the children dined with their parents, she was expected to join them there—never to speak or be noticed, just to be on hand to keep the girls in line and rush them away at the first sign of temper or tiredness. Always in a limbo between staff and family.

It had gotten lonely.

She'd spent the meal last night covertly watching Henry Ainsley, trying to place him. Not that she'd succeeded. The more she tried to

106

identify what made him familiar, the more she questioned whether he even was.

Her mother greeted the newcomers with a bright smile. "There you lads are. Success?"

Collins held up a brown paper bag, which must be testament to some errand they had run. "As you promised. Want some?" He grinned. "Telford will never know there's any missing."

Mam chuckled but shook her head. "I've never been one for toffee. But Mr. Dawe says Logan makes the best in England, and my husband's sweet tooth can certainly be trusted."

Collins grunted another laugh and tossed the bag on the table. "I've yet to meet anyone whose sweet tooth rivaled his lordship's. I swear I've visited every sweet shop in the country for him."

"Quite a hardship for you." Ainsley smiled, too, and pulled out a chair at the table. He was the elder of the valets, clearly, but she couldn't tell by how much. She guessed him to be in his mid-thirties, but Collins's age was harder to pinpoint. With his round face and smooth skin, he could have been anywhere from twenty to thirty.

Collins peeked into the pan Mam was tapping the air from. "That smells good. Almond?"

"Mm. Our lady mentioned her brother favors it."

"Along with any other cake. The true test . . ." He stole the mixing bowl from the workbench and ran a finger along that single line of batter. Made a happy noise. "It'll do."

Ainsley shook his head and reached for a few of the pea pods still awaiting their turn.

Senara's eyes went wide. "Oh, you needn't do that. I'll be finished in no time."

He turned his eyes, dark and calm, on her. "I don't mind. Reminds me of my own mother's kitchen, and happy hours spent there." With a well-trained motion, he opened the shell and poured the peas into his palm.

Senara moved the wooden bowl from her lap to the table so he could drop them in and then repositioned her chair to face it.

She ought to say something. Ask some simple, polite question that could show her a sliver of his mind. How did he like serving Lord Sheridan? Or what did he think of the Scillies?

But his steady gaze weighed her down like an anchor, and he spoke before she could. "Your father mentioned you've been a governess for the last decade."

She studied her next pea pod instead of his face and simply nodded. The loss of that identity was still so very fresh that she didn't quite know how to respond.

"For what family? Perhaps I know of them."

Oh, she prayed not—but wouldn't that be just her luck? She cleared her throat. "The Cliffords—the baron and his wife have three beautiful daughters."

Her fingers curled up at the mention of them. She ought to be tidying braids and tying pinafores, coaching eager little faces on what greeting they ought to give their mother when she came to spend her hour with them before she left for whatever calls she'd make that day.

"The Cliffords." Ainsley said the name slowly, thoughtfully. Dropped three more peas into the bowl. "Was the baroness a Griffith? Welsh?"

She gave a tight nod. The aristocracy was frightfully small— perhaps there was a connection between them and his employer. Perhaps she'd seen him in passing at some event or house party and that was why his name and face rang distant bells of memory.

He didn't smile—she peeked to see—but he didn't frown either. Just regarded her evenly. "They were summering together, weren't they? The Griffiths and Cliffords? My cousin mentioned it."

She lifted her face again. "Your cousin?"

"Mr. Griffith's valet—Rory Smithfield. Perhaps you met him."

A smile bloomed on her lips. That was it! Rory had mentioned his cousin a few times. That's why his name was familiar. And the two cousins bore a few features in common—not enough that their relation was obvious at a glance, but certainly enough to account

108

for why she'd noticed it "Oh, Rory! Yes, of course. Everyone at Cliffenwelle loves him."

How could they not? He was bright and cheerful, handsome and smart. Charming and cunning. All the staff looked forward to the Griffiths coming for every holiday and the whole summer, largely because it meant Smithfield would be there—entertaining all the fellows, flirting with all the maids.

How had she ever been lucky enough to be the one to snag his attention?

She felt Ainsley's gaze on her for another long moment. No doubt her affection for his cousin had come through in that explanation. Usually, she'd have made more of an attempt to keep her attachments guarded, but why bother now?

Besides, this was the cousin who Rory had spent Christmas with, wasn't it? At his employer's castle—that must be Lord Sheridan's home. They must be close. Getting to know Ainsley would be like seeing a new side of Rory—and wouldn't he be pleased when he showed up and saw that his cousin was here too? What were the chances?

Perhaps he'd even mentioned her at Christmas. Perhaps he'd written to his family of her. Perhaps Ainsley had thought *her* name sounded familiar when her parents mentioned her and now would laugh and put all the pieces together too.

He reached for more peas and angled a few degrees away. "Do you know when I ought to expect his lordship back, Mrs. Dawe? If he's been hiking over heather in that fog of this morning, he'll be wet and muddy when he returns and in need of a hot bath."

Or perhaps men didn't gush about their love interests in letters to each other as girls did. Heat stung her cheeks at her own foolishness.

Collins dropped into the chair beside Ainsley's. "And of an eighth pair of shoes for the day?"

"Now, Collins. Only the third. Thus far." Amusement laced his tone, where she'd have expected complaint. Rory, though cheerful, had certainly painted quite the picture of the excesses of his employer, and for good reason. Every outing of the masters meant more work for the servants—brushing and cleaning and mending—while the family swept on to the next game or meal or engagement.

Mam slid the cake pan into the heated oven. "Gracious, that's hard to say. It all depends on how long they're exploring. Our Beth can spend all day peering into nooks and crannies sometimes. Other times, she's back by noon."

Ainsley chuckled. "Well do I understand that. Lord Sheridan always has some excavation or another underway in the neighborhood, and there are days we're out from dawn to dusk. And then there are the times he travels in pursuit of some theory or discovery and we get to live in a tent if there isn't a reputable inn or hotel nearby. Always great fun, that."

Senara pressed her lips together. She had to admit she couldn't imagine the man beside her living in such quarters. "Just the two of you?"

"And his sisters. They're an invaluable part of his team." Another smile danced over his mouth. "They'll be cross if they find he's got caught up in another adventure here without consulting them. They always swear he makes a mess of everything on his own—and they may have a point. But you must have a knack for organizing children, Miss Dawe. Perhaps we can call on you for the role Ladies Abbie and Millicent usually play."

Her fingers stilled on the next pod. He was inviting her into their business? Perhaps Rory *had* mentioned her, and this was Ainsley's way of getting to know his cousin's chosen wife. Perhaps he wanted to sound her out before giving his approval. Hadn't Rory mentioned that his cousin was a bit too prim and proper? No doubt the sort, then, to want to form a sound judgment of her.

Well, with that single exception that had gotten her sacked, she'd made a career of living up to people's expectations for her. Surely she could impress this valet. She cleared her throat so she wouldn't sound too eager. "I'm not certain the skills transcend."

Collins hooted a laugh. "Don't worry, Miss Dawe. I assure you—taking care of our gents is *just* like keeping a couple of kids in line."

Mam rinsed her hands, dried them, and sent Senara an amused look. "Have I asked you both already how long you've been with them? If so, forgive me, for I don't recall the answer."

Ainsley answered first. "Twelve years, roundabout. Lord Sheridan was little more than a boy when his sisters hired me." He pulled another handful of pea pods toward him. "Then Lord Telford hired Collins a couple years later. It's fortunate we get along, since those two are together more than they're not."

Collins gave Ainsley a friendly elbow in the ribs. "Like the brother I never had."

Mam opened her mouth, but before she could say anything, a commotion at the front of the house clattered its way into the kitchen. A door slamming against a wall, raised voices, thundering footsteps.

"What in the world?" Senara shoved the peas aside and was on her feet and out the corridor in half a second, too used to leaping in to defuse any fray—because in her previous life it was usually one of her charges behind the shouting and rushing. Ainsley, Collins, and Mam were all hot on her heels, though—because in this house there were no children to be causing a ruckus, only ladies and gents.

Maybe they were right, and the groups weren't so different.

Oliver was tripping out from his study to investigate. Telford and Mamm-wynn appeared from the library, and Beth was already halfway up the stairs, shouting over her shoulder, "I'm not saying he *is*! I'm only saying you *aren't*!"

The front door slammed shut again, and a battered creature who might or might not have been Lord Sheridan under the dried blood, bruised face, and wet clothes yelled back, "And that's a fine reason to toss me in the sea."

"It was an accident!"

"Ha!"

"Good Lord above, have mercy." Ainsley edged past her and charged toward his employer. "What happened?"

"Scofield." Sheridan spat the name and winced.

It meant nothing to Senara, but clearly it meant considerably more to the rest of them, even her mother.

Mam pivoted on her heel. "We need ice and hot water. Senara, would you fetch towels?"

They'd need a whole clothesline's worth, given the ocean Lord Sheridan was dripping onto the floor. Senara nodded and dashed off for the linen closet, grabbing an armful of fluffy terry cloth. When she ran back to the entryway, there were only distant voices, trailing puddles, and Oliver waiting for her with an outstretched arm.

She let him take a few of the towels and begin to sop up the worst of the seawater. She handed a few more to Ainsley, who reappeared long enough to take them with an understandably distracted murmur of thanks. And then she stooped down to dry the puddle trail.

"So *what* happened?" she asked softly as she spread the towels over the floor.

Oliver shook his head. "From what I could tell, Sheridan and Beth had a bit of a run-in on Gugh with a fellow we've been keeping an eye out for. He's after Mucknell's treasure."

"Mucknell's . . ." She paused to look over at him. How very odd. The entire decade she'd been away, she couldn't recall thinking even once about those old pirate tales. But this was the second time they'd come up now in a week. Here and now, of course . . . and at Cliffenwelle, just a week ago.

When Rory had sat with her in the garden during her half-day off and said, *"You're from the Isles of Scilly, right, love? I've heard there are some entertaining tales from the days when pirates made them their headquarters. Tell me some."*

A coincidence that he had asked and that she'd shared the proper history she'd learned at school—and some of Mr. Gibson's outlandish stories besides. So, why did her stomach go heavy? "I always thought those were just stories."

Oliver opened another towel. "As did we all. But Beth found a map, and it led us to some silver. It seems this chap thinks there's more to be found, and he has buyers ready to bid on it."

"Buyers." Silver. Actual pirate treasure, and high-ranking gents trying to get their hands on it.

Rory's parting words, whispered to her when she was supposed to be rushing to the train station, came back to her. *I'll come for you, love. I'm going to resign soon, and I'll come for you. I've had a bit of a windfall, and I can finally get out of service. We'll make a home somewhere, together. Just wait for me in the Scillies. Go straight home.*

She shook off the terrible suspicions that sprang up like the worst fears always did, quick and full-grown. Ridiculous. Utterly ridiculous. How in the world would Rory ever have gotten mixed up with whoever these Scofields were?

"Mm. Sheridan was one of them. And some American whose identity we've yet to uncover." With a sigh, Oliver stood, the wet towels in his arms, and cast a troubled gaze up the stairs. "I should see to Beth."

"No, let me." She sprang to her feet, adding her wet towels to his stack. "I'm happy to. It'll be just like old times." And give her time to resign those outlandish thoughts back to the abyss into which they belonged.

His lips twitched at the corners, then settled into a neutral line. But his eyes were far from neutral. They looked deep into hers. Too deep. Too knowing. "I'm glad you're home, Senara."

She shifted toward the stairs. Tried for a light, dismissive smile, but it shook at the edges. He wouldn't be glad. Not if he knew why she was. "Me too."

She turned away, needing to escape his dark-eyed probing. It just wasn't fair that the lad she'd watched when he was little was now tending the souls of Tresco—and seeing hers in a glance.

She hurried up the stairs, feeling only a momentary pang of guilt for leaving the master of the house with the armful of wet towels. The Tremaynes had never been *that* sort of master's family, the kind that sat back and waited for others to serve them. And from what Mam had said, Lady Elizabeth never demanded a thing either. She would be the sort of mistress that this house—this village—

expected. The kind who loved first and asked only for what she couldn't manage on her own.

Senara rapped on the door at the top of the stairs. "Beth? May I come in?"

A squeak, footsteps, and then the door creaked open. "Since you're not an arrogant brat of a gentleman, yes."

The storm in her young friend's eyes was familiar enough to make Senara feel comfortably at home. She slipped in and let Beth close the door behind her, making no attempt to tamp down a smile. "Bad morning?"

Beth growled and stomped past her, throwing herself onto her bed just as she'd been doing all her life. "Why are men all such idiots?"

"The same reason women tend to be such fools over them, I suspect." She gathered her skirt and sat on the mattress beside Beth. "I can't quite wrap my mind around my little Beth having gentleman problems. You're supposed to be ten still. Twelve, at the most."

Beth flicked her a smile and rearranged herself to sit beside her. "Life was simpler then. And yet, when I was ten, all I wanted was to be twenty. To be a lady grown, like you, off on the adventure of my life. Now I wish I could go back and appreciate where I was."

"Don't be so hard on yourself." Senara tapped on the back of Beth's shoulder as she'd done hundreds of times—and then hundreds more to the Clifford girls. And apparently the old training was still ingrained, because Beth scooted around to put her back to Senara, presenting the braid in desperate need of tidying. Senara pulled the tie from the bottom and began fingering the weave and the snarls from the locks. "You took every possible moment of enjoyment out of your childhood—and borrowed a few more besides. Looking forward to adulthood is part of that joy, though, I think. Dreaming of all you'll do. All you'll see. All the people you'll meet and love. Of pirate princes and ladies fair."

Beth exhaled, long and hard. Her shoulders sagged. "Pirate

princes are better in fairy tales than reality. In a story, their exploits are glossed over with pretty words and heroic motivations. But in reality, you can't help but see the lives they wreck and the destruction they leave in their wake."

How true that was. Senara unplaited the rest of the braid and then stretched behind her for the hairbrush, where it sat as always on the dressing table. "And is that what happened on Gugh this morning? Did you get a glimpse of a gentleman's trail of destruction?" She'd spare her those lessons if she could. And yet, generally speaking, they all had to learn them for themselves.

Beth shrugged. "Reminded of it, anyway. I ran into a gentleman—quite literally. In the fog. And he was handsome and charming and we flirted, and for a moment . . . for a moment I actually entertained notions of love at first sight."

Senara's hands stilled with the brush only halfway through its first stroke. Beth had always been the sort to revel in such tales. But she also had a level head on her shoulders. She knew, didn't she, where stories ended and reality began? "But?"

"But it was Nigel Scofield. Emily's older brother, whom I've yet to hear a single kind thing said about. Who may have had something to do with Johnnie Rosedew's death."

"What?" She dropped the brush onto the bed and leaned around to peer at Beth's face. "Mam said it was an accident!"

"That's what everyone thought, until a week ago when we apprehended a fellow who admitted to it. A fellow who'd been working with Mr. Scofield." Beth reached up to rub at her eyes. "He's a cruel man. I know that. Emily has said so, and if anything, she ought to be looking at him through a lens biased in his favor. But when he was smiling at me, when I didn't know who he was—I felt something. Or thought I did. And now Sheridan's accusing me of being in league with him, when it's *him* who started all this by hiring both Lorne and the Scofields to begin with, and—"

"Wait a moment, Elizabeth. I think you had better start at the beginning of this tale. I don't have any idea who these people are."

Senara picked up the brush again, stroking it through Beth's long blond hair while her young friend filled her in on all that had happened since spring. Pirate maps and threats, mistaken identities and armed abductions.

The hair ended up glossy and well-ordered. The story was anything but. Senara was left feeling as heavy as the cannonball Beth said she'd found a few months ago.

And she still couldn't shake the oddity of Rory bringing up Mucknell with her just five days ago. But this tale of Beth's had been in motion long before that. *Rory* couldn't have told these Scofield people anything that she told him.

Coincidence. That was all. Obviously.

If only her churning stomach would get the message.

Senara slid the brush back into its place. She would simply have to accept Ainsley's invitation to join this odd treasure hunt. Learn everything she could. No doubt within a day or two, she'd convince herself that Rory couldn't have possibly had anything to do with it.

"Nara?" Beth turned to face her, questions clouding her storm-colored eyes. "Are you all right?"

Senara mustered a smile. "Sorry. It's a lot to take in."

Beth drew her lip between her teeth for a moment and gnawed on it—a habit Senara had thought she'd been broken of years ago. "What am I to do? Other than steer far clear of Scofield?"

"Yes, run far and fast from that one." Her voice sounded heavy to her own ears as she said it, a remnant of the thoughts she couldn't—wouldn't—put voice to. But she shook them off and focused on Beth. Young, pretty Beth. Headstrong, impulsive Beth.

Something more muted than panic but less controlled than concern clawed at her throat. She couldn't let Beth tumble into the same errors *she* had made. She'd learned firsthand the consequences for letting such emotions carry her away. "That sort of man is bad news for any girl."

Beth nodded, which wouldn't have eased Senara's feeling any. But her eyes went cool as steel, and that did. "You needn't tell me twice. He has proven himself violent and cruel. I have no use for such a man."

"Good. As for the rest . . . I think you ought to apologize to Lord Sheridan."

"What?" That was clearly not what Beth had expected. She pushed onto her knees, poised to leap to her feet if she thought it necessary to storm off or stomp a foot. Typical Beth. "Why should I?"

Senara gave her the arch look she'd perfected years ago. "For starters, because you purposely dumped him off the *Naiad* when you came round the point."

Beth pursed her lips, but her eyes flashed. "The cold water was good for his nose. Could even save him from black eyes."

Not from the glimpse Senara had gotten of him. "Moreover, because you had quite a hand in mangling his pride. First you were flirting with another man—a rival, if not an outright enemy—under his very nose, and then you accused him of being no better than said man after he lost a fight."

The storm clouds in Beth's eyes had darkened more and more with every word she spoke. "His pride can stand a bit of mangling. And why should he care if I flirt with someone?"

Senara laughed, then realized Beth was serious. "Oh, sweetheart. You haven't noticed? Why, when I peeked in the library window on my way past again yesterday, he was sitting at your feet like a puppy. He's sweet on you."

"That's absurd. We've only just met a week ago, and we've been arguing incessantly since."

As if either of those negated the other. But Senara held up her hands, palms out. "All right. Even if I misread it . . . when have you ever known a man who wasn't embarrassed and in need of a bit of coddling after losing a brawl? Yet you dumped him in the sea for his trouble, when all he was doing was trying to rush to your rescue. Like a proper knight when he saw a scoundrel near the princess."

Beth huffed and gathered her locks behind her head, twisting them into a coil. "He wasn't trying to rescue me. He was just sore

117

because Scofield lined up another buyer for the antiquities he's determined to have for his own."

Senara tilted her head, swiveling it to follow Beth when she rose and marched to the dressing table to jab a few pins at her hair. "Why do you dislike this one so much? From what you said, it's that Scofield fellow you ought to despise."

"Because." Hair in a tidy chignon, Beth spun to face her again. "This is all his fault. If he hadn't told them he'd purchase any artifacts dealing with Mucknell and Rupert—"

"Beth." Senara stood. Calmly, slowly. Met her eyes. "This is me. What is it really?"

Her young friend huffed and pointed at an empty shelf. "Lord Scofield sold him Mother's trinket box when I sent it to him to see if it was Prince Rupert's crest on the lid. And he refuses to give it back."

"Oh." That certainly put it more in perspective. "And it was *Scofield* who gave him the black eyes, not you?"

She hadn't solved any of her friend's troubles nor answered any of her own questions. But at least she brought a fresh smile to her lips.

"I'm glad you're here, Senara," Beth said softly. "I've missed you."

Senara smiled back. "I'm glad I'm here too." And perhaps it didn't need to be wasted time just waiting for Rory to come. Perhaps she really could help. "Ainsley suggested I may be of some assistance to everyone with my organizing skills. If you think . . . ?"

"Oh." Surprise flickered through Beth's eyes, chased by relief. "You know, that could be just the thing. It seems our group can't ever agree on what to do next."

"Not surprising, given how many of you there are, and all strongwilled." But she *did* have ample practice bending strong wills toward the best path. She smiled. "Brief me on absolutely everything. And we'll see what I can do."

9

Sheridan had scarcely emerged from his bedroom in the last thirty hours, but it wasn't because he was sulking—despite what Ainsley said. He'd been half frozen from the unplanned dip—never mind that tourists were frolicking in the same water in their bathing costumes on the beaches nearby. He'd been lying low because he'd been contemplating their next move regarding Scofield—never mind that he always did his best thinking aloud, and preferably with Telford.

And he'd had the worst blighted headache of his life, because his nose was most assuredly broken. And he had two streaks of bruising under his eyes.

If that didn't give him the right to isolate himself in his room for a day or so, what the devil did?

But by teatime on Friday, his mood was only growing surlier and Ainsley was threatening to shove him forcibly into the corridor, so he shrugged into his jacket, cast only one scowling look at his battered reflection in the mirror, and trudged to the drawing room.

Which was empty, despite the growling of his stomach saying it *was* teatime.

The back garden, then.

Though he didn't know why he was bothering. He could have

119

food delivered to him, like he'd insisted upon for luncheon yesterday. He'd felt too pained and ill to stomach anything for tea and had barely touched his supper, so obviously he'd made a sound call in skipping those meals in the dining room. Requesting a tray for breakfast rather than risk trying to take it with others and embarrass himself by getting ill in front of everyone had been purely sensible.

Embarrassing himself *more*, that is.

It wasn't as though Mrs. Dawe resented the requests. She'd delivered his food this morning herself and fawned over him, insisting on another dose of aspirin, even though his headache was only a dull thud now.

He ought to have ignored Ainsley's prodding. Because as he drew near to the back garden door and heard the happy voices of Beth and Mamm-wynn and Telford and Oliver, he was quite certain that joining them was the absolute worst idea he'd had since the one that had sent him down the hill on Gugh yesterday, convinced he needed to rush to Beth's aid.

Idiot. She certainly hadn't looked the least bit upset to be in Nigel Scofield's company. Which just went to show how foolish she was.

He stepped into the sunlight, which immediately pounded a stake into his skull. Blast it.

"Sher! Crikey." Telford materialized at his side. "You look like secondhand death."

"Thanks. Really."

His friend held out a full, steaming cup of tea. "I got a taste of his skills last week, if you recall. Full commiseration here."

It made him feel half a degree better. Or maybe that was due to his first sip of tea, brewed strong, just how he liked it.

Of course, it was also how Telly liked it, and Mamm-wynn had clearly made the cup for him.

Sheridan lifted it in a salute of genuine appreciation for the sacrifice. "Where did he learn that, do you think? Certainly not in London."

"Okinawa."

At Beth's voice, his every muscle tensed. He wouldn't even look at her. He was better off without her, if she was so senseless as to fall for a cad like Scofield.

She sat in the chair beside her grandmother, teacup cradled in her hands, and looked positively gorgeous in a dress of sky blue that teased the shade of it from her eyes.

Blast and bother. He dragged his gaze away again and stomped to an empty chair beside Oliver.

Beth sipped her tea. "Which you would know had you deigned to join us yesterday evening when Lady Emily came for supper. He apparently spent several years traveling Asia. It's called *karate*."

She pronounced each syllable deliberately. No doubt wanting to pay them special honor, since it was the chosen form of combat of her darling *Nigel*.

He slouched into his chair. "So sorry. I hope my absence, as I nursed a migraine from the broken nose her brother gave me, didn't dampen your evening with your friend."

Her smile was positively glacial. "Not at all."

"Elizabeth Grace." Mamm-wynn tipped the teapot over another cup and handed it to her grandson. "Mind your manners."

Telly, taking the other empty chair between him and Mrs. Tremayne, passed him a plate with a crumpet already slathered with butter.

Sheridan sighed around his first bite. "You're a true friend, Bram."

Beth muttered into her teacup something that sounded suspiciously like "As if he deserves one."

He would ignore that. He turned to the gentlemen, putting her out of his line of sight. "I assume someone made an attempt to locate Scofield or his yacht around the islands yesterday?"

Oliver nodded. "I took the *Adelle* around and recruited a few friends to help too. Enyon said he saw a craft matching Beth's description of the yacht near St. Agnes on Wednesday evening. It's called the *Chatelaine*. It was nowhere to be found by yesterday

121

afternoon, but he easily could have gone back to Penzance. With that motor, he could come and go as he pleases if he brings his own supply of fuel."

Cheery thought, that. He could show up again any time, without warning. Sheridan took another bite of crumpet. Perhaps it was just that he hadn't had anything more substantial than this morning's porridge since supper on Wednesday, but it tasted like ambrosia. "I'm going to steal Mrs. Dawe away."

Mamm-wynn and Oliver chuckled. Beth took another sip of tea. "Perfectly in character. Once a thief . . ."

He dropped the crumpet back to his plate. "I am not a thief. I *bought* that box."

"Which was stolen property. A gentleman would return it."

"Yes, well, I'm rather glad I haven't, or you'd probably have given it to that reprobate by now. He'd have smiled at you and you'd have—"

Telford's hand, steadying, landed on his shoulder. "Are we missing something?"

He snorted. Reached for his tea, then changed his mind and shoved away from the table. "Why don't you ask our lovely Miss Tremayne? She certainly seemed rather cozy with Mr. Scofield yesterday."

She put her tea down with a clatter too. "I *told* you. I didn't know who it was."

"Oh, so you just flirt with every stranger, then?" He pushed to his feet, shaking his head. "Well, how wonderful for you. No business of mine. I hadn't proposed yet, and I certainly won't be now. You'd probably have strung me along for those eight years and then announced you were engaged to him all along. Well, Abbie was right about you—or would have been. Had she met you, which she won't now."

That had come out all wrong. And shouldn't have come out at all. Oh well.

He turned for the garden gate. "Oh, never mind. You may be the prettiest young lady in England, but I've learned my lesson. If

122

you want another chance, you'll have to spend a decade begging *me*. So there."

A parting shot that may have been more satisfying if she didn't have an expression of complete bafflement on her face.

Well, she'd puzzle it out eventually. And see her mistake. Then she could spend countless hours trying to sort out how to propose to *him*. Maybe she should be the one to drop to a knee. Take his hand in hers. Say, *Marry me for Mrs. Dawe's crumpets and scones. You'll never regret it.*

He pushed through the gate and out onto the cobbled road. The pub. He'd order a cup of tea there, and something sturdier—though no doubt far less delicious—than a crumpet. And let beautiful Beth Tremayne go to the devil.

Though that may very well mean Scofield, come to think of it. And he just couldn't stomach the thought. He'd proven himself a miserable savior once already, true, but he may have to try again if her bad judgment persisted in that direction.

Quick footsteps gave him three seconds of warning before Telford appeared at his side. "That was interesting."

"She had it coming. I'm going to hold out for at least a year after that stunt of hers. Maybe two." He shoved his hands into his pockets. "All right, six months. She'll have to work hard, though, to win me back."

Telford snorted a laugh. "You do realize you said all that out loud, don't you? Perhaps you'd been having the conversation in your head before, but I'd be willing to wager no one else was part of it until now."

"You couldn't be more wrong." He turned his head, which made an ache pulse through his nose. He'd probably scare every child in Old Grimsby with this mug of his as he walked through the town. "I had at least half of it with Ainsley. And future Abbie and Millicent, who will have disapproved of her because she doesn't come from wealth or title. Wise women, my sisters. Well, not that she ought to be judged by that. I'll still defend the Tremaynes to them—you'll

123

soon be related, after all. Can't have your future brother-in-law maligned."

"Glad to have you championing him someday. Though we'll see how you feel after he's finished running you through the wringer for all that back there." Telford reached into his pocket, pulled out his handkerchief, and held it out.

Sheridan blinked at it. "What?"

"Your nose is bleeding again."

"Oh." He took the pristine white square and held it to his nose. Sure enough. "I've ruined a perfectly good waistcoat, too, you know. As if it's my fault." He dabbed a few more times, but it wasn't bleeding in earnest. Another couple steps and he was able to stow the soiled handkerchief in his own pocket. Telford had an endless supply anyway. "Do you know, there are valets in the world who don't lecture their employers?"

"Fascinating." Telford tugged him to the side as a horse and cart clopped lazily by. "And did you really *have* to go after Scofield?"

"It just isn't fair. I know far more about fairies than he ever could. He tried to guess that her name was Peaseblossom! As if every schoolboy doesn't know Shakespeare. Completely unimpressive."

"Usually I can follow your inanity, but you've lost even me this time, old boy." They turned at the corner, and Telford looked about them. "Where are we going, anyway?"

"I'm hungry."

Telford dug in his pocket again and came out with a toffee wrapped in foil. "Pub doesn't open for another hour."

"Blast." He took the toffee. "Couldn't you have put another crumpet in there?"

"Sorry. I was in a rush to catch up."

And if there was no pub at the other end of his walk, Sheridan saw no reason to keep his pace so quick. Which meant he soon drifted to a halt and stared up at the building before him for a long moment before realizing it was St. Nicholas's.

This was where he'd marry Beth, no doubt. If she convinced him.

Or he convinced her. Oliver would officiate. Though for Oliver's own wedding to Libby, he'd have to call in the vicar from the parish in St. Mary's. What was his name?

Unless Libby insisted, or Lady Telford did, that they marry near Telford Hall instead. That would be more expected, but somehow he couldn't imagine it. "The Abbey Gardens, more likely."

Telford lifted his brows.

"Libby and Tremayne."

Telford lowered his brows all the way into a frown. "Do you think so? Mother won't like that."

"But think about it."

Telly grunted. "I suppose I wouldn't argue. If they want a garden wedding, that means they'll have to wait at least a year."

"Or hurry it along and squeeze it in before autumn is over."

"Pessimist." Telford struck off again.

Sheridan held his place. It was a relatively new church building—he'd guess it to be no more than thirty or forty years old. But an older one would have stood in the same spot or a nearby one before it was built. An island that boasted two castles would most assuredly have had some sort of priory too.

Priories and churches kept records. Meticulous ones. And even if the old building were no longer around, it was still the same parish, and they were likely still in the care of the same parish priest—or vicar, now.

He pivoted back the way they'd come.

"Sher?" Telly jogged to catch up. "Now where are you going?"

"To fetch Tremayne."

"Because . . . ? You're ready for his lecture about his sister?"

The toffee was quite good, really. Though he usually preferred lemon drops. Or perhaps anything would taste good right now. "Don't be silly. He can lecture me about that any time. Right now, we need him in a professional capacity."

"You need spiritual guidance?"

Sheridan shot him a look. Ainsley would no doubt be thrilled if he had a heart-to-heart with a vicar on spiritual matters . . . and maybe he would, at some point. When his nose wasn't aching and he had the mental capacity to engage him in a rousing debate on why Christianity was often presented as so very dull, when its truth was far more interesting. In other words, not today. "No. I need church records. Preferably dating back to around 1650."

Telford was an intelligent chap. It only took him three steps to let loose a grunt of understanding. "You mean to test Beth's theory that Prince Rupert married an island girl."

"If he did, a clergyman would have presided. There'd be a record." It might take them nowhere. But it was a lead he could follow here on Tresco.

And since he didn't fancy another swim quite yet, leads on Tresco sounded like just the thing.

10

B eth had grown up with a vicar for an uncle, and now for a brother. But never did she imagine that it would result in their library table being completely covered with every parish record able to be dug up. Which, given the long history of the isles, meant a considerable stack of manuscripts, books, and ledgers.

Even so, they knew what range of dates they were looking for, and there were plenty of them to do the looking. They ought to have found the answer by now. But it had taken approximately forever for Oliver and Uncle Mark to unearth the key to whatever cupboard the old records were stored in, and then rain had blown in, and they hadn't wanted to transport them until it had passed. Then they'd had to eat, and they had only been at work for an hour before Sheridan succumbed to his headache again and retired, and the rest of them had stopped, too, out of sympathy. And because those old books smelled so strongly of mold that they were *all* getting headaches.

Which meant that here it was, midday on Saturday, and they were still paging through texts between sneezes—though at least the long stretches of time had given Senara ample opportunity to organize and assign. They'd come in today and found a nice little chart telling who to read what.

Beth scanned yet another faded list of births and deaths. Some of the dates were impossible to make out, but the ones she could be certain of said 1646. Close. They didn't know exactly what year to look for, but it ought to be sometime between 1648, when Mucknell returned to the Scillies after prowling the waters around Ireland for a while, and 1650, when he and Prince Rupert left English waters for a term in Portugal and Spain before going to the Caribbean. Any line could be the one that held the linchpin to her theory.

Beside her, Emily dragged the church's cupboard key in a slow circle, her eyes moving back and forth across another page. "Here's a Kerinda and a Robert in 1651. Rupert is a form of Robert."

"A year too late, though," Sheridan said from his chair on the opposite side of the table. "Mucknell and Rupert were in Portugal by then and would soon be on their way to the Caribbean."

"And if we consider every Robert, we'll never be able to narrow it down," Oliver added.

Beth forced her eyes back to the pages Senara had assigned to her, but her gaze kept wanting to drift to Sheridan. His bruises were even worse today, though the swelling around his nose was finally going down. He didn't have full black eyes, but the smudges still looked awful. And must feel even worse.

And clearly the blow had knocked something loose in his head for him to have spouted that nonsense yesterday. What had he meant, he wasn't going to propose? Why would he have? They barely knew each other.

And she certainly wasn't the prettiest girl in England. Nor would she ever spend a decade begging him for anything, most especially "another chance." He was mad, that was all. The only possible explanation.

Or Senara was right, and he was sweet on her. Which may in fact explain his otherwise inexplicable fixation with her having flirted with Scofield before she knew he was Scofield.

She sucked in a long breath and blew it slowly out. All her self-lectures on grace should have been more diligently applied. She felt like an utter heel when she looked at his mottled face and considered that he'd only earned the bruises because he'd been trying to rescue her. Spurred on by jealousy over her.

It was rather sweet, really. At least if one ignored the fact that he was still holding her trinket box hostage. No one had ever exchanged fisticuffs for her sake before. A bit brutish . . . and a complete failure . . . but sweet.

The mold was clearly getting to her. She sat back in her chair and rubbed at her eyes, which prompted Emily to do the same.

"You know what this reminds me of?" A ghost of a smile on her lips, Emily twirled the key in her fingers now. "Etiquette class at the academy, where we had to recite that endless list of titles from the peerage. Creation, extant, or extinct. So many names and dates."

Beth chuckled, following the movement of the iron with her tired gaze. "I had to tell myself stories about them to remember them." But she already had the story for the records she was looking for now. Just not the names.

Clearly as weary of eye as she was, Emily stared at the key too. "It's pretty, isn't it? Old keys are so much more interesting than the modern ones. All the scrollwork on the handle end. Almost looks like jewelry—and I suppose they were worn as such, back in the day. Grandmama still has an old chatelaine that's a true work of art."

"Mm." The church's key was indeed lovely, that scrollwork looking nearly shamrock shaped. "There's a box of keys in the attic to all the old trunks and chests. I loved to look through them as a girl just because they were so interesting. And because Senara had a necklace with a lovely old key for a pendant."

From her place at the table, Senara flashed her a smile. She was taking her newly appointed role as organizer quite seriously and had even joked that there'd be a ruler for the knuckles of anyone shirking their duties. Though with a check of her watch, Senara stood up now rather than lecture her and Em about chattering during their work. "If you all can carry on without me for a few minutes, I promised Mam I'd help with the bread."

Oliver chuckled. "I daresay we can stay on task without you for a while."

Senara sent him a playful scowl. "If not, we'll just have to tell Mabena to bring her schoolmaster here to keep you all in line."

Oliver snorted. He and Casek Wearne may be on better terms than ever in their lives, but no one was exactly surprised when Mabena had opted to spend much of her time with him at his family's home or her parents' rather than here. "Try it and I'll put all these records away in protest."

Senara laughed her way toward the door. "Not until I say so, Ollie. Keep at it. I'll be back soon."

Beth sneaked another glance across the table. By all rights, Sheridan's eyes ought to be more tired than the rest of theirs—he'd been at it this morning long before anyone else joined him. But then, he seemed to be more accustomed to digging through dusty old parchment than anyone else in the room. He had rocked his chair onto the back two legs and was currently holding a page up toward the window.

Had he really been thinking of proposing to her? After a mere week's acquaintance? It couldn't possibly be. She'd been nothing but rude to him. And he was a marquess. She was hardly a suitable match for him, which his sisters really were likely to point out if ever they met.

His chair came back down on all fours with a loud smack, and he shook the page in his hands. "I may have it. Mayday, 1650. A wedding recorded. Briallen Carew to R. Simmern."

Beth, much like Telford and Oliver and Libby and Emily, just stared at him. Telford then waved a hand in the air. Apparently that meant "more information, please" in whatever language it was those two spoke.

Sheridan tapped the page. "If he wanted the marriage kept quiet, Rupert wouldn't have put all his official titles. But he was of the Palatinate-Simmern branch of the House of Wittelsbach. *Simmern.* Not exactly a standard Cornish name to be here otherwise."

And *R* could be for Rupert. Beth scooted forward in her chair, closer to the table and the sheet of parchment he still held. "Briallen Carew." She said the name softly, reverently. Was that the fair island lass whose tragic love story her mother had told, and hers before her, back through the centuries?

"Carew is certainly a name still present in the area." Ollie tapped another line on another page, where presumably another Carew's name was written.

Briallen. Beth let her eyes slide closed and tried to imagine what she would have looked like. What her name would have sounded like when spoken in a heated whisper by a Germanic prince's lips.

When she opened them again a moment later, Sheridan's gaze was fixed on her. Held hers for two beats before he looked away.

Her chest went tight. Or heavy. Or hollow. Did he really believe in love at first sight?

"So, is that the answer to that question, then?" From beside Ollie, Libby shuffled her own stack back into neat order. "It sounds convincing enough."

"And gives credence to the oral tradition passed down through the Tremaynes' maternal line. Including the line common to the letters." Sheridan set the helpful sheeet of parchment back onto his stack.

"So then . . ." Emily slid the lovely key back onto the table and looked as though she'd like to fold in on herself and disappear. "Since we have the answer to that small question, are we ready to ask the one that's been looming over us? How my brother knew to investigate Gugh? The reason the rest of us thought it a lead not worth pursuing was because Nigel couldn't have known it, as he never saw those letters. But he was still there. So clearly we've missed something in the material to which he *did* have access."

A moment of silence greeted her. And then Oliver sighed and looked to Beth. "Lady Emily is right. We need to focus on the material we know the Scofields have. I assume you know which pieces you sent to them for authentication and reference and which they'd have no way of knowing about, especially among the letters."

"Of course." She certainly hadn't been willing to copy out each and every missive between Mucknell and his wife for them. "But don't we also want to have the edge? To use what we know that he doesn't to find this?"

"Yes." Sheridan.

"No." Everyone else.

Her eyes met his for another fleeting moment, a tentative smile passing between them. It seemed that in this, they were still the lone allies. But before they went off alone again and ended up with black eyes and broken noses, perhaps they ought to grant the others their say.

Sheridan huffed. "You all are forgetting that they have access to the archives that *we* don't have. Could be . . . well, could be that they've found something and didn't share it with Beth. Which would mean—that is, don't we *have* to try to find it first? With what's at our disposal?"

The others sighed and exchanged glances. Not exactly agreement, but not refusal either.

Beth shifted to Emily. She knew better than the others just how devastated her friend was by the telegram that had come for her a week ago, from her father. The one that had said, *Nigel tells us you hindered his investigation and betrayed his trust. Patch things up. Don't come pouting back to us until you have. It's time you remember you're a Scofield.*

As if Em had ever been able to forget she was a Scofield. It had been a constant specter hovering over her, a third party in the room every time they whispered and laughed together during their year of finishing school. If Beth had suggested an innocent joke to play on another girl or a teacher, Emily inevitably met it with "Oh, I mustn't! If Father found out, he would consider it a disgrace to the family name." When all the girls were dreaming about romances and courtships, Emily would be the one who sighed and said, "I imagine my father will choose someone. The Scofields have always been very particular about their alliances, and my parents will make no exception for me."

When first they met, Beth had envied the lovely redhead with her unending wardrobe and her enormous family estate and her stellar connections. But it hadn't taken more than a month for her to pity her for those things instead. Lady Emily Scofield had lived her life wrapped tightly in the invisible chains of expectation, unaware that she even *had* wings she could spread and glide away on. She didn't know what to do when a stout breeze blew, perfect for soaring. She had no Mamm-wynn whispering always in her ear, *"You're my little rosefinch, aren't you, dearover? You will fly away, you will see the world, but you'll always know to where you can come back. You'll always fly home."*

Yet for all the stifling influences, all her seeming kowtowing to them, there was still something in Emily's spirit that Beth's recognized. Something that had made them move quickly from classmates to friends. Something that had insisted last week that Emily stand firm against her brother, defying every familial expectation.

She reached now for her friend's delicate ivory hands and gave them a squeeze. "I don't want to ask it of you, Em, but . . . Sheridan is right. They could have information we don't. Or that they *think* we don't. Is there any way to learn if he does? Could you ask your mother, perhaps?"

Emily's wide, horrified eyes were answer enough. Her "Oh, she'd never tell me anything if Nigel's said I'm not on his side. He's the very apple of her eye" was superfluous.

"There's likely someone from your home who would be more your friend than his, though." Libby reached over to pluck her kitten from her brother's lap, snuggling the cute little tabby under her chin. Even from across the table, Beth could hear Darling's happy purr. He'd adjusted rather quickly to being a mobile cat, traveling in a basket from St. Mary's to Tresco with her every other day.

Emily drew her bottom lip between her teeth. "I can't think who. Our old nurse may have taken my side, but she's no longer with us. And there's Briggs, but she's here with me."

"Oh, but that could well be your answer." Smiling, Oliver brushed

133

his hand in a caress over Libby's. Really, they were so sweet it might give Beth a toothache if she weren't so ridiculously glad that her brother had found someone. "Briggs."

Emily frowned. "What about her? As I said, she's here with me. Not there to overhear anything."

"Yes, but she'll have friends among the staff who *are* there to overhear. Why don't we ask her if she'd be willing to test those waters for us?"

Emily looked genuinely baffled. "Friends."

Beth snorted a laugh and stood up. Obviously, Emily had not grown up idolizing the housekeeper's daughter and being best of friends with everyday people. "You *do* know your maid is an actual person, right? With feelings and thoughts and relationships?"

Emily's cheeks flamed pink. "Yes. It's only that I never paused to wonder what they may be."

Beth shook her head. In most of her acquaintances within society—which were few, granted—she found such attitudes maddening. But she had the distinct feeling with Emily that her thoughtlessness about the people in her family's employ was incidental, not deliberate.

Which meant she could learn. Learn to see them. Learn to appreciate them.

They might as well start now. "I imagine she's in the kitchen or thereabouts. If not, Mrs. Dawe will know where she's tucked herself. Let's go and find her."

"In the kitchen." Emily stood, but from sheer obedience, Beth suspected.

Libby hid her smile in the kitten's fur. She'd grown up in the same position as Emily, after all—an earl's daughter—but had far different opinions on appropriate interactions with her staff. Mabena had been serving as her lady's maid for two years but had also become her friend. That was how she'd ended up here for the summer, falling in love with Mabena's cousin.

Beth glanced—again, what was wrong with her?—at Sheridan.

He probably had stuffier opinions than any of them about such hierarchy. He was a marquess, after all. Below only a duke in the peerage. Two rungs down the ladder from a prince.

But he was grinning, too, and elbowing Telford. "She must have one of those unicorns. You know—the ones who don't lecture. Don't let Ainsley rub off on her then, my lady. He'll have your Briggs giving you sermons by week's end."

Beth lifted her brows. She'd met Ainsley, of course. He had a calm, steady spirit that shone from his eyes. "I can't imagine him lecturing."

Sheridan snorted. "He does. Such an expert at it, he rarely even needs words. Right, Telly?"

It being before noon, Telford merely grunted.

Emily frowned. "Forgive me, my lord, but if he's given to lecturing and sermonizing, why do you keep him on? My father would never suffer such audacity from a valet."

Sheridan opened his mouth, closed it, shrugged. Then tried again. "Because he's Ainsley. Everyone needs an Ainsley in their lives. If I didn't have his lectures keeping me straight, just imagine the mess I'd be."

Perhaps, aside from being a thief, Sheridan wasn't so bad. But that was a revelation she could ponder at her leisure later. For now, the kitchen. She linked her arm through Emily's and tugged her toward the dining room's exit, following Senara's invisible path. "Let's pay Briggs that visit."

Emily made no argument—until they were in the corridor, at which point she leaned close and whispered, "Are you certain this is a good idea, Beth? I don't think Briggs will appreciate us imposing upon her like this. I am certain she *does* have friends among the rest of the staff, but that life is to be kept separate from her service. And the same in reverse. The very thought of asking for such a personal favor . . ."

"Em." She halted them halfway between library and kitchen and looked her friend straight in the eye. "Do you want out of all this?

135

To just apologize to your brother and go home again? I realize we didn't present it as a choice, but it is. You don't *have* to be here, working with us. It's only treasure. It isn't worth sacrificing your family relationships for."

It was the truth, hard as it was to say. Beth had given months of her life to this treasure hunt, put her family in danger for it. But then, that was why she was so invested. Why she couldn't back out now. It was different for Emily, though. She had nothing at stake, and their friendship probably shouldn't be so valuable to her that she'd trade her place in her family for it.

Emily let her gaze drop for a long moment, a million thoughts parading across her expressive face. When she spoke, it was still in a whisper. "All my life, he's resented my very existence and tried his best to make me miserable. All my life, I've been less in my parents' eyes than him, simply because I'm a girl." Her eyes came up again. They were the same green that Beth had found striking in Nigel's face, and yet they looked nothing like his. There was no filter of charm. No pretense. Just bare pain still hardening into determination. "He's got away with so much, Beth. So many people he's misused and mistreated and hurt, and our parents have always helped him cover it up and get away with it. If I can't stand up to him, what chance does anyone else have? How will he ever be stopped? Or ever learn a different way?"

Beth clasped her hand, squeezed it hard. She couldn't imagine having a family like the Scofields. Couldn't imagine a brother who didn't champion and adore her—and tease her, yes, and try to find her nonexistent diary, and always make her feel guilty for wanting to taste more of life than the isles could offer. But Morgan and Oliver only acted as they did because they loved her. And never in her life had she had cause to doubt it. "So, you're with us?"

Another long silence, another million thoughts on her face. Another layer of determination over the pain. Then she nodded. "Let's go and talk to Briggs."

———————○———————

Senara pulled the bread from the oven with a long, happy inhale, hurrying the pans onto the stovetop before the heat could burn through the protective towel in her hands. Two loaves, fluffy and golden and perfect, were a testament to the early morning of laughter and kneading and earnest, honest work that she'd put in before joining the ladies and gents.

"Oh, that smells divine." Tommie Briggs was at her elbow, her smiling face wreathed in freckles. "If none of the masters favor the heel, I claim one. I can already taste it with your mother's strawberry preserves and a pat of butter."

Senara laughed and shut the oven door before its heat could do more than dampen the curls at her temples. She wasn't certain where Ainsley and Collins had taken themselves this morning, but it had been just the girls in the kitchen when she bustled in a few minutes ago to check her loaves—not that Mam would have let them burn. "I can't speak for the visiting lords, but Ollie and Beth never cared for the heel, and Mrs. Tremayne always joked that it was the fairies' portion, so it oughtn't to be eaten."

"Which," Mam put in from the table, "was her way of saying she didn't like it either. You're welcome to one, Tommie."

Tas would claim another, no doubt, when he came in from the grounds for his midday bite. That would be in another twenty minutes or so, if he stuck to the pattern he'd observed all her life.

Senara drew in another yeasty, golden breath. And wished she could just enjoy this—the everyday, the routine, the simple and lovely—without the specter of the unknown looming before her. When did Rory mean to show up? When he finally did, she'd have a few questions for him.

In the meantime, she was determined to impress his cousin, which was as close as she could currently get to making a good impression on his mother and sister. But she was finding that Ainsley and Rory were about as different as two cousins could be. Where Rory was all energy and passion, Ainsley was steady and stoic. She had no idea what he thought of her, or if he even knew that she would soon be his cousin by marriage.

But Rory had surely mentioned her. Hadn't he?

"There she is."

At Beth's voice, Senara and Tommie both turned round, though Tommie's smile froze on her lips. Beth wasn't alone in the kitchen doorway. She had Lady Emily with her.

Tommie dipped a quick curtsy, transforming instantly from bread-craving young woman into emotionless lady's maid. "My lady, forgive me. Did you have need of me?"

Senara sighed. It was a transformation she'd witnessed count-less times with the staff at Cliffenwelle—they all had it perfected. Their own feelings neatly buttoned. Their own lives folded away. Their own identities traded in for starched aprons and pressed liv-ery. Half the time even their names were checked at the door like an umbrella and something simple like Alice or Sally or Abigail picked up instead.

She'd witnessed it countless times, but never in *this* house. And it made Mam frown as surely as it made Senara sigh.

Beth gave her friend an elbow to the ribs, and Lady Emily stepped forward, looking everywhere but at Tommie. "No, no. I don't need anything, there's nothing to apologize for. Or rather . . ." She made a face, as though she'd tasted something sour, and then forced her gaze to Tommie.

Senara planted a hand on her hip. Was it really so difficult to look upon her own maid? With Tommie as sweet and bright as a jar of the strawberry preserves that she loved?

"I've a question, but you mustn't feel put upon to answer. It's about my brother."

Tommie went stiff as a tombstone. "Beg pardon."

Emily's eyes squeezed shut. "I'm bumbling this."

Which was more than Beth had the patience for. She huffed and gave Tommie a warm smile. "It's like this, Briggs. We all know he's a cad, and worse—a criminal, at least in his associations if not outright in his dealings. But quite possibly in both. And I have a feeling you and every other employee of the Scofields know it. Am I right?"

Pale as a ghost, Tommie said nothing. But her silence said plenty, as did the knuckles gone white as she gripped the workbench.

Even Lady Emily must have noticed. She'd opened her eyes again, and her face went fierce. It transformed her instantly from pampered miss to the sort of girl who could live out a legend in one of Beth's favorite tales. "We're going to stop him. He's going to answer for all he's done."

Beth's smile flashed again, this time with pride at the lady, before turning to Tommie again. "But we need to know what he's about. There's no chance Em's parents will tell us anything. . . ."

But not a thing went on in a master's house that the servants didn't know about. Senara studied Tommie's profile. They were asking her—all the Scofield employees—to take a risk. The question was whether it was one they'd deem worth it. Whether there was any benefit to them.

Apparently, Tommie thought there was. "What do you need me to do?"

Beth and Lady Emily seemed to think it the right question. They tumbled over each other in their answers, asking for letters or tele-grams and for friendships to be leveraged.

Senara bunched the towel into her fist and then tossed it onto the counter and stepped between them, a hand held up.

Emily blinked in surprise. But Beth knew well what the raised hand meant. She fell silent, yes, but also tilted her head to the side and looked Senara in the eye, waiting.

Senara lifted her brows. "She'll need a guarantee. Security. A promise that if this goes awry and they're caught scuttling around behind the masters' back and end up sacked or, worse, facing charges, someone's going to step in to protect them."

Lady Emily looked as though she might faint dead away, and

even Beth frowned, perplexed. Clearly neither of them had thought this fully through.

Good thing they'd invited Senara into their adventures, for sure. "I'll offer it."

The two young ladies jumped and spun, making room as Lord Sheridan, still bruised and puffy, stepped into the kitchen. He looked Tommie straight in the eye. "Anyone whose employ is terminated over this will have a position at Sheridan Castle. Or regardless, if they just want to leave. And I'll offer protection to anyone if there are charges. Well, I mean . . ." He grinned, though it looked as if the action hurt, and waved a hand. "Don't anyone go maiming or stealing or murdering willy-nilly. But you know."

It was good enough for Tommie. "I'll wire Dandy straightaway."

Senara exchanged a bare smile with Beth. Her young friend may still have an argument with his lordship over her mother's trinket box. But he clearly wasn't as bad as she'd been ready to believe.

11

S heridan might not have been as chock-full of virtues as some—Ainsley—would hope, but patience he had in abundance. And over the last two weeks, he'd had plenty of chances to put it to use.

While the others expressed frustration in the fact that Scofield had vanished again, Sheridan had used the time to send scads of notes to mutual acquaintances, and replies had begun trickling in. Their group here had gone out on multiple expeditions to Gugh, trying to determine what had drawn *him* there, but Sheridan wasn't put off by the lack of ready answers. He was well accustomed to spending weeks or months at an excavation, removing the earth layer by careful layer in search of whatever could be found.

Discovery would not be rushed. And moved on no one's schedule.

Besides, all this uneventful time gave the post a chance to bring a reply from Briggs's friends too.

And for Sheridan's bruises to fade a bit.

All well and good until the rain began nearly a week ago and hadn't let up. He had no particular problem with rain—either in working in it or in cozying up with a book by the fire instead. But Telford had been pacing the library like a caged tiger for the last three days, grousing about the minuscule size of the house again. Ainsley and Collins were heard bickering over whose turn it was to slosh along the street in search of a newspaper, and even Tremayne, who Sheridan had yet to see in anything but a pleasant mood, had grown sullen.

That one he could explain easily enough—the rain had kept Libby from making the sail from St. Mary's, and apparently five days without his lady love were not to be borne.

Beth sank down beside Sheridan on the sofa. Actually beside him. Of her own free will. And not at the other end either but on the space directly beside his. With a delightful little smirk on her face.

He'd only make her beg for four more months. He'd tell Tremayne to book the church. A Christmas wedding should do.

She even leaned closer to his side, her glance flicking between her sulking brother and irritably-pacing Telford. "I know what Ollie's problem is—but I can't think Telford misses his sister so keenly. You'd think neither of them has lived in England more than a month the way they're reacting to a little rain."

Sheridan chuckled and turned a page in his book on the Druid sites identified in the Lake District. It was sorely incomplete and had some of the most ridiculous theories espoused in it. "Telly is very much like Abbie's pug. All posturing and ferocity until the first splash of rain on his nose, then back inside he runs. Might muss his hair, you know."

The smirk turned fully to him. "Telly or the pug?"

"Yes." He tried to read the next paragraph—some absurd theory about the circle of standing stones at Castlerigg that made him question whether the author had ever even *been* there—but gave up after a moment. She was near enough that he could smell the scent of her soap. And her hair looked as soft as silk. And when she snorted a laugh at his joke, her eyes positively danced with the very light of heaven.

"What are you reading today?" She tilted the book up to answer her own question. Which meant her fingers were mere fractions of an inch from his.

He wouldn't even make her beg. She had only to drop to a knee and he'd agree to marry her.

She gave him a dubious look. "Weren't you reading a different book on Druid ruins yesterday?"

"Finished it. This one's rubbish, though. Better suited for tinder than reading material. Well, I mean—not that I'd ever do such a thing. One of the seven deadly sins, I'm all but certain. Have to ask Ainsley."

She smiled and leaned against the back of the sofa, making herself comfortable. Around *him*. That counted as a proposal, right? "Where did you even come by it? I don't recall that one being in our library."

"No, the Tremaynes have better taste in books than this." He closed it—though over his finger. There could yet be a nugget of insight worth considering, buried somewhere under all the rubbish. "I brought it with me. Trying to read all the existing texts about the liths and cairns in the Lake District. Research, you know. To pair with my own excavations."

"He intends to set the record straight and expostulate on his theories about Bronze Age monuments and burial sites in a book of his own." Telford dropped to a seat in the same leather chair he always chose and scowled at Oliver. "You should have a dog. What kind of English family doesn't have a dog?"

Tremayne didn't even look up from his own book. "I'm certain Darling would love that."

"My sister and her cat weren't part of your life until June. What was your excuse before then?"

Sheridan took a calculated risk and leaned a few inches closer to Beth. "He's a pug. I told you. Now he's nipping at others' tails."

She laughed. Her brother said something about a childhood wolfhound. Hardly mattered what. Beth had laughed again and still had her face turned his way. "Have you started the writing yet? Of your historical text?"

No lady in all his days had ever asked him about his research.

Even his sisters. Who rather made it a point to change the subject each and every time he brought it up. Which meant there were a lot of subject changes in the castle.

That definitely counted as a proposal. Who would she want as her bridesmaids? He'd send them telegrams himself, telling them to hasten to the isles, if they weren't here already. "Not yet. Well, notes. Reams of them. I don't know how I'm going to pare it down enough, honestly."

"Then you'll have to write a whole series, I expect." She plucked the current book from his unprotesting hands, careful to keep his page marked with her own finger but flipping to the table of contents. "If I have an arch-nemesis, it's a blank, empty page. Everything I try to write upon one seems as rubbish as you say this is."

She wrote too? Not research texts, he suspected. Much as she knew about island history, she seemed to lean more heavily toward lore. Legend. "Ah. Fairy tales. Like the one Libby read from *Treasure Island*."

She blushed and cast a look toward her brother. She'd presented him with a new copy of the book on the evening that Sheridan had closeted himself in his room with his broken nose and migraine, he'd heard. "I imagine you think such tales foolish."

"On the contrary. I find them critical parts of any culture. Often better indicators of how a people really lived than any other records can provide. Also." He lifted a finger, as if about to deliver a clincher. Which he was. "They're smashing good fun."

She smiled again. Not in amusement. Not because of the others' sniping or poking. But a smile as intimate as a kiss, and just as delicious.

Well. Perhaps not. Though he'd be up for the experiment whenever she was.

From the front of the house came the sound of a door blowing open, and a voice as blustering as the rain-soaked wind called out, "Anyone at home?"

Sheridan was on his feet in a flash. Fitzwilliam Gibson was without question one of his favorite people that he'd met on Tresco thus far, right behind his grandchildren. And their magician of a housekeeper. And of course Mamm-wynn, who he may have even considered tossing Beth aside for, if she weren't still in love with her late husband and old enough to be, well, his grandmother.

"Back here!" He strode to the library door to wave a hand, just in case his voice wasn't beacon enough. "Reading. And sulking. Depending on which of us you look at."

After a rustle and a thud that must be mackintoshes and wellies being shed, Gibson appeared in the corridor, his smile as sunny as the sky was not.

"Fitz, is that you?" Mamm-wynn emerged, too, from the drawing room, where she'd been trying to talk her fingers into wielding her knitting needles. He'd have opted for her company instead of the library this morning, except that she'd asked Senara to come and read to her while she worked. And it was difficult to concentrate on rubbish Bronze Age theories when someone was reading *Oliver Twist* aloud.

He hurried forward now, though, to offer her his arm. Beating Gibson to the punch by half a second. Sheridan celebrated the victory with a wink for the old man, who pretended affront, then clapped his hands together. "Decided the rain wasn't going to keep me housebound another day, so I thought I'd come and see the children."

"Good." Mamm-wynn twinkled a smile up at her old friend. "I can hardly stand all the dour faces today. They could use a distraction. Other than my pirate prince here, who seems happy as a puffin on Annet."

"Well, of course." Sheridan patted her hand. "I have you for company. Don't miss the ladies stranded on St. Mary's at all."

She laughed that magical laugh of hers. "Oh yes. All the credit is mine, without a doubt." She held him still rather than letting him lead her onward, poking her head back into the drawing room. "Thank you for reading to me, dearover."

145

Miss Dawe had drifted close enough to the door to be visible. "My pleasure, Mamm-wynn."

Gibson proffered an arm in her direction. "Join us, Nara?"

Her smile softened. "I should probably see if Mam has lost her patience with Ainsley and Collins yet. She had them pulling taffy, since no one wanted to dash to the confectioner's."

And heaven forbid Telly run out of sweets. "Tell them to come and hear whatever tale Gibson will tell us. Give your poor mother a reprieve." In most society, he wouldn't dare invite the valets to join them for the afternoon's entertainment. But this was far better than most society.

Mamm-wynn patted his arm as they started down the corridor. "You're a good lad, Theo."

He lifted her fingers with his opposite hand long enough to drop a kiss onto her knotted knuckles, then set them back on his arm and grinned. "Say that again when Beth can hear you, will you?"

———————○———————

"And the ship, with all its ghostly pirates, sank beneath the waves, never to be seen again by mortal eyes . . . but for in the light of a full moon."

Beth clapped at the close of her grandfather's tale, laughing at Telford's exaggerated shiver.

"I'll have nightmares for a week," he said, but with the first smile she'd seen from him in two days.

She glanced over to where Ainsley, Collins, and Senara had settled in too, still a bit surprised that they'd joined the rest of them. And especially that, as Mamm-wynn reported, it was Sheridan's idea.

The man was full of surprises. And not all of them dastardly.

Another prime example rested on his knee: the pad of paper and pen he'd pulled from his stack of books. She'd seen him taking notes aplenty on the texts he'd been reading since his arrival, but he'd jotted down key points of Tas-gwyn's story too. Apparently he really did think such tales worthy of attention.

She nudged him with an elbow, though, and leaned over to say in a stage whisper, "Don't look for any kernel of historical truth in that one, my lord. It came entirely from my grandfather's imagination."

"Not entirely." Tas-gwyn Gibson took a sip of tea and gestured toward the window. "There really is a rip current. And a moon."

Sheridan capped his pen. "Even if there weren't, it would be worth recording. You should consider a written collection of your stories, Gibson. For your grandchildren, if nothing else."

Beth sat up a bit straighter. It was a good idea. She'd probably be as miserable at catching the cadence of his words as she was the remembered one of Mother's, but it would be worth trying. And at the very least, it would be time spent together and enjoyed. "That's brilliant."

Sheridan beamed at her. "I do."

Had she missed something? "You do what?"

He grinned. "Weren't those your marriage vows?"

Her face heated. And laughter bubbled up. How in the world did a marquess get to be so self-deprecating that he'd turn an embarrassment of one week into a joke the next? The next elbow she sent into his side had a bit more force behind it. "You're ridiculous."

"Until death do us part."

Tas-gwyn was laughing, too, but soon sobered. "My girl already had that idea. The year you were away, Beth. Well, both of you, I suppose. You were still at university, Ollie. Your mam and Morgan and I spent the winter working on it. Wrote down all my tales and others from the islands as well. Went door to door collecting them, chatting with all the neighbors. Happiest time of my life, aside from when your mamm-wynn Kendra was by my side."

Beth's gaze flew to Oliver's. He was staring right back. "Mother wrote down your stories? And Morgan?"

"But . . ." Beth slid to the edge of her cushion, brows knit. "That would have been just months before the accident." She'd only been at finishing school from September through July, the year she was sixteen. And had been home again only three weeks when what should have been a leisurely trip to the mainland for her parents to check on Truro Hall had turned into a violent storm that had snatched their boat down into the Atlantic's jaws.

Ollie's breath slid out between his teeth. "And then Morgan, a year later." Leaving just the three of them in the house. Her and Ollie and Mamm-wynn.

Her grandfather nodded. "I know. That's why I hadn't the heart to ever ask where it had all been put. Hardly seemed to matter. When I'd already lost the people, the stories we'd put down didn't seem so important. Though that was a bit cruel of me in a way, I suppose. They're your mam's words as much as mine. You deserve to have them."

"Mother's words." There'd been so many things to sort through. To pack away. So many papers. She'd made no attempt to read them, or even to see what they were. Just shoved them all into boxes before the next bout of tears blinded her. She blinked at her brother. "We must have them still. We put it all away, but we didn't get rid of anything."

"They must be in the attic."

Sheridan stood and took four steps around the table, toward the door. Then stopped and arched a brow back at her. "Well? Have any of you anything better to do?"

Beth leapt after him, Ollie hot on her heels. She didn't much care what the others did or didn't do. All these years, they'd had Mother's words, island stories, Tas-gwyn's pirate tales closed up in a box, and she hadn't even realized it. She'd wasted paper trying to write it in her own hand instead, when all she'd had to do was go to the attic.

Sheridan stepped aside to let her through the doorway first, probably because he didn't know where the stairs to the attic could be found. But she did, and it only took a minute to reach them, climb them, and step into that world of dusty rafters and pattering rain and soft blue light filtering in through the small garret windows.

She moved into the center of the space to make room for whoever else had joined her—Sheridan and Oliver, Telford and Senara, Ainsley and Collins, by the looks of it. Only the grandparents had stayed behind. And then Beth looked around at the stacks of boxes and trunks and old, broken furniture not suitable for use but too dear to get rid of. "I have no idea where we put her papers."

Sheridan grinned. "Another treasure hunt, then."

He had a nice grin. Better than nice, really. She knew plenty of people whose faces looked better in repose than when they were smiling, but his grin carved creases into his cheeks and turned his eyes into happy slits that invited everyone in the room to smile along.

Though she hadn't better mention it, or he'd probably start naming their children.

She tucked a smile of her own between her teeth and turned to the nearest stack of boxes.

This hunt was considerably faster than the other. Within a few minutes, she'd located notes in her mother's hand that were clearly stories gathered from neighbors. And Oliver had found some in Morgan's that seemed to be more general island history. Senara read from yet another page one of Tas-gwyn's favorite opening lines: *"Once there lived and once there was . . ."*

"You know . . ." Beth fanned through the stack of pages in her box, Mother's beautiful script adorning them all. "If they'd really collected stories from all the neighbors, there could be more like the one about Briallen and Rupert. Or mentions of Mucknell— ones to which Tas-gwyn hasn't added ghosts and skeletons and ghouls and fairies."

"Oral traditions." Sheridan was sitting cross-legged on the dusty floor, flanked by open boxes.

Apparently Ainsley hadn't noticed it until that moment, because he turned around and made a choking sound. "My lord! Have a care for your trousers."

"It's only dust, Ainsley."

And only the finest of worsted wool that he was saturating with it. But she hadn't the urge to add any more sarcastic observations

149

about his lack of care to her silent litany just now. She'd been kneeling in it too, after all.

Senara stood. "We're going to lose the light up here soon. We either need to bring up lamps or to carry down whatever we want to look through."

Given Ainsley's three consecutive sneezes, right on cue, they opted for returning to the library, everyone with a box in his or her arms.

12

Senara had to admit that reading through the stories in Morgan Tremayne's careful hand was a more entertaining way to pass a rainy evening than she'd anticipated. Everyone in the house had taken a stack of them, even Mam and Tas.

She'd taken hers to their own kitchen table, which was smaller than the one at the Tremaynes', and less used too. But it was comfortable, and there would be fewer distractions here. Fewer people chattering over whatever they'd just read and exchanging opinions on what it might mean. She'd gather their notes on what each story was about in the morning and start making a catalogue of what was to be found, but for now, a dose of solitude was just what she needed.

Their little cottage was quiet, and she relaxed into the hard wooden chair. She'd shed her governess dresses with their tight sleeves and stiff collars right away, as she always did when she came home. Now she even undid the top button of her loose blouse so the relaxation would feel complete.

She had a small notepad beside her stack, and a pencil, much like the ones she'd made certain everyone else had too. She'd given them all strict instructions on what to include in their notetaking, amid the grins and chuckles and whispers about a governess clearly missing her charges.

She'd assured them they were all a sorry substitute for her sweet little girls, which had made them laugh all the more, as she'd intended. Get them smiling and settled and then leave them to their devices, that had been her plan. So that she could do her own reading alone.

Funny, that—she was so often lonely at Cliffenwell, especially after the girls were abed, when it was nothing but quiet. She'd had no one to talk to, no real friends there. Sometimes the ache had been palpable, and her room had felt as hollow and echoing as a dungeon.

Now she craved that peace and solitude like Lord Telford did his chocolate drops. She'd scarcely had a waking hour of it since she got home, as crammed as the Tremayne house was.

Her eyes focused upon the page before her. She'd learned straight off that Morgan had done a bang-up job of choosing titles for each piece that perfectly captured the essence, so she got off easy on her own notetaking.

Dear Morgan. He'd been the closest to Senara in age, only four years her junior. And when he was a small lad, he'd been just like any other. Boisterous and full of energy, constantly into mischief. Mam had frequently given her the task of watching over him, or at least following him about. They'd explored the garden together, and much of the neighborhood besides.

Then, when he was five, he got ill. And it was like . . . it was like he never got over it. One thing after another, every flu or cold or ague to go round found him and knocked him down. Constant infections. Incessant aches and pains. The poor child went from a healthy, happy boy ready to start school to an invalid.

But there'd been a change in his spirit too. A deepening. His infirmities had shaped him not into a bitter person who demanded sympathy, but into a young man determined to find every drop of joy that life could offer him. To love his family fiercely in whatever time God allotted him. To do anything in his power—absolutely anything—to make those in his world happy.

She jotted his title for this page down on her pad and started reading. More history than imagination, this one, about an old hermitage on one of the smaller islands and the monk who'd lived there.

One of the other chairs at the table scraped its way out, and then Ainsley dropped into view.

So much for solitude. But then, she'd not had much opportunity to speak with him without others about. She wouldn't complain about it now. Perhaps she'd even find a way to bring Rory up and see if Ainsley would let slip anything he may have said about her. And even if not, she'd been enjoying getting to know him. He was a wonderful man, the sort you couldn't help but like. He and Rory must be good friends as well as cousins—he was just the sort of steadying influence that would complement Rory's passionate personality.

She made a show of glancing at the old clock. "Don't tell me his lordship is abed already. With all this reading to do?"

His chuckle was both amused and indulgent. "Quite the opposite. He plans to stay up all night, so he told me I may as well go wherever I liked to do my assigned reading."

She breathed a laugh. "So long as you do your assigned reading."

"It's like being at school again." He situated his stack on the table too. Neat and orderly, as she'd come to expect of anything he touched. "Really, I think he just hoped I wouldn't see the fresh ink stain on his new summer jacket."

"A little bicarb and water will take it right out."

"And a little care would have kept him from getting it to begin with." But he said the words without any heat. Or, clearly, any expectation that such care was on the horizon. "How did you keep your charges in order, Miss Dawe? I could use some help."

She laughed and got up to fetch them some lemonade. "I'm not certain the techniques I used for a trio of lasses would be so very helpful on your grown marquess."

"Sometimes I don't think they're so dissimilar. Good hearts, fine intentions, but an utter lack of common sense."

She set two tall glasses on the table and pulled the pitcher from the icebox. "I don't know. He seemed rather practical-minded when it came to ensuring safety for the Scofield servants."

Ainsley still hadn't so much as moved his pages. His attention was on her, steady and even. It could have felt demanding. Unsettling. But it didn't. She put the pitcher away again.

"And he meant every word," he said. "All two hundred of their domestics could arrive in a parade asking for sanctuary, and he'd just start a new building project to house them all and welcome them aboard."

That was pride in his tone—unmistakable, almost paternal. Or fraternal, anyway. A far cry from the resentment that always underscored Rory's tone when he mentioned his employer. She'd never thought much about his unhappiness in his position before, but these last two weeks, she'd had far too much time to consider where that dissatisfaction could have led him. It had begun bothering her more than she cared to admit. A few times she had nearly mentioned it to Ainsley, but then she'd stopped herself. Perhaps because she didn't want to plant any suspicions of his cousin in him.

Perhaps because she feared what he might say. For now, she forced her mind back to him and Lord Sheridan. "He must be either loaded or completely irresponsible." She handed him one of the glasses.

He took it with a nod. "He spends widely, but not wildly. On anything, but with care. Anytime he sees a craftsman or artisan or student with a genuine passion and skill, he finds a way to contribute."

She held up her own glass. "A toast, then. May there be a thousand more just like him in the world."

Ainsley clinked his glass to hers, but before he could push any words through his parted lips, the kitchen door quaked under a hard fist.

Senara started, sloshing a bit of her lemonade from the glass, and spun toward the door. She could make out nothing but a masculine silhouette against the glass.

"One of your father's friends, I imagine. I'll step out—they tend to clam up when they see any of us incomers, as they call us." Sounding cheerful about his self-banishment, Ainsley strode quickly for the stairs and vanished up them.

Conscientious of him, to be sure—and accurate too. The islanders had a healthy respect for holiday-goers and the pounds sterling they brought, but they never wanted to air local business in front of them.

She slid her lemonade onto the workbench and moved toward the door, an easy smile on her lips for whichever neighbor she'd find in the drizzly evening.

The smile froze and then exploded into a laugh as she opened the door and the light fell on the man outside. *Not* a neighbor. Rory!

"Hello, luv." He stepped inside, as if he'd been here a hundred times before. Darting a glance over her shoulder, he leaned over to drop a kiss onto her lips. But then he pulled her toward the door still standing open.

She laughed again and tugged at him to stay put. "Where are you going? Come in! I'll introduce you to—"

"Not yet." He darted a glance past her again, and she finally gathered her wits enough to note that the smile on his face wasn't half as joyful as her own felt. "Just step outside with me for a moment, will you?"

For a moment? She let him tug her out into the dusk, but a thousand questions were vying for a place on her tongue. When had he arrived in the islands—and why was he only just now showing up on Tresco? All the locals would have been inside by now, not out in their boats this close to dark. Which surely meant that he intended to stay here tonight. Why wasn't he eager for an introduction to her parents, so that they could invite him to bunk with Ainsley?

Oh, wouldn't he be surprised to learn that his cousin was here too?

Once he had her outside, he dropped her hand, which left her fingers feeling oddly cold and uncertain. With his newly free one, he took his cap off and combed the thick waves she'd run her own

155

fingers through a few short weeks ago. Tucked the cap into his pocket and made a show of surveying the house. "So, this is home, aye?"

The drizzle had tapered off, leaving more mist than rain in the air. She smiled at his twilight-draped form. "It is. I always thought I'd see your home before you saw mine, given how far this is from everything. I'm eager to show you about, though. And where are you staying? We could squeeze you in here, I'm sure, with, of all people—"

"Slow down, Nara." Rory gave her a grin, but it was absent his usual cheer. "I didn't come for a tour."

Confusion twisted with dread and knit a shroud over her heart. This wasn't how their reunion was supposed to go, not this time. Not after the words they'd spoken, the kisses, the things she'd given him—and given up for him. He was supposed to sweep her into his arms, proclaim how much he'd missed her. He was supposed to march straight up to her father and ask for her hand.

He was supposed to make everything right.

She kept her smile in place, though her throat went tight. "Of course not. But you came, which is what matters, and you'll need a place to stay, won't you? Your cousin—"

"You've met him, then?" Now his eyes flashed, and he reached for her hand again. But it wasn't love or desire in his eyes—not for her anyway. "I imagined you would, given how small the islands are. What's he been about? How well have you got to know him? Do you think you can get information from him?"

"I . . . what?" Her fingers went limp in his. She'd thought it would be a surprise for him that Ainsley was here. But he'd known it all along. Known it and . . . what? What exactly was he asking of her? "Rory?"

Now he put back on his usual smile, full of charm. He sidled closer to her. "Don't look at me like that, luv. This is what you've always wanted from me, isn't it? To leave our positions so we can be together? Well, that requires cash. And I found a way to get some."

The windfall. He'd hinted as much back at Cliffenwelle. She'd thought he meant an unexpected inheritance, or that his paternal uncle had decided to retire and turn the shop over to him. Suddenly here, now, with a very different backdrop and her own weeks having been spent in pursuit of a pirate hoard, she had a very bad feeling that she'd assumed incorrectly.

"No." It was a plea, not just a word. "Rory, please tell me you didn't somehow get tangled up with the Scofields."

"Well you needn't blame *me*. It's saintly Ainsley's fault." He chuckled as he said it and cast a glance around their back garden. "Do you know where he's staying? I'd better avoid him. He won't be too keen on me having leveraged our relation."

She tugged her fingers free of his so she could reach up and press them to the sudden headache pounding in her temple. "You didn't. You wouldn't sell out your own cousin."

He pursed his lips. "That's an ugly way of putting it."

"Rory? What are you doing here?" Ainsley's voice, sounding from the kitchen doorway, made her jump half out of her skin. Though her own response was nothing compared to Rory's. He jumped, too, and a terrible look crashed over his face. He moved to the side, spun her to face his cousin, and then held her there with hands on her shoulders.

Putting her in between them. Using her as a shield.

Which was ridiculous, on the one hand—Ainsley would never raise a hand to anyone. But on the other hand, the absurdity didn't matter at all. Rory was supposed to be her hero, setting the world to rights. He was supposed to be as gallant as he was handsome, honorable, worthy of the love she'd given him.

Instead, he was cowering behind her.

"Guess that answers the question of where he's staying," he muttered, punctuating it with a curse. "Didn't think you'd have got quite *that* close to him, luv."

She stiffened under his heavy hands. "His employer is staying next door. My parents work for them, so they offered him a room."

He sucked in a breath. "Your mum and dad work for the Tremaynes? Blimey, how did I not realize that?"

How indeed? She'd mentioned it often enough over the years. Had he paid no attention?

Or . . . wait, had she ever said their name? Or had she done as she always did and called them Mrs. T and Mamm-wynn T and Beth and Ollie, just that?

His hands on her shoulders softened a bit, massaging instead of just holding her down. His voice was low and soft, undoubtedly meant to reach only her ears and not his cousin's. "Well now, that's perfect. You'll be able to help more than I dared to hope." Louder he said, "Good to see you, Henry. And you've met my girl, clearly."

His girl. A few weeks ago, she'd thrilled when she'd heard him call her that to another servant. Somehow, it felt very different now, with all this ugliness spilling out. And with Henry Ainsley staring them down.

"I asked you what you were doing here, Rory. Though I suspect I know, given that '*ugly way of putting it.*'"

There was something odd about his tone. Something she'd never heard in it before—a coolness, a reserve. Strange, because she would have told anyone who asked that Ainsley was always on the cool, reserved side. But his normal voice sounded downright tropical in comparison to his current one.

"Good to see you, too, cousin." Rory chuckled and slid one of his hands down her back, resting it on her waist. No less an anchor but somehow more possessive. And not in a way she particularly liked. "Actually, I owe you quite a lot of thanks. If you weren't such a stick-in-the-mud, I'd never have had this golden opportunity land in my lap."

If possible, Ainsley's spine went even straighter. He glanced momentarily to Senara.

She wondered what he saw. Did she look as undone by Rory's arrival as she felt? Could he see in a glance all the guilt she bore when it came to him?

Putting on the playful mood she'd once loved, Rory gave her shoulder a squeeze, still laughing. As if they shared a joke. "Is it any

158

wonder they couldn't get information from him? Sealed up tighter than that sarcophagus his employer has on display. But that's all right, old boy. Your reticence is my gain."

Ainsley's expression went utterly still. "Rory. What have you done?"

Rory laughed again. "What you hadn't the gumption to do. They said they approached you first, back in May. Just wanting a bit of information about your employer, so as to make the best business deals possible with him. Harmless, Hank. You ought to have seen it was—but just because *you* missed the opportunity doesn't mean *I'm* so dense."

"They." Ainsley took a step—one single step closer to his cousin. But it was a step so forceful that Rory stumbled back, pulling her with him. "The Scofields? What have you—you wouldn't. *Couldn't.* You don't know anything of interest to them."

Rory's laugh sounded thin this time. "*They* didn't realize that. All they knew was I'd spent Christmas with you. Two cousins, of an age. *Of course* we're the best of friends. They're happy to believe anything I tell them—and pay me handsomely for it too."

Senara's arms sagged to her sides. After all those years of flirtation, after an innocent stolen kiss last year, he'd finally focused his full attention on her this summer. Because, she'd thought, he loved her too.

But by that time, he'd already been in the Scofields' pocket. Tears stung her eyes. He must have remembered where she was from, at the very least. He may have forgotten she had a direct association with the Tremaynes, but he'd clearly known something about what Beth had gotten involved in. Was that all this summer had ever been to him? Were all his words of affection empty?

Had she compromised everything she'd ever believed in for a rake who was just out to use her?

Ainsley took another menacing step. "What information? What have they asked you for? I told them in May that I had no interest in betraying Lord Sheridan's trust."

Rory finally stepped a bit to the side, though he kept that one arm

159

around her waist. "I know you did. Probably even told his lordship that they approached you."

"Of course I did. He had to know that the people he was doing business with weren't above stooping to bribery."

Rory raised a finger, grinning. "Or extortion. That's why they came to me, you know. Not because they thought I'd know anything about Sheridan—because they assumed I'd know things about *you*. Things that they could use against you to get what they needed about him, if it came to that."

Ainsley didn't take another step. But his hands curled into fists.

Senara sucked in a breath. "Rory. How could you?"

He rolled his eyes. "Relax, Nara. It isn't as though I gave them any *real* weaknesses of his to exploit. Couldn't—he hasn't got any, you know. Pillar of virtue is Henry Ainsley." His tone dripped mockery.

The breath she'd pulled in felt like a rock in her chest. She'd thought . . . well, that the cousins *were* friends. That she ought to get to know Ainsley because he mattered to Rory. She'd come to admire this man she hoped would be her cousin soon, for every sterling quality Rory was now mocking.

She'd misjudged him so. Not Ainsley—Rory. How? How could she have been so blind?

A muscle in Ainsley's jaw ticked in the light spilling through the kitchen windows. "What have you told them?"

"Nothing you need to worry about. Blimey, Hank, I wouldn't put you in danger. I may want to make a few quid, but I'm not a monster. And really, you ought to be thanking me. Since they think they found a fount of information in me, it means they're not pressing your mum, or mine. I'm a blighted *hero*."

Exactly what she'd wanted him to be. A hero worthy of any of Beth's tales. But he didn't seem the hero now. Heroes didn't sell information to the villains for a few pounds. Heroes didn't mock the virtues of their cousins.

Heroes didn't seduce a girl just because he thought she might be useful.

She shuddered. Maybe these suspicions were wrong. Surely. *Please, God.* But what if they weren't? Was she really fool enough to have fallen for such a charlatan?

Ainsley was drawing in slow, careful breaths and letting them out again with the same careful measure. "Tell me everything you've told them, Rory. Now."

Rory took a step to the side, pulling her with him. "I didn't come here to listen to your lectures, thank you. I came for my girl." He flashed her a grin. "Just like I said I would, luv. Flush from my good fortune and ready to start a life together. We can go anywhere in the world you want."

Blast it, why did tears have to sting her eyes? Why did hearing the dream tumble from his lips shatter her heart? "Rory." This wasn't a conversation she wanted to have in front of Ainsley—in front of *anyone*. It wasn't a conversation she wanted to have at all. But she needed to know. "This summer . . . is this all it was about? My connection to the Scillies?"

"Tell me about Mucknell, luv." Tapping her for information, so he'd have something true to pass along to the Scofields, something other than whatever tales he'd told them about Ainsley and Sheridan.

His smile didn't falter, but something flashed in his gaze. "Of course not. How could you think so? You know I've always fancied you."

Did he? She had always fancied *him* . . . but he'd never singled her out until recently. He'd flirted, stolen that one kiss, but he flirted with *all* the girls.

She pulled away from him, needing a bit of space. Needing the fresh, rain-scented air to bring reason to her mind. *Think, Senara. Piece it together.*

He'd asked her outright, just five short days before her dismissal, about Mucknell, yes. But before that? He'd certainly shown more interest than he ever had before in her history, her family, where she came from. She'd thought it was because he was coming to care for her. That he wanted to know all he could about her, as she did him.

161

But how could she know if it was sincere or if he had ulterior motives the whole time? *Lord* . . . Only when she breathed the name in a silent prayer did she realize how long it had been since she had done so. Months. Because it had been Rory, not God, filling her thoughts this summer. And because Rory lured her into things that made her squirm every time she tried to pray.

Probably answer in itself, but that was ultimately *her* fault, her failing, not his. *Lord, I know I have so much to answer to. I know I've failed you. But please . . . if you could show me his true nature. Whatever it is.*

"Nara." He tried to ease closer again, but that just sent her another step back. He spread his hands, palms open. "Why are you looking at me like that? It's all been for you. For us. So we can build that life together, just like I promised. Everything else—that's just steps on the path. Things that had to be done to get where we wanted to go. Lying to a few blue-bloods with more money than sense, giving up our positions . . . sacrifices we needed to make, that's all."

She frowned. "I didn't *give up* my position."

He breathed a laugh. "And never would've, despite all your talk about a family of your own. Those brats had you wrapped around their little fingers. But now that you've been free of them for a while, you're no doubt thanking me for seeing to that too."

For a long moment she could only stare at him, mouth agape. What was he saying? That he wasn't just the one who'd talked her into a situation she'd known better than to be in, but that—that he was the one who'd tipped off Lord Clifford? He was the reason they'd been discovered, so that she'd be sacked on the spot?

The horror of it was paralyzing.

Not that he suffered from the same blow. He eased closer again, that smile she'd always loved on his lips. "Come now, luv, you know it was for the best. And I'm willing to marry you, like I said. I just need to finish this business first, then you can show me about and introduce me. We can decide where we want to go—anywhere in the world."

162

Her nostrils flared. "Here."

He winced. "Anywhere in the world away from these blokes who will eventually know I've pulled the wool over their eyes."

Ainsley stepped forward, making her aware yet again of his presence. Only now she saw the strangest thing in his eyes—a fire she'd never beheld in them before. "No. Miss Dawe, don't let him convince you to leave with him. He won't play you true."

Rory spun on him. "Just stay out of it for once in your life, Henry."

Ainsley glowered at him. "I watched you break enough other hearts at home. I'm not going to stand here while you do the same to her. What of all those other girls you bragged about at Christmas? And *she* wasn't the one you mentioned in your last letter to your mother!"

The blow struck not high in her heart but low in her stomach, making it churn.

Rory waved it away. "Haven't written to her since I fell in love with Nara, that's all."

So much for *always fancied her*. Her eyes slid shut. That was her answer, she supposed. And she should have known, shouldn't she have? Who was she to gain the attention of someone like him? She ought to have known she was nothing but a diversion, one in a long string of girls—until she became useful to him.

Even so, he said he'd marry her. If she could convince him to honor that, wasn't she obligated? She'd given him a part of herself she could never get back. He had to make it right. Otherwise, what did she have left?

Nothing.

Someone stepped to her side, but she knew before she opened her eyes that it wasn't Rory. "You deserve better than what he'd give you, Miss Dawe. More than a husband who would always be entertaining others on the side."

Rory's snort of laughter agreed. "Oh, I see what this is. You fancy her. Well, Hank, you'll want to look elsewhere. She doesn't live up to your sterling standards. Did she mention why she was dismissed? Caught rolling in the hay—"

"Will you shut up, Rory?" Ainsley sounded more annoyed than she'd ever heard him.

But Rory wouldn't have to say more. His implications were crystal clear, and they'd sink fast and deep into his cousin's mind. Just as they sank straight to her dormant conscience.

Rory turned to her again and leaned close. "I'm your choice now. And if you want to keep it open, don't drag your feet. I'm not hanging around here long. If you're not ready to come with me next time I stop by, then you're on your own. But if you *do* want to come"—he fastened a smile to his lips, but there was no charm in it now—"then come with information. Eyes and ears open, luv."

She shook her head, though it still felt dazed. "I won't betray them."

"They'd betray *you*. Just like Clifford, ready to turn on you at the first sign of imperfection. They're all the same, all the masters. You think they'd suffer your being around them if they knew the truth about you?" He shook his head. "Bet your parents wouldn't be too pleased either. I'm it, Senara. So focus on *us*, not them."

Ainsley remained standing, solid and straight, at her side. "Not everyone is as fickle as you, Rory. Don't listen to him, Miss Dawe."

Rory laughed and backed up a step. "She knows the truth." His gaze arrowed into her, stripping her down to her hopes, to her shame. "Don't you, luv?"

She couldn't convince her lips to move.

It was his turn to shake his head, looking disgusted with her. "Think about it. I'll give you two weeks to weigh your choices while I see about some other business, and then that's it. If you don't come with something useful, I'm gone. *Then* what will you have?"

She didn't dare to answer. It didn't bear thinking about.

He melted into the night, and Senara didn't stay a moment longer to make sure he left the garden. She spun back toward the door, the horror of it all too heavy. And to think that Ainsley had witnessed it all! How could she ever hold her head up around him again, much less look him in the eye?

"Senara." Ainsley stepped into her path, apology in every line of his posture. "Don't let anything he says bother you. I know better than to believe a word that falls from Rory's lips."

Somehow hearing him so ready to dismiss the accusations undid her.

Because she didn't deserve his high regard. Not in the least. She had trusted a man bent on using her. She had let love for him blind her to her own morals. She had given what she could never take back. And she'd lost everything.

"Excuse me." The mutter came out halfway to a sob. She sidestepped him and flew through the door, ignoring her father, who was just stepping into the kitchen with questions on his lips.

Up the stairs, into the room that had always been hers. It was dim inside, but she didn't need to see. She just needed to disappear. She closed the door behind her, fingers hovering for a moment. And then she did something she hadn't done since she was fourteen and crying over the loss of her grandmother. She turned the skeleton key in the old iron lock.

It squeaked a protest at being shifted in its bed, but then a solid clunk assured her the bolt had moved.

She pulled it from its hole and then just stared at the dark outline of it against her pale palm, its details smudged by the rainy twilight coming through her window. Never in her life had she bothered taking the key from the lock. Because her door didn't need to be bolted, certainly not from the inside. She'd never had any secrets to lock away. Never had any danger to keep out.

Now, she had both, and the truth of it was cold and rusty in her shaking hand.

Though she sat slowly, her old mattress still protested her weight, the springs rattling. She set the skeleton key on her knee for a moment, long enough to reach under her collar for the long silver chain she'd worn for the last seventeen years. She slipped it on every

165

morning, off again every evening. Lifted it now, a familiar whisper. But then she undid the clasp. Fed one end through the loop end of the iron. Fastened it again.

The door's key slid down, gravity pulling it until it clanked against the pendant key. The one so ornate, so lovely, so promising. *"Your life,"* Mamm-wynn F had said as she pressed it to her palm in her last moments, *"is whatever you make of it. Just remember that family is the key to it all."*

But she'd squandered that hope, that promise. Thrown it away on a man who'd proven himself unworthy of it.

And this was what she had left. A stark, cold reminder that doors could be locked too late. And that if one's secrets were already loose, then the dangers were already waiting.

13

Never had Beth imagined that she would resent the first rays of sunshine after a week of incessant rain. She'd been rather looking forward to another day tucked away in the library, Mother's words looping before her. But instead, the sunshine had brought Mabena and Libby and Lady Emily back to Tresco, so the day had been spent with them.

And it had been a wonderful day, she granted, as she padded back down the steps on bare feet, long after she should have been asleep again. They'd shown the girls all they'd found in the attic. Briggs had pulled out three letters from the Scofield servants that had arrived during the previous week, sharing far more gossip about Nigel than they really needed to know—including the fact that he hadn't been back to the family estate in more than a month, but that he'd made appearances at the London townhouse several times.

And then Mabena had gone for a stroll with Casek and come back with a ring on her finger and a flush in her cheeks, so naturally supper had been an all-family celebration, including uncles and aunts and cousins and more or less the entire village "just happening by."

Island village life. She loved it, in general. And wouldn't have traded it in this case especially, since Mabena certainly deserved all the happy wishes and the happy future they were certain to usher in.

It had been dark before that petered out, which meant it was too late for anyone to sail back to St. Mary's. Libby and Mabena had already been planning on spending the night with the Moons, but Emily and Briggs were left little choice. Em was asleep now in Beth's bed, and Briggs had gone home with Mabena.

A wonderful day. But the craving for the stories kept nipping at her, snatches of words swirling around in her mind after Emily's breathing had evened out. So, she and her candle were creeping toward the library at one in the morning. She'd read a few more pages of Mother's notes, and then perhaps sleep would come.

What she'd read last night after their haul from the attic had been tantalizing. Mother, Morgan, and Tas-gwyn really did seem to have talked to all the main island families. Stories had been dusted off and shared that probably hadn't otherwise had voice put to them in decades.

It was a worthwhile thing they'd done. Important. Lasting.

And she'd boxed it all up after the funerals without even looking at it—and Morgan had let her. He'd never made a peep.

Perhaps it had hurt him too much to look at it all. Or perhaps he'd known that someday she'd find it, someday she'd look, and when that day came, it would mean all the more because of the years of silence in between.

She paused just outside the library. The doors were closed all but a crack, which they never were. And from that crack spilled golden light.

She wasn't the only one up for a midnight reading session—and she had a reasonable guess as to who the other might be, which made her glad she'd slipped back into her day dress instead of just shrugging on a dressing gown over her nightgown, as she'd considered doing.

There was still a part of her mind that whispered, *Turn around, tiptoe away. He'll never know you were here, and you won't have to spend a moment with him that isn't necessary.*

But that part was small and quickly shushed by the part of her that thrilled just a bit at an hour in his company without the others around. And then by a third part that said she'd probably get herself all worked up and then walk in to find Ollie there, his nose in a MacDonald novel and his thoughts on Libby. She nudged open the door.

Sheridan glanced up from the sofa against the far wall, his smile instantaneous. "Perfect. I saved you a seat." He motioned to the dozen empty chairs and cushions throughout the room.

What was she to do but breathe a laugh? It wasn't her fault he was worming his way past her anger with him. How in the world was a girl to resist being greeted so joyfully? Being smiled at so single-mindedly? Being flirted with so creatively?

She blew out her measly little candle as she stepped into the lamplit room. And that's when her own thoughts really struck her.

Theodore Howe, Marquess of Sheridan—two rungs down the ladder from a prince—had set his sights on her. *Her*. Beth Tremayne, simple island girl. And he had made it rather hilariously clear that if she crooked a finger, he'd fall at her feet.

So, she did the only reasonable thing. She slid her candleholder on the table, picked up a stack of notes in her mother's hand, and settled into the chair that sat at ninety degrees to his sofa. "Have you learned anything revolutionary?"

"That it's quite possible that the Scillies are what remains of the lost island of Lyonesse, home of Tristan and Isolde. But if you mean in the Mucknell and Rupert search, I'd have to say no." He didn't sound too put out about it. "Plenty yet to read, though."

And he'd obviously planned to do just that all along. He still wore the same dinner jacket he'd worn for the impromptu feast, the only change that he'd made being to untie his bow tie and leave it dangling around his collar.

She clucked her tongue. "Ainsley would be appalled." She indicated her own collar to tell him why.

"Shh." He made a show of looking over his shoulder. "If he senses it's come undone, he'll be in here in a heartbeat, retying it."

"And lecturing you."

"With his *eyes*." He narrowed his at her, though if it was an accurate imitation of Ainsley, it was a wonder his valet ever convinced him to wear a tie at all.

A cluster of giggles bubbled up in her throat. No doubt as much to blame on the hour and the evening's celebration as his antics. She shook her head and smoothed a hand over the topmost page. "So many stories passed down through the centuries. Surely one of them will help."

"Even if not, they're a treasure of themselves. Or—too sappy?"

"No." Though Beth of three weeks ago would have sneered in disbelief and made some comment about him saying the right words but only putting his money behind the hunt for silver and gold. Beth of three weeks ago would have been wrong, though. From what she'd gathered during the last fortnight, he put his money behind all sorts of worthy endeavors. "Oliver and I had a few minutes to talk about it all this morning, before the girls arrived. We're going to finish their work. Put them into a book. I don't imagine anyone will pay us to publish it—"

"I will. Or, well, you know." He drew a spiral in the air with his pen. "Fund the production. That's what I mean to do with my Druid studies."

She'd known he would offer. And while pride said she ought to refuse, she wasn't sure her own pride ought to have any place in her mother's and brother's legacy. But this *was* still Sheridan. She couldn't just agree with a humble thank-you.

She pursed her lips. "I don't know, my lord. If you're going to basically act as my publisher, I *will* demand some compensation. In the form of a mahogany box, engraved on the top with the crest of one Prince Rupert of the Rhine and leafed in gold."

He slanted a hard look at her and turned back to his paper. "You clearly need an education on how this publishing business works. I may slide some jewelry onto the table as a bargaining piece, but the box is mine."

She muttered, "Unapologetic thief." But the *jewelry* idea stuck. Rupert would have had jewelry too. Even when in exile, he likely carried more wealth in the hilt of his sword or on his pinky finger than any islander would have earned in a lifetime. After all, he'd had a trinket box with him. Chances were good it had been filled with trinkets. Cuff links. Rings. Gemstone brooches.

Her gaze moved back to Sheridan's. "What do you suppose was in that box when he gave it to Briallen? Jewelry?"

Sheridan tilted his head. "Possible, but it would have been more difficult for her to liquidate and use, if his intent in giving it was to provide for her. Coins are more likely."

But stories were less likely to be written about coins. "Rats."

"No, rats are far *less* likely. He was in love with her, remember?"

She laughed again and leaned back in her chair. "So, you'll pay me for the stories in jewels, will you?" It was dangerous, flirting with him like this—it must be, to get her heart hammering as it was.

His glance flicked up, tangled with hers, and then returned to the papers he held. "Any you like. What's your fancy? My vault at the castle is positively bursting with choices. Though—really, it's unfair of you."

Her brows shot up. "What is?"

"That you haven't eyes the color of a jewel, so that I can wax poetical about how this or that set would match them. But I haven't any storm-cloud jewels to offer."

She clucked her tongue. "Well, that's a deal-breaker, isn't it? If you've none to match my eyes, I'm afraid I can't accept them as payment. You'll have to give me the trinket box instead."

"You drive a hard bargain. I suppose I'll have to commission a chemist somewhere to develop me a new jewel. A silver diamond, we'll call it. Or—what do you think? A Beth diamond?"

It seemed she couldn't be in his company without laughing every minute or two. "I'm certain that would be immensely popular. You really know how to give gifts."

"Better than a prince in your estimation, clearly. I wouldn't give

171

you rats, though you thought Rupert would have." He sent her a wink and turned a page in his notebook, jotting something down.

"Ha." She shook her head. Did nothing ever nonplus him? "What if I *wanted* a rat? For a pet."

His brows rose, though his eyes sparkled more with amusement than surprise. "Rats are not pets. If they were, they'd follow Telly around like he was the Pied Piper, like all the cats and dogs. Parrots. Horses. He has a veritable menagerie trailing him most days."

It was all she could do to tamp down her grin. "I've yet to see parrots following him."

"Because all the pirates in the islands are long dead, that's all. Were they here with their Pollys, Telly would have one on each shoulder."

She chuckled at the image, though her mind wandered back to her imaginings of the black-haired prince presenting his island lass with a parting gift. The trinket box was special . . . but still it seemed terribly impersonal to stuff it with nothing but money. "Not even a necklace or ring, you don't think? To Briallen, I mean?"

"Anything's possible. Why, have you some ancient family heirloom of a jewel you think may be linked to the story?" He sat up straighter, looking ready to go investigate her jewelry box then and there.

Funny how it made her grin now instead of wanting to slap at him. "No. But someone else could. We could go knocking door-to-door, asking other families."

He checked his pocket watch. "Probably bad form to start that just now."

"Probably," she agreed on a laugh. It turned into a yawn. "No mentions of anything like that in Mother's stories?" She glanced down at the page she held but couldn't even convince her eyes to focus on the words.

"Not that I've seen. Though one never knows when discovery will leap off the page." He motioned to the small stack of them in her hands.

It was true. But she hadn't realized how tired her eyes were. At the moment, she didn't trust them to note anything of interest, seeing how Mother's script blurred before her. "I think I'd better come at it fresh in the morning, actually." She stood, casting a tired gaze over the table as she returned her pages to it. Usually, Senara came in to tidy up after them at the end of the day, but the chaos of papers said that their organizer had not been in this evening. Odd—but she must have been distracted with Mabena's announcement. Which meant all the letters of Mucknell were still strewn across the surface, along with Mother's stories. Or, at least, the ones she'd sent copies of to the Scofields. She'd been hoping something would jump out at her as to what they'd seen in them to propel Nigel to Gugh.

No luck, though. And if not earlier, when her mind and eyes were fresh, she certainly couldn't hope to find anything now in those water-stained pages. She smiled at Sheridan instead. "Good night, my lord."

"So soon?" He looked up from his page, disappointment there instead of a smile. "But I had at least four more good rat jokes brewing. You'll miss them all if you leave now."

She slipped out of the room as she'd entered it. On a laugh.

No, Sheridan really wasn't so bad. In fact, she'd rather come to depend on seeing that grin of his every day.

She tucked her own grin away in the corner of her mouth and turned for the stairs. What would he do if she flirted first? Or did something as audacious as kiss him? The thought sent a flood of heat through her. Maybe one of these days she'd have to find out.

She darted a look over her shoulder, to where she knew he sat behind the walls. Poring over texts, making notes, thinking up jokes just to earn a smile from her.

Maybe someday soon.

———————○———————

Sheridan gave up on reading shortly after Beth abandoned him, cruel creature that she was. He'd been primed for an all-night session, but she'd utterly destroyed his desire for hours spent with text and paper simply by walking into the room and smiling at him. Laughing. Sitting close enough that he caught a whiff of her soap.

And her hair had been down. That ought to be illegal. Even after nearly a month under the same roof, this was the first time he'd seen it spilling down her back like waves of sunlight, and all he could think of as he stared blindly at the page resting against his knee was sliding his hand through that sunlight, anchoring her head, and kissing her senseless.

He tossed the handwritten version of Tristan and Isolde's tragic tale onto the table and strode from the room, down the corridor, and then out into the back garden. Perhaps he'd be able to return to tales of love-potion victims after a breath or two of fresh air.

"Ha," he said to the stars that twinkled down at him. Maybe *he'd* been struck with a love potion. Maybe that was why he'd been so consumed with thoughts of Miss Elizabeth Tremayne ever since she first collided with him in the entryway.

Well. If so, at least he'd have a better end of it than poor Tristan. Beth wasn't betrothed to his uncle.

And there was something remarkable about a night sky after a week of rain, as if the very air had been scrubbed clean. Each star shined down from its place in the cosmos, a pinprick to him here. And yet a sun to its own planets.

"Any particular reason you're laughing at the stars, my lord?"

He spun with a frown, his eyes taking a long moment to pick Ainsley out from the shadows in which he sat. There—he was on the bench tucked into the flowers, leaning forward with his forearms braced on his legs and his hands clasped between his knees. Relaxed in a way that he only ever was when Sheridan came upon him in the middle of the night out of doors.

Which, given the many excavations on which he'd dragged along his poor valet, was more times than one might think.

Sheridan repositioned one of the chairs to more or less face him and settled into it, tipping his head back to keep those far-off suns in view. "Not at the stars. At their claim that they could clear my mind of Beth enough to then read more."

Ainsley's puff of breath might have been a laugh. Or it might just as easily have been exasperation at having his midnight garden invaded. Well, if he wanted solitude to finish his prayers, he'd just say that Sheridan had better get to bed. It was his code for *"Leave me alone, you oblivious dolt. Can't you see I'm trying to escape from you for a few minutes?"*

Diplomatic even in his dismissals, that was Ainsley.

But instead of sending him away, Ainsley sucked in a long breath. "It's a lovely spot, isn't it? At night, with the village sleeping, you can hear the surf on the shores even from up here."

"Mm." Sheridan linked his hands behind his head. "One of the loveliest we've seen. We'll visit often, I expect. With Telly, to see Libby. And if I convince Beth to propose to me, for her sake too."

Definitely a laugh, that second puff. "You're incorrigible."

He grinned up at the sky. "Seriously, though. I'm glad you like it here. I do feel bad, dragging you around to places you have no desire to see. I'll never forget the look in your eyes after a week in Egypt."

"If God meant me to live in the desert, He wouldn't have made me an Englishman." A smile laced his voice at the memory. "I'm not sorry you didn't discover that your true passion lies in Egyptology. Druid cairns I can handle. Especially if there's an inn near them."

A sound of fabric on stone had Sheridan briefly tilting his head forward, just long enough to see that Ainsley had stretched himself out along the bench so he, too, was staring up at the stars.

The silence was summer-warm, rain-fresh, and comfortable. Though Sheridan could practically hear Ainsley thinking, so he wasn't surprised when he said, "I won't mind visiting here. Though Miss Dawe might mind my coming, if she doesn't find another position elsewhere."

Sheridan pressed his lips together. He'd known that Ainsley and Collins were spending most of their time with the Dawes. And he'd thought he'd caught his valet looking a bit longer than necessary at

175

Senara—understandably. She was a pretty woman, and she knew her mother's crumpet recipe. So quite a catch.

But now that he mentioned her, she hadn't been among the group of family and neighbors today, which was odd indeed. She ought to have been one of the first to embrace Mabena Moon and congratulate her.

Was Ainsley saying it was *his* fault, somehow, that she'd been avoiding them today? Unthinkable. Unless . . . "Did you preach too loudly?"

"I didn't preach."

"Not even with your eyes?"

Another snort of laughter. "No. But—do you remember my cousin? Rory Smithfield?"

Sheridan made a face, though Ainsley wouldn't be able to see it. "Hard to forget that one. Not my favorite of your relatives, I confess."

"Yes, well, Miss Dawe knows him. Quite well, apparently. He showed up here the other night, thinking to lure her away to marry him."

"I beg your pardon?" Sheridan nearly wished he'd been tilting his chair back so that he could slam it down on all fours again. As it was, he had to settle for tipping his head to its normal angle. "She said no, clearly. Having some sense."

"She did. Though she hasn't said a word to me since, no doubt because I witnessed a scene between them that would have been embarrassing." Ainsley sighed. "And it gets worse. I've been debating how best to bring it up."

"Oh dear." It must be bad indeed, whatever it was, if Ainsley had to debate how to talk to him about it. Sheridan leaned forward. "What is it? Has Smithfield tried to sell all our secrets to Scofield or something?"

Ainsley propped himself up on his elbows. And frowned at him.

Sheridan blinked. "Well, I can't have guessed it. That would be absurd. He doesn't know any of our secrets."

With a snort—a dignified one, somehow—Ainsley lowered

back down to the bench. "That apparently doesn't stop my cousin from making things up. He's convinced the Scofields that he's my confidant—that they can get at me, and hence you, through him. Now he wants to draw Miss Dawe into it, too, and have her provide him with actual information in exchange for his affection and a marriage proposal."

"As if that would be a prize." Sheridan would have muttered a few other choice words, had he not known that his valet would lecture him on it. "Well, I'm not concerned that she'll turn on the Tremaynes—they're family. But your cousin himself is a different story. What's he told them?"

"He wouldn't say. Except to point out that I ought to thank him for blathering on, since it meant they weren't pressing my mother or aunt for information instead."

Worry wove through Ainsley's words, and for good reason. They made Sheridan's chest tighten too. He hadn't been exactly surprised when Ainsley had told him back in May that the Scofields had tried to get information out of him. They were, after all, good business-men. Just trying to know as much about their buyer as they could. It had been little more than amusing at the time.

It felt far more sinister now. Knowing what he did of them, he wouldn't put them past extortion. "Well, that won't do. We can't have your family in any sort of danger just because you work for me. Did you check with your mother? Is she all right?"

"I wired her first thing this morning and had a reply this after-noon. She said some strange men have been around, here and there. One tried once, months ago, to get her to talk about you, but you know Mother—she isn't one to ever have loose lips."

Chuckling at the memories of the times he'd met Mrs. Ainsley—and their very opposite personalities—Sheridan let his head tilt back again. "Nothing for it, though. We have to keep your family safe. Maybe—what do you think? Move them to the castle until this all blows over?" They'd had a smashing good time at Christmas. Mrs. Ainsley had even said so.

"Generous of you, my lord, but what good would that do? Especially given that we're here."

"You have a point. If the Scofields are looking for people to pressure into spilling our secrets, the castle would be the first place they'd try. So then. Paris it is."

"So then—what?" Ainsley shot up to a sitting position. "What does Paris have to do with anything?"

"Your mother said she wanted to go. See the Eiffel Tower. Don't you remember? Part of that game Millicent had us playing on Christmas Eve, where we all had to name the place we'd most like to see. She said Paris. So, let's send her and your aunt and that cousin who wasn't a blighter to Paris until all this blows over."

Ainsley blinked at him. But there was no lecture in this one, not that he could discern. Just surprise. "You would send my family to France for weeks or months?"

Though *why* he was surprised, Sheridan couldn't fathom. "Obviously. It's your *mother*. That's sacred, you know. We'll let a few rooms at that hotel we stayed at two Aprils ago. They'd like that, don't you think? Close to all the attractions and museums. And I'm certain the manager will remember me. He'll see they have a fine time. I can ask Abbie and Millicent to take care of it, give them something to do. They'll be happy to make arrangements—we won't mention why, though. No need to get them worried."

Ainsley breathed a laugh. "I admit, I would feel better if they weren't at home to be threatened. Thank you, my lord. I'll wire her again tomorrow. Tell her to expect to hear from your sisters."

"And I'll compose a note to wire to Abbie and Millicent, whenever you go. Now—back to Miss Dawe."

Ainsley groaned. "Must we? She was like a ghost all day today, barely present. I could practically *see* her hurting, and I . . . I don't know how to mend it. And what's worse, my cousin saw in a glance how I feel—he'll try to leverage that. No doubt a note will arrive soon, saying if I want to keep *her* out of this business then *I* had better supply him with information."

178

Sheridan stole another glance at Ainsley's profile in the moonlight. "You care for her."

Ainsley just sucked back in the breath he'd heaved out. "It doesn't matter if I do. I thought I'd be a help to her the other night by coming out, but clearly I've made things worse. She won't even look at me now. It's as though my mere presence is a reminder of it all, and everything I say upsets her further."

In the light of day, in a lighter way, discovering that prim and proper Ainsley was sweet on a girl would have deserved all sorts of poking and prodding and teasing. Perhaps a jest about how if he and Beth had six children, they'd certainly need a governess.

But now wasn't the time for any of that. "Ains." Sheridan leaned forward again. "Even if you have upset her . . . sometimes we *need* to be upset. Sometimes that's the only thing that will convince us to let down our walls and allow someone in. Or even to turn to God."

"And sometimes it builds the walls higher."

"Yes, sometimes. But my valet—he's rather wise when it comes to such things—would say that every time we make a mess of things, every time we take a wrong step, it's just an opportunity for the Lord to meet us in an unexpected way. He would say that if you really care for her, and if she's hurting, then the best thing you could possibly do is put her in God's hands and just pray that He'll give you the honor of being one of the people He uses to heal her."

"I want to be. I always want to be one of the people He uses, but especially this time. I'm just afraid I've ruined it."

Sheridan sighed. "I'm always afraid I've ruined it, every time I open my mouth. But God is bigger than our mistakes, I'm told. In fact, I'm fairly certain my wise valet would say that the best thing we can ever be is a willing instrument in His hand. That we ought to stop worrying that our every word is wrong and instead let the Master Craftsman wield us however He will. There may be stray chisel marks, the times we slip. But He'll still set the stone where it belongs. We just need to remember our lives are a monument to Him, not to ourselves."

Even in the darkness, Sheridan could see Ainsley narrow his eyes. "You really aren't quite a heathen, for all your obsession with Druids."

"I keep telling you that. It's just that I don't much care for the sanitized Christianity that society has embraced. They've tried too hard to make it civilized."

Those eyes just narrowed more. "You're not about to become a heretic instead of a heathen, are you?"

"On the contrary. They're the heretics, not me—the people who try to make Christian history tidier than it is, I mean. Have you read all those stories of the martyrs? And the Old Testament! The Druids have nothing on Judeo-Christianity when it comes to mysticism and odd rituals."

"Sheridan."

"Well, think about it. How many times have you seen a lady blush and skip verses when she's reading aloud from the Bible? It's far too raw for Millicent in some places. Not 'Christian' enough—come now, even you have to admit that's ironic."

Ainsley stood, shaking his head. But a starlit smile played on his lips. "I'm not quite certain how the conversation has taken this turn, but I'm going to go in to bed before any stray bolts of lightning come this way. Good night, my lord."

"Night."

Ainsley started for the side gate that connected the Tremayne garden to the Dawes'. But he paused a few steps away. "And thank you. For protecting my family, but also . . . I needed that reminder about being an instrument in God's hands."

Sheridan grinned. "Don't thank me. Thank my valet. All wisdom is his."

"See, I told you I heard voices back here."

Sheridan spun in his chair at Telford's voice, raising his brows when he saw not only him but Tremayne rounding the house from the front, both still in their dinner dress. "What are you two doing out in the middle of the night?"

"We heard a few noises from the general direction of Piper's Hole while we were walking Libby to the Moons'." Tremayne nodded a greeting to Ainsley, who gave a wave of farewell and then proceeded through the gate, and pulled out a chair. "So, we decided to investigate, given all the shenanigans there this summer."

"I don't suppose you found Scofield hiding out by the pool." Sheridan used his foot to push a third chair away from the table for Telford.

"No, just the burnt remains of a few crackers." Telford shook his head. "Lads enjoying their third-term break. Or seizing the opportunity to celebrate their headmaster's engagement with a bit of mischief."

Tremayne grinned. "They should have lit them on Wearne's doorstep."

Telly snorted. "You're friends now, remember."

"Ah. Right. Easy to forget."

Sheridan shook his head. It was that rivalry between Oliver Tremayne and Casek Wearne that had, in a strange way, convinced Telly that Tremayne was deserving of Libby's heart. He'd tossed himself in front of a bullet to save Wearne's life, after all, even though they'd been lifelong enemies.

Just imagine what lengths he'd go to for the lady who held his heart.

Perhaps Telford was remembering the same thing. He looked for a moment at their host, his gaze thoughtful. Then glanced toward Sheridan and donned a crooked smile. "Have you exercised your brotherly duty yet on Sheridan, Oliver?"

"Hm?" Tremayne had been looking up at the stars but lowered his head at the question. "What duty is that?"

"Trying to scare him away from your sister. Making certain his intentions are honorable."

Sheridan's ears grew hot, but at least the darkness concealed any accompanying redness.

Besides, Tremayne chuckled, sounding utterly unconcerned. That was a relief. Or was it a bad sign? Did he think Sheridan's chances with Beth so slim that they needn't even be addressed?

"I believe our friend's intentions have been made quite clear, given that proposal the other week."

Sheridan lifted a hand to rub at the back of his neck. Just to pat out any flames that had sprung up. "It was a *retraction* of a proposal, thank you very much."

"And I don't have any reason to think him after her dowry." This Oliver delivered dryly, with a pointed look at Telford that arrowed even through the darkness.

Of course, Telly just batted it away. "Even so. Shouldn't you be sounding out his faith? That ought to be rather important to a vicar, I'd think."

Sheridan blew out a breath. It was one thing to insist to his valet that he was neither heathen nor heretic. He wasn't certain his musings on the ancient Christian mystics would hold up so well with a vicar, though. "Whose side are you on, Bram?"

"He's just punishing you for not making a protest over my stealing Libby from you."

No doubt Oliver was right about that. But how was Sheridan supposed to have insisted Libby marry him when it was clear that she was in love with Oliver Tremayne? And when Sheridan didn't really *want* to marry her? And when Beth collided with him and knocked all thoughts of any other woman from his head? "Blame the love potion."

His old friend blinked at him. Puzzled it out. "You were reading the Tristan and Isolde story, I suppose."

Sheridan grinned and leaned back to study the stars again. "And for the record, Tremayne, I'm not a heathen."

"I should think not."

"Nor a heretic, as I was just explaining to Ainsley before you joined us."

"Mm-hmm."

And really, Telford had a point. Tremayne really *should* be giving him a harder time, and the fact that he wasn't was downright cruel. Now he'd be worrying endlessly about whether even a century would be enough to convince Beth to convince him to give her another chance. "And it's not that *real* Christianity is boring. It's just that people have made it so."

"I couldn't agree more."

Sheridan huffed. "Well, stop it, will you? It's a mean trick."

Tremayne's laughter just rolled up into the night.

14

Beth slid a lovely blue-and-grey feather into her pocket for Mamm-wynn and turned her face into the wind. No one else had been awake yet when she padded down the stairs at home—even Mrs. Dawe had only just slipped into the kitchen. Usually, unless she had secrets to recover from Samson, Beth preferred a more leisurely start to her day. But something was nagging at her. Something that propelled her outside into the soft morning light, toward the coast. Something that kept her walking until she stood here looking over at the shapes of Teän and St. Martin's playing hide-and-seek in the mist.

She'd explored them both countless times, including this summer. She'd dug for what she thought could be a clue on Teän only to come up empty—except that that was where she'd run into Johnnie Rosedew, who was following the same old clue to the same empty ground. They'd realized, then, that they'd both been hired to find the same thing. That was when they'd compared notes—after she pushed aside her irritation that someone, presumably the Scofields, had invited others into *her* search. They'd tried to make a plan.

A week later, he'd been dead. Poor Johnnie. Her chest still went tight when she thought about it, thought about him. He deserved better than this. And how many hours had she lain in her abandoned cottage on Samson and wondered what they could have done differently? How many times had she wept, crying out to God to somehow respool the thread of time and erase it? So many things she wished she could undo. Johnnie, of course. And she'd have warned her parents against trying to sail to the mainland that day. She still wasn't sure what they could have done to make Morgan healthy and well, but had she known he was so near the end of his life, she might have chosen not to leave the Scillies for finishing school.

Although then she'd never have met Emily.

How strange were regrets. So many things she hated, yet without them, things she loved would never have been.

She took another step onto the wet sand, into the damp wind. It wasn't regrets that had woken her up at the first scarlet breath of dawn, though. No, it was the question of why Nigel Scofield had been on Gugh. A question they'd all asked countless times already, and nothing had seemed a satisfactory answer.

But he'd been there. So, an answer there must be. And she'd woken up thinking, feeling, remembering *something*. Something that had propelled her out of bed and out the door, where perhaps the fresh air could tease it to the fore of her mind.

Another billow of morning mist rolled between Tresco and the nearest uninhabited islands, making them nothing but hulking shapes for a moment, before they turned into rock again. She'd tried to sketch them, though art had never been her strong suit. Beth could never quite perfect the way they rose out of the water just so.

Who was she kidding? She'd never even been able to draw their outlines correctly when they had to make maps at school. Her lips tugged up as she remembered stomping a foot when she was all of eight, arguing with the teacher that maps were stupid. That the islands were so much more than an outline, flat and . . .

She sucked in a breath and spun around, darting back up the path. *An outline.* Last night, as she left the library, she'd glanced at the papers still strewn over the table. Noticed the water stain on one.

Or what she'd thought was a water stain. But the shape. *The shape.*

It took her only a few minutes to dash back to the house. It was still quiet in there, aside from humming coming from the kitchen, along with some lovely scents. But she aimed for the library, barely even smiling as she recalled her exchange there with Sheridan just a few hours before.

No, she moved directly to the table and then stopped, breath balled up in her chest. There, right on top. One of the letters from Mucknell to his wife that she'd sent a copy of to London. She'd been meticulous in her copying, tracing both Mucknell's script and every oddity on the page—including the water stain.

But what if it *wasn't* a stain put there by the centuries in Tasgwyn's foundation? What if it was something Mucknell himself had traced?

Perhaps that explained why it bore the strangest resemblance to St. Agnes and Gugh.

She'd never noticed it before, in all the times she'd looked at it. But now, seeing it upside down—it was unmistakable. Wasn't it? Pulling out a map of the islands to check it against, she was all but certain.

That could be no coincidence. No quirk of water over time. Mucknell *must* have put it there on purpose. And the portion that was Gugh . . . only one word crossed into it. The word *again*—did that mean something? Or was it more about location? Because unless she was mistaken, the portion of the island that the word crossed was the very spot where she'd literally run headlong into Nigel Scofield.

It could be how he knew to check there. They could have seen this in her copy.

She spun out of the library again, charging into the breakfast room. She needed to show Sheridan. Or even Ollie would do. Someone who could either tell her she was mad or that this was worth considering.

But only Emily and Mamm-wynn were there. She huffed out a breath. The gentlemen were usually up well before she was—other than Telford. Why today of all days were they not?

"Behind you."

Beth stepped into the room, out of Senara's way. Her old friend had a platter of food in her hands . . . and circles under her eyes that made Beth frown. "You look exhausted."

Come to think of it, she hadn't looked much better yesterday—Beth just hadn't paid all that much attention, given the arrival of sunshine and the girls from St. Mary's and then Mabena with a ring on her finger.

What kind of a friend was she? New regret pierced.

Senara offered a bare smile. "We'll blame it on the gents keeping me up all night with their laughter."

Beth's frown deepened. "Telford and Sheridan? Where were they, to keep you up?"

"Back garden. And your brother too." Senara slid the platter onto the sideboard. "I don't think they retired until four o'clock."

Well, bother. They weren't likely to be making an appearance for breakfast any time soon, then. How was she to tell them about her discovery if they were imitating Telford and staying abed until noon?

"Do you think we could get going soon?" Emily asked as she lowered her teacup. She sent a frown out the window. "Those are some rather dark clouds on the horizon, and while I'd love to spend another day with you, I'm hoping there will be a reply to the telegram I sent my mother the other day." Though it wasn't *hope* exactly in her tone—not with that shadow of doubt darkening it.

Beth offered a soft smile and went to fill a plate. "Let me get a quick bite, and then we can leave."

Perhaps the fellows would be awake by the time she returned. That was apparently the soonest she could expect to see them unless she wanted to march through the corridors with a pot and a spoon. Her lips twitched at the thought.

They ate quickly, with Emily darting continual worried looks out

187

the window. It did indeed look like more rain, which was enough to make Beth sigh. One day of sun hadn't been enough.

Emily took the last sip of her tea and stood, sending a smile to Mamm-wynn. "Thank you for yet another lovely visit, Mrs. Tremayne."

Her grandmother's fairy-bell laugh filled the room. "Oh, dearover, you know you're welcome anytime. And Beth." Mamm-wynn fastened her gaze on Beth and blinked. A strange, clouded something drifted over her eyes but vanished in the next blink. "Don't tarry too long or fly too far, little rosefinch."

"Of course not." Her heart still twisted whenever she paused to let herself think of how she'd worried her grandmother and brother when she vanished back in June. She paused now to drop a kiss onto Mamm-wynn's soft, creased cheek. "I love you. I won't be but an hour—two at the most. We'll see if the gents have roused themselves by then."

Within ten minutes, Beth and Emily and Briggs were striding down the streets, out of town and toward the *Naiad*. Beth had grabbed a few mackintoshes on her way out the door, just in case the clouds outpaced them.

She and Emily chatted of unimportant things as Beth got the *Naiad* under sail, but by halfway through their trip, her friend had fallen silent and was staring off into the water in a way that Beth had seen her do before, at school. Whenever talk among the girls turned to families and holidays at home and all the fun they had planned, Em would get quiet, distant. Not because she didn't have a family with holiday plans that could outdo anyone's. But because, from what her friend had said, her parents never really greeted her with any notable joy. It was her brother on whom they'd hung all their affections.

Beth's hand tightened on the tiller. Plenty of parents unabashedly had favorites—she'd seen it often enough and had forgotten to bite her tongue about it a time or two when it was an island family. But her own had always been so different. Each of them had always been loved for exactly who they were. They were all the favorites, and they all knew it. Their favorites in all the world, but never in competition with one another.

Now here sat her friend, all but exiled from her parents until she made amends with the brother who had manhandled her and threatened her. Yet still she'd kept reaching out—like this latest telegram to her mother. The one to which she'd been awaiting a response. "Em? Are you all right?"

Emily sighed. "There won't be anything. Not from Mother. Even if she wanted to reply—and I don't know she would—she'd never go against Father, and he's made his stance clear. Nigel is right, I am wrong, and I'm not to be forgiven until I admit it."

Beth reached over to give her friend's shoulder a squeeze. "I'm so sorry you're going through this." She barely kept herself from saying the next thing on her mind—that they were idiots for clinging so blindly to their adoration of Nigel, given the many times they'd had to bail him out of trouble. And that, worse, it might not be blind. That if the underhandedness the earl had demonstrated in selling Beth's trinket box was an indication of a pattern, Nigel might in fact have learned his ways from his father.

Emily wasn't ready to hear that, though. She resented her brother, but she still longed for her parents' affection as anyone would.

Briggs shifted, stealing Beth's attention for a moment, and looked as though she were about to say something and then thought better of it. Apparently, enlisting her help hadn't bridged any major gaps between her and Emily. Though whether it was her own reticence or Em's demeanor was anyone's guess.

How glad Beth was to have grown up in a family where such lines weren't only blurred, they were deliberately stomped all over. Mamm-wynn had always been that way, so far as she could tell, but even more so after Father and Mother married. Mother, after all, was just an island lass. No social connections whatsoever. She was no better than anyone else on Tresco, even if she did live in the second-largest house after her marriage.

189

Which meant Beth had been free to look up to Senara. Free to hold Mabena as her dearest friend. Free to share her heart with whomever she pleased. But then, she had other advantages, too, ones that Briggs had no doubt been denied. She was also free, thanks to her father's landed status, to dream of a society match. A prince who could sweep her off her feet.

Or, perhaps, someone two rungs down.

Emily chuckled, snapping Beth from her thoughts. She realized with a start that she must have been caught up in her mind for at least ten minutes, given their current position, and something on her face must have pulled Emily out of her own reverie. Her friend was grinning at her in that way every girl knew, and knew how to do.

"Why do I get the feeling that it isn't Prince Rupert you're thinking of with that dreamy look on your face, Beth?"

Beth's cheeks went warm, despite the damp air blowing against them. "I have no idea what you mean."

The sparkle in Emily's eyes called her bluff. "Mm-hmm. Have you begun practicing yet?"

This time, Beth really didn't have any idea what she was talking about. "Practicing what?"

"Signing your future name. *Lady Elizabeth Howe, Marchioness of Sheridan.*"

Had they been in the dormitory at their finishing school, Beth would have tossed a pillow at her head. Having none handy, she settled for narrowing her eyes and laughing. "Watch yourself, Emily. Or I'll give you a dunking as I did him."

"I'm terrified."

At the very least, she was cheerful again, distracted from her family woes. Which made Beth's hot cheeks worth it. She let the sound of water against the hull speak for a moment and then let out a long breath. "What do you think of him?"

"Other than that he's madly in love with you, and so has good taste?" Emily leaned over to bump their shoulders together. "I like him. Not in the way *you* have clearly begun to—but there is much to

190

admire about him, and he's without question entertaining. Though top of the list is frankly the way he looks at you. You deserve that kind of devotion."

Did she? Beth turned her face into the wind. When she thought of devoted couples, her parents were always the first to spring to mind. And she had never wondered why her father had married Mother instead of going back to the mainland for a more "suitable" bride. She was everything bright and joyous. Everything deep and true.

Then there was Beth, constantly frustrating her brother with her yearning for something else, something more. Oblivious to the work her mother and eldest brother had been doing in what turned out to be their last year all together. So focused on adventure that she brought danger to the doorstep of those she loved best in the world.

"Sometimes I think I'm too selfish to deserve that kind of devotion." She spoke it softly, into the wind, and didn't turn to see if Emily even heard her.

She must have, though. She shifted closer. "Selfish? You? Don't be silly. You were always the first to offer what you had to anyone who lacked. Always the first to tend to the hearts of your friends."

"And also the first to run off on some new adventure, with no thought to how it may impact others."

Emily shook her head. "It isn't the same. And you *do* consider others. Those weeks you spent in hiding—it wasn't to save yourself, it was to save your family from my brother and his associates, who are the ones who actually do what you're afraid of. You don't leave a trail of hurt and destruction in your wake, Beth. Not like he does."

Kind words, but were they true? They were what Beth had told herself. But as she huddled in that hovel on Samson through lonely hours, as she explored in solitude and played a constant cat-and-mouse game, she'd had plenty of time to question her every motive.

"But we're not talking about Nigel. We're talking about Lord Sheridan. And he clearly thinks you're deserving of all his affection."

The corners of Beth's lips pulled up. She couldn't help it. "No one's ever . . ." She didn't even know how to finish the sentence.

Other gentlemen had let their gazes linger before, but their attention never lasted past learning that she had only a minuscule dowry and no grand connections. Or else it shifted into something that set her teeth on edge and brought her temper to the fore. None had ever been interested in dreaming of adventures alongside her. No one else had ever thought she was worth fighting for.

Emily grinned again. "And to think, you only have to beg him for a few months, and he's yours."

Laughing, Beth followed the deeper channel toward St. Mary's quay. She'd also never met a man who jested about marriage quite so much. What would he do if she did beg for a second chance?

Another experiment she'd have to add to her list. It may pair rather well with that kiss she had entertained the thought of last night.

The *Naiad* wasn't the only vessel making for the quay, so she directed her attention to the task at hand. Soon enough, she'd brought them safely to anchor and they'd all scurried to shore.

A glance at the looming clouds, complete with veil of rain over the water moving ever closer, made Mamm-wynn's words echo in her mind. *"Don't tarry too long or fly too far, little rosefinch."*

"You'll come in for a minute, won't you? To see if any new post or telegrams arrived?" Emily linked her arm through Beth's, eyes hopeful. As eager as she'd been to come back to St. Mary's for that purpose, she seemed to prefer having company.

Beth sneaked one more look at the sky. The rain would catch her regardless, and she had her mackintosh. She could spare a few minutes to spend with her friend. "Of course."

It was Ollie who had arranged for Emily and Briggs to stay in the little flat over Mrs. Gilligan's millinery shop, just before Beth had come out of hiding. There'd been nowhere else to let for the rest of the summer, but her brother had a remarkable way of pulling favors out of people and somehow making them feel like it was they who had been blessed. She'd had a hard time, at first, imagining Lady Emily Scofield tucked away in these small rooms, with only her maid for company. But as she trailed her friend up the steps and into the cheerful space, she thought it seemed to suit her quite well.

Which was good, since she'd apparently be here until she could make peace with her brother.

Briggs turned immediately toward the small table just inside the door, where Mrs. Gilligan must regularly deposit their post. A stack of it waited, which was enough to raise even Beth's heart rate. That many letters *must* contain something of promise.

Emily crowded close to her maid's side, but the girl soon cast her an apologetic look. "They're all from the other domestics, my lady. I'm sorry."

A resolute smile chased away the disappointment that flashed in Emily's eyes. "That's nothing to apologize for at all. It's excellent news."

Though clearly as unconvinced as Beth was, Briggs held out one of the letters. "From the housekeeper at the country house. Would you read this one while I begin with one from your mother's maid?"

Tossing her mackintosh onto a chair, Beth followed Emily to the sofa and sat beside her to read the note too. Her eyes skimmed over the household chitchat that meant nothing to her, slowing again when she saw *Master Nigel* in the narrative. It seemed he had made an appearance in Bedfordshire last week, though only briefly. He'd arrived without warning in the evening, demanded a meal, and then vanished into the study for hours. He was gone again after breakfast the next morning.

"Well, here's some good news," Briggs said a minute later. She hadn't sat but was leaning against the wall and looked over at them with bright eyes. "It seems the friend whose yacht your brother had been borrowing has taken it back—he had a trip of his own scheduled, I guess. Your brother was fuming about it."

Emily sucked in a breath. "If he wants to come back here, he'll have to take the ferry."

"That's the best news yet." Beth had friends at the ferry office whose help she'd already enlisted. "He won't be able to arrive again without our knowing it. Not unless he has other friends whose yachts he can borrow." She lifted her brows at that.

Emily shook her head. "Not that I know of. Or at least not who are currently here to lend them. A few others are lounging about the Mediterranean on said yachts even now, but that is hardly helpful to Nigel."

"Perfect."

When Briggs offered another envelope, Emily reached out to take it. "So, is he still in London, then?"

Her maid shrugged, flipping over the letter she still held. "No mention is made of his leaving again after his trip to the country. I suppose that means he's still there." Briggs held out another letter to Beth with a small smile. "If you don't mind, miss."

Mind? She grinned. "Of course not." She'd been given a missive from a fellow who went by Haversham—the earl's valet. A short few paragraphs, but they had her pressing her lips together. "Seems your father and brother have been spending quite a lot of time in the museum's archives and records after Nigel's last return from the Scillies. Haversham says couriers have been coming night and day with copies of files."

Copies. She never would have thought to worry about those. Now she did, though, after Emily pointed out that copies meant people doing the copy work. People whose loyalty could possibly be bought.

Was that something they should try to leverage? Beth frowned and pulled her bottom lip between her teeth. She certainly didn't have the resources for bribery, never mind the moral questions involved that would likely be of more concern to her brother than the coin. But it seemed like the sort of thing Sheridan might randomly throw some pounds sterling at, if it gave them answers. Like what the Scofields knew that the rest of them needed to.

And what other buyer they had lined up to bid against Sheridan on whatever artifacts Beth had found. The owner of the yacht called *Victoria* that hadn't been seen in these waters since the silverware was found. Who was it? She didn't like not knowing such a vital piece of information. And why hadn't Sheridan and Telford been using their considerably greater resources to discover it already?

She would ask them as much this afternoon. After she shared her epiphany about the supposed water stain.

By the time they finished reading through the letters, soft rain drummed against the windowpanes, though a bit of sunlight still shone outside too. Thus far, at least, the weather was half-hearted. With a bit of luck, it would stay that way. She pushed to her feet after briefing them on the last letter she'd been given. "I had better go before the rain gets any more earnest."

Emily sighed her way to standing too. "I suppose you must. Though if ever you want to stay here with me on St. Mary's for a night, just say the word. I'd love the company."

And usually, she'd have jumped at the chance for a change of scenery and a short escape from the monotony of Tresco. But it had only been a few short weeks ago that Mamm-wynn had fought her way back to health. Beth couldn't bring herself to leave her grandmother's side for more than a few hours here or there just yet.

To her friend, she offered a smile. "Thank you. And perhaps soon. I'm a bit fearful to be away from Mamm-wynn so long. I know she'd chide me for it, but . . ."

"I understand completely." Emily held out Beth's mackintosh for her. "And I'm certain it is only that and has nothing at all to do with a certain handsome houseguest of your own."

A chuckle tickled her throat as she slipped her arms into the raincoat. "Nothing at all."

"But if ever you want to make his heart grow fonder with your absence, I'm a willing conspirator."

"I have no doubt of it." And it was nice, really, to be able to joke like any two friends would and put aside the larger questions for a while here or there. Perhaps she *would* take the time to stay over a night.

Soon. Just not *too* soon.

She said her farewells and pulled the hood up over her hair as she stepped out into the drizzle. Even though it wasn't the time of day for one, she cast her gaze around in search of a rainbow as she strode back along the puddle-ridden streets toward the quay. The air was still warm despite the rain, making her coat uncomfortable in a matter of minutes. The sun either needed to win the battle or lose it, that was all.

Her step quickened when she saw the *Naiad's* mast bobbing happily in the water. Perhaps the gentlemen would be awake when she got home . . . though that was debatable, given their late night. They may not put in an appearance until midday. Which made anticipated frustration surge in her veins. Wouldn't it be predictable for her to rush home only to find them all still abed?

Her gaze drifted to the southwest. St. Agnes and Gugh weren't far. Not even three miles—much closer to St. Mary's than to Tresco. Why not make a quick detour now, just to see if her suspicions about the placement of the word within the outline of Gugh could be right? She wouldn't stay long, and she didn't really expect to find anything in the place where she'd collided with Nigel Scofield before.

But investigating it would be more entertaining than hurrying home just to wait for the sleepyheads to wake up. And it would be perfectly safe. Scofield had no way of sneaking around now, and if any other suspicious characters had arrived on the ferry, one of their many friends would have let them know.

It was perfectly sound reasoning. She thought so as she got her sloop under sail, she thought so as she anchored it off the shore of Gugh, near where Scofield's borrowed yacht had been before, and she thought it still as she hiked up the incline, muttering at the rain that decided to let loose a torrent just then.

She thought it up until she crested the hill and saw the last thing she could have expected to see.

A tent, pitched in a little dip so it wasn't quite visible from the water. With a mahogany-haired man smiling a charming smile from its flap.

Drat and blast and bother. Maybe Oliver was right—she was a rosefinch who needed to have her wings clipped to keep her from flying straight into the teeth of danger.

15

Sheridan had expected to sleep until noon, given the ungodly hour at which they'd finally retired, but he found himself in the breakfast room at nine on the dot and looked around to see which mischievous soul had come knocking on his door fifteen minutes prior. He'd have wagered that it was Beth—he *hoped* it was Beth. That would be the sort of joke that spoke of new camaraderie, wouldn't it? But if it had been her, she'd then vanished. He'd already peeked into the library, the drawing room, and the garden, but she hadn't turned up anywhere.

Tea, then, was the obvious order of business. Still groggy and bleary-eyed, he turned to the sideboard and the hot water.

A grunt of greeting behind him alerted him to Telford's presence. Which made his brows knot. "What are you doing up this early?"

In reply, Telly grabbed a cup and elbowed him out of the way of the water urn.

Sheridan stepped aside. He'd learned long ago that it was a fool's mission to stand between Telly and his tea when he first stumbled from bed. To hold himself over the thirty seconds necessary, he reached for a piece of bacon. "I didn't expect to see you until noon. Frankly, I didn't expect to be up myself until then. Until some jokester knocked on my door."

Telford froze, then turned a questioning eye on him. Not the kind that said, *"Who would have knocked on your door?"* No, the kind that said, *"Yours too?"*

Sheridan's brows felt even knottier. "Wait. Someone woke *you* up? I can't fathom it. Everyone's learned long ago not to rouse the sleeping bear."

Another grunt as Telly added a heaping spoonful of sugar to his cup.

There was nothing like his best friend's daily foul humor to restore his own. "Well, it's hardly an insult if it's true. Though I do wonder who the culprit was if they woke both of us." While he could imagine Beth pulling such a prank on *him*, he couldn't think why she'd do it to Telford.

After a sip of tea, Telly moved on to filling a plate, leaving the space in front of the water urn open to Sheridan. He fixed his cup, looking toward the door when he heard footsteps. Two sets of them, from the sound of it.

Tremayne and Mamm-wynn filled the door a moment later. Their host was frowning. "She couldn't have waited until we were all up before she went?" he said.

Sheridan's fingers went tight around his cup. He had the distinct feeling they weren't frowning over Mrs. Dawe.

Mamm-wynn shook her head. "Lady Emily was ready to go home, and it seemed wise to let them beat the rain there. They left about an hour ago. But . . ." The lady lifted a trembling hand and pressed it to her chest. Her gaze moved from her grandson's face to Telford and then Sheridan. She looked relieved to see them all there. And yet too worried to be truly relieved. There was something strange in her eyes, which looked nearly unfocused. "Oh good. You all heard my summons."

Sheridan put the cup back down. "*You're* the one who woke us up?"

The lady's gaze locked on his and sent a shiver down his spine. "A good prince ought to go and find the fair damsel in such a time. Don't you think?"

199

He had no idea what *such* this time was, but he set his teacup back down on the sideboard. "Right. Where are we off to, then? Do you think she tried to run and hide again?"

Her eyes seemed to bore straight through him, but she pressed her lips together rather than reply. And reached that trembling hand out toward him.

Sheridan darted a questioning gaze at Oliver but, at the chap's blank look, simply took Mamm-wynn's hand in his own and let her squeeze it. Which she did, hard and long. Pointedly. Which probably oughtn't to have made panic boil up in his chest, but it did.

He'd heard Oliver and Libby murmuring about the lady's second sight and how it had played such a role in the events earlier that summer. But he hadn't quite expected to see its reemergence now, to be perfectly honest. And he wasn't entirely certain that's what this was. But it felt momentous somehow. Grave. Urgent.

He squeezed her delicate fingers in reply and turned his eyes more steadily on Beth's brother. "You'll have to man the sails, Tremayne. I don't know the waters well enough. And offer the boat, of course. I daresay your uncle hasn't yet finished the one I just commissioned."

Oliver was still frowning at his grandmother, but after a moment he refocused on Sheridan and nodded, looking less convinced than concerned.

During this exchange, Telford had taken a seat at the table and was hunkered over his plate and cup like a brooding bear. Sheridan released Mrs. Tremayne's fingers and slapped him on the shoulder. "Hurry up, old boy. Down the hatch. We leave in five minutes."

Apparently fully set on his bear persona, Telford emitted what could only be termed a growl. Sheridan chuckled and turned back toward the door and the Tremaynes. His friend might grumble, but he'd be ready to leave with the rest of them.

For his own part, he'd better go and fetch his mackintosh and wellies. Though he paused beside Mamm-wynn to press a kiss to her silk-soft cheek. "Don't worry, lady fair. We'll bring the princess home again directly."

She rewarded him with a wobbling smile and a brush of her hand over his cheek. "You're a good lad, Theo."

He thanked her with a wink and jogged toward his guest room, trying to convince himself that the tightness in his chest was merely for her sake. Or at the prospect of a small adventure. That it wasn't worry for the yet-again-missing Beth. Because really, if she'd only been gone an hour, there was no real cause for alarm. She couldn't possibly have even been due back yet, unless she tossed Lady Emily to the quay at St. Mary's and sped immediately home again, without taking any time to visit with her there.

That logic did nothing to convince his heart to beat at its usual pace. He banged his way through his door, muttering an apology when it made Ainsley start where he stood reorganizing something or another in a drawer. "Mackintosh. Wellies. Then I'll be out of your hair."

Ainsley blinked at him. "You're not meaning to go out in this." He motioned to the window, which revealed a new deluge streaming down from the heavens.

It was enough to make a man think another jaunt to Egypt might be just the thing. Well, once Beth had begged him for another chance to convince him to marry her. It would be much more fun with her by his side. "No choice," he said cheerfully to Ainsley. "Mamm-wynn's worried about Beth being out. We need to go and see she's well."

"Why wouldn't she be? I heard her leave only an hour ago, and if she sailed through that pea soup of a fog a few weeks ago, she can certainly handle a little rain shower."

"True. But who's going to argue with Mamm-wynn?"

In answer, Ainsley handed over his raincoat and boots. "Try not to take an unscheduled dip in the Atlantic this time, will you?"

Sheridan just grinned and spun toward his door.

"My lord."

He paused, turned back.

Ainsley was frowning. "I had a note waiting for me when I woke up from my cousin. I was right. He wants to chat with me this morning, and I have no doubts at all about what he'll say. He'll try to get me to give him information. I didn't want to go without telling you."

Sheridan grinned. "Feed him something ridiculous to pass along to the Scofields, then. Something that will have them looking the other way while your mother goes to Paris."

A bit of a smile overtook Ainsley's frown. "And I'll see to that wire you composed for your sisters about said trip. Thank you again for that."

Sheridan tried his best lecture-in-a-blink. "As we already established, Harry, it's your *mother*." Which meant nothing more needed to be said on the matter—and he trusted Ainsley implicitly to know what to say to Smithfield.

For his own part, Sheridan would concentrate on Beth. He hurried back down the corridor and was the first to convene at the front door, but Telford soon stomped his way there, too, face darker than the storm clouds outside. Oliver was only a moment behind.

Their host looked as worried as Sheridan was trying not to feel. "I'd love to tell you both that I'm certain this is nothing, and that we'll probably pass Beth a few minutes out. But . . ." He looked over his shoulder, toward the house at large. "But Mamm-wynn has a strange history of being right about this sort of thing."

"Indeed. Proving, as we were discussing last night, that God and Christianity aren't half so boring as people today try to make Him." Sheridan took the liberty of pulling open the door, thereby letting in a gust of warm, wet air. "I don't suppose she mentioned where we ought to begin looking for Beth, though?"

Tremayne sighed and shook his head, leading the way outside. "I was rather hoping she'd whispered something in your ear that I didn't catch. I asked her, but she just got that look in her eyes and said something about her little rosefinch always flying too far."

"Hm." Pursing his lips, Sheridan stepped out into the rain, hoping against hope that it would drill an idea into his head. Given that he'd forsaken his tea, he might require the rain's help in that department.

As they hurried to the quay and onto the *Adelle*, he let everything spin through his mind. He was the last one of the three of them to have seen Beth, so if she were in any kind of trouble, perhaps she'd let a clue drop last night. Though when he recalled their conversation, all he could really remember was the way she'd smiled—at *him*. And even laughed. The way her grey-as-the-storm eyes had flashed with amusement instead of lightning. The graceful lines of her figure he might have admired more than necessary while he was coming up with more rat jokes.

He suddenly felt as though a giant took hold of his heart and squeezed it tight. Nothing could have happened to her in this short amount of time since she had breakfast with Mamm-wynn and Lady Emily . . . could it?

He sank down onto a wet bench, knowing well that they'd get under sail faster if he and Telford stayed out of Tremayne's way. Which, just now, was fine. He wasn't quite as adept at prayers as Ainsley or Oliver and preferred to give them his full attention, rather than undergo them while he was doing other tasks. So, he bowed his head against the rain and clamped his eyes shut.

Lord God . . . we don't know where Beth is. But you do. Keep her safe, protect her if she's in any danger. And if she's still safe and well, then just whisper in her ear, as you seem to do in her grandmother's, that she ought to come home now. Let her know she has us worried.

"What are you doing?"

Telford's voice, still gravelly from disuse, elbowed its way into his awareness and made Sheridan sigh. "I'm *praying*." Shouldn't it have been obvious? Bowed head, closed eyes, clasped hands?

"Why?"

Sometimes his friend was downright obtuse in the mornings. "*Because* . . . Beth may be in some sort of danger, if Mamm-wynn is so alarmed."

"So? Since when does such a thing inspire you to pray?"

With a huff of pure exasperation, he opened his eyes and looked at Telford. "I am *not* a heathen. I pray!"

Telford's brows were furrowed. "When? All these years, I've not seen it."

"Because I usually do it in private. Is that so difficult to fathom?" Maybe it was a miscalculation, though. He'd always preferred to undertake such tasks with no eyes watching him. After all, he was no vicar or saintly valet or theologian to make a proper example of it, so he preferred to approach the King of kings without anyone around to tell him he was doing it wrong. But did his best friend really think he just never prayed?

Such a thought would have been amusing even yesterday. Just now, it seemed horrific. If absolutely everyone in his life thought him so faithless, then he was clearly doing something wrong.

He'd have to fix that. Turn over a new leaf in his outward behavior to better reflect his inward life. And yes, all right, work on the inward too. Because that must not be quite as robust as he liked to think if no one could detect it in him. Perhaps he ought to spend a bit more time thinking about God and of what He'd ask of him rather than where *he* wanted to go for his next dig.

He shut his eyes again. *Forgive me, Lord. I don't think it's ever occurred to me that I'm failing you by not making faith a more active part of my life—which is ridiculous of me, given that you've put Ainsley in my life as an example. Forgive me. And lead us to Beth, please. Help us to find her quickly and, if she needs help, to be able to give it.*

He paused, ignoring Telford's next muttering altogether, barely even registering that the sloop was moving through the water now. *And it hasn't even crossed my mind that I ought to pray about my feelings for Beth either. I suppose I am rustier at this than I thought. Forgive that, too, please, while you're forgiving me for the rest. No one has ever stirred my heart like this, Lord. I want . . . you know what I want. And you know, as I certainly don't, how she feels. Take all of it. My heart and hers, our feelings or lack of them. And work your will there. I don't know if she's really the one you'd have be the next Lady Sheridan, but . . . but I hope so. You know how I hope so.*

"Are you all right, Sheridan?" Tremayne's voice this time.

Telford snorted. "He's *praying*. One would think you'd be able to tell that, Mr. Vicar."

It probably wouldn't be righteous of him to shoot out a foot and find Telford's shin with it, but Sheridan was tempted. Sorely.

"Wise of him. Keep it up, Sher. I'll add mine to yours, and perhaps the Lord will give us guidance on where we ought to point ourselves. For now, I'm setting a course for St. Mary's since we know she'd have gone there first."

Sheridan opened his eyes but kept his head down. At least *someone* offered simple approval instead of mockery. And St. Mary's was certainly the logical place to begin. They could knock on Lady Emily's door and see how long ago Beth had been there. Perhaps they'd even find her there still. If the Lord was going to whisper a warning to Mamm-wynn, why not early enough that they could *prevent* trouble instead of just finding her in it?

He saw Mamm-wynn's eyes again, troubled and clouded. Felt the squeeze of her hand as she held his.

Holding hands . . .

The words echoed in his mind, making his brows draw together. That had been her sole reaction when he asked for direction from her. To hold his hand. Though that couldn't possibly *be* an answer, could it? It was just an emotional reaction.

Holding hands . . . with St. Agnes.

"Gugh." His murmur was lost to the drumming of the rain, or at least drew no reaction from either of his companions. Which was fine by him. He had no idea if this thought was inspired by God or just a desperate grasping of his own mind.

But Gugh—it was where they'd last seen Scofield. Why? Why had he been there? Something had taken him to the little hunk of rock off St. Agnes's shores.

Could the same something bring Scofield back again? Could the question of it have lured Beth back there this morning?

It wasn't impossible. That didn't make it likely, but . . . He looked up, toward her brother. "Gugh," he said again, more loudly this time.

Oliver looked over at him with lifted brows. "She's already been there and found nothing of interest. What would draw her to it again?"

Though he opened his mouth, Sheridan wasn't certain what answer to give him. He shrugged and summoned a few words, paltry though they might be. "It's where he was. That alone would be enough to make her wonder why, wouldn't it? And if she had a question about it, why *not* explore a bit while she's so near, after dropping Lady Emily at St. Mary's?"

Their captain granted that with a tilt of his head that sent a stream of water onto his slicker-clad shoulder. "As good a theory as any."

Telford didn't look quite so convinced. "Really? Your sister would just go off for another random investigation in this weather, without letting anyone know?"

With a laugh, Oliver faced forward again. "If you have to ask, you've not spent enough time with her yet, my lord."

Despite the weight of his worry, Sheridan grinned. He'd never met a young lady so prone to adventure. She was exactly the sort who would be eager to join him on excavations anywhere in the world. She wouldn't complain about the dry heat in Egypt or the strange food in Greece. She wouldn't faint at the thought of hiking into the Andes or give a dreadful shiver at the very suggestion of catching sight of the northern lights while he researched something in Iceland. She'd thrill at the chance to see those places, to explore and discover. And rough living for a few weeks at a time wouldn't deter her a bit. She'd resorted to just that this very summer when she was in hiding, after all, of her own volition.

There was no girl in the world like Beth Tremayne.

"Oh, egad." Telford, with that exasperated declaration, made a show of clamping *his* eyes shut and clasping his hands. "Lord Almighty, spare me the sap and moon-eyes of all these lovesick fools."

His future brother-in-law laughed. "Careful what you pray for, Telford. Perhaps I'll spare you by giving you a toss into the drink like my sister did Sheridan."

16

I knew you would make an appearance soon."

Beth stood rooted to the heather, her shock at war with her common sense. She knew she ought to turn and run back to her boat before Nigel Scofield could come a step closer, but instead she blinked. How could he be here? *How?* She must be imagining it.

But her imagination never would have conjured him up like this, dressed in clothes better suited for an Amazonian expedition than a jaunt in the islands, ducking out of his tent with nothing but a hat to protect him from the rain. And grinning. Still grinning as he'd done the day they met.

"I knew it was only a matter of time after I discovered your name. Surely a magical binding works over distance, to pull the fairy to her captor. It's only logical."

Water dripped from the hood of her mackintosh, across her vision. She managed a step backward. "I beg your pardon, sir. I didn't expect anyone else to be here."

He pursed his lips, though if he made any noise, it was lost to the rain. And shook his head as he took a step toward her. "Now, Miss Tremayne—or may I call you Beth? Why wouldn't you have expected me to be here?"

She winced a bit at the sound of her name on his lips. No magic bound her to him at the speaking, but even so, it left her with a bare feeling. Exposed.

He'd realized who she was—not just some random "Beth" of Sheridan's acquaintance, but the very person his father had been communicating with all spring. Which meant he'd likely also realized who Libby was, and that she and Oliver and Telford had pulled the wool over his eyes that day outside Cromwell's Castle, when he'd forced them to Piper's Hole to trade Mabena for a piece of Mucknell's treasure.

But she'd learned quite a bit in their time apart too. Maybe even something that would make *him* proceed with care. "Well, I suppose, Mr. Scofield, that I simply don't expect to find earls' sons making camp on an unoccupied island in a rainstorm." And from the looks of it, he'd been there more than just a couple hours, given the small cookstove and assortment of items set up. At least a day. Perhaps he came during the fair weather yesterday, though she still couldn't think how he'd managed it without anyone knowing.

He came to within a foot of her and offered his elbow. "I don't know why not, given the particular earl I'm the particular son of. I've certainly set up camp in far worse conditions than this. Did Em ever tell you about our expedition to Peru when she was twelve? Not that she and Mother left the hotel in Cusco."

She glared at the proffered arm before spinning back toward the *Naiad*. "She did, yes. She said that it was a hot, muggy, miserable fortnight spent all but locked up in a room with her mother while you and your father were off gallivanting about in search of Aztec temples." And gold that the conquistadors had missed, no doubt.

She hadn't gone but a step before his hand closed around her slicker-covered elbow and forced her to a halt. It was an iron grip, too, despite the warm, friendly sound of the laugh he let loose.

"Emily never had a stitch of adventurousness in her bones. Neither does Mother. I admit I thought it was typical of all ladies. But you're a different sort, aren't you, Elizabeth Tremayne? You've certainly proven that this summer, with all the artifacts you've sent to us. I could scarcely believe it was one young lady collecting it all." He gave her a tug, turning her to face him. A dark glint shone in his eyes. "Or a young *woman* anyway."

Her nostrils flared. She'd come to expect such jabs at her family line from people like him. She'd once defended herself, then learned to let it roll off her. But in this case, she had a feeling that letting him think her too lowborn would only give him leave to behave badly. "You were right the first time. As you ought to know, given the fact that I know your sister from finishing school."

He breathed another laugh, this one scoffing. "Only the London one. Not the Swiss château she went to the next year."

Tempting as it was to spit on him or grind her heel into his toe, she forced a smile through the rain. "Oh, you mean the one where she met my future sister-in-law, Lady Elizabeth Sinclair. The Earl of Telford's sister." Well, not entirely true—Libby and Emily had missed each other by a year. But still, they'd gone to the same place. And it made the point she was trying to make. Beth's mother may have been "only" an island girl, but that didn't mean he could stomp all over her. If connections were all that mattered to him, he needed to know she had some too.

He didn't look terribly impressed, though. He waved a hand through the rain and tugged her forward. "All that hardly matters, darling. The point is that I was hoping you'd come by again soon. I want to show you something."

She tried to dig in her heels, but that just resulted in her slipping in the wet heather and mud. Which further resulted in him taking *both* her elbows to steady her and then standing there far too long, facing her, inches away, looking down at her with that smile she'd thought so charming two and a half weeks ago.

How had she not seen that it was mocking? Self-satisfied? Arrogant?

"Come, Beth, don't be that way. I'm not trying to be an ogre. I only want to show you what I discovered last night before I lost the light. The fact that you've come back, too, tells me that you've also

210

identified this as a place of interest. You must be curious as to what's here." He eased closer still. "Unless . . . unless it was thoughts of *me* that brought you back here?"

What she wouldn't give to hear Sheridan's shout echoing down the hill again. She'd appreciate it this time as she hadn't the last. And if he got another black eye for his efforts, she'd soothe him and baby him and lavish him with attention instead of tossing him into the drink for his troubles.

As for the gentleman in front of her now . . . she lifted her chin and glared at him with all the icy fury of a winter fairy. "Don't flatter yourself, sir. I prefer men *without* the blood of my friends on their hands."

Something flashed in his emerald eyes. It wasn't regret, that was obvious. But she had no word for what it *was*. Something dark. Something warning. "It's a shame what happened to the lad." His voice was smooth, polished, and utterly devoid of any true emotion. "That Lorne bloke who Lord Sheridan hired was certainly volatile. And ruthless. But I didn't even join forces with him until directly after the incident, so you can hardly blame *me*. It seems if you're going to be angry at anyone for that, darling, it ought to be Sheridan."

"I have anger enough over it to go round." And he was lying, from what she'd pieced together, about when he began working with Lorne. The only timeline that made any sense involved him and Lorne teaming up just *before* Johnnie was killed.

And Sheridan hadn't even realized Lorne had come to the Isles of Scilly until after the tragedy. Perhaps a few weeks ago she was willing to believe he was complicit in it, but now? No. Sheridan valued life too highly to have condoned anything violent.

Apparently, her fury amused Scofield. His lips twitched up, even as he let go of one of her elbows and moved to her side again. "You really do have the fire of a fairy princess, don't you? I suppose I should have believed my sister when she told me how enchanting her island friend was." He dropped her other elbow, but her freedom was too short-lived for her to act on it. In the next second, he'd taken her hand and linked their arms together, resting her fingers against his soaked forearm and then pressing them there with his own.

A move her father had made, her brother, her uncle. One she could imagine Sheridan making with a warm smile and a hopeful gaze. Strange how the same innocuous action felt like a threat just now.

"Now." He grinned down at her through the rain as he led them down the hill, leaving her little choice but to go along or risk another slipping attempt at escape. "Allow me to prove wrong whatever rubbish Em has told you about me. You oughtn't to listen to her, you know, not about this. She's always been jealous of the attention Father pays me. It colors her every view of me. I promise you, I'm a stand-up chap. One who shares your interest in history and archaeological discoveries."

And why was he trying so hard to win her favor? Their first flirtation was one thing—it was anonymous, nothing but a moment of fun. But he knew who she was now, knew that she knew far too much about him to ever want to spend another minute in his company. Why was he so determined to detain her?

She wasn't likely to find out by spitting vitriol at him every moment. Though it required some gritting of teeth, she gave him a tight smile and kept pace. The *Naiad* was still right there. She'd wait for a moment when he wasn't likely to trip her up and then get away. Sail home. "I can hardly argue about our common pursuits. Though I find it a bit hard to believe my little discoveries here are really of such interest to your family. From the way Emily talks, you're usually off exploring pyramids or lost cities or something far bigger than one pirate's missing hoard."

"This could well *be* a lost city. Lyonesse." He shrugged as if dismissing it, but there'd been a note of genuine intrigue in his voice. "And your pirate was one of the greatest to haunt the seas. How many others had an entire pirate fleet? The moment I read about him, I was fascinated."

She lifted her brows. "Were you? Your father led me to believe your interest was solely on behalf of the mysterious patron who wished to purchase any Mucknell or Prince Rupert artifacts—Lord Sheridan."

"Sheridan." His voice was a sneer, though she couldn't see much of his face through her own mackintosh hood and the rain to discover if his expression matched his tone. "He doesn't deserve to have such things in his collection. That man makes a mockery of exploration—as you no doubt know, having been forced into his company these weeks. He'll fund absolutely any expedition, no matter how ridiculous, and then get excited about beads and pottery shards. He's wasted a veritable fortune unearthing liths and cairns, as if the Druids ever buried anything worthwhile in them. He'll never discover anything noteworthy."

Were they rivals in this world of digs and expeditions? It hadn't ever occurred to her that such animosity existed, not until Johnnie got caught in the cross fire. "I suppose that's why you've brokered a deal with the American, then." It was a rickety limb, that line of questioning. But if she was going to be stuck in his company for a few minutes, she might as well ease her foot out along it and pray she learned something.

Pray. There was an idea. How had the response that had become second nature during her weeks of solitude fallen away again so quickly in society? Especially when most of the society she'd been keeping turned to it so readily? *Father God, you know I didn't come here looking for this. I thought . . . I thought it would be safe. But here I am again in need of your protection.*

Scofield chuckled. "Stroke of luck, really, that there is someone else willing to waste untold amounts of silver on Mucknell's treasure. One can never underestimate the power of a bidding war either. And if it's a way to needle Lord Sheridan, all the better. My father seems to have liked him well enough before now, but I can't say as I was ever inclined to make friends, knowing what I did of him. And I think I had the right of it."

Well, drat, she was hoping he'd let slip the American's name. Too much to expect, she supposed. Perhaps a different tack, then, would reveal some new information. "How did you know to look on Gugh?"

"How did *you*?" He shot her a challenging look.

Adages about flies and honey filled her mind, and she forced a smile that she prayed was a good imitation of the one she'd given him on their first meeting. Even tossed in a little chuckle of her own. "Now, now, my lord. I asked first." And she wasn't about to tell him about the mention of "the old man" in the letters she hadn't even sent to him. There was probably little harm in pointing out the water stain in the one she had. "Though to show goodwill . . . there was a mark in one of the letters. Or, rather, an outline."

He lifted his hand from hers just long enough to wipe away some of the rain that had made it under his hat, then covered her fingers again. "Quite a good representation of the islands, wasn't it? I was surprised, at first, at how closely it matched the map we have. But I suppose I shouldn't have been, given that Mucknell was a captain. He would have had charts aplenty at his disposal, and they had every inch of the islands mapped, I daresay. Even so." He sent a wink her way. "An outline alone probably wouldn't have been enough to send me here. But we found mention of the island in a deposition we dug up. One of Mucknell's crew was eventually arrested for piracy, and he named Gugh as a place where items of interest could be found."

Beth's heart lifted—he was sharing information! But then it sank again. "So, the authorities knew about it. Which means if it had been a site of part of his hoard, it's likely been recovered already."

The clucking of his tongue mixed with the drumming of rain on stone.

Wait—stone? On this part of the island? Beth blinked and then squinted through the driving drops. The heather and bracken should have been muffling all such sounds, but . . . what was that, just ahead? A dark, gaping opening . . . just where that word had been on the not-a-stain.

214

"Such pessimism!" Scofield increased their pace. "The mention was no more specific than that—and named other possible locations as well. I highly doubt anyone came out here and dug up the whole island at that point in time. But coupled with Mucknell's own directions . . ."

Beth sucked in a breath as the image reappeared through the rain. The dark gap she was seeing was a dig. A shovel lay nearby to prove it. And if the rain was hitting on stone, it could just be the granite bedrock.

Though would he really be dragging her forcibly over here to look at bedrock?

Despite the company, her pulse quickened. And then *because* of the company. First, because he might have found something. And then because *he* might have found something.

She sucked in a quick breath when he drew them to a halt at the edge of a five-foot-deep pit. Far deeper than one could dig in most places on Gugh, where the soil was but a thin layer over the granite. But he'd found granite, to be sure. Straight, perpendicular lines of it. A wall, and a barely dug out corner at its end. "A cairn."

Sheridan would be delirious with joy if he were here. A cairn, previously undiscovered, unexplored. Known to no one else on the islands. He could set up an official excavation and see what could be found inside it, what mysteries of the Druids it could reveal.

Except that Scofield had gotten here first.

She darted a look up at him and found him staring down into the pit he'd dug as if it had already revealed mounds of treasure.

Maybe it had. She swallowed and eased her hand away from his arm, a bit surprised when he let her go. "Have you found anything of interest yet?"

"Perhaps. I am rather glad you came by, in all honesty. I could use a pair of educated eyes. Do you mind?"

For the first time in their albeit brief acquaintance, he sounded perfectly earnest. No façade of either charm or sneer. Just a man interested in something but not quite certain what he'd found.

And she was here already. She might as well gather as much information as she could to tell the others when she got home. "What is it?"

His answer was to crouch down and then jump into the hole, landing with a splash in the puddle that formed its bottom. He held a hand up for her, but she ignored it.

She could jump into a hole no deeper than her own height without a man's assistance, thank you very much. Even when encumbered by skirts. She did so in the next second, only wincing slightly at the sound of water and mud greeting her, no doubt painting the hem of her dress. Oh well—she'd soaked her own clothes before, to avoid Mrs. Dawe's ire, and she could do it again.

Her pulse rocketed once more as she looked around. He'd dug out quite a bit of dirt, proving he'd been here awhile. The hole was about as big in circumference as it was deep, making for tight quarters for the two of them. "You've been busy."

"I've had a few days to do it. Carefully. And covertly." He nodded toward the mounds of muddy soil he'd dug out, which weren't just piled helter-skelter above him as one would expect, but which he'd taken care to shape in such a way that it didn't look odd from a distance.

He must have been working in the rain, which didn't seem quite safe. Her brows knit. What exactly had that arrested pirate said was buried here, to make it worth the risk of digging in these conditions? "I suppose you didn't want the neighbors poking about."

Scofield laughed. "Preferably not—and the rain has been helpful in that goal, I must say. No one has ventured to Gugh in the last week that I know of, and if there were any danger of my noises reaching all the way to St. Agnes, it's covered it up."

A week? He'd been here a whole week? He must have been slow and precise in his excavations, then—not surprising for a trained archaeologist, but she hadn't honestly expected him to bow to anyone else's wisdom. He seemed more the type to plow hard and fast into whatever he wanted, consequences be hanged.

Her gaze traced the lines of the granite slabs he'd found—the main one, and that corner, set at right angles to each other. That was more indicative of this being a burial chamber meant to be underground rather than a standing stone that had sunken or fallen over. Probably—though it wasn't her area of expertise. She'd need Sheridan's opinion on that.

But the question more pertinent to their situation—had Mucknell discovered this same chamber and buried something not-so-Druid within it? "Quite a discovery, my lord." It was easy to inject admiration into her voice this time—for the discovery if not the discoverer. "Any idea what we're looking for in here?" The *we* was deliberate.

"Hard to say exactly, though we can be sure that if Mucknell ferreted something away, it was worthwhile and not given to rot. Precious metals, jewels maybe. Not quite as interesting as Queen Elizabeth's silverware . . ." He angled a playful look at her that was likely masking anger, though she couldn't detect it in his eyes. "But perhaps you'd be willing to work out a trade with me, to at least share that set. No reason for Sheridan to take home the whole prize, is there?"

"No." She had, in fact, wasted hours' worth of breath arguing with him at the start about why he had no right to claim or even to purchase the silverware. It had no direct link to Prince Rupert, and it would be more suited for a museum. Its historical value far outweighed even the pure worth of the silver, which was quite high on its own. But add in the story of it being first a gift for Queen Elizabeth and then stolen by pirates, and that made it virtually priceless.

She wasn't about to say she wouldn't ever put any of it into *his* hands either.

A bit of mud gave way and slipped down into the hole. Beth watched it sag to a halt and then examined the sides of the excavation more closely. Where he'd hit granite slabs seemed secure enough, but the other two sides looked as though they could go the way of that stray clump any moment. She edged a bit closer to the granite. "So, what is it you wanted my opinion on?"

"I'm wondering if I've discovered the wrong side of the cairn and should begin digging over there instead—if this is the outside instead of the inside of the chamber wall. See here?" He pointed at something in the granite slab. A large crack, one that traced the entire height of the stone. It looked deep, too—deep enough to mean the whole slab was split in two.

She sloshed over to his side. Two steps, that was all. But the bedrock must not be entirely even here, because the second step was a deeper puddle than she anticipated, and she stumbled, sank to a knee, and bumped into the granite.

It shouldn't have mattered. The granite should have been well anchored in place, held there by the soil on the other side if nothing else. But she felt it give, shift, move away from her at the base.

"No!" A thousand thoughts crashed through her mind like surf on sand. Part of the slab was falling. She had to get out of the way. She lunged toward Scofield—or where he'd been a second ago, anyway—out of the granite's path, but the mud and water sucked at her, slipped away from her when she tried to find purchase. "Help me!"

Weight. Groaning. Mud and muck and water and a desperate stretching, scratching. She couldn't even process the sensations for a long moment. "Mr. Scofield!"

"Tut tut. What a shame." His voice came from what seemed a great height. "How fortunate it hasn't crushed you already—though I daresay if that little ledge of dirt it's stuck to on the opposite wall gives way . . . Well, I'd better go for help."

He was calm. Too calm. That's what sliced through the panic in one moment, though it only managed to multiply it in the next, rather than subtract from it. Had he planned this? Deliberately dug out around part of the broken slab so that it would fall? Measured the opposite wall's distance so that it would just barely catch it? Pinning her without killing her outright?

218

Was he that devious? Surely not . . . and yet here she was, trapped in the mud and water, untold pounds of rock holding her there as effectively as a giant hand. She strove to match his calm, but her very soul was quaking. "Sir, please. If you but get the shovel . . . use it as a lever . . . I'm certain I can scoot out."

"And risk bringing the whole thing down those last inches on you? Oh, I'd better not, darling. This calls for help. I'll just take your charming little sloop and find someone, shall I? Of course, I need someone who understands some basic engineering. Daresay I won't find that on St. Agnes."

Bedrock was beneath her, however uneven it may be, so how was it that his words made her feel as though she were sinking lower and lower? Cold seeped into her, compounding by the second. Partly from the rain and the mud and the water and the stone. Partly from the utter lack of any emotion in his tone. "What is it you want from me? Just tell me, and then help me."

"Want from you?" He chuckled, and it came from a bit farther away. She couldn't see where he was. No matter how she craned her head, she could see only the edge of the hole above her, and he must have been standing beyond it. "You think I did this on purpose? Here I am, ready to risk life and limb to save you, and you're accusing me of vile intentions. Well, despite that, I'd better do my part to play the hero. I'll be back, Miss Tremayne. Stay calm."

Stay calm? He was stealing her boat and leaving her here, trapped in a puddle deepening by the minute. If the granite didn't crush her, she could well drown in a few hours. Or die of hypothermia. "Please." Desperation colored her voice, but she couldn't care about that.

She didn't want to die. It would destroy her grandmother. Devastate her brother. "*Please.*"

"I'm going for help now. Sit tight." She heard the sound of feet moving off through mud and heather as he laughed at his own joke.

He was leaving her here. Actually leaving her here. He hadn't tried to bargain with her for the silverware or anything else, he was just *leaving*. "Scofield! Come back!" Her shout turned to a sob, and then a scream.

Had the slab sunk another inch downward? Or was it her own panic crushing her? She tried to twist, to wriggle forward or backward, but the weight was too great. She tried digging with her hands, but her palms scraped against rock.

Sheridan's face flooded her mind's eye. Smiling at her in that way he did. She should have wakened him with a clang of spoon on pot this morning, so she could tell him her theory. She should have given him some solid indicator last night that her heart had warmed. She should have done so much differently.

Perhaps it was summer, but that generally mild temperature would only prolong the inevitable if she didn't get out of here. The cold and wet were slinking in around her mackintosh, sloshing into her boots from her frantic scrabbling. How long before the mild shivering turned to clattering teeth and bone-jarring quakes? How long before that pain she felt in her ribs and leg intensified? Or maybe it would go numb.

Maybe whatever was holding the slab up on the opposite side would indeed give way, and the full force of the granite would crush her into the bedrock. By the time anyone found her, she'd be flattened. Flattened or dead from exposure or drowned if the rain didn't slacken and this hole filled. It wouldn't take long to achieve it. Her only hope was discovery—but no one would come here. No one had any reason to. And if Scofield was taking her boat, it wasn't as though anyone would spot that and think to investigate.

She was stranded. Alone. And no one even knew she was missing.

Curling her fingers through the mud, she slammed her eyes closed. "Lord God. You know. You know exactly where I am. Whisper it to someone, please. Send help. I beg you."

They were perhaps ten minutes from St. Agnes and Gugh, within sight of the dual islands with their now-invisible tombolo, when

Sheridan peered through the steady rain and swore he saw a sail disappearing around the far side of the island. He held out a hand toward the other two. "Spyglass?"

Someone, after a moment of fumbling, put one in his hand. By the time he lifted it to his eye, he couldn't make out more than the top of the mast and the stern of the boat before it slipped out of sight. But even that glimpse was enough to tie his stomach in knots. It *could* have been the *Naiad*. Right size, right shape, right colors. But he could think of no good reason for Beth to be sailing in *that* direction, away from the rest of the islands.

Which only left bad reasons.

And it might *not* be the *Naiad*. So, what should they do? Follow the sloop? Or their original plan to investigate the place on Gugh where they'd originally found Scofield?

He looked over at his friends and told them briefly what he could make out, putting the question to them. But their silence was as loud as his own.

What he wouldn't give for one of Mamm-wynn's whispers right about now.

17

Senara glanced out the kitchen window, telling herself for the twentieth time that Beth was *not* like little Paulette or Josephine or Rose. The fact that she was "missing" according to Mamm-wynn wasn't *really* cause for concern. She told herself that her friend was a woman grown, one who knew the islands like the back of her hand, and that even if she *had* found a bit of trouble, the gents would set it all to rights.

Senara had no cause to worry. Still, she found herself scrubbing the porridge pot with enough force to earn her an arch look from Mam when she came back in with the last armful of breakfast dishes from the dining room. Because capable and grown woman or not, there were clearly some shady characters lurking around the islands, mixed up in this same business. Shady characters like one Rory Smithfield, apparently.

She'd spent the last two days forcing her mind to wrap around the horrid truth. She was nothing to him aside from what she could bring him. He may speak of marriage, but did she even dare believe it? What if he took her away from here only to abandon her?

And all of that was a moot point, regardless, because he said she'd have to purchase his loyalty by turning on her friends. Which she would never do.

How had she got herself in this fix?

Her hands stilled in the wash water, and her eyes squeezed shut. Ever since he'd shown up here thirty-six hours ago, she'd felt as though a monster were feasting on her insides. Guilt—gnawing at her, devouring her from the inside out.

The fact that he was here, mixed up in all this, wasn't exactly her fault. It was his connection to Ainsley, not to her, that had gotten him involved. That only made the guilt bite harder, though. Because she kept seeing Ainsley, looking at her with that serious, respectful look of his. Ainsley, who was as different from his cousin as day from night. Ainsley, who made her feel like a criminal just by assuming her innocent.

No, not a criminal. Just a sinner.

Her hands stilled on the pot, and she had to sniff the sudden emotion from her nose.

Mam came to a halt beside her, close enough that Senara could feel her there, feel the warmth of her. "Why," she said softly, "do I have the feeling that this upset isn't only about Beth?"

Because she'd always been too perceptive, that was why. Senara could only shake her head for a long moment as she tried to swallow down the sob that wanted to rise. At last she managed to choke out, "I've ruined everything, Mam. I've—I've ruined *myself.*"

Her mother's arm came around her, tight and strong. "There now, little love. Tell Mam all about it."

She didn't want to. Didn't want to confess to this woman who had always been everything upright and good that she'd fallen so far. She squeezed her eyes shut and braced her palms against the edge of the sink. "I . . . I can't. I'm so . . ." She had to search for the word, the one that summed up this tightness in her chest, the burning there each time she recalled the way Ainsley had looked at her, ready to believe the best of her.

No, that wasn't right. He hadn't ignited the feeling. He'd just made her aware of what had been there already, buried under the layers of anger and betrayal. Ever since that night when she had forgotten herself and let Rory's kisses lure her where she knew she shouldn't go.

"I'm so ashamed." That was the only word that would do, though it scalded her lips even to say it. How many times had she tossed the word out at a child who had been naughty? *Did you steal that biscuit from the jar? You ought to be ashamed of yourself. Did you strike your sister? Did you lie? Shame on you.*

Mam stroked her hand over Senara's arm. "Rory?"

Senara jerked a nod. "I never meant to let it go so far. But . . ." But she was lonely. And she loved him, or thought she did. And that he loved her. She'd thought they'd be married soon, and that while that didn't excuse it, it made it less grievous a sin. "I hadn't let myself think about it. What I'd done, what I'd sacrificed. Now it's hitting, though. All at once." She splayed a damp hand over her heart. "He showed up the other night. Here. Made insinuations in Ainsley's hearing, and Ainsley dismissed them. Assured me," she said on a dry laugh, "that he'd never believe it of me. Only he *should*. I'm not what he thinks me to be. *Who* he thinks me to be."

"Senara, dearover. Sit down." Never one to let her commands go unheeded, Mam nudged her over to a chair. The same one she'd been sitting in that first full day home, snapping peas, when Ainsley and Collins came in.. Mam sat beside her and gathered Senara's fingers into her own. "Look at me."

She'd rather have studied the grain of the table's wood, but she did as she was told. Mam held her gaze. "You were always such a good girl—we never really had to speak of these things. But shame, Senara . . . it's for a purpose. It's there to strike our consciences, to remind us of the standard of the Lord. It's there to let us know we've sinned."

Senara's gaze dropped away. "I know I have." She did know it. But it had been buried these weeks under the lies—that it would all be glossed over as soon as she married him. That the interim didn't matter if it ended in the right place.

"Then your next step must be to repent of it. And I don't mean the cursory 'I'm sorry' that we let children get away with. You have to mean it, dear one. You have to regret not only the consequences but the sin itself. You must regret not just your own pain, but the grief you've caused—to those girls who will feel you've abandoned them, to the other servants who will see your example. To Rory, for not showing him that you're a woman of integrity."

Her eyes flashed back up at that, and no doubt fire flashed in them. "What? You can't expect me to apologize to him!"

"Sins committed together are also committed against each other." Mam lifted a brow. "And against the Lord. Repenting to Him is sometimes the easiest part. But He asks us to make right what we can too. That generally means facing those we've wronged."

The pressure squeezed and flared hot again. She'd done wrong, yes. But not like him. He'd pushed her too far. He'd seduced her. He'd whispered promises he had no intention of keeping. He'd used her for information. And then he'd betrayed her.

But she'd proven herself too weak. Too susceptible to flattery. And how could she ever trust herself again now? How could she ever return to what she'd once been, as pure and innocent as Ainsley had assumed her still to be?

Mam's hand stroked over her hair. "And after the repentance, dearover, comes the truly hard part—you must learn how to let the shame go. It has its purpose, a right and needful one. It can take us to life and repentance and return us to God. But if we're not careful, it can just as easily carry us away and drown us. Others will try to force us to live in it still even after we've repented, after Christ has washed us clean. They will try to push *their* guilt and shame upon us, if we let them. Guard against that. But only after you are once again clean." Mam dipped her head down to catch Senara's gaze. "Aye? You must take it to the Lord, Senara. And then let Him truly take it from you."

And how was she to do that? She nodded, because she knew the words were true . . . but then she pushed herself up. "Do you mind if I go for a walk?"

Mam didn't even mention the rain coming down. "Of course not. Go on with you."

She gathered her rain gear and slipped out the door, opting to let the drops soak her hair instead of covering her head with the hood or a brolly. Maybe it would do that cleansing work Mam said she needed.

She *did* need it. She knew that. But water alone couldn't wash her of this stain. And she didn't know how to let the Lord do it either.

Her feet took her to the street, aimed her toward the Abbey Gardens. When she was younger, that had always been where she went to clear her mind. Maybe it would work now too. Neighbors were out and about, clearly not willing or able to let the rain's return hinder them, but she didn't spot any unfamiliar faces. Good. At least the incomers wouldn't be in her path.

She'd waved a greeting to Mr. Menna, caretaker of the Gardens, and found a secluded path to wander, when familiar movement caught her eyes. She turned to see what it was and frowned. Ainsley? She'd never known him to slip away for his own pleasure, even when Lord Sheridan was off about other business. Usually, he was home with his brushes and his bicarb, trying to work the latest ink stain from jackets and trousers. Or running errands with Collins. She couldn't think what errand his lordship would have sent him on to the Gardens.

She didn't really mean to follow, but her feet tugged her down the same path. Curiosity or dread, she wasn't sure which.

Though she had her answer the moment she heard that other familiar voice call out, "Hank! Knew you'd come."

Rory. She couldn't see either of them at the moment, as Ainsley had gone through an arched opening in the wall, and that was fine by her, as it meant they couldn't see her either. She slipped up against the wall, where she could hear them over the patter of rain on the path but stay out of sight.

"We're family." Ainsley sounded tired. Defeated? Had he given up resisting and decided to let Rory lead *him* into a life of sin too?

226

Her fingers curled into her palms. It wasn't like him. Or maybe it was. What did she really know about him?

Rory's laughter slithered through the rain. "Don't pretend that would be enough to make you see things my way—it never has before. And you weren't exactly leaping to my defense with Senara the other night, were you?"

Ainsley said nothing, though she could imagine how he would look. He'd be still and steady, not even blinking out of turn.

Rory went on, voice low. "Well, it's like this, cousin. I need some actual information, and she's my best chance of getting it. And the amount they're paying me—well, it's certainly worth a few vows that don't mean much anyway."

"You are such a reprobate." The words snapped out in Ainsley's voice, full of leashed feeling.

"Sticks and stones, Hank. But if you want to spare her poor heart, you know what you have to do. If you want to keep her out of it, you have to take her place."

Senara stared with horror at the stone before her. Not just at how little she meant to Rory, though it still stung. But Ainsley . . . he wouldn't be drawn into Rory's scheme. Not for *her*.

Would he?

The silence stretched long, thin, taut. It felt like an eternity later that Ainsley gusted out a breath audible even over the rain and said, "If I help you, do you swear to stay away from her?"

Rory's laugh slid into her ears like poison. "You have my word."

"Is that supposed to satisfy me? We both know how much your word is worth."

"Now, Henry, don't go insulting me or I'll change my mind."

Ainsley made a low, frustrated noise. "Just tell me what you need."

Rory chuckled. "Just feed me a bit of reliable information, that's all. They have specific questions, you see. Questions that I can't make up the answers to or they'll know and cut me off."

Silence. And then another heaving breath. "Such as?"

227

Senara let her eyes slide shut. No. This couldn't be happening. Ainsley wouldn't turn on Sheridan just to try to spare her a future with his cousin. She couldn't possibly be that important to him.

Or maybe . . . maybe she was just an excuse, like she'd been to Rory himself. Maybe it was the money tempting him. Maybe he'd gather the information they wanted but then not turn it over until Rory cut him into the deal.

A gust of wind tore through the Gardens, sending rain sluicing off leaves and onto the path. The patter turned to a drumming, overpowering any other sound. Senara pressed closer to the wall, trying to hear Rory over the noise.

". . . archives. They didn't realize it until the bloke vanished, and now they can't trace who paid him. Was it Sheridan?"

Archives? Senara sent her mind back through all the tidy lists she'd made over the last weeks, all the things the others had asked her to note. Lady Emily had mentioned a concern about the archives—not in Senara's hearing, but Beth had relayed it later. That someone was doing all the copy work for her family. Which meant someone else knew everything they did. Sheridan had lit up at that, proposed that they ought to be the ones to leverage it— but Telford and Oliver had insisted it was an unnecessary expense and not quite aboveboard, respectively. But that didn't mean the marquess hadn't done it anyway.

"I have no idea," Ainsley said evenly. Though he would. He knew everything Sheridan did. "But I'll see what I can discover. What else?"

"They're still a bit miffed that some bloke initially hired by Sheridan but then recruited by them was arrested last month."

"Lorne."

"Yeah, that sounds right. Anyway, they're convinced Sheridan has more people out there working from different angles. They want to know who they are."

Senara pressed her hand to the ivy-covered stone behind her. Sheridan didn't, in fact, have anyone else working on this—Lord

228

Telford and Oliver had both asked him point-blank if he had, within her first day home. He'd assured them both that they were now the only ones researching the questions from his end. And she couldn't imagine him lying to his best friend.

But Ainsley said, "Of course he has. At least three that I know of. I'll have to poke through his papers to get you their names and how to reach them."

Three? Senara frowned. Had Sheridan lied to his best friend?

Rory chuckled. "I knew you'd come through for us, old boy. How quick can you get the information to me?"

"It shouldn't take long. A day or so. Where are you staying?"

"Penzance. No rooms to let here, so I've been ferrying over. I can come back tomorrow."

"Better make it the day after. I don't want to have to rush and risk getting caught snooping. Sheridan is all the time in his room, hovering over his materials."

She squinted through the rain, as if that would help her make sense of the words coming from behind the wall. Sheridan was scarcely *ever* in his room.

And she was an idiot.

It wasn't his employer who Ainsley was playing for a fool—it was his cousin. He was feeding him misinformation, and no doubt he'd report back to Sheridan what he'd said and promised, so they could devise what to tell him when he came again.

Well, that made sense, then. He wasn't sacrificing anything, much less his own standards, for her.

For a moment, something akin to disappointment flooded her. But she banished it quickly. She didn't *want* Ainsley to compromise his morality for her. She'd have been disappointed in him if he had, especially when it would endanger them all.

She just wanted to mean something to him. To anyone. That was all.

"Fair enough. I'm supposed to check in with them again on Saturday, so that'll be fine. But, Henry—make sure it's all accurate or our families will be the ones to pay for it. These people . . . they pay well, but they don't mess around."

"Understood."

Was it? Because Senara's throat went tight at those words. What was he doing? It was bad enough that all of them here were at risk, clashing with the Scofields outright. Why in the world would Ainsley put his own family in the cross fire, too, when he wasn't even there to protect them?

The cousins said their farewells. Senara debated whether to try to dart away, but if one of them came back through the arch, he'd see her for sure. Better to wait here and trust that the rain would force them to keep their heads down and keep them from looking all around.

It was Ainsley who came back along this path. But he *did* look around, and he spotted her in about half a second. Quirked a brow. Stepped off the path to her side.

She didn't know what she meant to say to him. Not until she opened her lips and the whisper tumbled out. "Why would you risk your mam for him?"

But Ainsley only smiled. "By the time Rory delivers the information I give him to the Scofields," he whispered in return, "my mother and his, and his sister, too, will be on their way to France, under Sheridan's protection."

She wasn't sure if it was relief she felt, knowing he wasn't betraying them, or some second sort of twisted disappointment that he really was as good as he appeared. Which cast her in such sharp contrast.

His brows drew together, and he came half a step closer. "Miss Dawe . . . what have I done? To offend you?"

And even better—here he was, clearly ready to apologize, when she was the one on whom all the blame rested. She shook her head. Stepped away from him, onto the path. "Nothing."

"Senara." He was at her side, pleading in his voice. As if it grieved him that she was upset. As if she mattered. "Clearly there's some-

230

thing. You wouldn't speak to me all day yesterday. Please—I only want to be a friend to you."

That twisting, burning feeling clamped her in its teeth again. She came to a halt, looked up at him, and let it have its way with her words. "All those things your cousin said about me, the things he insinuated—they're true."

He blinked, but that was the only response he made.

The only one she waited around to see, anyway. In the next second, she darted away, down another path. If he tried to say anything more to her, the rain ate up his voice.

If only it could quench the fires still feasting on her soul.

———————o———————

One time, when they were children, Beth and Mabena had followed the boys into one of the sea caves without their knowing it. It had been a grand adventure—at first. But trying to stay out of sight meant that they put themselves in a rather risky position. The tide had turned, and the cave had begun to fill up, and while the boys scampered easily out, Beth and Benna had found themselves stuck, their escape route already flooded.

It was the first time she remembered the excitement of an adventure turning so drastically to terror. Seeing that dark water surge and crash on the rocks, knowing the waves would pound *her* into them just as easily. Though usually Beth wasn't one to scream and cry, she'd done it then. At the top of her lungs. And praise God, Oliver had heard her. He, Enyon, and Cador had come back and helped them escape.

But there was no Oliver here now, nor Enyon, nor even the despicable Cador Wearne, whom she'd sworn never to speak to again after he broke Mabena's heart two years ago. She'd happily forgive him if his face appeared in the space above her now.

And the hole was filling. Not as quickly as a sea cave at high tide, but steadily. The water that had been an inch deep when she landed in this pit was two inches deep now, as the rain collected here from

231

the runoff of the hill. It had seeped up under her coat, into her boots. She was soaked, and the shivers had already begun, despite the air temperature being summer-rain warm.

Father God, Lord of all, help me. Please, God. Help me.

She'd tried wriggling, praying the growing mud would give her enough room and lubrication to pull free, but without luck. All she'd managed to do was get wetter and muddier and make pain throb its way up her side.

Then the slab of granite had shifted—in the wrong direction. When it slipped that fraction of an inch closer to the ground, pinning her all the tighter, she'd gotten the message. No more wriggling.

Rain pounded on her coat, deafening in its threat. Fear pounded in her heart, numbing in its certainty.

She could die here. Because of her own stupidity, her own impulsive choices. Because she'd listened to that ever-alluring call for adventure.

And now what? How long would it take a local from St. Agnes to find her? It could be days, if the rain kept up. A week. She'd be dead by then.

And Mamm-wynn would just be sitting at home, staring out the window and worrying the edge of her shawl, that vague look Ollie had described in her eyes as she waited for Beth to come home.

"Don't tarry too long or fly too far, little rosefinch." When, when would she learn to heed her grandmother's warnings?

She might not ever have the chance to heed them again. Nor to see Oliver smiling at her. She—heaven help her—she might not live to see her brother's wedding. And what would that do to Ollie, to lose yet another sibling, another family member to what would look like a freak accident? At a time when he ought to be filled with nothing but joy?

It wasn't fair to him, nor to Mamm-wynn. *Please, God . . .* She didn't know if she was praying for her own salvation or for His mercy for their sakes. Both.

And Sheridan. Her eyes slid shut. What potential lay undiscovered there? She'd only just begun to appreciate his sense of humor. The joy he found in everything. Only just begun to crave his stories. What if she never saw him smile again or heard his laugh tangled up with hers? What if he never again got to offer one of his ridiculously flirtatious comments?

What if she never had the chance to kiss him?

Her fingers curled into the mud, nostrils flaring. She wouldn't cry. She wouldn't. It wouldn't solve anything, and for all she knew it would make things worse—send her more quickly into shock or something. She had to think. There must be an answer. There was always an answer. She could get out of this.

Except this wasn't a matter of being faster or hiding better than her friends. She wasn't strong enough to lift this slab of granite, and that was all there was to it. Her only hope was in the Lord, that He would send someone to—

"Beth?"

For a second, she thought it must be her imagination, her own desperation making her hear one of the voices she most craved. Because there was no other reason for her brother to be calling for her.

"Beth!"

But Sheridan's voice joined Ollie's, and her heart galloped. "Here! Over here! Carefully—a granite slab has fallen on me and pinned me!"

Footsteps joined the pounding of the rain, and a minute later three faces, all equally horrified, appeared above her.

Her brother looked positively fierce. "We'll get you out. We saw a camp. Perhaps there's something there to help."

"Scofield's." She reached a muddy, shaking hand as high as she could. "Be careful—I assume he's gone with the *Naiad*, but he could circle back."

Sheridan shook his head. "We saw the sails vanishing. He's not here. But he was?" His brows crashed down, and the look of doubt slid down his face as ferociously as the rain, even as he eased himself carefully into the pit.

233

Oliver vanished again. "He must have something. I'll be back directly."

She let her hand fall. "I didn't realize it until I'd come. I saw something in one of the letters this morning and wanted to see . . . I was so close on St. Mary's already, so . . . I shouldn't have come. I'm so sorry." The tears she'd managed to hold off a minute ago clogged her throat now.

Stupid, stupid, stupid. The pressure in her chest just made her ribs ache and her limbs feel even weaker.

Sheridan crouched down in the mud beside her and took her muddy hand in his. "It's all right." It wasn't, he surely knew it wasn't. But still his voice soothed her like honey. "We'll get you out of here. That is—Telly! What are you doing? Helping Oliver?"

The lack of response seemed answer enough. Sheridan offered a tight smile. "See there? Between the two of them, I daresay . . . well, they'll find something. And if they don't, I'll lever this off you myself, Atlas style. You'll be very impressed. Begging me to give you a second chance, you know, when you see my inhuman strength."

A laugh tangled up in her tears and choked her. "You're so ridiculous." And what she wouldn't give for a few decades to listen to his absurdity. She held his hand as tightly as she could. "I don't want to die here, Sheridan."

"You won't." His face went as fierce as Oliver's had been. "I swear it." His attention then moved around the pit, no doubt taking in more in a glance than she could in an hour. "Tell me what happened. With Scofield."

She did, briefly, though her teeth chattered a few times during the telling. Sheridan never let go of her hand, nor did he stop sending his gaze over every line of the place. No doubt taking in the stones, guessing at what each one's placement meant to the Druids who carved them and set them here. Probably a burial site.

But not hers. *Please, God.*

When he reached over to the base of the slab that was pinning

234

her, though, her panic ratcheted up again. "No! Don't touch it, it could slip more!"

"I'm not. But . . ." He frowned and poked at something she couldn't see. "He'd dug out around the base of this stone. No reason for him to have done that. I mean—well, unless he *meant* for it to fall."

A trap? But how could he have known she'd even be back?

Never mind. No doubt if she hadn't come on her own, he'd have sent her a message to lure her here. Something to flame her curiosity—or threaten her family. She wouldn't have been fool enough to come *alone* in answer—probably—but her own drive had led her here without the need for his creativity.

"That snake." It was the kindest thing she could think to say about him.

Sheridan rocked back on his heels, frowning. "Does he realize he's dug out the wrong side of the cairn, I wonder?"

She didn't get the chance to answer. Oliver and Telford reappeared, their bright faces telling her they'd found something useful even before they held it up.

"Is that a jack?" Sheridan sounded as incredulous as she felt. "The man comes prepared."

And, therefore, really had no reason at all to leave her here and *"fetch help."* As if she'd needed clarification on that.

But as her brother lowered himself into the hole with that precious hunk of metal, Nigel Scofield's treachery fled her mind entirely.

She wasn't going to die in this pit after all—news that brought the tears back to her eyes.

18

heridan had been sitting in the same position so long that his back and neck screamed at him. He wasn't about to complain, though. Not when he was ninety-eight percent certain that the only reason Mamm-wynn had set up Beth's sickbed down here in the drawing room was so that he could take a shift at her side without bending the rules of propriety. He didn't believe for a moment that it was so that *she* didn't have to go up and down the stairs to tend to her. And he was beyond grateful to have been entrusted with even a sliver of the vigil.

Not that she needed a vigil, per se. She was, praise the Lord God Almighty, in no danger of dying on them. Though by the time they'd gotten her home again, into a hot bath, and then looked over by the doctor, she'd been completely exhausted and had promptly fallen asleep. As she'd remained for the last three hours while he sat here hunched over at her side, praying like he'd never prayed before.

He could have lost her. Had Mamm-wynn not sent them looking before she had any "real" reason to worry . . . had they not decided to follow his hunch and go to Gugh . . . had they chased after the *Naiad* instead of continuing on their route . . . she could have died in that pit. By the time they'd jacked the slab up enough to ease her out from under it, the water had deepened another inch with runoff and rain. Another hour of this pounding torrent, and she'd have drowned.

He could have lost her, and he'd never even had the chance to beg her to beg him for a second chance. To come up with a way to convince her to marry him. *Marry me before one of us gets trapped in a Druid burial chamber, will you?*

Probably not the romantic proposal a girl like her had dreamt of.

Prayers had seemed a better recourse than going over and again in his mind how she'd looked down there, covered in mud, only half visible beneath the granite, desperation on her face. It wasn't a sight he would ever forget—nor a fear that would let go of his heart.

She could have died there, and they wouldn't even have known it for days. And for what? Pirate treasure? It wasn't worth it. Nothing was worth it, no excavation or discovery or expedition.

He'd always known his chosen pursuits came with a few risks. But somehow natural ones—cave-ins or slips or tropical diseases—felt different. But knowing that a *person* had caused this, had done it deliberately, had done it out of greed or spite . . . entirely different. Mr. Scofield was seriously pushing the bounds of Sheridan's cheerful nature just now, igniting all sorts of dreams of burying *him*—figuratively, of course. His reputation. Not *literally.*

Why would anyone think to do it literally? What must be broken in his soul to have left Beth there like that?

Ainsley would probably say he ought to pray for the blighter's soul, if he thought it broken. So, he'd tried to. Experimentally. And discovered within about ten seconds that his furious heart had gone from *"draw him to your truth"* to *"and smite him with a taste of his own medicine."*

He'd have to work on that when his anger had cooled a bit.

For now, he soothed himself by reaching again for her hand where it rested against the cushion of the sofa she slept on. He had no right to take her fingers in his. But she'd held fast to him during the entire jacking procedure and then all through the sail back to Tresco, so he couldn't think she'd mind terribly. That is, she'd clearly just needed something to cling to—and now he needed the same. She wouldn't begrudge him that, would she?

Well, Beth of four weeks ago certainly would have. But Beth of last night, when she'd laughed and smiled at him, wouldn't. Probably.

And the feel of her fingers in his, reassuringly warm and alive, eased a bit of the tension in his chest. Earlier, they'd been frigid. Slick with mud and rain. Now, they were yet again the hands of a lady, with dirt scrubbed out from under nails that were neatly trimmed.

Would it be pressing his luck to lift her hand to his lips and kiss it? Probably. Especially when she wasn't awake to slap him if so. Hardly fair of him. Best to content himself with the liberty already taken and marvel at how small her hand was compared to his. He wasn't exactly a towering giant of a man or anything, but her fingertips barely reached his second knuckle if he aligned the bottoms of their palms.

He'd never really considered himself the nurturing sort—his sisters were so much older, and he'd never taken in every stray dog like Telford pretended he didn't do but *always* did. So why did seeing Beth Tremayne like this, bruised and battered and overcome with exhaustion, make him want to take care of her? Protect her? Champion her? She wasn't the sort who *needed* a champion, generally speaking. She'd proven she could take care of herself.

Still. He wanted to help her achieve her goals. Watch her back, if nothing else. Ward off broken-souled antiquities hunters, at the least.

Not that he'd done a stellar job of scaring Scofield off in the past, the mere thought of which made his nose ache. He scowled down at their fingers. Maybe he should take up that ka-rot-whatever-it-was that Nigel Scofield had mastered, just in case they ever had another encounter like that. Or he could learn something even more impressive. Deadly. Surely there was some fighting method out there that would render one's opponent unconscious by the sheer force of one's will. Or a single finger expertly placed. Or—

"That is the most ferocious scowl I've ever seen you wear." Beth's voice emerged as a whisper, scratchy and faint.

His gaze flew to her face, where her eyes were open to half-mast. Her fingers flexed against his but didn't pull away, so he held them a little more tightly. "Contemplating which new form of combat I should take up to render that snake utterly useless next time we meet. There's probably some ancient Aztec method I could learn. Or Ethiopian—they're fierce warriors, I hear."

Her lips curved up a bit in the corners. "You mean the Druids don't have any methods you could learn?"

"Well, possibly. But I've yet to meet one who could teach me." Now that she was awake and it was fair, he risked raising her hand to his lips and pressing his lips to its back. She didn't slap him—though maybe she was just still too weak and tired. "I wish I'd been there. I would have traded places with you."

She shifted, winced, and settled again. "I wish you'd been there too—though not so that you'd feel as I do now. Just so you could've kept me from running into him again at all."

She didn't wish him to be in pain? They were making great strides of progress. He might as well send an order for wedding invitations to the printer. "I still can't believe there's nothing broken. Though you must be miserable." Her grandmother had reported that her whole side was black with bruising, and the doctor thought it likely a rib or two was cracked, though not broken fully, so far as he could tell through the swelling.

Still. She'd be forced to rest for a week or two, at least, before she could reasonably expect to go out exploring again. And the shadows under her eyes spoke of severe pain.

"Is there anything I can do?" he asked. "To take your mind off the pain? Or relieve it somehow? Fetch some healing waters from Mount Olympus, perhaps? Or, given that I'm really not a pagan, perhaps a relic from some ancient church, guarded by some secret order of the Knights Templar? I know—I'll track down a mystic physician from—"

Her laugh was weak, but it still brought a smile to his heart, especially when she squeezed his fingers. "I don't think such a quest would be of any help. But . . . I would certainly appreciate a distraction. Why don't you tell me about your other adventures? You've been all over the world, haven't you?"

"Well." Stories—those he could give her. He could tell her every story he'd ever lived and make up a few besides, if she needed him to. "Not *all* over. I've yet to make it to the Americas, either North or South. Or Central, for that matter. But I've been all over Europe, especially Scandinavia. Africa—including a memorable trip to Egypt that Ainsley has made me promise we'll not repeat. Not a desert-loving chap, apparently. And India, of course."

"Of course." Her eyes drifted closed again, though a ghost of a smile remained on her lips. "How old were you when you went on your first adventure? And was it a trip designed for exploration and excavation, or was it travel that inspired your interest in archaeology?"

He pulled his chair a few inches closer to the sofa. "Fourteen. And for the purpose. I'd been studying the ancients in school, you see, and an old friend of Abbie's sent a letter saying she would be touring the ruins of Pompeii that summer and invited us along, and we could even take part in some of the ongoing work if we liked."

"And you liked."

"I *so* liked. There's nothing to compare it to, is there?" He looked away from her face for a moment to gaze out the window instead. The garden, the sea beyond it, the world beyond that. "There is so much to discover. So many people who have lived before us and left clues behind about what sort of lives they enjoyed. So many stories of tragedy and victory, love and loss, just waiting to be uncovered. Seeing Pompeii like that—have you? I mean, pictures, at least? Fiorelli's work was absolutely astounding. He realized that some of the voids in the ash were where human bodies had been, so he injected plaster into them. And they *were*. You can see them now, if you go.

These plaster forms of people curled up, defensive. Trying to take cover. Protecting themselves and each other."

He shook his head, though it was a memory he wasn't likely to ever forget. Twelve years later, it was still vivid as daybreak in his mind. "I knew that summer that this was what I wanted to do with my time and resources. Resurrect old stories. Rediscover history. Share that history with the world."

"Find some pirate treasure?" She'd opened her eyes again, and if he wasn't mistaken, it was teasing that lit them.

He shook his head. "A bit of fun, that. To be sure. I mean, who wouldn't be interested in pirate treasure? But it's the discovery I crave, not the gold."

He nearly jumped—largely from joy, though partly from shock—when she ran her thumb over his knuckle. "And the fame? The credit for the discovery?"

He snorted a laugh. "Hardly. Do you know who's sent the world rocking with his discoveries of old Druid sites?"

Her brows arched. "No."

"Exactly. No one does—no one cares that much. And that's all right. It's still worth knowing."

For a long moment, she just looked at him. Steadily, silently. Heavily. Then she shifted again, winced again, and settled back against her pillows with a long, pain-ridden sigh and closed her eyes once more. "Tell me about Pompeii. And then Egypt—and I want details."

A request surely meant to woo him. And it worked. "I'll ask your brother to book the church."

She cracked one eye open. "Pompeii, Sheridan."

"Really? I thought you'd prefer to marry here on Tresco." It earned him a laugh, which brought a grin to his lips. And a story. "All right, all right. So, as I said—it was Abbie's friend who started it all. We had no idea what we were getting into on that first trip. It was Millicent and Abbie, their maids, me, of course—and Ainsley, who had only just been hired. And nearly resigned then and there . . ."

241

———————○———————

Beth had intended to let his stories lure her back into sleep, but they had the opposite effect. Two hours later, she was sitting up straighter and listening with wide eyes as he described how he'd found a way into a Viking tomb in Holland four years ago after spending a week deciphering some runes he'd found nearby. And how, the moment he realized he was indeed inside it, he rushed back out to go and wake the Dutch professor he'd been working with—a professor who was still excavating in that area even now, and was counted as the leading expert on the subject, thanks in part to that discovery.

Sheridan hadn't been kidding when he said he wasn't in it for any glory. He'd made it sound as though the professor was the one who'd done all the deciphering, and all he'd wanted was to bring home a small souvenir from the dig. Which stood in stark contrast to the base motives of fame and fortune that obviously fueled Nigel Scofield.

And watching his face as he recounted the tales of his adventures . . . that was entertainment in itself. He lived his life with a passion she rarely saw in anyone, Scillonian or incomer. A passion she still couldn't quite believe he was willing to let her share.

She wanted to, though. If any lingering doubts had remained before, the simple act of listening to his stories removed them. This was a man she could imagine exploring her way through life beside. A man she knew she could count on to cherish her, who would always treasure the right things. A man who would seek adventure with her in whatever neighborhood they found themselves, here or the Lake District or Antarctica.

"And, really, that's what sparked my interest in the Druids. Especially knowing that they were even more present here on British soil than in Scandinavia. I could start an excavation—well, anytime, really. On school holidays. Any season. Whenever Abbie looked away for a moment. You name it." He chuckled and leaned back in his chair. "Something to be said for that, you know. Convenience, I mean, not dashing away from one's sister the moment her back is turned. Although there's something to *that*, too, at least when one's sister is Abbie."

She could only laugh. Again. Carefully. Even that quiet version kicked up a fire in her ribs, but how could she *not* laugh? Perhaps it had been a bad idea to ask him to tell her stories. She'd had to reclaim her hand an hour ago so she could brace her side as she listened. Which was just as well, because he'd needed his hands to gesture with as he talked, anyway. "Your sisters sound like quite the pair. I'm a bit surprised they didn't follow you here to search for pirate treasure."

"Ah. Well." He cleared his throat in that way he always did. "May not have told them, exactly, what I was up to. What with—well, Libby, you know. They rather liked the idea of a match with her, and they all but kicked me to the drive when Telly said we should come and fetch her home. If they'd known I agreed in large part because I wanted to come and see about the Prince Rupert and Mucknell artifacts . . ." He winced.

She did, too, though hopefully he would think hers was either empathetic or a result of her aches and pains. When really, it was at the reminder that he'd come here because of the engagement Lord Telford had been trying to arrange between Sheridan and Libby.

She'd been thinking she'd like to meet his sisters . . . but they might not be so keen on meeting *her*. If they wanted a bride for their brother like Lady Elizabeth Sinclair, sister of the Earl of Telford, then they certainly wouldn't be happy with Miss Elizabeth Tremayne, nobody from nowhere.

And had someone told her a few weeks ago that she'd be worrying over something like that, she would have laughed in their face. Yet here she sat, wondering if she could convince him to hold her hand again. Wondering what he'd do if she started playing along with his joking references to marrying her. Wondering how she could win his sisters over.

"Well." He slapped his hands on his knees. "You look exhausted. I should let you rest. I suppose. I mean—of course I want you to rest. And recuperate. But I'm also happy to, at any time whatsoever, tell you another story. Or go and fetch you something to eat or drink. Or hire a Sherpa to lead me up a mountain if you decide a quest for some miracle potion is in order after all."

She chuckled again. She probably *should* send him away for something or another and give herself a reprieve from him before she gave in to the urge to start planning their wedding. And now that she paused to consider it, why had no one else come in during all this time? It wasn't exactly proper that they'd been left alone for hours on end. She frowned. "Where is everyone else, anyway?"

"Oh, ah." He lifted his fingers, ticking them off as he said, "Your brother went out to try and hunt down the *Naiad*. Telford went with him—and I think they meant to stop at St. Mary's and let Lady Emily know what happened. See if she or Briggs had any ideas about where Scofield would have gone. Libby and your cousin Mabena dropped in while you were still asleep and said they'd be back to check on you again this evening. And your grandmother . . ." He frowned. "I've no idea. She usually takes a nap after tea, though, so I assume she's resting. Bit much excitement for her, I think. She looked pale as a ghost when she saw the doctor out."

Guilt bit just as deeply as the pain. The last thing she'd wanted was to cause her grandmother any more stress. "Poor Mamm-wynn. Would you see if she's up yet so I can tell her again how sorry I am? And I would love some tea."

"Straightaway." He sprang to his feet. "Tea and Mamm-wynn and—wait, just tea? As in the beverage? Or would you fancy tea, complete with Mrs. Dawe's crumpets? Or cakes. Or whatever she's made for today, I don't frankly know, I couldn't even think to ask at the time. Though now that you mention it—or now that I have, if you only meant the beverage—I could use a bite myself."

And if no one had been there to eat the food Mrs. Dawe would have prepared as her own means of stress relief, then she was likely

244

fit to be tied. Although at least she'd have had Ainsley and Collins and Senara to feed, and hopefully Mamm-wynn ate something as well. "You know, a full tea sounds like just the thing. I've had nothing since breakfast."

"Then a full tea you shall have." With a grin and an exaggerated salute, he spun on his heel and made for the door.

She couldn't have said what it was about the action that tied her heart into a knot. Maybe it was the light in his eyes at having a mission. Maybe it was the shadows that underscored it. Maybe it was the way he strode through her house, perfectly at home as he aimed for the kitchen like a family member instead of the highest-ranking guest they'd ever entertained. Maybe it was the way his shoulders looked as he moved, or—no. It was the mud stains that still stretched across them, from where he'd put shoulder to granite to stabilize the stone while Ollie pulled her out.

He really had been willing to play Atlas for her, if it would help. And since they had returned home, he'd not taken the five minutes to change into fresh clothes. Because he'd been too focused on her, even when she was with the doctor or soaking in a hot tub. Senara had said he'd been pacing the drawing room like a caged lion that whole time, which was what inspired Mamm-wynn to set her up this little sickbed down here instead of in her own room.

"Sheridan. Wait." She pushed herself up a few more inches, heart pounding from her own thoughts more than the effort. Her throat felt tight as he turned back around. She didn't know what she wanted to say, exactly. She could thank him. Or ask him why in the world he was so good to her when she'd been utterly horrid to him at the start.

But he'd already addressed that, hadn't he? She lifted a hand. "What was it you said I'd have to do to convince you to give me another chance?"

For a second, he stood as still as a monolith in the doorway, his face frozen. Then, in the next, he was flying back across the room so fast she feared he meant to leap at her. But no, he just dropped to his knees at her side, and his hands came up to frame her face, his own so close to hers. She could scarcely swallow. He smelled of rain and earth and adventure. "I believe there was begging involved." Her voice sounded strange even to her. Low. Hoarse.

The fault, no doubt, of his eyes and the way they gleamed as his gaze caressed her face. "Only for a decade. And I'm willing to negotiate on that. We can cut it down to five years. Or minutes. Or perhaps, since I'm feeling rather generous, a second or two."

Well, that was only fair. She nodded as much as his hands allowed. "Sheridan. Theo. I am so sor—"

His lips pressed to hers, cutting off the apology.

An interruption that made her blood hum in her veins. She leaned toward him until her ribs and the bandages they were wrapped in protested, resting a hand against his chest and nearly smiling against his mouth when she felt the pounding of his heart beneath her palm.

How was it possible that she had this effect on him?

Regardless, he had a matching one on her. She kissed him back, kissed him again, or let him kiss her again, or . . . it didn't much matter who initiated each new touch of lips. Only that they continued, and her pulse raced in time with his galloping heart, and for a few moments she forgot the pain and the bruises and the questions and the fears.

This. This was the adventure she'd always craved. The feeling she'd always sought. The discovery she'd always longed for.

Her brother had been right, in a way. Finding it wasn't about the *where*—because here they were, in her own drawing room.

It was about the *with whom*.

She hadn't known to ask the question that way. But now she had her answer. All the adventure she'd ever need could be found with him. Theodore Howe, Marquess of Sheridan. Her very own prince.

Well. Close enough, anyway.

19

Sheridan eased shut the door to his room, letting the soft click act as punctuation to his thoughts. Letting it still them. Solidify them.

He'd known the moment he dropped to his knees at Beth's side what he had to do. Well, after kissing her. And kissing her made all other thoughts fly from his head. Then, after he'd eventually convinced himself to break away, he had to go for tea. And enjoy it with her. And then kiss her again before their little bubble of privacy popped into the usual chaos of brothers and best friends and cousins and Dawes and grandmothers.

But after that, there'd been no question at all. Into his room. Over to the little desk against the wall. Into the chair. And out with the paper.

Even so, he stared at the blank page for a long moment before he unscrewed the cap of his fountain pen. Not because he didn't know what he wanted to write, but because there was so much of it, he wasn't exactly sure where to begin.

Well, that wasn't altogether true either. So, he started with the obvious.

Dear Abbie and Millicent. Or Millicent and Abbie. Can't recall whose turn it is to come first, so my apologies if I've mixed it up.

His lips tugged up a bit as he lifted his pen, remembering how serious he'd felt as a lad of eight, away at school for the first time and debating for an eternity over whether it was fair to always put Abbie's name first just because she was eldest, or if Millicent would be offended. He'd explained in that first letter that he would alternate the honor from then on, and their return letter had thanked him most eloquently for his conscientiousness.

They'd probably had a good laugh about it, which he was old enough now to know. Even so. Tradition was tradition, and usually he could keep it straight—but his mind was a bit muddled right now, so they'd just have to forgive him.

> *First, thank you for your quick action on behalf of Ainsley's family—knew you'd come through. You surprised even me by how quickly you replied, though. Thought I'd have to wait at least a day for a return telegram, but it was waiting for me when I got home from . . . an outing today.*
>
> *Are you two bored in London yet? I hope so. Or you know what I mean. Or will. I need you to come to the Isles of Scilly as soon as you can arrange it. Well, after a detour to the castle. And bring all my Rupert artifacts, if you would. You know which ones they are, don't you? Millicent, I know you do, you were there chattering about feathers or fringe or something while I was cataloguing my collection a few months ago. Remember? The catalogue is in the library. Use it as your guide. Everything should fit in a trunk or two.*
>
> *Make sure you don't forget the latest addition—the trinket box.*

He paused to drag in a deep breath. This, of course, was his whole reason for writing a letter to them, rather than just another quick wire of thanks for their help with squiring away Ainsley's family. Perhaps Beth had softened, perhaps she even liked him now, perhaps she'd just helped nudge their relationship into an actual courtship and out of his one-sided imaginings. But she wouldn't be able to fully forgive what had made her detest him at the start until he righted what she saw as his gravest wrong.

He had to return the box to her.

And he didn't mind, not really. It was just a box—interesting, and he'd loved the thought of owning it. But it was nothing compared to her. He'd give her that and anything else she wanted if she'd just look at him again as she had when she asked him for another chance.

He bent over the paper again.

> *The trinket box is on the shelf in my bedroom at the castle, not with the other items in the gallery. Which the catalogue would tell you. Six inches square, three high, has Rupert's crest engraved on the lid, gold-leafed. You know the one. I'd love if you'd bring it yourselves, but if you can't, could you at least send that? But not by post—can't risk damage. You'd have to send a courier.*
>
> *So, really, you might as well come yourselves. Easier that way, and of course I'd love to see you. And you'd love to see the islands. And . . . well. Some bad news. No, not bad. Actually. Good news. Lady Elizabeth is engaged to a local here, the Reverend Mr. Oliver Tremayne. Stand-up chap. I quite like him, and she adores him, and he her.*
>
> *Now, don't start with any of the "poor Theo" nonsense, all right? You know I wasn't . . . that is . . . she's Telly's sister, and a fine young woman, and it would have been an easy thing, but I wasn't attached, exactly. And especially am not now. There's someone else I've met while I've been here, and . . .*

What should he tell them about Beth? *Nothing*, that was what. If he gave them any information, they'd just use it to compose all those arguments Ainsley was sure they'd have, and he did hate arguing with his sisters. Better to let them meet her first and come to like her. Then he'd share his feelings, along with his own carefully constructed arguments for why they should approve of her. Which he'd accomplish best in person, when he could ply them with sweets pilfered from Telford's stash and smile and remind them of what a charming lad he was and how much they adored him.

Some things just didn't belong in a letter.

Just come, will you? And I'd be grateful if you wouldn't dawdle about it. No doubt you have morning calls and balls and soirees and such rot every day of the week, but cancel a few, won't you, for your dearest darlingest little brother? I'll repay you with some pirate treasure hunting. And my eternal gratitude, of course.

Yours,
Theo

There. He gave the ink a minute to dry and then folded the page and slid it into an envelope, doing mental calculations as he scrawled the address of their London house onto the front. Even if they left London directly upon receiving it—which he doubted—it would take them at least a day to travel home. They'd go by train—they'd just had their private car refurnished that spring, after all—but even so. His sisters didn't exactly travel light, which meant they didn't travel fast.

So, a day to home. A day *at* home, packing up his things. He could have asked them *only* for the box, but he wanted to show Beth the rest of the Rupert and Mucknell collection too. Then, another day of train travel to Penzance.

He had at least a week before they'd get here, by his estimation. Possibly more, because despite his wheedling, they probably wouldn't hurry away from London, given that he hadn't said it was an emergency.

For a second, he considered opening the envelope again and saying it was. But that didn't seem like a good idea. Then they'd be in

250

a panic, and when his sisters got in a panic, things got left behind. They'd probably get themselves here in a hurry but not even bother to go home for the box, which would defeat the whole purpose.

Patience was clearly the better course. And before he could change his mind on that, he took the letter to the table in the entryway where outgoing post was left for whomever was going to the village next. Ainsley would take it in the morning when he went for the newspaper, if no one did before.

His valet slipped to his side even now, face somber. "My lord, I didn't want to interrupt you while you were sitting with Miss Tremayne. But if you have a moment, you'll be interested in what my cousin wanted."

Sheridan could hear Mamm-wynn's silver bells of laughter coming from the drawing room where Beth was, so he knew he wouldn't be missed for another minute or two. He nodded. Ainsley briefed him quickly on the conversation from the Gardens and what he'd said.

Sheridan's lips twitched up. "Lying. Tsk-tsk. What would Ainsley say?"

Ainsley slanted him an unamused look. "Feeding someone false information in order to prevent a crime is hardly *lying*."

He had to chuckle. "Stroke of genius, really. Send them off every which way chasing false leads while Beth recovers—not that we knew that part at the time. That she'd have to recover. But God did, clearly. Quite amazing how He's working all this out."

That Ainsley granted with an inclined head. "Perhaps this evening we can work out the details we'd like them to chase." He glanced over his shoulder at the front door, behind which clattering footsteps could be heard approaching. Tremayne and Telly coming back, no doubt.

Sheridan nodded. "I'll be thinking on it."

Ainsley nodded, too, and then opened the door, rain and wind and fellows blowing inside with the dusk. Sheridan grinned. "Weather's still lovely, I see."

Tremayne greeted him with a fleeting smile. "I think I saw the clouds breaking up on the horizon."

Telford snorted. "*I* think he saw his own wishful thinking. But his uncle's big toe predicted an end to the storms, so I'm not permitted to argue." Despite his gruff tone, Telly looked genuinely amused. "We had some success, though." He nodded a thanks to Ainsley, who closed the door behind them again. Who knew he'd make such a fine butler?

"Excellent. You can update us all at once. Mamm-wynn is sitting with Beth." Sheridan had to assume the success wasn't having apprehended and arrested Scofield the Snake or they both would have been far more excited, but even so. He turned toward the drawing room.

And had to rub damp palms over his trouser legs. The doctor hadn't given Beth any mind-and-heart altering medications, had he? To account for her letting him kiss her? He'd still been too foggy-brained to consider that question when he'd rejoined her after their kiss for tea, but now . . . well, she'd had at least fifteen minutes out of his company to come to regret her apology. And she had food in her stomach now. If she'd just been under the influence of opiates and hunger, she might get those visual daggers back out and slice him to ribbons.

But when he stepped into the room, she greeted him with a smile. Not exactly a bright one, but its warmth made up for its tightness. And while it was possible he was imagining things, he was quite sure the light in her eyes shifted, lost a bit of that glow, when she looked from him to her brother and Telford, who came in behind him.

"Did you find the *Naiad*?"

He could hardly blame her for asking about her sloop first and foremost. He'd been sick at the thought of it being stolen from her, even as he also recognized that it would give them an actual crime to pin on Scofield. Boat thieving was an arrestable offense, even for an earl's son.

Oliver nodded. "In the quay at St. Mary's. No harm done to it.

I left it for now, but Jacob and Pat said they'd bring it over on their way out in the morning."

Sheridan didn't know who Jacob and Pat were, but Beth didn't seem to mind the thought of them sailing her sloop. "That's kind of them," she said.

Mamm-wynn laughed. "You know no one ever refuses Ollie a favor."

Very true, so far as he had seen. And it brought another tight smile to Beth's lips. "I do indeed. What of Scofield, then? He didn't go to Emily's flat, did he?"

They both shook their head as they chose chairs. Oliver let out a long sigh. "His first stop was the authorities, where he reported that you'd been in an accident . . . on Annet."

Beth scowled. "Annet?"

"Well, 'that little island to the west of St. Agnes' is what he told them. Gugh, as you know, being to the *east*. A mistake, they called it, when I told them where you really were."

"And he was 'clearly distressed,'" Telford added in a decent imitation of a Cornish accent.

Oliver looked about as convinced of that as Telly had sounded, and as Sheridan felt. "Right. So distressed that he went immediately to the ferry and was gone before we even would have had you home."

Beth gusted out a painful-sounding sigh. "So, it's my word against his when it comes to his intentions. The water in the pit will have washed away the evidence Sheridan saw of obvious digging around the slab—or they'd chalk it up to normal excavation. And he neither stole my boat nor, in the eyes of the authorities, left me for dead. And being so clearly distressed, they'll overlook the fact that he had a jack a few feet away and didn't see fit to get it to help me."

"And no one seems to think anything of the fact that he hired a few chaps to tear down his tent and stow all those supplies either." Telford's nostrils flared in obvious disapproval. "Had the presence of mind for *that*, but no one batted an eye."

253

"But the joke's on him, isn't it? We found you." Oliver moved his smile from Beth to Mamm-wynn to Sheridan. "And I deem that a testament to God's mercy and providence. He kept you from serious harm, whispered in Mamm-wynn's ear before logic would have had any of us worrying, and then inspired Sheridan to know where to go."

Had He?

Well, of course He had. It certainly wasn't his own brilliance that had made him decide Gugh was the most likely destination. Which made new warmth spread all through Sheridan's chest. So far as he could recall, God had never used him in such a way before. But then, he'd never sought Him as earnestly as he had that morning.

Quite a feeling, this. No wonder Ainsley was so devout. Drawing closer to the Lord, being directed by Him, used by Him to help someone else . . . that was quite a feeling. Heady and humbling all at once. To think that they served a God who could and would do such things—and use them to accomplish it.

To think that he could have so easily waved away the impressions and thoughts as foolish.

To think that God had trusted him to listen. To act. To help save this beautiful young woman who had captured his heart so completely.

Yes. Definitely heady and humbling.

"So then. What now?" Beth shifted down a few inches on the sofa, gritting her teeth as she did so.

Which was clearly not lost on her brother. "Now you heal. You take it easy. And . . . we wait. Seeds have been planted, this garden plotted out. We wait to see what grows."

Beth somehow managed to make closing her eyes look like a scowl. "*Waiting*. Not what I was hoping for."

"Waiting like a *gardener*," her brother corrected. "That doesn't mean we're idle. It means we're patient. And that we're clearing weeds and checking soil acidity and guarding against pestilence as we wait. We can't make the plants shoot up faster, but we can certainly prepare the garden for when they do."

Sheridan cleared his throat. "More seeds were planted today than those, actually." He gave them the short version of Ainsley and his cousin, summing up with, "So, we can decide later today where we'd like to send them off chasing a few wild geese. It'll distract them. Give Beth time to heal."

"Perhaps they'd enjoy a trip to Portugal." With a chuckle, Mamm-wynn rose slowly from her chair. She moved into the space between Beth's sofa and Oliver's chair, reaching out a hand to each of them. "Don't fret, my darlings. That young man is chasing after the wind, even without Theo and Henry's distraction. And he doesn't stand a chance—not against my favorites. Speaking of which . . ." She craned her head enough to send Sheridan an arch look. "Where exactly do you intend your sisters to stay, Theo? I'm afraid we don't have any more room here."

He could only open his mouth, no words there for his tongue to lay hold of.

Telford sighed. "You invited your sisters to join us? Really, Sher. You know well they'll take over."

"Well, I . . ." No, still no words. Not intelligible ones. He looked to Beth for some fortification, sure she would understand. Wouldn't she? They had to come, obviously. Meet her. So that he could convince them that she would make a most excellent marchioness.

Yes, she certainly understood. Which was no doubt why panic lit her eyes. Bother.

He directed a playful scowl to Mamm-wynn. "How did you even know that? I've only just written the letter—it's still on the hall table. You wouldn't have even seen it yet."

She only laughed again, that sound of silver and magic, and released her grandchildren's hands so she could come over to him. She patted one cheek and utterly charmed him by leaning down to kiss the other. "You're a good lad, Theo. And your sisters are lovely girls. I do so like you all."

How she could like them when she hadn't even met them, he didn't know. But there was really only one reply he could make. "Thank you, Mamm-wynn. I assure you, the feeling's mutual."

———————○———————

Beth battled her way out of sleep, the pain pulling her from that blessed oblivion like a tugboat. She blinked her eyes open, winced at the bright midmorning light, and tried to sound out her current aches without moving.

It turned out that twenty-four hours after being nearly crushed by a granite slab, one was more aching bruise than sound flesh.

The whisper of shifting fabric drew her gaze to her left, where she fully expected to see an auburn head bent over a book. But the hair was redder, longer, neatly pinned into an elegant style. Beth frowned and tried to push herself more upright. "Em? When did you get here?"

Emily's head jerked up, eyes wide, red, and swollen. "You're awake!" She scooted her chair as close to the sofa as she could get it and reached out to clasp Beth's hand in both of hers. "Oh, Beth. I'm sorry. So, so sorry."

She sounded more than sorry—she sounded more miserable than Beth felt, which inspired her to try to find a smile. "Last I checked, you weren't there pushing that granite down onto me."

"He's my brother." Misery paired with shame now in her voice. "And he tried to *kill* you."

A reality as shocking as it was unprovable. Somehow, even though Beth had gone into hiding because she feared this very thing, she couldn't quite wrap her mind around it. That Nigel Scofield himself—not a hired lackey known for ruthless tactics, like Lorne— had done this. He had plotted, planned, dug out that slab, and lured her into the pit for the express purpose of injuring or killing her.

Even more chilling was the realization that her friend had lived under the same roof as that monster for so many years. Beth squeezed her fingers. "You are not at fault for what he does."

"Am I not? I'm a Scofield. Scofields—"

"Stop. Em." Beth pushed herself up a little more, wincing with the effort. "As long as I've known you, that's been your reason for *everything*. You're a Scofield, and that comes with expectations. With duties. With—"

"Because it does!" Tears pooled in Emily's eyes. "Isn't that what all those stories your mother and brother gathered prove? We cannot escape our families. They shape us and define us. We share a fate."

"Not always." She'd come so close yesterday to following after her parents and Morgan. But God had spared her. And she had to believe that He, being merciful and loving, would spare Emily, too, from the fate her brother was hurtling toward.

Emily shook her head, a sad, slow pendulum. "We've never been like you and your brothers—you know that. I've never . . . I've never *liked* him. And he's certainly never shown me the slightest regard. But he's my brother. And whether neighbor or enemy, I'm supposed to love him. Right? That's what *your* brother said."

Beth's face twisted. "Sounds like Ollie."

Emily's tears spilled out onto her cheeks. Her voice emerged as a strangled whisper. "I don't know how, Beth. When I think of him, of our father, even of Mother—all I feel is this terrible anger. Why have they chosen this path? Why?"

Though Beth opened her mouth, she had no answer to give.

Emily sighed and leaned over until her head rested against their hands. Her tears fell warm and wet against Beth's fingers. Her back trembled. "I have to stop him. I have to. Before he goes so far there's no coming back from it."

"Oh, Em." Beth rested her free hand on Emily's head, like Mother had always done when Beth threw herself in a tearful fit into her lap. Usually over something the boys had done—teased her or pulled her hair or tried to exclude her from a game. Such petty things. Nothing at all compared to her friend's troubles. Morgan and Oliver had always been so easy to love. They'd been her champions. Would she ever have had the strength to spread her wings if she didn't know she had such a rock-solid home to fly back to? "That may be the bravest thing I've ever heard anyone say."

"Brave?" Emily tipped her face up. "I'm not brave. You are."

Beth shook her head. "I may be bold. Sometimes—foolishly—even fearless. But that's not bravery. Bravery is seeing the fearsome thing and standing firm when you want to run." Her chest ached, and not just from the bruising. "That's never been me. I'm the rosefinch—quick to flit away."

"I wish I knew how to fly like you do." Emily gave her a weary smile and sat up straight again. "I'm so glad you came to London that year for school. I don't know where I'd be if I'd never met you."

"Probably not in the Scillies, at war with your brother." All but disowned by her father.

Emily sighed. "Exactly. But I think—or at least I hope—that this is precisely where the Lord wants me to be." She squeezed Beth's fingers and then stood up. "I'll let Mamm-wynn know you're awake."

Beth nodded and let her leave, knowing her friend needed the moment alone to compose herself.

Frankly, Beth could use the moment too. All of a sudden this wasn't about the treasure or besting Nigel Scofield or solving a mystery or even exploring her mother's favorite story.

Beth drew in a long breath and tried to find a comfortable position. She'd begun this journey alone, thought she liked it that way. She'd gone to extremes to try to preserve that and keep everyone else out under the guise of keeping them safe.

But she'd been wrong—and maybe that's what those weeks of solitude had really shown her, as she had no one but the Lord. That it wasn't about what she could do on her own. It never had been.

It was about how much stronger she was in community. With her family, with her friends. With the one who had sparked a fire in her heart. Nothing mattered without them.

If only it hadn't taken such tragedy for her to realize it.

20

| 7 August 1906

S enara refilled the glass of water on the end table, humming the last bars of a ballad as she did. And chuckling when she looked over at her charge and saw Beth's scowl. The drawing room had become Beth's prison over the last week, and she knew well her young friend was ready to burst free of its walls and spread her wings again, even if only to another room of the house.

But she had to admit—to Mam, certainly not to Beth—that it had done her own heart good to have someone to take care of. Organizing them had been interesting, but it had never been that which fueled her. It was caring for *people*. She took a minute to open the windows to the sunny summer breeze and took her seat beside Beth's sofa again with a smile. "There now. Too beautiful a day for you not to enjoy it."

"I'd enjoy it far more if I were out in it." Probably thinking to prove it, Beth pushed herself up and walked with careful steps to the window. "Just for a few minutes?"

Poor thing. She was healing, but her movements were still stiff, and she was clearly sore, though better than she'd been a few days ago. "A morning in the garden does sound like just the thing, doesn't it? Let me fetch our hats and we'll go out."

259

Five minutes later, they were settled on the wrought-iron chairs—Beth's padded with cushions—and Senara had pulled out some mending that she'd offered to do for Mam. "Did Lady Emily mention when she'd come again? Not that you could possibly be tired of *my* company."

Beth laughed, at least. "Tomorrow, I think. She wanted to get caught up with her correspondence today. Not that anyone in her family has responded to a single letter from her, but she won't give up on them."

Senara could only shake her head and jab needle into cloth with a bit more force than necessary. She knew firsthand how some families could be. But it was one thing to dismiss their employees out of hand, without entertaining thoughts of forgiveness. It was another thing entirely for them to treat their own daughter that way. She couldn't fathom it. Here Senara was, having legitimately done something wrong, and her own parents still stood beside her. "I don't understand why they're acting so with her. What's she done, that they're giving her such a silent treatment?"

Beth shook her head, gaze distant. "Chose a side other than her brother's. She tried to tell them that he'd behaved atrociously here last month. That he was involved in Johnnie Rosedew's death and had threatened me. This was their answer—she was grievously mistaken, Nigel is a saint, and until she apologizes to him and patches things up with him . . . Well, I believe their words were something along the lines of, '*It's high time you learn what it means to be a Scofield, and you're not welcome with us again until you do.*'"

It didn't ease Senara's frown any. "The tack they should be taking with *him*. Not *her*."

"Exactly so." With a gusty sigh, Beth leaned forward and snatched from the mending basket an apron whose hem was unraveling. "I'm bored enough to think sewing looks interesting. Where are the needles?"

Senara chuckled and passed her one. Beth had always had a fine hand with sewing, when she bothered with it, but the call of the out of doors had usually been stronger, at least in the days when Senara lived at home. She'd become a bit more domesticated in recent years though, Mam had said. Not that Senara had really seen it this summer, what with all the treasure hunting.

It took only a few minutes of surreptitious glances, though, to see that Beth's childhood skill had increased with age as one would expect. She'd probably stitched a slew of lovely, useless samplers at finishing school. The Clifford girls hadn't yet mastered such skills—but then, they were still so small. Needles looked so awkward in their little hands. And oh, the way Rose had always stuck the tip of her tongue out when she was concentrating on it!

She missed them. She missed them so much. She missed tucking them into their beds and singing lullabies, she missed chasing them around the grounds, she missed looking deep into their eyes as she gave them their instructions for their next visit with their mother and seeing their sweet spirits flashing there.

It struck her down to the bone just now—she'd never see them again. Those precious girls. She'd never get to watch them sew years from now and see how they'd progressed. She'd never get to measure their heights against the doorframe again. She'd never more get to kiss bumped knees or soothe angry tears.

This was the price of sin.

"You could tell me, you know." Beth's voice came softly to her ears, gentle as a breeze and just as inviting. "Why you can't go back. I can see you're missing them."

Senara drew in a long breath and kept her gaze on the patch she was affixing to Tas's trousers. Her instinct was still to protect Beth from such truths, as she'd have done a decade ago. But Beth was a young woman now—a young woman who had been looking in a new way at a young man. A young woman who needed to know, then, what consequences there could be for the choices she made.

Not that she was equating Lord Sheridan with Rory. She couldn't imagine him ever behaving so selfishly. Even so. "I . . . made a poor choice. With a man. And was dismissed for it."

There. She managed to say it with an even voice.

"Oh, Nara." Beth's hand moved into her vision and covered her own. "Was it that Rory chap?"

Her gaze flew up.

And found Beth's face earnest. "There was always something about the way you mentioned him in your letters home."

She sighed out the breath she'd drawn in and looked down again. "I was a fool. I thought he loved me, that we'd marry. I thought . . . I thought he was my path, Beth. That with him I could have a family of my own, that . . ." She let her needle still. Let her eyes slide shut. Reached up and tugged her necklace from under her collar so she could squeeze the key into her palm, as she'd always done when such thoughts troubled her. "It's all I ever wanted, you know. A family of my own. Much as I love the Clifford girls, I'm not their mam. I was just a hired servant dismissed in a moment, despite all the years of love I've poured into them. And now I've squandered it all, ruined it all. Lost my chance for the only thing I ever wanted."

"Oh, Nara." Beth squeezed the hand still in her lap. "Don't give up on the future yet. If the Lord can redeem the mess I made of everything, He can certainly use your failures too."

So easy for her to say, especially when she had a marquess staring at her as if she were the only girl on the planet. A marquess who had made good on his promise to keep Ainsley's family safe. A telegram had come just this morning saying they were settled into their hotel in Paris and having the time of their lives.

He was the sort of man Beth deserved. He'd treat her right, cherish her, take care of what was hers every bit as much as what was his. How did some men seem to know how to do that instinctually, and others never learned it at all? "Maybe I'll just come along with you when you marry. Take care of the passel of children you're sure to have."

When the flush worked its way into Beth's cheeks, it made Senara aware of how pale they'd still been before. "On the one hand, I can't

262

imagine anything more perfect than you at my side to teach me how to be a good mother. But on the other hand, it would entirely defeat my point. Or . . . maybe not." A mischievous little grin stole over her lips. "If ever Sheridan and I—well, a certain valet of his would probably be quite happy if you tagged along."

She could feel the flush in her own cheeks now—turnabout, she supposed. But hers had the sting of shame underscoring it.

A fine man like Ainsley deserved better than her. His utter kindness proved it over and again. She'd expected him to avoid her in the last week, but he hadn't. She couldn't think why he kept smiling at her, speaking gently to her, when he knew well what she'd done. And it wasn't for any foul motives either—not Henry Ainsley.

No. Not Henry Ainsley. "That can't be. He's Rory's cousin, you know."

Beth's fingers stilled. "What? That's an odd coincidence, isn't it?"

"Not as odd as you may think. He only paid attention to me because he realized I had a connection to the Scillies, and hence all this business of yours. He's tried to sell you all out, Beth. He made the Scofields think they were confidants." She squeezed her eyes shut. "He meant to make me help him. Thought I would turn on you, too, for the promise of money and marriage."

She opened her eyes to find Beth gaping at her. Senara sighed. "You see, then, how ugly and convoluted it all is." She lifted her hand again to touch the key on her necklace. "I don't know what my future will hold—but not a family. Not any time soon. Certainly not with him."

Beth's expression went contemplative. "I'm trying to remember the story of your necklace, but it's been so long since you've told it to me. It's old, though, isn't it?"

A happy distraction from the emotions ready to swamp her, and may God bless Beth for the subtle redirection. "So said Mamm-wynn F, when she gave it to me." Her lips turned up as she remembered her grandmother's words. "She told me my life could be anything I made it to be, as long as I remembered that family is the key to it all."

Beth wouldn't even remember Fiona Dawe, though. She'd been naught but a mite when she died. It was a wonder she even remembered there *was* a story to the pendant—she couldn't have been more than six the last time Senara told it to her. "According to my grandmother, the key once belonged to a grand house—that's why it's so pretty. It unlocked something just as beautiful, though she didn't know what. Only that it was first given to some beautiful island lass by her true love, and she passed it to her daughter, and on it came down the line. A reminder that the grandest thing we can ever seek is love. Riches will come and go, be found only to be lost again, but family . . . family stands the test of time."

Beth picked up her needle again but then just sat there holding it, brow creased. "It's odd, isn't it?"

Senara blinked. "What is?"

"That none of your family's stories were in the ones Mother wrote down."

It was, now that she mentioned it. "I suppose that *is* strange."

Beth set the sewing down and looked as though she was about to stand.

Senara stopped her with an upheld hand. "Rest. I'll ask her." It wasn't as though she had to go very far to do so. Mam had the kitchen windows open into the garden, so she only had to cross the flagstone path and get to the right side of it, then step carefully into one of the flower beds that Ollie and Tas both tended. "Mam? Are you in there?"

Her mother's face appeared, looking half amused and half horrified. "Get out of the gladioli, dearover, before your father sees you there. What is it?"

She motioned toward Beth and stepped carefully back out of the bed. "Beth pointed out that in the collection of stories her mother had put down, there were none from our family."

"Oh." Mam's face took on that somber mask that always descended when the talk turned to the late Mr. and Mrs. Tremayne, or to Morgan. She nodded and reached for something. "Give me just a moment and I'll come out."

Senara hurried back over to the garden table and pulled out a third chair, just in time for her mother to join them. She'd brought a pitcher of lemonade and glasses with her, because that was Mam. She couldn't ever arrive empty-handed. It made Senara smile.

Beth, too, as she accepted a glass. "I was just thinking a taste of your lemonade would be perfect. Thank you."

"Oh, it's no trouble. Now, your mother's stories." Mam poured herself a glass and took a sip from it. "We'd always *meant* to take the time. But it seemed foolish to set up an official one, as she did with everyone else. Why bother, when we could just sit down of an evening and chat? We'd made mention of doing it countless times through that winter, but we never quite got to it. Then you were due home from finishing school, Beth, and Master Oliver from university, and . . . well, she put the whole project aside for a while to get everything ready for you both, and then there you were, home again. The whole family together. I'd heard her and Morgan whispering about the project again, though, just a few days before the storm. And I said how we ought to make it a point to have our time soon too. But then your father got that note from Truro Hall, and they had to make the trip to the mainland, and we decided it could wait. Again."

When her mother's face went tight like that, Senara could all but see it playing out again before her eyes. She'd have been worried when the storm kicked up unexpectedly—it was her way. She'd have looked out every window, as if answers would come. Praying. Waiting for those bullying clouds to break up and speed away.

Mam traced a finger around the edge of her glass, teasing a mournful note from it. "That storm—you weren't here, Senara, and I don't know that I ever had the stomach for telling you about it, after. But it was horrible and took us all by surprise. Even

Jeremiah Moon hadn't felt it coming, and you know that's saying something. We tried to tell one another they'd have made it to the mainland before it hit, that they were well enough ahead of it. We tried to tell ourselves they were perfectly well, and that we'd have a telegram from them any minute, assuring us of it. They always sent word as soon as they got there, always. Morgan would fret otherwise."

Beth swallowed, her gaze just as unfocused as Mam's. "But no word came. And no word and no word. Night fell. We thought they must've just forgot—that it was a difficult crossing, and it took them too long, and by the time they reached shore, they were tired. That it slipped their minds."

Mam lifted her eyes, brimming with tears and aimed straight at Beth. "If I could turn back the clock, that's the day I'd go back to. I'd do something, say something to keep them at home."

"I know." Beth scooted slowly to the edge of her chair and reached over to grip Mam's hand now, as she'd done Senara's a moment before. "We all would."

The rest of the tragedy Senara had pieced together years ago. When the Tremaynes didn't arrive at Truro Hall by the next morning, another telegram had come here for them, asking after them. That was when the family had known their worst fears had come true. It was simply made fact when one of the fishermen found their sloop adrift out at sea and towed it back. No sign of either of the Tremaynes within it.

Every islander in the Scillies with a boat had gone out looking, as they always did when someone vanished like that. But they never found them.

Senara shivered. It was one thing she'd never missed about island life. Every place had its dangers, true enough, but the sea . . . it could snatch life just as quickly and just as easily as it provided for it. Swallowing those who loved it best. "I'm so sorry I wasn't here and couldn't come for the funeral." She'd tried, but the Cliffords had never been exactly generous with allowing time off, and as it wasn't her own mother who had died, they'd refused her plea. And little Paulette had just been born. They'd needed her.

But so had her family here.

"Anyway." Mam sniffed and dabbed at her eyes with one of the linen napkins she'd brought out. "Morgan asked me, once, if we wanted to sit down with him and tell our tales. We were some of the only ones around who hadn't done so. But . . . well, none of us really had the heart. Even him. Especially him. And really, what stories would we have to add that hadn't already been told? They'd spoken to my cousin already. And to your aunt Nancy."

Senara touched her pendant again. "No one told the story of the key."

Her mother pursed her lips. "I suppose no one thought of it. Mother Fiona had been the one to have it for all those years, and you weren't home to remind anyone it even existed. She was gone by then, of course."

Beth sucked in a breath and looked from one of them to the other. "Would you tell me? Now? I want . . . I want to finish their work—Mother's and Morgan's. And the tales of the isles aren't complete without the Dawes' stories."

"Well." Mam smiled, banishing her tears with another sniff. "We'd be happy to. If you think it's worth your time, with all else that's going on."

Beth had the strangest look on her face as she glanced over at Senara's necklace again. "I think it's worth it. And more . . . what do you think the chances are that the Dawes and the Gibsons have a common ancestor?"

Both Senara and her mother lifted their brows as Mam said, "All but guaranteed, I'd say, on an island the size of Tresco. Why?"

"Because that key, supposedly from a noble house—well, none of the other stories involved any noblemen. None but *ours*, with the trinket box. Makes me wonder if perhaps your however-many-greats grandmother who passed down the key was a sister of the one who passed down the box."

Senara laughed at that. "Don't be silly, Beth. Not that I doubt we share a relative somewhere along the way, but I've heard your theories about that box. And I can't possibly believe . . ." She couldn't even say it, it was so ridiculous.

But Beth had no such qualms, as her grin attested. "That we may both be descended from a prince?"

21

"This counts, you know."

Beth looked up from the book of parish records she'd dug out again, failing utterly at tamping down her grin when she saw Sheridan had made himself comfortable on the library's leather sofa, much as he'd done that night when she'd come down here in the middle of the night and found him reading.

That felt like an eternity ago, made all the longer by wondering if he'd kiss her again. Which he hadn't done, though that could well be because Senara had been taking her chaperoning and nursing duties *far* too seriously.

They were alone now, though, here in the library on this Monday afternoon. Now that Oliver had run back over to St. Nicholas's to look for a record book they seemed to be missing in the stack they already had here.

"What counts?"

"This. Poring over old documents together. As a date." He grinned at her over the top of his book. "That's what modern couples do, you know. They go on dates. As part of their courtship. Alone together, out on the town. Only we haven't much town to go to. And a drive isn't exactly necessary around here. But we've gone for a sail, so that was our first date."

She laughed. She couldn't help it. "You mean the one where I 'accidentally' tossed you into the sea?"

He waved that off. "I choose to remember it as the one where I gallantly rushed to your defense when you were apprehended by the snake."

"Ah yes. That one." She made a note of what she'd just read before she forgot it and then rested her chin in her hand, grateful she could make the simple move now without wincing in pain. She'd begun to think her ribs were never going to stop complaining, but these last two days she'd felt nearly herself again.

And she'd certainly been enjoying looking at him, even if they'd not had any time alone together until now. He really was a handsome man. How had she failed to focus on that at the start? Frustration with him had absolutely blinded her. Though even then, she'd noted the power of that grin of his. The one he gave her now, which had her insides positively melting.

"And then there was the midnight library date. Not exactly pre-arranged, I grant you, but even so. Nothing more romantic than a library by lamplight, is there?"

"When the conversation is about rats? Absolutely not." How long would Ollie be gone? Probably at least twenty minutes, and he'd only just left.

Sheridan chuckled. "Perhaps that one could even be termed a tryst. That's a critical part of courtship in some cultures, you know. Ancient Sparta, for example—a couple was expected to steal out at night to meet. They recognized that the feeling of secrecy was, well, exciting. Even when it was approved. So that's what they would do. Meet in secret, I mean."

"Fascinating." She pushed her chair back and stood. If he put his feet down, there'd be plenty of room on that sofa for her too. "And what about sickbed vigils? Is that a critical part of courtship in any culture? Perhaps fabricating an illness or injury when one doesn't occur naturally?"

His gaze tracked her as she came closer, and his feet hit the floor, freeing up that cushion beside him. "Ah. Well. Not that I've yet learned about. Per se. Though Mrs. Bennet certainly recognized the power of such a thing, didn't she? Hence the ploy to make Jane walk in the rain. To Bingley, I mean."

It was the second time she could remember him referencing *Pride and Prejudice*, which was downright hilarious. She'd never have taken him for the sort to read romantic novels. Usually, he had his nose in the driest history texts to be found in their library. "And Mrs. Bennet's tactics are *certainly* ones we should all emulate."

"Well now, we needn't go that far. But still, the sickbed vigil most assuredly counts." He reached for her hand and, when she moved to sit beside him, tugged her toward him instead, so that she landed on his lap.

A squeal slipped out, more of surprise than protest, though it soon turned to laughter when his grin went mischievous.

"And this, lady fair, most definitely counts too. Even if the library isn't lamplit."

His right arm supported her back, his left came around her waist, anchoring her, and he could probably hear the way her heart crashed against her chest, but that was all right. She could hear his too. She did her best to keep her smile serene. "Studying historical records together is the *most* romantic date of all."

"Obviously. And even if some troglodytes disagree, no one can argue that a meeting involving a kiss is anything but a true milestone of courtship."

She felt as though she might just fly to pieces. "Kissing? I seem to have missed that part. I could swear we've only been reading and taking notes."

"Ah, well. Patience, you know. That's the next phase of my brilliant plan, now that I've got rid of your brother." He wiggled his brows.

Hers shot up. Then, as she caught sight of the edges of paper sticking out from behind his cushion, laughter bubbled up again. "Devious man, aren't you? I *thought* we'd already brought that book over."

"Desperate times. I've been trying for days to get you alone again, but . . ." He trailed off, frowning. "It wasn't on purpose, was it? I mean—you weren't making sure to keep others around? To avoid this—me? If so, I—"

"Sheridan." She set a finger on his lips to silence him. And then leaned close, gaze locked with his. "Back on topic, please. I believe we were discussing a kiss."

The blaze of uncertainty settled back down into his previous amusement. "Right. But, you see, I'm not just a man of words. I believe fully in the need for field research. So, less talk, as they say."

And more kissing. She met his lips with her own, grateful that this time she could lift her arm without pain and settle her hand on his cheek. Send her fingers into the light auburn of his hair. Hold him there just a moment more when he made as if to pull away.

"Definitely, definitely counts," he whispered a moment later, as he trailed his nose over her cheek.

Gracious. "Well, if you're set on adding dates, I think we need to schedule a few more. A walk after supper, perhaps, in the Abbey Gardens." He feathered a kiss over her jaw and made her breath catch. "And now that I'm feeling better, another sail—and I promise not to send you overboard. Probably."

"Mm." His lips trailed down to her chin. "You can if you want. I'll just take it as a declaration of your undying affection."

"You would. Incorrigible man." Praise God he was that, and patient enough that he hadn't turned and fled in those first few weeks.

"Well, I—"

Footsteps in the hall cut him off and brought a scowl to his brow. She slid to the cushion at his side, the racing of her heart shifting a little. A man's step, without question. Was Oliver back already?

No. Telford had finally deigned to join the land of the awake and entered with a teacup in one hand and a telegram in the other. "Did you see this, Sher?" He didn't even glance over at them.

"I haven't seen anything today. I was busy plotting. Which you've ruined, thank you very much."

That brought Telford's gaze up. His lips twitched upon spotting them, no doubt well able to imagine what they'd been up to. "I may not be sorry about that, but I'm certainly sorry about this." He held up the yellow slip of paper and then held it out. "They'll be leaving Sheridan Castle tomorrow."

His sisters. Beth's stomach turned to a rock, and she eased away a few more inches. Sheridan had received a letter a few days ago saying they'd be coming, but they'd offered no definite date. And Beth had let herself think that maybe they'd get distracted and go somewhere else instead.

Because she had only to remember all the sneers she'd received from the aristocracy while she was at finishing school to know that, happy as the marquess was to steal kisses and talk about courtship, his sisters weren't likely to approve of a match between him and an island girl.

An indisputable fact that didn't seem to faze Sheridan at all. He took the telegram with a smile. "Oh, good! I was beginning to think they'd never come."

Was the look Telford sent her commiserating, or was she imagining it? "Still not sure why you invited them, old boy."

"Had to."

"Did you?" She didn't really mean to say it. It just slipped out. Probably the fault of the acrobats doing flips in her stomach. Obviously if this was really a courtship and it progressed, then she'd have to meet his sisters at some point. But did it have to be so soon?

And obviously Sheridan knew exactly what she feared. He took her hand, lifted it, and kissed her knuckles like he'd done the day of the accident, as she'd taken to calling it. "I did. For you. You'll see."

Would she? Because right now it didn't seem like he'd given any thought at all to how she would feel about the invitation. Yet the way he was looking at her . . . clearly he believed it was for her benefit. Somehow.

Telford sank into his usual armchair. "Well, if it puts your mind at ease any, Miss Tremayne, you can at least tell them that we've all but proven you're the descendant of a prince, which puts you in the heiress category, even if your inheritance has been lost over the centuries." He offered a cheeky grin. "I intend to break out that argument if Mother gives me any guff for not objecting to Libby and your brother."

Her gaze drifted back to the table, fully covered with papers and books and records. Other than on Sunday, she'd spent the last several days tracing out a family tree for both the Gibsons and the Dawes, and Saturday night she had found the linchpin to her theory—a single common ancestor, yes, two hundred years ago. The Gibson line traced back to a woman named Morgelyn, and the Dawes to her sister, Jenna. The two children of—she could still scarcely believe this—Ruperta, daughter of Briallen—who had no father listed.

But *Ruperta*. The very name that, more than a decade after their Ruperta's birth, Prince Rupert's mistress gave to their illegitimate daughter, who went on to marry a Howe, thereby guaranteeing Sheridan's interest. *Ruperta*. Clearly a feminine form of Rupert. Which was *not* a variation of Robert otherwise present in Cornwall or the Scillies.

"It doesn't make me heiress to anything but a good story. And it isn't proof that anyone's likely to accept, besides." It seemed the reasonable thing to tell herself, because really, who would honestly care that her many-times-great-grandmother had secretly married a prince?

"I don't know why not. If one cares so much about bloodlines, I mean. Which I always thought was rot. For the record." Sheridan winced. "I mean, not that I mean to insinuate that you ought to be defensive about bloodlines, because—ah, blast. You know what I mean, don't you? I adore your family, prince in its line or not. And you're an heiress of the only thing that matters—an amazing family. That's worth treasuring."

She squeezed his fingers. A month ago, she probably would have tried to turn it into an insult. But she *did* know what he meant.

"I adore them too—both sides. And I've still been thinking about Senara's key." A far happier thing to contemplate than what witty insults Sheridan's sisters were likely to devise for her. "I find it quite plausible that it dates back to Jenna. To Ruperta. To Briallen. It could have been something Rupert left with her. It could be a literal key to a chest of pirate treasure."

"It could just as easily be the key to the loo." Telford hooked his ankle onto his knee. And held up a hand just as Sheridan opened his mouth. "I know, sorry. Cynical of me. And unlikely to boot, as I daresay no one put a fancy lock on their outhouse. But seriously. Even if it *is* the key to an actual treasure chest, I don't see why it's cause for excitement. If it's a literal wooden chest that's been literally buried as you two seem to think, then I daresay a key won't be necessary. The thing would have rotted by now anyway, just like the crate of silverware you dragged up last month."

He had a point. Which was another dash of cold water. She'd had quite a fun time dreaming about unearthing a pirate chest and brandishing Senara's key to unlock it. She leaned close to Sheridan again and said in a stage whisper, "Is he always such a killjoy?"

"Yes," Sheridan said without hesitation, even as Telford slammed his foot back to the floor and said, "I am not!" Then frowned at his friend. "Am I? I'm only trying to be reasonable."

"Well, but that's the thing, Telly. Reason is greatly overrated." With a conciliatory look on his face, Sheridan snatched up a ball of discarded paper from the floor and lobbed it at Telford's head.

Telford snatched it from the air. And smiled.

Men were such odd creatures sometimes. And it was going to take her a lot more than a month to learn the language these two spoke, if ever she had a hope of doing so.

She let herself sink against the back of the couch, ignoring the lingering twinge in her ribs at that move. "Regardless of whether we'll need the physical key, it's still too strange to be a coincidence, isn't it? That in one branch of Briallen's line a key has been passed down, in another a box that was unquestionably from Prince Rupert, and that his associate Mucknell kept using the phrase '*the key to your future*' in letters to his wife?"

"But the key wasn't left to Elizabeth Mucknell." Telford held up both hands, this time, against their dual glares. "Well, it wasn't!"

"Even so. Rupert could have known where Mucknell stashed some of his loot. He even could have slipped the key to a chest from him sometime and given it to his own bride. A sort of insurance policy, if you will, in case he never came back."

"Or came back too late." Sheridan ran his thumb over hers. Another something those records had shown them. Briallen's death, a mere week after the record of Ruperta's birth. "Do you think he knew? About his daughter?"

Sheridan shook his head. "Not a chance. If he had, he would have come for her. Raised her as his own, as he did the other Ruperta. The stories, you know—about how he loved her. My Ruperta, I mean—well, you know. The one who married a Howe. He doted on her, boasted of her childhood accomplishments to all his friends. He was a good father, despite never marrying her mother. He'd have been the same with *this* Ruperta, if he knew of her."

"Well, I don't understand why no one would have told him, especially if they told him of Briallen's death." Telford tossed the paper straight up, caught it again. "One would think her remaining family would have wanted her to have what he could give her."

"Don't be so sure, my lord." Beth stood when noise from outside worked its way into her hearing and moved over to the window. Sure enough, Mabena and Libby and Lady Emily were laughing their way up the walk. She turned back to face the gentlemen. "Island life may look dismal to incomers. Deprived. Harsh. But those who stay here do so because the islands are part of them. I can't imagine my family or neighbors ever making a choice that they knew would send their children away from here forever. From their point of view, Ruperta was *theirs*. A daughter of the Scillies, like Briallen was. They loved her, and so they kept her with them, probably knowing well that society would never have accepted her fully."

Sheridan stood, too, and pulled the hidden record book out of the cushion, probably so he could return it with an apology to Ollie when he got home. "They could have given society a bit more credit. I mean, because they did. Accept his other daughter."

Sometimes he was just adorably naïve. "Oh, Theo. Just because they let her into their balls and dinners and a decent man married her doesn't mean she wasn't parrying catty comments about her mother every day of her life. Not to mention that while actresses were scandalous, they were also the accepted mistresses of rich men, who frequently acknowledged those offspring. An island nobody would have been quite a different thing."

"You can't know that."

And sometimes he was just frustrating. "I think you mean that I know it better than anyone! That year I was in London at finishing school—it was miserable. I was no worse off than plenty of other girls there, but you have no idea the things they said to me. Just because my mother wasn't a gentleman's daughter. Just because we live here instead of on the mainland."

"Then why have you been so determined to go back?"

She jumped at Oliver's voice from behind her. He stood outside in the front garden, on the other side of the window. When had he gotten back? She hadn't seen him coming up the walk with the girls. And the girls weren't there with him now, either, though she could hear them coming along the corridor.

He had that dark gaze of his set fast. Looking, as always, so much like Mother. And so *serious* as he tried to understand her. She sighed. "Because I didn't think there was anything left to find in the Scillies, Ollie. I didn't fall in love with any of the local boys like all my friends here did, and it didn't seem likely that my own prince would ever come to the islands. I imagined I'd have to find him myself."

"Ha. Well, as Ainsley would say . . ." Sheridan slid to her side and slipped a bold arm around her waist. "You ought to have had a bit of faith."

Her cheeks felt hot as the sun itself. He'd been so restrained the last several days, she'd rather thought it was because he hadn't wanted to give anything away to her brother quite yet. But here he was, all but announcing their relationship to everyone.

And no one looked the least bit surprised. Oliver, in fact, just snorted a laugh. "That she should have. Well, I'm coming in. Didn't find the book, though."

"Oh. Right, that. Sorry. Found it here after all. Buried, you know."

Oliver didn't examine it too closely, though whether it was because he was just in a hurry to come inside with Libby or he thought it a reasonable explanation she didn't know.

Nor did she think about it overlong. When she faced the newly arrived girls again, she noted at once what she hadn't when they were outside. All the laughter was from Mabena and Libby. Emily kept herself a step behind and was, just now, seemingly trying to melt into a bookcase. She looked pale, her eyes downcast.

"There you are, Darling." Libby had crouched down to set her basket on the floor and flipped the latch that held the top down. It was all the invitation her little tabby kitten needed to poke his head up and then leap out. With a happy meow, he rubbed against Libby's ankles for a second and then ran straight for Telford.

"There you are." Telford chuckled as Darling leaped onto his lap and stretched up to bump his head into his chin. "I missed you too. I keep telling Oliver he needs to get a dog to keep me company when you're not here, but he won't listen."

Beth shook her head. Oliver had always loved dogs, and they'd had several over the years. If he wasn't listening, it was likely just for the point of it. Telford had been a bit of a bore when he first arrived, after all.

But *she* had to determine how best to get over to Emily and get her to tell her what was wrong, not get dragged into a conversation about the merits of a puppy. Emily would never breathe a word about what was bothering her in company, though. Not unless no one was paying attention to them.

So then. A distraction. And the yellow paper still sitting on the arm of the sofa provided just the one she needed. "Sheridan received word that his sisters will be here in two days." She lifted her brows and turned to him. "Have you addressed Mamm-wynn's rather cogent point of last week?"

He blinked at her.

She motioned to the house. "They need a place to stay. And as we have already well established, all the holiday cottages and hotels are booked for the summer, and we're already bursting at the seams."

His face screwed up. "Right. That."

As she'd expected would happen, everyone had an opinion or suggestion, and while they talked them over, she slid away from Sheridan and skirted the table, gave a hello squeeze to Mabena's elbow and a grin to Libby, and then worked her way to Emily's side.

"Oh, but I don't mind at all!" Libby was saying. "I love staying here on Tresco with the Moons. Your sisters are welcome to stay in my cottage as long as they like. Only . . . well, I don't know that they *would* like. It's rather basic, and they're . . . not."

Laughter rang out from Sheridan, Telford, Libby, and Mabena— the ones who clearly knew the Howe sisters.

Those acrobats in her stomach took up a new routine. All sorts of gentry and nobility took their holidays on St. Mary's in the cottages outfitted for the purpose. What made these two less likely to enjoy it than all the others?

She rather dreaded finding out.

But that wasn't the point. Emily. She tucked herself close to her friend's side and leaned close. "I didn't see Briggs with you. Did she not come?"

Emily's nostrils flared. "She'll follow later. The Wights are touring the Gardens this afternoon and offered to bring her. She had letters to answer."

"You've had news."

Still, Emily didn't look up. Just to the side. "No. *She* has had news. That Nigel had been back in London after that trip to Portugal chasing Sheridan's false leads, and the house has been a veritable flurry of activity ever since."

"Oh, Em." She leaned in until their shoulders touched, unable to imagine how it felt to be completely ignored by her own family. To have to hear from her maid what her own parents and brother were doing. "I'm so sorry they're acting this way."

Emily squeezed her eyes shut and then, when she opened them again, fastened on a smile that was trying too hard. Or not hard enough. "Well. I can't really worry with that right now. We have bigger considerations." The false smile slipped away. "They report that something big is happening, though they don't know exactly what. Only that my family has been running around like mad, and they've been told to prepare the house for a special guest."

"What? Who?"

Emily shook her head. "They don't know. My parents just keep calling him 'the American.'"

The American. Beth let her breath hiss out. "The same one who owns the *Victoria*, do you think? Who would bid against Sheridan for anything I found of Mucknell's?"

"I imagine. I don't know what other American it could be."

She sighed and looked back toward the others. No one was going to like this. Not one little bit.

22

Sheridan settled into his usual seat in the library with a long exhale. They'd spent the morning on St. Martin's after the Wednesday gig race—him and Beth and Oliver and Libby—bird-watching and walking the coast. Telly, of course, hadn't had the least desire to get out of bed early enough to join them. And Sheridan hadn't tried too hard to convince him, truth be told. It was rather nice, an outing with just the four of them. Especially since Libby and Oliver had been so focused on the birds and each other that they hadn't even noticed when he and Beth had kept on walking. Hand in hand.

He might manage to wipe the grin from his face. Eventually.

She actually liked him. She laughed in all the right places and joked back just as she should. He caught her looking at him at odd moments. And though she'd flushed beautifully on Monday when he all but called himself her Prince Charming, she hadn't argued, then or later.

He'd convince her. And not even just eventually. Soon, perhaps. He'd land on the right way to propose one of these days, and she might possibly accept.

But before that . . . there was the issue of Abbie and Millicent. Which was why he hadn't invited himself along when Telford said he was walking to the sweets shop after luncheon, nor had he joined the ladies and Oliver in the garden.

His sisters would be arriving on St. Mary's on the last ferry today. The Peppers would greet them and see them to the cottage they'd let to Libby—and would be catering for them for the duration of their stay, because neither Abbie nor Millicent nor their maids knew the first thing about cooking—and then tomorrow morning, someone here would go and fetch them to Tresco.

They'd all offered—Mabena Moon, Oliver, Beth. But he hadn't decided yet who the wisest choice would be. Oliver had quite a knack for putting people at ease, but he'd also "stolen" Libby from Sheridan, which they might not be too quick to forgive. Mabena they could likely ignore, given that they'd still look on her as a servant . . . except she didn't look much like a lady's maid anymore, and that could put them on their guard.

And Beth was out of the question, obviously. No way he wanted them to meet her before he had a chance to talk with them.

Hence the list he'd been working on last night. He dug the notebook out and unscrewed the cap from his pen. Even looking over what he'd already written made him smile.

She's the most amazing girl in the world. You'll see.

She loves to explore.

She can survive in harsh situations. She first spent a solitary week on an uninhabited island as a child, with her parents' blessing, and repeated the adventure this summer. She would make an excellent addition to my expeditions.

She wants to see the world.

She has a heart for adventure and can find it everywhere.

She actually enjoys it when I talk about the Druids.

No, really. She does. I've seen the fascination in her eyes.

I am not imagining it.

She has a keen sense of humor and enjoys mine.

I'm quite serious. Stop laughing.

She has a kind and caring heart. Every time she goes to another of the islands, she returns with a small token for her grandmother—a shell or a piece of sea glass or a beautiful feather.

Speaking of her grandmother, she has the sweetest one in the world, and I think you'll soon want to claim Mamm-wynn as your own, just as I do.

She comes from a wonderful family. The Tremaynes have an estate in Cornwall, and Mamm-wynn is the daughter of a viscount's second son. See? Excellent bloodlines, if that matters to you. Her brother is vicar here on Tresco, a post he kept even after he inherited the estate. You won't have to wonder why after you've met him. He is a true minister of souls.

She is a woman of deep faith.

She is quite likely descended from Prince Rupert! (Telly told me this one should clinch it.)

She's beautiful. I know it's shallow of me to list it, but I can't help it. From the moment I first saw her, I've just wanted to go on staring. Even though Telly says she's only a normal sort of pretty. I completely disagree. She's the most beautiful woman ever to live.

That was as far as he'd gotten last night, because the next words that had wanted to spring forth from his pen wouldn't do at all.

I love her.

It was true. And they'd know it just from the other items on the list. But it didn't seem right to simply write it down and read it off to them. He ought to tell Beth first, after all. And not tell his sisters in some studied way.

But he'd thought up a few more items in the meantime, so he added those now.

She's intelligent—can't believe I didn't mention that one earlier. You'll note it right away.

She's strong. In spirit, but not only. I know you're always sticklers for fitness in a young lady, and she has a reputation on the island for being able to outrun anyone. I haven't seen it myself yet, but that's just because she doesn't run away from me. Anymore, I mean.

She's an expert sailor. I know how you admire such skill.

She can even navigate without visual aids, just with a compass and watch, true Nathaniel Bowditch style. See the item about her intelligence.

She is bursting with life. Imagine the vivacity she could bring to the castle.

Which naturally got him imagining her in his ancestral home, strolling about poking at the suits of armor and making jokes with him about how he'd soon have to add another wing to expand the gallery if he didn't slow down his collecting. Then imagining the laughter of children ringing through the halls. He'd never really bothered imagining such a future before. But the old stones could do with a bit of new mirth to soak up, couldn't they?

Well, blast. Now he was back to wanting to write down that he loved her. He tossed the pen onto the table before it could betray him and leaned back. No, standing. Standing was better. He followed the course of his pen to the table, pacing around it simply for something to do. Given her distraction with taking care of Beth, Miss Dawe hadn't been quite on top of keeping everything tidy in here. Which was just as well, since he would have pulled it all back out every evening anyway. He loved nothing better than the quiet hour or two he took in here after the house was asleep.

Well, that was a lie. He loved even more that time Beth had joined him. Maybe, now that she was healed and looking herself again, she'd repeat it. Another tryst to add to their courtship.

A gust of wind tore through the open window, inspiring him to spin toward it and pull the sash down. A bit too late, though. The rustling of papers all throughout the room told him he had a mess on his hands already.

The downside, he supposed, of leaving everything out when no one was using it.

Hopefully nothing had been blown out of place too much. He turned again to make sure of it.

And nearly stepped on a stray page right away. A folded one. He bent to pick it up, realizing in an instant that it wasn't one he'd seen before. It was in Beth's hand, but not arranged in the form of an outline like most of her notes were. Perhaps it had come from the book that had blown open on the floor.

He scooped it up, too, so he could close it. *Treasure Island.*

Ah! Fascinating. The stolen copy, no doubt, that she'd written in. He very nearly opened it back up. Had to dig his teeth into his lip to stop himself. Curiosity had to give way here, though. The last thing he wanted to do was make Beth angry at this point in time, over something so trivial.

He slid the book onto the shelf beside her favorite chair and then glanced at the paper. *Had* it been in the book? If so, he ought to refold it and slip it back inside. But it could just as easily have blown from somewhere else. How was he to know?

He glanced at the first line, just to get an idea of what it was.

Once upon a time, in the islands called Scilly, lived a girl called Elizabeth, who everyone called Beth. Brought up on the sea and the granite and the isles, Beth sought adventure above all. And she found it. First by exploring every rock and rill of her island home. And then, when the call of romance grew loud in her ears, she turned her sights toward the mainland. But no true love awaited her there, and so home she came once more.

Well now. Unable to control his smile—and not honestly trying—he leaned against the wall. She'd written herself a fairy tale. He ought to add *She's utterly charming* to his list next. He read on, thoroughly enchanted by her lyrical prose.

Then, one day, this island lass found a treasure map hidden away in her grandfather's house, once the home of a pirate king. "Could it be?" said she. "The long-lost treasure of Mucknell the Menace?" Knowing not whether she dare to hope, she remembered her dearest friend from her years at school—sweet Emily, whose father was of great renown. "A trustee is he," thought Beth to herself, "of the greatest museum in all the land. If it be true, he will know, and if false, he shall advise."

And so off she sent her map to grand old London Town, where the earl of renown declared, "By Jove! Follow this map, dear girl, and it'll lead you to the pirate's hoard! And anything you find, you may send my way. For I have a friend who will pay you well."

Visions of Seasons swimming in her head, fair Beth set out to unlock the secrets of the map. But wanting to keep her family from thinking her foolish, she convinced her brother, Good Vicar Oliver, to let her spend the summer on the next island over, so in secrecy she might search.

Little did she know that this friend of the earl was none other than the Nefarious Marquess of SheriDoom. And when he heard that pirate treasure could be found in the isles, in he sent his henchman with vile intent.

"Sheridan? What are you reading!"

It was panic more than question, which drew his gaze up in time to see Beth flying through the room, eyes wide. She snatched the sheet from his hands.

He let her. "Wind blew. Papers went everywhere, I all but stepped on it."

"I assumed the wind had made a mess, that's why I came in, I . . ." She was looking at him with horror. Absolute horror. "It isn't—I wrote this ages ago. When we first met."

"That's your excuse?" He lifted his brows and slung his hands into his pockets. "The Nefarious Marquess of SheriDoom? Really?"

Though she'd been out all day in the sun and had come home with pink cheeks, they washed pale now. She clutched the paper like it was a life preserver in a raging sea. "I was angry. You know I was angry."

His pockets wouldn't do after all. He pulled his hands free and folded his arms over his chest instead. "I don't care how angry you were. Some things—well, they're just beyond the pale."

"I didn't honestly think you a villain!" She winced, like she'd been doing last week when her ribs hurt. Except he knew those had healed. "Well, perhaps I did, briefly. Or wanted to. But I couldn't think it for long."

"You thought I was a villain?" Now his arms fell stupidly to his side. "An actual villain?"

Her expression twisted. "Well . . ."

"And the best name you could come up with was *the Nefarious Marquess of SheriDoom*?" He shook his head, nearly ruining his performance with a grin. "Really, Beth. I expect better from you. It doesn't even alliterate. Shouldn't I have been the Shadowy Sheri-Doom? Or Shifty? Shameless? Sh . . . piteful?"

She let her arms fall to her sides, too, and her face cleared right up. All the way into relief. Or perhaps annoyance. Hard to tell, sometimes. "You think it's funny."

"You could have even done the double *D*, for that Doom part— that was a nice stroke, really. Dastardly SheriDoom has a nice ring to it. Devilish. Demented." He struck the most demented pose he could think of, baring his teeth and raising his hands like claws, but it didn't seem to strike any fear into her heart.

She laughed. Or maybe growled. And slapped him in the arm. "I thought you were upset!"

"I am! With your complete lack of imagination in my villain name. I mean, how many people get one of those? And SheriDoom itself I do quite like. We just need a better adjective. Don't worry, darling, I'll help you come up with one."

With a roll of her eyes—which he was all but certain was meant to hide a grin—she spun to the table and tucked the page under a stack of others. "No thank you."

"Oh, it's easy. Though not, perhaps, as easy as finding an alliteration for *Beth*." While her back was to him, he seized his chance and boxed her in, a hand on each of the chairs that flanked her. "Beautiful Beth. Bold Beth. Brave Beth." He pressed a kiss to that spot that was already one of his favorites, there where jaw met neck just below her ear.

"You're ridiculous." But she was smiling now. No denying it.

"Beaming. Bewitching." He moved his hands to her waist and kissed his way down her neck. "Though occasionally belligerent."

She laughed and wiggled out of his arms. "I'm insulted."

About as much as he'd been with SheriDoom. His lips twitched as he stepped her way again. Though she retreated a step, sparkling eyes locked on his. "Brash. Brilliant. Bodacious."

Another laugh as she backed away. "Just stop."

"Bossy." The grin won possession of his mouth.

With a totally unconvincing huff, she made a dash for the door. Though either everyone had been lying when they said how fast she was, or she didn't truly mean to get away, because he caught her in two steps and swung her around. "Bellicose!"

Though he was laughing then, too, as he put her back on her feet and pulled her close. "And the absolute, without a doubt, *best*."

Her hands settled on his chest. "You're really not upset? About the story?"

Surely she could tell that from his grin. But just to make sure, he leaned down and kissed her. "I love your story. You can write me as a villain any time you please. Or a hero. Or a sidekick. Or an amusing puppy, I don't care, so long as you're thinking of me enough to put me in there."

One of her hands moved up and rested against his cheek. "I find I'm always thinking of you these days," she whispered.

Well, if she was fishing for another kiss, he was happy to oblige her. Though when he pulled away a minute later, that same urgency found his tongue that had threatened his pen. And this time he couldn't think of a good reason to fight it back. "I love you, Beth." Well, *now* he could think of a few. Too soon, she hadn't been in love with him as long as he had her—assuming she even was, which he shouldn't. Liking him—kissing him—was a far cry from love. Or could be.

He'd probably scared her off with those four little words.

But she kissed him again. Probably to shut him up.

Only then she whispered, "I love you too," and he was pretty sure his heart would just give out then and there.

He rested his forehead against hers. "Are you sure? Because,

288

well—I could have just worn you down. You know, *Northanger Abbey* style. It could be more that you like the idea of me being in love with you, which you obviously knew I was."

He could listen to that low laugh of hers for eternity and never grow bored of it. "I thought I was supposed to fall in love with you for your house, *Pride and Prejudice* style. Or perhaps you have a few other Austen references to draw out?"

"Not at the moment. Give me some time, though. It's been a while since my sisters read the others aloud."

"Well." She kissed the tip of his nose. "No need. It's not the idea of your love that's won me, Theo. Or your castle, though I'm certain it's lovely. It's just . . . *you*."

Him. As it should be. And yet . . . He lifted his head, narrowed his eyes. "Are you sure no love potions were involved? Those wear off, you know, and usually come with some nasty consequences. Just ask poor Tristan."

She lifted her brows. "Because I fell in love with you so very quickly? Don't be silly. If anyone drank a love potion, it was you. You're the one who's been tripping all over himself since we met."

She had a point. And that cheered him right up, since he could be fairly certain no one had slipped anything into his tea that day she came home. The only one he'd expect it of was Mamm-wynn, and she'd been unconscious at the time. "Very true. No potions even then. Which leaves a simple miracle. That you, Beautiful Bold Beth the Best, care for me, the absent-a-good-adjective SheriDoom."

With a happy little sigh that made him smile, she rested her head on his shoulder and wrapped her arms around him. "How could I do anything but?"

She'd done a fine job of it those first few weeks. But he decided not to remind her of that again just now. Better by far just to hold her close. And marvel.

23

It had seemed like a brilliant idea that morning as she sipped a solitary cup of tea and nibbled on a piece of toast. It seemed a bit less of one now as she stood before the cottage door.

Beth indulged in a moment of utter nerves, smoothing a hand down the skirt of her dress and trying to imagine exactly how unruly her hair was under the brim of her hat. She had to look a fright. Such was the way of things after the sail from Tresco to St. Mary's. Why hadn't she thought of that before she decided she'd just remove the question from Sheridan and come to get his sisters herself?

Because, she had to admit, all she'd been concerned with was his quite obvious hesitation when she'd offered. A hesitation that had done the same thing to her that disapproval had always done at finishing school—made her straighten her spine, lift her chin, and determine to show the whole world what she was made of. Sisters of the Marquess of Sheridan included.

Only now did she pause to remember that she was made of island gumption rather than London breeding, of last Season's fashions, and of windblown ease. There was no way these ladies were going to be impressed with her. Which Sheridan clearly knew, hence why he'd said last night that Mabena was probably the best choice of ferry operator.

Oh, why had she gone this morning to tell Mabena to stay at home and leave this trip to her? Her cousin had shot her a dubious look even as she relented—because Mabena was a wise girl, and a caring one, and clearly she'd known this was a bad idea too.

But it was done now. She couldn't exactly come all this way and *not* announce herself and take them home.

Dear Lord . . . She didn't know quite what to pray, so she breathed out a long sigh and gave herself another moment to consider it. *You know better than I do what's at stake here. I want them to like me—if not this very moment, then soon. I want them to accept me. I want them to realize that I'll do whatever it takes to make them proud and do honor to the Sheridan name. To see that I would do anything, absolutely anything for him. He's so amazing, Father, all I ever wanted and yet nothing I thought I wanted. He's . . .*

She shook herself. If anyone knew Sheridan's virtues and endearing features, it was God. He didn't need her to enumerate them for Him. Though standing here listing each thing she'd come to love about him would be far more fun than knocking on the door.

"Chin up, Beth," she muttered to herself. "Shoulders back. Smile with grace. You can do this."

She lifted her hand to knock. And then jumped back with a gasp when it opened before her knuckles could connect with wood and a somewhat familiar male back greeted her vision. "Mr. Pepper?"

A grunt was her answer as her former landlord backed out of the door, followed by a trunk that must be quite heavy, given the continued grunting and the shuffling of his feet. And then his son-in-law emerged, arms around the trunk's other end and strain upon his face. "What's he got in here, anyhow? Rocks?"

From somewhere inside the cottage, a cultured female voice answered, "Don't be silly. We didn't touch his rock collection. It's merely cannonballs you're feeling."

Mr. Pepper grunted. And then cast a glance Beth's way. "Ah. The *Naiad*, then?"

For a split second, Beth could only gape. Sheridan hadn't mentioned

291

that it wasn't just his sisters who were coming. What had he done, instructed them to bring his entire collection of Rupert artifacts?

As if she needed to ask. *Of course* he had instructed them to bring his entire collection of Rupert artifacts. She nodded. "That's right. Are you quite all right to be carrying that, Mr. Pepper? Your back—"

"Is fine enough for a moment. We've a cart there behind you."

So they did. She hadn't even noticed the handcart as she'd walked toward the cottage that had briefly been her own, so distracted had she been with worry over whether the Howe sisters would dismiss her in a single glance.

Still. Mr. Pepper wasn't as young as he used to be. "Can I help you in any way? Steady the cart, perhaps?"

Kindness peeked through the strain in his eyes. "Good of you, Miss Elizabeth. But nay. Don't want to go soiling that pretty frock of yours."

A woman filled the doorway the moment Mr. Pepper's son-in-law left it, though she was clearly not a Howe. She wore the high-necked grey dress, prim and plain, that declared her a lady's maid. And her eyes looked absolutely exhausted as they turned to Beth. "Who might you be, if you'll pardon my asking?"

It took Beth a moment to place the accent. Yorkshire, perhaps? Somewhere to the north. They didn't hear too many of those down here at the southernmost edge of England. She found it far easier to smile at the maid than she'd anticipating doing for the ladies and dipped a quick curtsy. "Miss Elizabeth Tremayne. The marquess has been staying with my family—I've come to bring his sisters to Tresco."

"Brilliant. They've been champing at the bit." Rather than either invite Beth in or close her out, the woman stepped aside, opening the door wide. "Miss Tremayne has arrived to take you to Tresco, my ladies."

In her mind, she'd come up with what she deemed a reasonable image of Sheridan's sisters. She knew the younger was in her late thirties, the elder having just turned forty. She knew they were both unmarried, and that they'd raised Sheridan themselves after their parents died when he was four. She knew that they frequently traveled with him on his expeditions. And so it had seemed likely that they'd look a bit like him but be showing their age. That they'd emerge from her holiday cottage—or rather, Libby's holiday cottage, now—dressed in field-worthy clothing. Perhaps they'd be a bit plump. Or too wiry. Matronly.

Her expectations, however, couldn't have been more wrong. The only thing she'd gotten even close to right was that they looked a bit like him.

The two women who stepped into the lane could have been stepping out of the pages of *Vogue*. They were . . . well, they were stunning, both of them. Had she not known their ages, she would have thought them thirty at the most. Beautiful faces, largely untouched by lines. But saturated with elegance. Their dresses were the absolute pinnacle of fashion—one was a soft aqua shade with the most exquisite embroidery Beth had ever seen, the other a bold red-and-white stripe that drew the eye directly to the lady's enviable figure. They both had glossy hair in shades close to Sheridan's, though it was a shade darker on the taller of the two, the one in aqua. She couldn't tell who was the elder.

She dipped another curtsy, a bit longer this time, and told herself not to run a self-conscious hand over her own dress again. It was perfectly fine. Pretty, even. And something like what these two wore would have been completely useless aboard the *Naiad*. She'd never be able to man the sails in either of those dresses.

The shorter one in red dipped her knees in response. "How do you do, Miss Tremayne? So kind of you to come for us. I'm Lady Millicent Howe, and this is my sister—"

"Lady Abbie Howe," the owner of the name interrupted, offering a smile and a curtsy of her own. She then patted her leg, and a pug trotted over to her side, tongue lolling. The maid held out a leather leash, which the lady casually wrapped around her hand.

"How do you do?" Beth had no trouble calling a smile to her lips. Something about their voices put her at ease just a bit.

"A bit aghast, truth be told." Lady Millicent cast a look over her shoulder, into the cottage, and gave an exaggerated shiver. "It's like living in one of Theo's tents."

"But without our chef, who usually travels with us." Lady Abbie speared the cottage with a glare of her own and then took another step away from it, her dog following. "Not that we're impugning the islands themselves, of course, Miss Tremayne."

"Absolutely not! They're quite beautiful. What we've seen of them."

"Which is precious little." Lady Abbie offered Beth a smile just as sweet, and just as mischievous, as Sheridan was wont to do. "I don't suppose this trip to Tresco includes a bit of a tour, does it?"

"Not that we need to get off the boat, mind you. We'd just like to see what can be seen from its decks."

"Exactly."

Her attention had been bouncing from one sister to the other. When they actually paused to await a response, she found herself grinning. "I would be absolutely delighted to show you about the islands—from the sea this time, but if you spot anything you'd like to examine on land, say the word and I'll take you back another day."

"Perfect." As if in punctuation, Lady Millicent snapped her parasol open. "Now then. Lead the way to the quay, my dear girl. I'm afraid I paid too little attention to the path last evening."

"We were far too busy taking in the view of the sea every time it appeared. Absolutely stunning."

"The waters are so blue! It's like being in the Caribbean."

Lady Abbie chuckled. "I was rather hoping Theo's search for Mucknell and Rupert would take us there soon. But you know, this is just as lovely, and so much closer to home."

"I do see why it's become a popular holiday spot. Mostly." Lady Millicent cast one more nose-wrinkled glare over her shoulder at the cottage. "Though the cottages *do* leave something to be desired. What are the hotels like, Miss Tremayne?"

"Other than booked solid at this point, she means."

Gracious, having a conversation with these two was a bit like watching a tennis match.

Luckily, Beth had always quite enjoyed the sport. "Charming, though probably not up to London standards. Though I daresay you'll find them to be on par with some of the places along the Mediterranean that Lord Sheridan mentioned you've enjoyed."

"Perhaps we should have Boynton see about rooms in the autumn. Or perhaps the spring." Millicent lifted her brows and hooked an arm through Beth's. "I hear the Scillies are enchanting in the spring. Flowers abloom everywhere."

Beth nodded. "A prettier sight you're unlikely to find outside of the tulip fields in Holland."

"Excellent." Abbie gave a decisive nod of her own. "We ought to plan to holiday here for Easter."

"Assuming Theo wants to return then."

"Or rather," Abbie corrected her sister, "you mean if he can be pried away in the meantime."

The sisters shared a laugh. Beth smiled, but otherwise her pounding heart muted her mirth a bit. These ladies might not be quite so eager to joke about Sheridan's staying here for a while if they realized she was part of his reasoning.

Millicent's mirth faded, too, and she sent a frown Beth's way. "Just a moment. Is Lady Elizabeth Sinclair where we'll be going?"

Abbie huffed. "I certainly hope so. I've been looking forward to giving that girl a piece of my mind. She clearly has no sense at all, to refuse dear Theo as she's done."

"Abbie!" Millicent blinked at her. "It's Miss Tremayne's brother she's engaged to now. Isn't that right, dear?"

Beth nodded. And said a quick, silent prayer for wisdom in how to discuss the subject of her soon-to-be sister-in-law with these ladies who were put out with her. Not that Abbie gave her a chance to speak on the matter.

"And no doubt Mr. Tremayne is as wonderful a chap as Theo

says—but even so, it wasn't right of Lady Elizabeth to run away from our brother as if he had the plague. They would have been a perfect match! She the sister of an earl, and his best friend. And Lady Telford and I had such grand plans for a winter wedding."

"That's hardly the only thing that matters." The words were out of Beth's mouth before she could think to stop them. And the interjection somehow—perhaps miraculously—managed to silence the sisters. Beth lifted her chin a few degrees. "With all due respect, Lady Abbie, Libby and Sheridan can scarcely tolerate each other. Is that really what you'd wish for your brother? A match that looks perfect in the society pages but results in a marriage in which he and his wife are always at cross-purposes? They both deserve better than that."

The buildings of Hugh Town were crowding around them now, but the Howe ladies weren't looking at the charming shops or the other tourists. No, they were both staring at her as if she were a particularly daring gown illustrated in their fashion magazine—interesting, but perhaps a bit scandalous.

Millicent gave her parasol a little twirl. "I suppose you'll say Lady Elizabeth has found that 'better' with your brother."

"She has." No room for debate on that, as she'd be happy to proclaim to absolutely anyone. "She's found a place for herself in the islands—she's flourishing here, and everyone adores her. She and Oliver complement and complete each other. I think you'll agree within minutes of seeing them. And Sheridan deserves the same, doesn't he? Someone who appreciates him for all of who he is, including the things about which he's so passionate."

"He certainly does." Abbie let out a breath that crossed a huff with a sigh. "I'm sure you're right, dear. Lady Elizabeth *looked* like a perfect match on the surface, but how many times have we mourned her lack of fashion sense, Millicent?"

The younger sister laughed. "And the girl hasn't the gumption to ever squeak a protest when you start lecturing her on it either."

Beth shook her head. "She's learned a bit of that since she's been here too. Though she is certainly a seeker of peace—a quality I appreciate."

Abbie granted it with a tilt of her head. Or dismissed it, Beth couldn't be certain which. "She is a peculiar girl. You ought to see the . . . the *apparatus* in her bedroom at the cottage!"

Beth blinked at her for a moment before realization dawned and came with a laugh. "You mean her microscope?"

Abbie waved a hand. "Whatever it's called. It looks positively dreadful with all those knobs and mirrors and tubes and trays."

"Well, it helped us locate a bit of pirate treasure last month, so don't be surprised if your brother decides he must have one for himself."

Millicent chuckled now too. "I see you've come to know Theo well. Tell me, Miss Tremayne—you've seen clearly that Lady Elizabeth doesn't fully appreciate him, but what do *you* think of our brother?"

She could only hope her face didn't go all dreamy, as Senara and Em both joked happened every time she thought of him lately. "I think there's no other person in the world quite like him." She looked from one sister to the other, noting not only the characteristics that were obvious to the eye, but what she was sure Ollie would have seen, were he here. "And I think he was very blessed to have sisters like you. It was an amazingly selfless thing you chose to do, putting your own lives on hold to raise him."

She had assumed before meeting them that these spinster sisters had probably always been destined to remain single, but that assumption—a rather ridiculous one for her to have made in general—flew to pieces upon meeting them. They were all the things society best loved: blue-blooded, wealthy, beautiful, fashionable. They could have had their pick of matches, if their parents' deaths hadn't interrupted what would have been their first Seasons.

Millicent smiled. Abbie sniffed. "There are those who say we ruined him."

"Then they're fools."

"Oh, I like this one, Millicent." Abbie winked at her sister around Beth. "You're obviously a young lady of taste. Which we knew the moment we saw you. All elegance and ease, isn't she?"

"I do love that color." Millicent brushed an appreciative hand over the pale blue of Beth's sleeve. "In general, but most especially on you, my dear. You've the complexion for it."

"And the lacework of this shawl!" Abbie touched a finger to the heather blue wrap that was folded over Beth's arm. Out on the water, the early morning air had made it a welcome addition, but once she'd been walking about on land, she hadn't needed it.

Though even glancing down at it made her smile. "Thank you. My grandmother made it. She has a true talent for knitting lace."

"It's stunning. Where did she find the pattern? I do a bit of knitting myself, though I've never attempted anything so intricate."

"Oh, she creates her own patterns. Each of her pieces is unique."

Abbie's eyes went wide. "That makes it even more stunning. I'm an absolute dunce about that sort of thing. I can follow a pattern, but if it requires creativity, I am guaranteed to make a mess of it."

They were walking through the heart of the village now, so Beth decided she may as well start playing tour guide, pointing out the Polmers' bakery, the hat shop above which Lady Emily was currently staying, and a few other shops she thought might interest them. They nodded along, interjected a mild exclamation now and then, but Beth found it interesting—and endearing—that their loudest exclamation was over the *Naiad* when they saw Mr. Pepper loading the trunk onto it.

"Oh, that is the most beautiful sloop I've ever seen! It's yours, dear?"

Beth nodded to Millicent's question, unable to keep from smiling. "Isn't she lovely? My uncle crafted her, and a matching one for his daughter, named the *Mermaid*."

"I see talent runs in your family. You uncle is a true artist." Millicent stepped over to view the sloop from a different angle, then turned bright eyes on her sister. "You know what Theo should do?"

"Commission one for our lake at home. I completely agree. We'll have to recommend it to him."

What a family these three were. Beth chuckled as she stooped down to pick up a shell with a lovely pattern of pink and white that Mamm-wynn would appreciate. "You're too late. He already has." She gave the pug a pet while she was on its level and then stood again, saying, when Abbie gave the shell in her hand an odd look, "Oh, for my grandmother. I always bring her a little something back whenever I'm away from her. Just a silly tradition."

Abbie's face moved into an expression that Beth didn't quite know the name for. "How absolutely lovely."

"Oh!" Millicent came back over to them, brows furrowed. "Did you get the note to George written, Abbie? Did we need to visit the telegraph office before we go to Tresco?"

"I left it with Payne. She said she'd walk there directly after we'd gone."

"Good. We all know Theo wouldn't have thought to write to him, don't we?"

Beth had no idea who George was or why Sheridan should have written to him, but she had no trouble believing he'd have forgotten a letter to someone in the face of pirate prince lore and Druid cairns abounding. She smiled as she tucked the shell into her pocket. "Well, ladies. I think our tour ought to start with Peninnis Head, visible there at the mouth of the sound. They say it's . . ."

24

What the devil was taking Beth so blasted long? Sheridan reached one end of the Tremaynes' back garden and spun so he could pace to the other. Again. Beth was mad, that's what. A raving lunatic, to willfully go around them as she'd done and put herself in the cross fire of his sisters.

Didn't she have a shred of fear in her? She should know better. Abbie and Millicent were not to be treated lightly, and the grim look on Ainsley's face when he heard that Beth had gone off at the crack of dawn to bring them here from St. Mary's had shouted that truth just as clearly as the knot in his own stomach.

He loved his sisters. He'd be happy to see them. But he knew better than anyone how overbearing they could be. And didn't Libby all but cower in a corner when they were in the same room? They could be terrifying. And while Beth no doubt could hold her own, she shouldn't have to, not so soon. Not until after he'd had a chance to present his list to them and convince them of how perfect she was.

"I don't believe I've ever met a young lady as strong-willed and headstrong as Beth Tremayne," he muttered to the roses.

From the table, Oliver chuckled behind his newspaper. "You knew that before you didn't propose to her."

He grunted and turned back to the thatch anchor in the corner of the garden. Practical thing, that, though he'd rather hoped when he first spotted them all over the islands that they had more interesting stories to tell. Like the Betrothal Stone in the Abbey Gardens—in many ways a scaled-up version of these small granite slabs—with its history dating back to the Druids. "And perhaps I admire it about her. In general. But I do hate the thought of her and my sisters butting heads without anyone else there to smooth things over."

The newspaper rustled. "Are you saying you don't trust that my sister's charms are sufficient to win your sisters over as quickly as they won you?"

"Well now." That wasn't quite fair, was it?

"Or is it your sisters' fair-mindedness and good taste that you're doubting?"

He winced. If ever they heard their taste being called into question . . . "Neither. Or both. That is . . . see here, Tremayne, it's fear. It doesn't have to be logical, does it? And Ainsley is quite certain that I have a fight on my hands. I mean, I know they'll *like* her. I just don't know if they'll *approve* of her. Like Telly, you know. With you. At first, I mean. You had to prove yourself, and I don't want Beth to have to do the same so soon."

Oliver just chuckled again. "We can walk to the quay if you'd like. Rather than wearing a new path through the garden."

"No, no. They said they'd meet me here." If they'd wanted him to meet their boat, they would have said so. No, for whatever reason, they didn't.

Perhaps because they intended to take a blighted eternity to get here and didn't want him waiting hours for them. He made another pivot and aimed himself toward the colorful daisies that were Beth's favorites. "Probably have her taking them round the coast of every island, you know. Telling them all the local lore. They'll have her out all day. Can never get enough of touring new locales, those two. Always eager to see one more place instead of taking a minute to examine the previous in any detail." It always took forever to drag them to the actual site they were aiming at.

Maddening.

"Well, Beth certainly shines when sharing the local lore. I imagine she'll dust off all Tas-gwyn Gibson's best tales for them."

His lips couldn't help but tug up at the thought. They'd definitely like her, especially after a storytelling tour. But what if hearing all the local tradition from her lips made them think her all the more "just" an island girl?

But it would be all right. He had his list, which he'd expanded still more last night. He'd included rebuttals to every single argument Ainsley had said they were likely to make. And given Abbie's penchant for organization and Millicent's merciless focus on solving every problem under the sun, real or imagined, they ought to be so impressed by the effort he'd made that . . . that . . . well, come to think of it, being impressed with his effort didn't guarantee they'd be won over by the arguments themselves. Which were sound, but even so.

Sometimes when they got protective of him, sound arguments weren't really their specialty.

He turned again, just in time to see Mamm-wynn easing through the door. He rushed to her side so he could steady her and help her to a chair. Her chuckle said she didn't need the help, but he would give it anyway. Sometimes she tottered a bit on uneven parts of the path. Other days she walked all the way to the Abbey Gardens and back, it was true, but he didn't know which sort of day this was yet.

"Thank you, dearovim." She clutched two neatly rolled bundles of yarn to her chest, setting them on the table after she settled into the chair beside her grandson. "They'll be coming up the path about now, I think. Go round and bring them back here, Theo."

He didn't need to be told twice. And sure enough, the moment he rounded the corner of the house, he saw his three favorite women coming under the trellis. They were laughing together, which was surely a good sign and not a warning to brace himself for how much harder the blow would strike if their admiration turned to scorn upon realizing he intended Beth to be the next marchioness.

"There you are!"

They all looked his way, not a one of them seeming the least bit chastised by the clear note of frustration in his tone. Beth led them off the path and toward him.

He made himself keep scowling. "I say. I expected you hours ago—"

"Well, that was silly of you." Abbie reached up as she drew near and patted him on the cheek. "You know we like to see a place in its entirety before we settle into one destination."

"Or as much of its entirety as we reasonably can." Millicent stretched up to kiss him on the cheek opposite the one Abbie had patted. "What lovely islands, Theo! It's no wonder you're content to spend the summer here."

"Well, I—"

"Though we ought to be put out you waited so long to invite us." Abbie slid her hand around his elbow and tugged him after Beth, who was still walking round the house. Though she was shooting a grin at them over her shoulder. "Trying to keep it all to yourself?"

"Of course not. That is—"

"Perhaps he knew how we'd complain about those holiday cottages." Millicent laughed and took his other arm. "Really, dearest, they're minuscule! I wasn't certain at first if there would even be indoor facilities, though praise the Lord there are."

"Well, they are designed for tourists. That is, just not—"

"I suppose we're not your average . . . what is it the Cornish call us again, Beth dear?"

Beth turned, walking backward. Still grinning like Alice's Cheshire cat. "Incomers."

"Right." Abbie nodded. "And we are most certainly incomers, and perhaps exacting ones. But we do also have a reputation for appreciating the true beauty of each place we visit. Isn't that so, Millicent?"

"Absolutely. And so, tiny cottages notwithstanding, brother dearest, you ought to have invited us to join you sooner." Millicent gave him a playful—mostly—slap on the arm.

He sighed. And looked behind them. "Where's the—"

"The trunk? Oh, some local fellow offered to bring it up for us. Beth called him En-something." Abbie gave a small tug on the leash when her pug stopped too long to sniff at the flower bed. "Don't worry, she assured us he's responsible and wouldn't make off with all your pirate loot."

"Actually, I believe she said he'd term it junk and was more likely to toss it into the sea than try to steal it." Millicent chuckled. "We told him it was fragile, part of your collection, but didn't mention what it contained."

Sheridan blinked his way through all the information. "Ah. Enyon?"

"Oh, that's right," Abbie said with a nod. "I do love the Cornish names. They have such a ring to them, don't they?"

He'd never really given them much thought. "Enyon is Oliver's—"

"Best friend, we know. That's what Beth said."

Beth had vanished around the back corner of the house, but it took them only a few steps and one more pull of the leash to join her and her family in the back garden.

"Oh, how beautiful." Millicent let go of his arm in favor of stepping closer to the climbing roses and leaning in for a long whiff.

Beth was grinning at him from behind Mamm-wynn at the table, and Oliver had stood. Beth set her gaze on his sisters. "My ladies, allow me to make introductions. This is my brother, the Reverend Mr. Oliver Tremayne of Truro Hall, and this is our grandmother, Mrs. Adelle Tremayne."

As how-do-you-dos were exchanged, Mamm-wynn stood, holding out both hands to his sisters, who had the good grace to step forward and each take one. She smiled up at them with perfect delight.

"How lovely that you could join us. I do believe I knew your great-grandfather in my childhood."

Well, that was news to him. While Sheridan frowned at Oliver, who shrugged, his sisters made questioning exclamations. Mamm-wynn, chuckling, motioned them to take seats and sank back into her own. "I just pieced it together this morning as I was contemplating your names. You see, my father and your great-grandfather were good friends, and my older cousin Millicent was the marquess's first wife. She died within a year of marriage, poor thing. But the next marchioness had been a friend of hers, and when they wed some years after Millie's death, she insisted upon naming one of their daughters Millicent. That would be your great-aunt, I believe?"

Millicent looked astounded. But she nodded. "We have a portrait of Great-Grandfather's first wife in the gallery, haven't we, Abbie?"

"A beautiful young lady. And your cousin, you say!" Abbie smiled. "I am constantly amazed at how small our world is. Theo, why are you just standing there? Pull out a chair for Beth." She leaned close to Mamm-wynn across the table. "I promise you, we taught the boy manners."

Now that he considered it, Telford might have had a point about them taking over everything the moment they arrived. And though he shot an amused-and-annoyed glance at Oliver for commiseration, his new friend couldn't offer quite the same amount of it as his old. He only grinned.

Sheridan pulled out a chair and presented it to Beth with a flourish.

She gave him the absolute prettiest smile as she sat. "Why, thank you, my lord."

He took the chair beside her and leaned close enough to whisper, "What in blazes took you so long? Where did you take them?"

They were still talking to Mamm-wynn about the original Millicent and Great-Grandmother Lucille, so they didn't hear him. Luckily.

Beth kept her gaze on them. Perhaps to make sure they didn't look their way—she was, after all, clever enough to realize they'd steal the conversation if they heard it happening. "Everywhere but

the eastern isles. Around St. Agnes and Gugh, then Annet, which
meant we passed Samson on our way here, so I showed them where
I'd been staying and how I hid the *Naiad* while I was there."

A huff of protest slipped out. "You've never shown *me* that."

Now she looked at him, with light dancing in her storm-grey
eyes. "Well, they aren't nefarious marquesses with vile-intentioned
henchmen."

"Dastardly. I prefer dastardly. And I'm fresh out of henchmen.
Unless one counts Ainsley. Which one really can't do, you know. He
absolutely refuses to hench." He would have liked to lean in for a
kiss—how could he not, when she was looking all sunny and full
of life and smiling at him like that, after first treating his sisters to
a morning of sightseeing and storytelling? She'd made their day,
no question.

She chuckled. "No, one certainly can't. And perhaps, my lord,
if you behave yourself . . . perhaps I'll show you sometime soon."

"I'm free tomorrow."

She lifted her brows and then glanced toward his sisters. "Are
you certain about that?"

Well, now that she mentioned it . . .

The pug let out a short bark, his curly tail wagging furiously. He'd
stationed himself at the door, his leash dragging along the flagstone.

Abbie breathed a laugh. "Do pardon Lancelot, madame. He must
have caught Lord Telford's scent—Bram always steals his attention
the moment he enters our home."

Mamm-wynn chuckled. "Our Libby's kitten seems to prefer him
over everyone but her as well."

"And he's been harassing me endlessly about needing a dog,"
Oliver added.

Which of course had Millicent laughing too. "Give him a few
more weeks and he'll likely find a stray to bring home to you, Mr.
Tremayne."

"Or rather, a stray will find him. They always do." Abbie sent
Sheridan a wink. "We used to tease that that's how he and Theo

306

became friends, you know. Theo just followed him about like every other lost puppy, and Bram took him in like one more mutt."

Sheridan folded his arms across his chest. "Oh yes. My very favorite joke. I'm all laughter."

Everyone else was, though. And he didn't really put up any more of an argument. Because, truth be told, he *had* just started following Telford around when they were lads at school, because . . . well, because he seemed a good chap and hadn't immediately joined the herd of other lads who had seemed to take an immediate disliking to Sheridan. It had made him a prime candidate for a friend.

And his instincts had been right, hadn't they? So what if they were the same instincts that stray animals had for Telford? He'd simply claim he had the senses of a bloodhound. A wolf. A—

Ruff! Ruff!

A curly-tailed pug. Sheridan chuckled to himself and looked behind him. "Did Enyon say when he'd bring the trunk, perchance?" Not that he meant to toss up its lid and present the trinket box to Beth the moment he arrived—it deserved a bit more pomp and circumstance than that—but he'd feel better when he knew it was here.

"He was unloading a few things for his mam first. He'll probably be about half an hour. Oh!" Beth reached into her pocket, pulled out a seashell, and slid it across the table to Mamm-wynn with a smile.

Her grandmother took the offering with a smile of her own. "Well, if we're giving gifts now . . ." She reached for the two bundles of knitting and handed one to each of his sisters. "The red for you, Lady Millicent. And Lady Abbie . . . I debated a good long while and decided the cream would suit you best."

He'd seen his sisters in many situations over the years—trying ones, fun ones, unexpected ones, boring ones. He'd witnessed their composure, their resilience, their grit, and their grace. But never had he seen either of them—much less both at once—reach out with such looks of reverence on their faces.

"Mrs. Tremayne." Abbie unfurled hers first, her tone as awed as her face. "It's exquisite. You can't mean for us to keep these?"

"Please, my dears, do call me Mamm-wynn. Everyone does. And I do." She sat back, content as Libby's kitten when he was curled up on Telford's shoulder. "I don't knit as much as I used to, but I've been saving up my work for its rightful recipients. I always know it when I've found them."

Millicent had unrolled hers as well and was running her fingers over the pattern. "It's lovelier than anything I've ever bought in Paris. You do us great honor, madame."

Abbie turned to Sheridan so abruptly that he leaned back against his chair, half expecting a cuff to the ear—not that she'd given him one of those since he was nine and experimenting with some of the more colorful language he'd picked up from those lads at school. "Theodore, it must be said."

He grimaced. She only ever pulled out his full name when he was in serious trouble. "What have I done?"

"I don't exactly know, given how little you told us in your letter. But you led us to believe you'd fallen in love with a young lady on the islands, and if it is anyone but Beth, then you're an absolute dunce."

He didn't know which part to take issue with first. "Now wait a moment—"

"She's absolutely right." Millie wrapped her new shawl around her shoulders. It matched the stripes in her dress. "She's perfect for you, and her whole family is clearly just as delightful. We'll not permit a single argument from you. Not on something as important as your future happiness."

Was he still sleeping? He could think of no other explanation. He reached into his pocket, where his list rested, wrinkled and apparently superfluous. "But—"

"But nothing." Abbie sliced a hand through the air. "I know we promised we wouldn't interfere when it came time to choosing a wife, but clearly we must."

"We must indeed!" Millicent scooted to the edge of her chair. "If left to your own devices, you would have let Telford bully you into marrying Lady Elizabeth."

"And the two of you can hardly even tolerate each other." Both of them were shaking their heads now, that look of superior maternalism in their eyes. "Didn't we warn you?"

Now, that was just too much. "No, actually. You didn't. You were too busy gushing about how perfect it would be."

Abbie lifted her nose. "We do not *gush*, Theodore. Really."

"And you misunderstood our enthusiasm. We were laboring under the apparent misconception that you'd been nurturing secret affections for your best friend's sister. You have to know we want nothing above your happiness." Millicent reached over Abbie, hand outstretched.

He'd been too well trained not to reach back. Though not so well that he could contain his huff. "Well, yes, but—"

"And, Theo, dearest." Abbie's hand landed on his outstretched arm too. "You will have that with Beth. She understands you. We could see it straightaway as she spoke of you."

"And she has the love of adventure and exploration that your future bride will require."

"She's so very intelligent—and imaginative! She had us on the edge of our seats while she was telling us the island stories." Abbie shot a smile past him, presumably at Beth.

His neck was absolutely on fire. Did it not once occur to them that if he *hadn't* already declared feelings for Beth, they would be putting him in quite the spot? "I'm quite aware of how—"

"She's strong and resilient—"

"And beautiful!"

"And I swear to you, Theo"—Abbie leaned close—"she sounded intrigued when she mentioned one of your theories of the Druids in relation to the cairnfields."

"You'll never find another young lady like her, not in a thousand years."

Sheridan slapped his list to the table. "Now see here, that's quite enough. I already know all that—and I was set on convincing *you*." He tapped a finger to the list. "It's all written out—why'd you have to go and ruin it? Don't you know you were supposed to object? I mean, it would have been stupid of you, but—but blue blood and family lines and all that. Ainsley promised me it would matter too much to you, and I'd have to . . . to . . ."

Abbie looked at him as if he'd been speaking in Gaulish. Which was absurd, because he'd only learned to *read* the Druid language, he couldn't speak it. "So, the lady in question *is* Beth? Is that what you're getting at?"

He pulled his hand free and sat back with a whoosh. "Of *course* it's Beth! Who in blazes else would it be?"

"Well then. We're all on the same page. Ah, and there's Bram, awake at last." Abbie stood, her hand extended long before she reached the door Telford was just stepping through, a teacup clutched in his hand and Lancelot all but climbing up his legs in his excitement.

A bit of Sheridan's mood turned to glee at watching Telly try with valiant effort to will Abbie away. A losing battle. Within a few seconds, he sighed and took her hand with his free one, bowing over it. Though Sheridan could only see his sister's back, he knew well the arch look she'd be giving Telly.

Who'd closed his eyes for a second. And, upon opening them, managed, "Lady Abbie."

"There now. Was that so difficult? As I keep telling you, Bram, you are perfectly capable of intelligent conversation before the hour of noon—you simply must *try*." Abbie pivoted back to them and motioned with her hand.

Millicent sprang to her feet too. "Quite right, Abbie. It's high time we see what our lads have been up to. No doubt they've made an absolute mess of their search and we'll have to bring some order to it."

Beth leaped up, too, though a glance at her showed him that it was panic in her eyes now. "Oh, but no! It's all ordered, I promise you. And most of it was mine."

His sisters kept on smiling, Millicent saying, "Perfect. Then you can give us the tour of it all, like you did the islands."

"Millicent." Sheridan tried to halt her with a hand on her arm, but it was a losing battle. Wasn't there a Scripture somewhere about grasping after the wind? The Lord had surely been talking about trying to stop his sisters once they'd set a course.

She did pause—for a moment, anyway—to pat his left cheek and chuckle. "You really made a list? You are adorable, Theo. Absolutely adorable."

Millicent was at Abbie's side a moment later, and somehow Mamm-wynn had gotten caught up in their momentum and was on her feet as well, offering to start the tour with the collection of whatnot Beth had brought her over the years.

Sheridan sighed. Though he was mostly mollified when Beth leaned into his side. "Well, she is right about that. You *are* adorable."

He grinned down at her. "She's right about you too. They both are."

"Clever ladies, those. I quite like them."

"Good." Though he still felt a bit like the wind had been knocked from his sails. He fingered the useless list. "It was quite thorough, you know. All your virtues and charms. Took me forever to list them all out."

Telford dropped into one of the vacated chairs, Lancelot jumping happily into his lap the moment said lap presented itself. He leveled a hard glare on Sheridan. "Everything."

"Yes, I know. They *do* take over absolutely everything. But . . ."

"But they're wonderful," Beth said, glaring right back at Telford. For a moment anyway, then she turned a smile on Sheridan. "And really, I think you're overlooking the most important thing."

That they'd given him their blessing? Well, yes, that was definitely worth celebrating. And he would, once he got over the windblown feeling.

Beth grinned. "Ainsley was *wrong.*"

The rest of his cheer came surging back. And was it any wonder he loved her? He laughed and dropped a kiss onto her forehead. "You're right—how could I have overlooked that? Ainsley!" He charged toward the back door, knowing Ainsley would likely be in the kitchen. "Hey, Harry! You couldn't have *been* more wrong!"

And he'd rub it in while he could. Heaven knew it didn't happen very often.

25

There had been a day not all that long ago when Beth had bemoaned how empty their house felt—how empty the whole isle of Tresco was, with Mabena on the mainland serving Libby, her parents and Morgan gone, so many of her childhood friends having moved away, and Emily living in London.

Now their house and the island felt altogether bursting. Mabena and Libby both here, Emily on St. Mary's, Senara home, and Telford and Sheridan staying with them. Toss in the Howe sisters, and she really began to wonder if little Tresco could hold so much personality. It was with a self-indulgent laugh that she sneaked back into the library while everyone else was still outside, enjoying the cake Mrs. Dawe had served with tea.

She'd liberate a piece from the kitchen later, if there was any left. But first she'd see what the two cyclones Sheridan called sisters had done with all her books and letters and maps and reams of notes.

She really did like them quite a lot—but Telford was right too. They were a force to be reckoned with, and they didn't appear to know how to see a situation without trying to bring their own version of order to it.

She strode first to her usual place at the table, where the parish record books and Mother's stories were still right where she'd left

313

them. Well, more or less. They were a bit neater, with the edges all perfectly aligned, but nothing was out of order.

"Didn't ruin anything, did they?"

Beth looked up with a smile. Sheridan lounged in the doorway, hands behind his back. "Not that I've spotted yet. Just tidied things up a bit—they must not have been able to argue much with Senara's order. Although even if they'd rearranged it all, I'd forgive it. Given how much they love me."

He grinned and pushed off the frame, advancing a few steps. "I suppose I should have given them more credit. How could they not see in a glance how perfect you are?"

"Perfect! Hardly." A perfect person wouldn't have let adventure put her family in danger. Wouldn't have treated him so ill at the start. Wouldn't have let herself be trapped by Scofield.

"For me, that is." He paused on the other side of the table, his hands still behind him. Which was rather strange. "I know Telly thought me mad for inviting them, but I really did need them to come. To bring me something."

She told herself to breathe normally. Not to flush. Not to let her imagination run ahead of her. Because really, it's not like he would have asked them to bring any family jewels or anything, right? He might joke about proposing, but they'd only known each other a month and a half. And while it hadn't even taken that long for Oliver to propose to Libby, such lightning wouldn't strike their family twice in the span of a summer, would it? Sheridan wouldn't ask her to marry him already—and especially, he wouldn't have planned to do it before knowing if they'd have his sisters' blessing. He clearly loved and respected them too much for that.

Still. She felt a bit detached from her body as she rounded the table, as if her feet were more on a cloud than the library floor. "Oh?"

"Mm." Gaze locked on hers, he advanced another step, too, until they were only an arm's length apart. Then he dropped to one knee, making her breath tangle up in her chest. "My lady fair, would you . . . forgive me?"

He pulled his arm forward, revealing not a piece of jewelry or a small box that would house one . . . but a box still. Larger, and a treasure in itself. She sucked in a quick breath. Her trinket box was resting on his upturned palm.

"Oh!" Better by far than a family jewel. Tears stinging her eyes, she cupped the precious wood between her own palms. "Sheridan. This is what you wanted them to bring?"

"Of course I did. It means far more to you than it ever could to me. Well, aside from the fact that it means so much to you. That obviously makes it important to me too. And—well, I ought to have returned it sooner. But it was at the castle, and they were in London, and I didn't trust just any courier to bring it, and . . . well, there at the start I may have been a bit stubborn about it. Because you were so set on being Beth the Belligerent, that is. But it was wrong of me, and—"

She leaned down and pressed her lips to his, making no objection when he tugged her onto his knee for a better angle. Though he'd probably collapse if they stayed like that for more than a minute. So, she pulled her mouth away at the first wobble of his leg, standing and pulling him up with her. "Thank you. And of course I forgive you. And pray you'll forgive me, too, for being so . . . belligerent."

Oh how she loved the way one corner of his mouth tugged up. "Well. Perhaps I will. If you beg enough. On your knees, hands clasped before you, I want the whole show—and it must go on for at least a month. I'm a hard one to win over, you know."

He brushed a stray wisp of hair from her face as she laughed. "Oh yes. You have certainly proven yourself to be ever so stingy with your affections and forgiveness."

A bit of a shadow overtook his face. "I admit I'm having a harder time of it when it comes to those who would hurt you." His fingers lingered in her hair longer than they needed to—not that she was complaining. Her own fingers were tracing the familiar crest on the box's lid, not quite able to believe it was back in her hands.

Somehow, even after everything had changed between them, she'd not been able to think that the box was anything but lost to her.

He'd returned a part of her family to her and valued it enough to ask his own sisters to bring it. She pressed the box to her chest with one hand and wrapped the other arm around his waist. Far better to focus on that than on Nigel Scofield. "I suppose we need to return that hundred pounds to you."

She loved his laugh too. All the more when she could feel it in his chest and not just hear it. "You know, I'd consider it a fair trade if you'd tell me a story about the box."

"A story?" She tilted her face up. "I've already told you the story that goes with it."

"Well, with the actual box, yes. I meant *your* story—the one that goes along with the slip of paper in the hidden compartment."

"The . . . what?" She pulled away, only vaguely aware of the din of many footsteps coming their way. "The what in the secret what now?"

He was frowning now—even as the pulse she could see in his throat pounded harder. "You don't—but you must have known about it. I thought it you who must have put it there. A slip of paper. Barely tall enough for a single letter, but long and written on both sides."

She was shaking her head long before he finished. "I've no idea what you're talking about. A secret compartment?" She held the box flat again. "Where? Mother never mentioned it—and surely she would have. That would have been part of its story."

"I assumed . . . here. Let me show you." His hands trembled as he reached for the box, which was no doubt why he breathed a laugh and shook his head. "Sorry, just—if you didn't know. If your mother didn't . . . it could mean *no one* did. It could—well, it could mean . . ."

She glanced at the doorway and the family and friends spilling through it, then back to him. To the realization in his eyes that mirrored her own. "It could mean that no one ever opened that

316

compartment, not since it was held in the hands of Prince Rupert of the Rhine. Until you."

Another nervous breath of laughter puffed from his lips, but his hands steadied as he turned over the box, twisted one of the legs, and then eased up the bottom piece.

Oliver stepped close, Libby with him. "What in the world?"

Beth reached for the slender slip of paper curled in the tiny compartment. It wasn't deep enough for much else—perhaps a necklace with a flat pendant, but nothing thicker than a quarter inch. The compartment was so shallow it was likely no one had ever guessed it was there.

Not paper. The texture was wrong for that. Parchment, much like the map that had led them to the silverware earlier in the summer. But where the map had looked aged and the ink had been faded by time and water, this slip, having never seen either light or elements, was pristine.

"What does it say?" Libby asked.

Beth shook her head, more at the string of letters than her friend. "I have no idea. It's just random letters." She lifted her brows toward Sheridan. "Or is it? Have you decoded it?"

"Me?" He shook his head. "I just said I wanted the story from you, remember? I thought perhaps it was a secret code you'd written as a girl, when you were playing pirate. I didn't honestly spend much time trying to work it out. It looked too new to be that old."

Beth pulled out a chair and sat, still staring at the slip. "I'm afraid I'm not an expert at secret codes, but everyone grab some paper and a pen. I'm sure one of us, or all of us together, can crack it."

There was a flurry in the room as everyone raced to obey. She looked up from the slip long enough to see that Mamm-wynn wasn't among the group—it was her usual nap time—but that Senara and Ainsley and Collins had slipped inside. And Mabena, too, though Beth had assumed she'd leave after tea.

"All right, Beth, read the letters to us," Oliver said from the chair to her right.

She read them off slowly, one by one, giving everyone the chance to write them down. First the line on one side, and then on the other.

There had to be a message in there, right? From Rupert to Briallen. She stared at it for a long moment, willing words to jump out from the jumble, though none did. She reached for a pen of her own as Oliver and Sheridan and Telford all started scratching notes onto their papers. The ladies, on the other hand, all seemed to be thinking through their tactics first.

Beth smiled a bit at the difference. She didn't even know what tactic to try, to be honest. She was only vaguely aware of the different encryption methods used in history.

"Ah! Miss Tremayne!"

At Ainsley's exclamation, she froze, not sure what he was objecting to until she followed his gaze down to her hands and realized she'd curled the slip of parchment around her pen. "Oh, how stupid!" The last thing she wanted to do was damage it!

"No, no." Ainsley motioned at the pen and parchment, looked to Sheridan as if expecting him to say something. Squeezed his eyes shut for a moment. And then shouted, "Scytale!"

Lady Abbie shook her head. "Really, Ainsley. How is it Italy?"

"Ah!" Sheridan slapped a hand to the table now and spun from Ainsley to Beth and back again. "Not 'it's Italy,' Abbie. *Scytale.* You know, the encryption tool."

Abbie blinked at him. "I'm not sure I do."

"Of course you do." He sounded nearly as exasperated with her as he had when she made his list moot.

Though, for the record, Beth had slipped his list off the table when his back was turned and read it, and it had made her heart positively sing.

"Sparta, remember?" He reached for the slip, though he paused before just taking it from her. Beth relinquished it with a smile. "We learned about it four years ago during our dig there. Surely you recall—you loved that trip, both of you. Even Ainsley. Remember, we had that delicious *amygdalota*—you'd have loved them, Telly. They're an almond biscuit—"

"Sheridan." Beth, laughing, rested a hand on his arm. "Biscuits later. Scytale now."

He grinned at her. "Right. It was a really simple method of encryption. One would wrap a thin piece of paper around a cylindrical object, like a stick or stylus." He carefully wound the parchment around his own pen, lining it up so that there were no gaps between the coils. "Then one would write straight across as usual, scrolling the paper up a bit like we do in a typewriter these days. But when you unwound it again, all those letters were out of order."

Simple indeed, and they could probably work out the meaning simply by trying to rearrange the letters that were a set distance apart from each other. Though it would require quite a bit of trial and error.

Telford leaned forward. "And Rupert would have known about this method?"

Sheridan scoffed. "Of course he would have. He was considered an expert in cryptography in his day. And it was a simple enough method that he quite reasonably could have left it with his bride, knowing she could decode it. All she'd need is a cylinder of the right diameter."

Beth's pen slipped from her fingers.

"So, we have only to gather up cylinders of varying widths." Oliver gathered a few of the pens and pencils lying about and pushed them toward Sheridan.

"None of those are going to work, Ollie." Beth smiled. "We already know what it should wrap around."

Sheridan blinked at her. "We do?"

"We do." She looked over to where Senara leaned against one of the shelves. "The key to your future, remember? Your *key*, Senara. Or the shaft of it, anyway."

Senara winced a bit at all the attention suddenly leveled on her, but she'd always been a good sport. With a fluttery "Oh . . ." she pulled her pendant out from its usual place under her blouse and slipped the whole necklace off her head as she walked over to Beth's chair. "Do you really think so?"

Beth accepted the key, its metal warm from where it always rested above her friend's heart. "One way to find out, and easy enough to try, isn't it?"

Sheridan slid the parchment back toward her, too, and she picked it up with a long inhale.

It took her a minute to determine how best to start coiling it. A minute in which a thousand questions crowded her mind. What if it said nothing important? What if it clearly *wasn't* a message intended for Briallen? What if it was in German or something and she wouldn't even know when it was producing words?

What if this was just one more clue that amounted to nothing, as so many had before?

It took her a few tries to coil it properly and for the letters to line up. But line up they did, row after row. She anchored each end with her thumbs and spun the whole key around to try to determine where a message might begin.

"There!" Sheridan halted her hands with a gentle touch. "Words— 'fro . . . from where Ik'—obviously not. 'I kissed you goodbye.' 'From where I kissed you goodbye.'" Eyes ablaze, he grinned at Beth. "Flip it over. I think we must have begun with the second part of the sentence."

She obliged, her own hands shaking a bit now. And the parchment, having curled in one direction, fought her a bit in trying to curl the opposite, but she won and lined it back up. "Here we are. 'On then'—no, 'on the norths' . . . 'the north shore of Gugh, due south.'"

Sheridan was scribbling it down on a clean sheet of paper. "'On the north shore of Gugh, due south from where I kissed you goodbye.' Ha! I knew it. Definitely a message to his bride."

"And quite possibly instruction on where she could find something she might need for her future, like coins or jewels." Letting the parchment unravel, she handed the key back to Senara with a smile.

Her friend took it, but her brows were furrowed. "There's just one problem, Beth. How in the world are you to know where he kissed Briallen good-bye?"

26

S enara trailed her fingers down the familiar chain, along the familiar iron scrolling, over the familiar shaft. Familiar . . . yet all this time it had been part of a secret she never could have guessed at. Never. Not in a million years.

She'd taken part in the conjecture all through the afternoon and evening, feeling for the first time that she wasn't just an overseer, a governess—she was an actual part of this story. How could she not be, when it was her key that had proven to be, well, the key?

But as darkness fell, she slipped away from the group and came out here, to the spot on the hill where she'd once brought Morgan and Ollie and Beth when she was in charge of them. She sat on the grass and set her eyes on the water, dark but for where the moonlight danced over its surface in flashes and ripples. Magic, that's what it looked like. The Scillies made it easy to believe in all the fairy stories that Mr. Gibson so liked to tell. And yet, she'd always had a practical core. She'd always known they were just stories.

It's what she'd always thought Beth's mother's anecdotes of noblemen falling for island girls had been too. But there was truth to the tragic tale. Truth that somehow saturated her own family history as well as the Gibsons'.

Truth playing itself out again now. Senara closed her eyes and let the ever-present breeze off the water caress her cheeks. Perhaps Beth wasn't *quite* as common an island girl as Briallen had been—she had Tremayne blood, too, after all, and noble connections, thanks to her grandmother. And Lord Sheridan wasn't quite nephew to the king. But even so, it had echoes of that first tale.

Echoes that she prayed, even now as she clutched the key in her palm, would fade away before any tragic endings could repeat themselves. She couldn't bear to think of Beth and her lovestruck young lord having only a single taste of happiness before life separated them.

Praise God that the Howe sisters had accepted her so quickly, and with such enthusiasm. That would pave the way to a happy future. But . . .

But still Senara couldn't help the worry that had buried itself in her heart. Beth was so young. And she had turned so quickly from anger with Sheridan to love. Which was, yes, perfectly in keeping with her personality. But what if her affections turned again? Or what if Sheridan's faded? She didn't know him well enough to say they wouldn't. What if he . . . if he simply used Beth, toyed with her heart, and then left, as so many noblemen before him had done with girls not quite suitable for their wives?

What if he—if they—let their feelings carry them away into more than the kisses she'd seen them sneaking? What if Beth ended up just like Briallen, heartbroken and alone?

No, not like Briallen. She at least had a secret wedding ceremony. What if she ended up like Senara? *Ruined.*

"Nara?"

The familiar voice had her jumping to her feet, searching the darkness for the darker shape she'd rather hoped never to see again. When he didn't show up exactly two weeks after his ultimatum, she'd convinced herself that he wouldn't come back here again at all, not after Ainsley fed him the false leads. That he'd realize he'd been played for a fool and slink away before the Scofields could turn on him. That he'd just forget about her, as he'd clearly been willing to do for the right price anyway.

She'd had a moment's pang over the thought of him being in danger when she'd heard their plan—she could admit it. But Rory Smithfield had always been a master at getting himself out of trouble . . . usually at someone else's expense. She could see that now, looking back on the years she'd known him. "What are you doing here, Rory?" It was the second time he'd shown up at night after the last ferry had gone. Where did he stay when he was stuck here?

Remembering Ainsley's warning about Rory's lack of fidelity, she decided she didn't really want to know.

He came closer, so that the moon's silver light gilded his handsome features. "I said I'd give you one more chance, didn't I? Before I go."

He said it with finality, as if he was talking about more than returning to the village he'd once called home. "Go where?"

He motioned to the sea. "America. Far away from those Scofield blokes—their last note was none too happy. Seems my cousin's 'information' wasn't so sound." But he didn't sound angry so much as amused. "Didn't think Hank had any deception in him—but my offer to you still stands. Tell me what they actually want to know, and there'll be enough for passage for two."

"To *America*?" Her incredulity slipped out without any conscious effort. It had been one thing to dream of marrying him when it would mean nothing but a train ticket and the ferry ride to reach home again. But a transatlantic passage was something else entirely.

But that wasn't the real reason she had to say no to the dream she'd held dear for so long. The dream that, with him at least, had never been anything but a delusion. "I'll not betray my friends or my family for vows that you yourself said mean nothing."

He folded his arms over his chest. "Did Henry tell you I said that? You can't believe him, you know. He's just jealous."

"I heard you myself, Rory. In the Abbey Gardens."

"I just knew how to play my cousin, that's all. Come now—you said you wanted a husband. I'll give you that." He sidled closer and smiled into the night. "We could have fun together, you and I. See the world."

This was the man she had hoped to make a future with. It was why she'd done what she shouldn't have. It was why she'd gone too far. And now . . . would marrying him redeem her? Make an "honest woman" of her? Rid her heart of this terrible feeling that sprang upon her at odd moments?

His fingers caught hers, stroked them. Two months ago, when he'd done that, it had turned her to a puddle of wanting. She caught her breath, almost hoping it still would. That she really did love him. That she could just say yes, apply for a special license, have Oliver marry them tomorrow, and then . . .

Then what? She couldn't imagine, anymore, spending her life by his side. Perhaps because she'd come to realize, over these weeks at home in disgrace, that he didn't make her better. He didn't encourage her as her parents did each other, as she remembered the Tremaynes doing, as Beth and Sheridan did. Still, that slithering voice inside, the one that came from the place where shame burned, whispered, *"You have to marry him, if he's offering. You have to. You gave yourself to him. It's the only way to make that right."*

She even took half a step closer, breath caught in her throat. But then she saw the flash in his eyes. Not of joy but of . . . something else. Something a few shades darker.

This man couldn't redeem her. There was only One who could.

"Rory . . ." She had to swallow and drag in a long breath. "I've done you wrong."

He dropped her hand as if it scalded him. "I knew it—Ainsley, right? Old Hank—"

"No!" Exasperation nearly took the place of the contrition she'd been feeling, but she squeezed her eyes against it. Drew that breath in again and reminded herself of Mam's words. "I did you wrong before—at Cliffenwelle. When we—I should have been stronger than that. I should have helped *you* be stronger than that. I should have fought for us to do things the right way. But I failed and . . .

and I'm sorry. Sorry I didn't respect either of us enough to do right."

He just stared at her for a long moment. Then he breathed a mocking laugh. "Oh, that's rich. Henry *has* sunk his claws in you. He must have done, for you to be talking like that. Spouting all his holiness nonsense."

"It isn't nonsense." And she didn't need Ainsley to "spout" it at her—she knew it all herself. Had heard it all her life. Had taught it to her girls.

When had she stopped living it? Stopped walking in it? Stopped craving it?

Rory laughed again. "Come on, Nara. We both know life's only about what you can get out of it. And we've wasted years enough concerned only for other people's happiness. Don't we deserve to take some of our own? To seek our *own* life instead of some lord's or lady's? This is our chance. Our chance to grab hold of the future for ourselves, not be tied down by other people's brats."

The key to your future. Her fingers fluttered up to touch the key and then dropped again. *Family.* But family wasn't created by seeking your own good. Family was created by doing good for others. "Don't speak that way of my girls."

"They're not *your* girls!"

"They are—or they were." Not by blood. But she loved them. She'd been more mam to those sweet darlings than their real mother ever had been—and she'd let a moment's pleasure steal them from her.

But there was a path through it. A path that would lead to faith and family and future, if she was brave enough to tread it. "I'm sorry, Rory. I am. Sorry that I never showed you that faith is the better way. I'm sorry I was weak. That I didn't love you well enough to seek the best *for* you, not just *from* you."

He looked at her through squinted eyes and then shook his head. "Blimey, you *do* sound like Henry. You've never been like that before."

Hadn't she? She pressed her lips together. No, she hadn't. Not with him. After spending all day with the girls, instructing them in kindness and morality, she'd been too lax in her free moments. And that shamed her too—because if it wasn't what she lived when the Cliffords weren't watching, then could she really claim it as her own?

Forgive me, Father. The words, silent and sonorous inside her, set loose something she'd kept locked away. Something that made her quake, made her gasp, made her press a hand to her mouth to keep a sob from ripping through her. *Forgive me.*

Rory backed away, still shaking his head. "Is that your answer, then? You're not coming? Just as well—I don't need a wife who'll preach at me, nag me night and day. Though if you think Henry'll give you a chance, ruined as you are, you're bound to be disappointed. He's too high and mighty for that. He'll want an innocent girl, if ever he settles down. You know that, right?"

She winced as if he'd struck her. "This isn't about Ainsley." It wasn't—it was about her and her own failures. But she'd be lying to herself if she said she didn't like him. Didn't wonder, now and again, whether someday . . . but she was in no place, mentally or emotionally, to even think about such things.

"Right." Was it jealousy in his tone, or just derision? "I'll find someone else for that second ticket. Don't think I won't."

It pierced, the thought that he could replace her so quickly, so easily—that he had other girls even now just waiting for a chance to be Mrs. Smithfield. Lost dreams always stung. But she didn't want a husband who valued her so little.

Though she would have to mourn quite a while yet that she'd given something so precious to someone unworthy.

"Good-bye, Rory. I'll pray the Lord keeps His hand on you."

Now *he* recoiled. "Don't waste your breath. I'm done with lords for good, earthly and heavenly both."

Strange—for as much trouble as he had caused her, as much pain and shame, as she watched him melt back into the night, it was pity that settled in her spirit. Pity that he couldn't see the beauty of what mattered most.

She heard his footsteps setting pebbles skittering down the path, and then it was only the shush of the waves, the sigh of the wind.

Then more steps, hesitant ones, coming from the direction of the house. She knew even before he eased into view that it would be Ainsley. And that he'd no doubt heard every word.

She brushed a stray tear from her cheek and motioned him to join her as she took her seat again in the grass.

He would probably try to talk of serious matters—but she couldn't, not just yet. She needed a moment first. "I'm still trying to reimagine my life, now that I know I'm a princess." She aimed for a light tone, but it fell a bit flat.

Still, he chuckled. "I can imagine it easily enough. Give his lordship and Miss Tremayne long enough, and they'll probably unearth a diadem or two for you ladies both to wear."

Her laugh was little more than a breath. But it was welcome, nonetheless. "I can't quite imagine you on excavations with him. All those places the two of you have mentioned! Do you help him dig, or just stand in the tent, clucking your tongue over all the dirt he's collecting on his clothes?"

Ainsley chuckled and propped his elbows on his raised knees, his face toward the fairy-kissed water. "Whatever he needs me to do. Which is only occasionally digging—that's the part he likes best. I organize his finds, mostly. Arrange transport and meals and lodging . . . that sort of thing."

Far more in line with what she imagined of him. Senara touched the key again and drew in a long breath. "He won't hurt her, will he? I mean . . . he isn't like Rupert—quick to fall in love, with no qualms about moving on when the time comes."

Ainsley turned his face toward her. And let a few seconds pass before he answered, proving he wasn't just offering the first platitudes to spring to his tongue. "He has never looked at a young woman as he does your Beth. Never—it was why I was so worried for him.

He's never given his heart so fully nor so quickly to anyone else, and the thought of it coming between him and his sisters . . . I couldn't bear it. But he wouldn't have turned from Miss Tremayne, even had the ladies disapproved. He isn't the sort. He would sooner take the hurt than give it, Senara—for anyone, but most especially for her."

Senara sighed. "She's the closest thing I've ever had to a sister. Not exactly the same, I know. I always knew my family were the servants, even though the Tremaynes never made us feel that way. I knew she was more my charge than my sister. But even so."

"I completely understand. I never meant to remain in service so long, you know." He reached down and plucked a blade of grass, twirled it between his thumb and forefinger. "I thought I would take the position for a year or two, send some money home to my parents, and then move on to something more exciting."

Her lips twitched at the thought of Ainsley wanting excitement. But then, a decade ago he would have been a young buck, eager to make his way in the world. Just like she had been. "Little did you know that you'd find all the excitement you could ever want with him."

He chuckled. "I learned it quickly. And felt . . . he needed me. I joke about him being like a lad in the nursery, but there's a bit of truth to it. He has an innocence to him, despite all the places he's gone, all the people he's met. Something no one has ever been able to rob him of—and I wanted to make sure no one ever could. It's the same reason his sisters have never married, why they never just shipped him off to school or left him in the charge of a tutor and went their own way. There's something bold and bright about him that deserves to be guarded. Your Beth is a lucky young lady to have won his heart. I know I'm biased, but it's true."

She nodded and let the wind and sea whisper for a moment. "They'll be good for each other. And I'm glad of that. They both deserve such happiness, just as Ollie and Lady Elizabeth do."

"They aren't the only ones who deserve it." He said it so softly, she nearly missed it over the shushing of the waves below.

329

She turned her face toward him, studied his silhouette in the moonlight. Elegance edged in silver. He spoke of her—because he was a kind man and a good man and one who had that same instinct to nurture and care for others that she had. But he'd just highlighted the difference between Sheridan and Senara. His lordship had an innocence about him—that was what drew people to him, what inspired such loyalty in Ainsley.

Innocence was the very thing Senara had given away.

She shook her head. "You're a kind man, Ainsley. But you know what I've done. And while the Lord and my family may forgive me, that doesn't mean . . ." She didn't know quite how to say it, not in a way that he wouldn't immediately argue against. Because he was good and kind and wanted to make her feel better.

But that couldn't change facts.

He sat up, letting the blade of grass fly into the wind, then leaned back a bit so he could dig a hand into his pocket. She had no idea what he was about until he pulled something out and held it toward her on his open palm.

Even so, she *still* had no idea what he was about. She reached toward the white sphere glowing in the moonlight. "A . . . bead?" It was the size of one of the peas he'd helped her shuck that day when she'd first come home, and it looked like the sort of bead she used to save her pennies to buy so she could sew them into her shawls or onto her hats.

But this one had no hole bored through it. And it didn't quite feel like the costume jewelry she knew.

"A pearl."

She drew her hand back just before picking it up. "Are you quite serious? A real pearl? It must be worth a fortune!"

He shrugged and kept holding it out. "Perhaps. I wouldn't know—I've never had it appraised."

He was the steady sort. Reasonable. She hadn't thought him capable of shocking her with something so . . . so utterly *un*reasonable. "So, what then, you just carry it about in your pocket?"

His teeth gleamed, white as the pearl, when he smiled. "For the last six years, yes. That's precisely what I've done."

When it became obvious she was not going to pluck the pearl from his palm—what if she dropped it and lost it? It had to be worth a month of her old salary, if not more—he moved his hand so that it rolled into his fingers and he could hold it up to the moonlight.

"We were on a dig in Tuscany. Truly beautiful country, and I was quite enjoying myself. His lordship was helping excavate a tomb of one of the ancient Etruscans, and he was going forever on about how they were masters of jewelry-making. He'd not found anything of true note yet, though." A hint of a smile settled in the corners of Ainsley's mouth. "Each morning, one of his sisters or I would lead the whole team in a Scripture reading and prayer, and that day it was my turn. I admit I didn't put a great amount of thought into my selection. I just read the next passage after the one I'd done the last time, from the Gospels. And it was about a pearl."

Senara tangled her fingers into the grass. "The one about not tossing one's pearls before swine?"

He shot her a reproving look. "No. The parable about the pearl of great price. You know the one—how the kingdom of God is like a man who finds a pearl of great price. And he sells all that he owns so that he can purchase the pearl. Just as we're to give up anything He asks of us to follow Him."

She nodded, though it was slowly. "And this went from a parable to a physical pearl how?"

"Well, later that day, his lordship had me moving the pieces they were digging up—mostly pottery shards and the like—from the ex-cavation site to one of the tents for cleaning and cataloguing. I saw this clump of mud beside the pottery and tossed it away. But Lord Sheridan caught it—" He interrupted himself with a laugh. "You ought to have seen him pluck it out of midair, absolute horror on his face. And he said, '*Ainsley, old boy, don't you know what this is?*' Well, of course I did—a clump of mud."

Senara felt her own lips tug up. "I suspect not."

"I didn't, not at the time. I knew mud when I saw it, after all. But he slapped it into my hand with that grin of his and said that perhaps I ought to make sure it was only mud before I threw it out like rubbish. I was curious then, and as I took it to the tent, I caught a glimpse of white that had peeked through the mud on one side. It only took me a few minutes to wash it clean. And there it was. A pearl."

"He knew. And then he let you keep it?" She didn't know many employers who would be so generous.

"Insisted on it, given the passage I'd read that morning. He said it was clearly meant to be mine. A reminder of the kingdom of God. But more than that." He looked at her again now, and though she couldn't see much of his eyes when his back was to the moon, she knew well what light would be in them. The same light that always was. "It was a reminder to me of what His salvation really means. I think . . . I think too often we compare our souls and our sins to a grass stain. We think that His sacrifice is sufficient to knock off the clumps and blades clinging to the outside of us, but not quite strong enough to get rid of the stain in the fabric."

She could barely swallow past the lump in her throat. That was exactly how she felt.

"But we're not fabric, Senara. We are pearls." He reached for her hand, turned it over, and set the pearl onto her palm. This time she didn't argue. Just looked at it, gleaming so brilliantly. White and clean and beautiful. "I realize I risk preaching here like his lordship always accuses me of, but it must be said. He makes us with great worth. Creates us that way intrinsically. Our sins, our bad choices, perhaps they coat us like mud. But the mud cannot take away the value He instilled in us. Mud does not make a pearl any less valuable. If it did, then why would Jesus have deemed us worthy of the sacrifice of His life? But He loves us, as does the Father. Because we are valuable. And the blood of Christ, when it washes us clean, fully restores us to what He created us to be. A pearl cannot be stained. No matter how many centuries it sits in the mud, wash it in a bit of water and it's gleaming again."

Her nostrils flared, and she blinked a few times. He was right—they were words he had to say. Words she needed to hear.

He closed her fingers around the pearl. "*You* are a pearl of great price, Senara Dawe. I could see that as soon as I met you. You are a woman of deep heart, of great love, of beautiful spirit. It is an honor to be counted among your friends." He drew his hands away, leaving her clutching the pearl.

She shook her head and held it back out to him. "Don't leave this with me. I may drop it."

"You won't. And if you aren't comfortable keeping it forever . . ." He stood and brushed off the seat of his trousers.

She scurried to her feet, too, holding the pearl tightly so she didn't lose it.

He turned to face her, stepping just a bit closer than he would normally stand. "You may return it to me after you've let its meaning soak into your soul. But only then. And if, when that day comes, when your heart is mended from the damage done by my selfish donkey of a cousin—" He hissed out a breath, shook his head, and then visibly calmed himself again. "If when that day comes you don't find me a tiresome Puritan . . . well, I would treasure the opportunity to see if perhaps we would suit as *more* than friends."

Tears stung her eyes, and she wished she could banish them with a simple blink, but they wouldn't be chased away so easily. How was it possible that this man—this good, kind, handsome, perfect man—could look at her and see anything beneath the dirt?

And if he did, how could he make that offer so gently, so easily? That he would give her any time she needed to heal. That he valued the state of her heart and soul above any relationship they might someday forge.

"Ainsley." She didn't know what else she meant to say. She knew only that she couldn't let him walk back to the house without a single word from her. She wanted to say that if ever her heart healed, if ever she could fully grasp the lesson he so generously gave her, then he would be the only man she could imagine trusting enough to walk beside into the future. But she didn't know when she could give him that, only that it wouldn't be fair to make promises now when she could only deliver him pieces.

But perhaps she didn't need to say anything beyond his name. Perhaps he heard in it all she wanted to say and couldn't, all she hoped but dared not speak quite yet. He smiled, perfectly at peace, and offered his elbow.

She first slipped the pearl into the pocket of her skirt. And then she tucked her hand into the crook of his arm.

27

On the north shore of Gugh, due south from where I kissed you goodbye. The words had become a constant tapping in Sheridan's mind, keeping time with each step he took. The day had dawned warm and beautiful—too beautiful to spend it cooped up inside—so he'd lured Beth out for a walk around the coast, saying they could spend the time trying to find a hint as to where Rupert and Briallen had said their farewells.

If they could come up with a good guess, he'd take it and run. Or, well, sail. To Gugh, and then just start digging. He didn't much care where. Truth be told, his hands were just hungry for the taste of dirt and a good shovel. Even if they didn't begin in the right spot, he just wanted to *begin*.

"I do wish there was some record of where they lived." Beth, her hand tucked snugly against his arm as they walked, looked not to the sea or the beach, but up at the roofs of the cottages barely visible over the waving seagrass. "Or at least Briallen's family. It's likely they stayed there after their wedding, don't you think?"

Sheridan made a face. "Spending one's wedding night in a two-room cottage with one's new in-laws? I can't say as that would be ideal, no."

But the mention of it brought a beautiful flush to Beth's cheeks, even as she laughed. "Perhaps not ideal, but I don't know how many empty cottages were just lying about at the time."

"Nor do I, but let's not forget he was a royal. He probably could have bought a few nights of privacy, even here."

She granted it with a tilt of her head and a pretty little hum. "Which means we really can't narrow it down at all. They could have let pretty much any cottage for a few days. So, if he kissed her good-bye there . . ."

"I don't know that he would have, though." Sheridan paused when a glint caught his eye in the sand, just near the high-tide line. He bent down, scooped up the piece of blue sea glass, and handed it to Beth. Mamm-wynn had quite a collection of sea glass, and her eyes always lit up when Beth brought her a new piece.

Beth smiled and slipped it into her pocket. "Perfect. And why not kiss her good-bye at a rented cottage?"

"Because." He dusted the damp sand off his fingers, onto his trousers. It would fall off long before they got back to the Tremayne house and Ainsley's eagle eye. Probably. "If we'd just married and I was sailing away without you, would you really say good-bye to me at the house?"

When she lifted her chin and raised her brows, he was reminded again of why he'd tumbled head over heels in love with her within minutes. Or at least hours. "If we'd just married, you would *not* be sailing away without me, Lord Sheridan. Make no mistake about that. I'd stow away in the ship's hold if I had to, but your future adventures would include me right by your side."

As they most assuredly would. It would get a bit complicated once children came along, but what child of theirs wouldn't enjoy hopping about the world from excavation to excavation? And then coming back to doting aunties and a wise uncle and great-grandparents to regale them with all the stories they could ever want? They'd make it work—though it may require a few extra hands. They'd definitely have to bribe Senara into joining them. It was that or see if Ainsley would play nursemaid.

He grinned at the thought of Ainsley changing nappies and scanned the sand for more treasures. "I didn't say Rupert wasn't a fool. But my greater point was simply that Briallen wouldn't just wave farewell from the doorway, would she? She'd have walked with him."

"I can't imagine her kissing him good-bye right at the quay, though, with all his crew watching."

She may have a point. "True. And due south of the quay isn't on the north shore of Gugh anyway." He glanced over his shoulder, in the general direction of said quay, though they couldn't see it from here. They'd already passed by Piper's Hole and were making their way to the southern point of the island. "But that's where his ship would have been anchored, isn't it?"

"Hm." Her brows wrinkled in thought. "That depends on the size of the ship. There was no anchorage around Tresco at the time that was deep enough for the large vessels. They had to anchor at St. Mary's."

"Well, Rupert's ship was large. Not quite as large as Mucknell's *John* had been before it was sunk, but it would have had a fairly deep draft." So, it likely would have been at St. Mary's. But that didn't make perfect sense, did it? He let out a long breath and toed a shell that looked promising—no, it was just a sliver. "We know Mucknell and his wife lived on Tresco, though, at the house Tasgwyn Gibson now calls home. And Briallen's family was on Tresco as well. So even if his ship was anchored at St. Mary's, he must have been staying here."

"The locals have always had small boats to use for hopping between the islands." Beth motioned at a few sails out upon the water even now. "And we've never minded ferrying people about, either from island to island or from island to ship—that's actually where the gig racing began, did you know? Locals racing the sailors to their ships. He could have been staying here and then gone in a rowing boat or sloop to his ship. It even could have sailed out of the harbor in Hugh Town and come as close to Tresco as possible to fetch him."

Well now, that was an interesting thought—both the actual one about Rupert and that such things were what started a tradition reaching even into the present. "And where would he have met it? The quay in Grimsby? But you'd already said she wouldn't have kissed him there."

"We obviously can't know for certain. But . . ." Beth pressed her lips together and shot him a wide-eyed look.

He hadn't quite mastered reading her mind so well, though. He could tell she liked whatever idea she'd come up with—but he hadn't a clue what that idea was. "Yes? But? Don't leave me hanging, you know. It's cruel. And you're not angry with me anymore."

She tugged him into a faster pace. "But when one is coming from St. Mary's and not looking to dock for long, there's a far more likely location. On Tresco's southernmost point."

"The one at the end of Carn Near Road." He matched her new pace quite happily. They could look for more shells on their way back from the little docking area. "It's certainly nearer to St. Mary's than any of the others. I've seen it, of course, and walked by it, but we've never used it."

"Well, no, not since we keep our sloops in the quay. But so far as I know, it's been in use for centuries."

"Well. Let's see if it has any locations near it perfect for a kiss, shall we?" He wiggled his brows at her and pulled her a little closer to his side for a step or two.

She laughed. "Sounds like a perfectly scientific experiment."

"Absolutely. And, really, we'd be remiss in our duties if we didn't explore each possibility in search of the most likely one."

Though as they neared the southern tip of the island, where the road terminated at the sand, he began to see Beth's point about Briallen not just kissing her pirate husband farewell in any old place. The shoreline grew busier here, and several boats were either making use of the dockage, just leaving it, or sailing toward it even now.

One of which looked rather familiar. "Is that your brother and my sisters already?"

Beth lifted a hand to add a bit of extra shade to the narrow brim of her hat as she peered to the south. "I believe so. They made good time. Your sisters must not have requested another tour today."

He snorted a laugh. "I can't think why not. They ought to have been clamoring to be taken to the Eastern Isles this morning. Your uncle's toe didn't predict a storm, did it, that would make Oliver override them?"

She shook her head. "He predicts clear skies for the next few days. And Ollie was planning on showing them about, I know. He told Libby he wouldn't see her until afternoon, hence why we passed her on her way to the Gardens."

With her sketchbook and magnifying glass and a field guide or two in hand. Habits he found quite a bit more amusing now that he knew she wouldn't be interfering with his every excavation for the rest of his life, telling him he couldn't possibly dig *there* because there was some precious, rare something-or-another growing that could be found nowhere else in the world—even though it looked exactly like every other something-or-another to be found absolutely everywhere.

Why had he ever let Telford talk him into considering a match with her, anyway? Though he couldn't be entirely sorry he'd entertained the notion. It was part of why he'd come here with Telly, after all, which was how he'd met Beth.

He did love the mysterious ways in which the Lord worked. So very interesting in all their coincidences and surprises.

"The beach is a bit crowded here." He nodded toward a few sloops' worth of tourists who were meandering about. "Probably would have been then too. With sailors, I mean. So . . . up?" He motioned toward one of the paths through the grass, up to higher ground.

Beth led the way, letting go of his arm so they could travel single file. By the time they reached the crest, the *Adelle* was sailing past them, on its way to her usual slip on the north side of the island. Sheridan waved a hello, though no gesturing arms indicated that they'd seen them here.

Beth wandered a few steps away, her eyes on where another boat was coming in. "They'd have had a good view of any ship anchored off the shore here . . . though the same could be said for just about any spot on the top of this hill."

And the top of the hill would probably give a good enough starting point to draw their line due south on the map. "Ah, but we have another criteria that must be met." He joined her where she stood and slipped an arm around her waist. "Is it a good spot for a kiss?"

Rather than just turn in his arms and try it out, she looked around. And shook her head. "Too close to the road. Anyone happening by would see. Here, come with me." She tugged him onward—really, sometimes she was no fun at all—across the road, and to the other side of it, where the hill was a bit steeper leading down to the sand, and a dip in it created a little spot that was more protected.

Sheridan drew in a long breath once they came to a halt on the bluff, the sea beckoning him, the wind whirling about them, and the most beautiful woman in all the world pressed against his side, her eyes bright with a smile.

"There," she said. "Much better. Now, my lord—the experiment?"

Well, who was he to disappoint a lady? He obligingly drew her close, sweeping his hat off his head with his other hand so their brims wouldn't collide, and leaned down to claim her lips with his own.

He didn't know if this was where Rupert had stood with his Briallen. But as he kissed Beth, he wondered again how he could have done it—left her here and gone off in search of treasure. Hadn't he realized he held the most precious thing in his arms already? But then, Sheridan didn't know how desperate life really was on Tresco at the time. Perhaps staying here simply hadn't been possible.

He just knew that Beth had the right of it. He'd never sail off without her. Not now that he'd found her.

When finally he pulled away, they shared a smile. "I rather like this spot. But there could well be an even better one. There. Or there. Or . . . somewhere. We ought to test out more of them."

340

"Mm." She came up on her toes and pressed another kiss to his mouth. "We certainly want to be thorough . . . wait." She frowned and spun to the north. "When the *Adelle* went by—did you count how many people were on board?"

"Um. Well, that is . . ." He hadn't. But he tried to remember now. It had looked a bit full, hadn't it? "My sister's maids could have come along. They may have wanted to see the Abbey Gardens."

"Yes, but I think there were even more than that."

Sheridan pursed his lips. "Lady Emily, perhaps?"

A perfectly logical possibility. So why did it light a spark of concern in her eyes and make her leap back toward the crest of the hill? "She was supposed to be doing something with Lottie's family today. If she's here instead, it could well be because they've received word about her brother."

Well, blast. He could hardly insist they try out more good-bye-kiss locations if important news was coming. Though how Scofield managed to interfere when he wasn't even *here* . . . Sheridan hurried to catch up with her. "I suppose that could explain why my sisters weren't insisting on seeing the Eastern Isles."

"We'd better take the road back into the village. It'll be faster."

Five minutes later, Sheridan was fairly certain it wasn't the fact that the road cut any straighter a line that made it faster—it was just that Beth could run on it better than on the sand. He was finally getting a glimpse of this speed she was known to have, and it would have been far more fun to watch than it was to try to keep up with. Not that he couldn't run—he enjoyed some fine sport as much as the next chap—but she didn't just *run*. She dodged this way and that, around obstacles, under lifted arms, through the legs of horses . . . all right, that one was an exaggeration. A bit.

Even so, he was rather glad he knew his way back to the Tremayne house, because she lost him halfway through the village. Because he dared to halt for a moment when a wagon passed in front of him, rather than simply leap over it in a single bound as she probably would have done.

He was smiling as he puffed his way to the house. She really was amazing. He could just imagine her on expeditions with him. She'd be in the lead, blazing trails. Outpacing the guides.

Just now, though, she stood in the front garden, clasping the hands of a very worried-looking Lady Emily.

"Wha . . . what . . . is it?" He sucked in a long breath and came to a halt just past the trellis.

His sisters were there, too, and both their maids, and Oliver. Millicent turned to him with a scowl. "It's that annoying Dutchman again, that's what."

Sheridan frowned. "Dutchman?"

"American," Abbie corrected. "But originally Dutch."

"His family." Millicent marched over to him. "Don't tell me you don't recall him, I won't believe it of you. Not given the thorn he was in our side in Europe. Vandermeer, Theo. Donald Vandermeer."

"Vandermeer!" He hadn't even thought of him in years, but the mere mention of his name brought a score of scorching memories to mind. He looked to Beth and Lady Emily. "Is *he* the American your family is working with?"

Lady Emily released the lip she'd been gnawing on. "So it seems—though I don't really know anything about him."

"Do you?" Beth, looking from him to his sisters.

Abbie snorted. It was, of course, a ladylike snort. The kind that screamed high-born disdain. "Far too well."

Sheridan let Millicent pull him farther into the front garden. "He's a fellow antiquities hunter. That is—"

"An antiquities *shark*, more like." Millicent shook her head, tossing the length of tulle attached to her hat over her shoulder.

Why the devil had she chosen such an extravagant hat for a sail to Tresco? It must have been tangled about her the whole way. "Well—"

"He isn't underhanded or anything, let it be noted." Abbie moved toward the front door, pulling the rest of them along in her wake by the sheer force of her will. "He simply employs a vast team of people, which meant that he was quite frequently a step ahead of us when we were exploring a lead."

Sheridan smirked at Millicent as they joined the others. "Which Millicent took as a personal insult."

She ignored him. "We haven't bumped into him in years, though. Not since Theo decided to focus on the Druids. The Dutchman has no interest in them."

"American," Abbie corrected again. She turned to the others from her place on the doorstep. "By way of the Dutch West Indies, which is where his family made their fortune in sugar and rum. I believe it was Mr. Vandermeer's father who decided to move to New York as a young man. His son was born there. And therefore is *American*, as my sister well knows."

"Allow me." Oliver bypassed the rest of them, including Abbie, and opened the door. "After you, my lady."

She rewarded him with a sweet smile. "Thank you, Mr. Tremayne. Now." Abbie pivoted again and marched inside, beckoning them to follow with a raised hand.

Sheridan took a bit of pleasure in seeing that Beth and Lady Emily obeyed that flutter of her fingers every bit as quickly as he, Millicent, and their maids did. Always good to know it wasn't just *his* spine that was a tad weak where she was concerned.

He tried to hang back so he could fall in beside Beth, but Millicent didn't relinquish his arm. Which meant he simply craned his head around instead and nearly tripped on the doorstep. "So, *what* is it? About Vandermeer, I mean. He's in London? With your family, my lady?"

Emily shook her head and cast one of those fretful gazes of hers at Beth. "That's the thing, my lord. He's not there anymore—none of them are."

"They're on the way here." Beth delivered the death blow calmly. Coolly. But he could hear the strain in her voice just as clearly as he could see it in her eyes. "They'll be here tomorrow."

343

"Tomorrow!" He paused, even though it made Beth bump into him—shame, that—and Millicent tug on his arm. Then he charged forward, shaking free of that sister and surging past the other. For all he knew, she meant to march into the drawing room or something and request some tea to aid them in their planning. But that wouldn't do at all.

The library. Their maps. That's what they needed, and they hadn't a moment to lose. "Hurry, then! No time to waste. Abbie— and Millicent."

They were right behind him, already pulling out papers and pens. Sheridan unfurled the most detailed map of the Scillies that the Tremaynes had. They'd already pored over it last night, trying to guess at which section of Gugh's northern coastline might be the correct one. But now he had something more to go on—at least he hoped he did. They had only to draw a line.

"Beth—where were we?"

She didn't ask him what he was doing. Just slid to his side, glanced at the map for a moment, and rested her fingertip at a spot on the southern end of Tresco. He would have guessed nearly right, but she obviously knew the island far better than he. He held out a hand toward his sisters.

Millicent slapped a ruler into his palm. He set one end of it on the spot Beth indicated, then lined it up with the north-south arrow on the map's compass rose. He looked to Beth again. "Look reasonable to you? As a location, I mean? You know Gugh better than the rest of us."

She stared at the map for a moment, closed her eyes.

He held his breath. Well, for a second. Then huffed it out. "Tell me it's not. Where he was already digging, I mean."

She shook her head. "I don't think so."

"Beth." Oliver's voice was hesitant. And had a warning in it. "One line isn't enough to go on. We can't exactly dig all along it."

"Well. We don't just have one line, though, do we?" He nodded toward Beth's stack of papers. "We've got the clues that led us there to begin with. Mucknell mentioning the Old Man. And that part of his watermark map with the word in it."

"Perfect." Abbie moved over to the stack he indicated. "Three points will allow us to triangulate with precision."

It took them a bit of doing to put it all together on this one map, however. It wasn't exactly drawn to the same scale as the one Mucknell had put down by hand on his letter. But between the two clues the pirate had left for his wife and the one the prince had for his, they soon had it.

A beautiful dot on a beautiful map. And nearly twenty-four hours' head start. Surely that was enough time to dig up a pirate hoard, all evidence to the contrary not worth considering. At least since Telly wasn't awake yet to remind him of it. Once he drew a circle around their place of choice, he looked up with a grin. "Well, then. Time to get digging."

28

Considering the fact that a swarm of people she didn't trust a whit would be descending upon them any moment, Beth probably shouldn't have been having quite so much fun. But as the sun burned its way from the mist the next morning and spilled its gold onto their site, she couldn't help but grin.

She'd thought, when she set out on this adventure three months ago, that it was hers and hers alone. She'd thought she had to hide it from her family—and then hide her family from the people who would take it from her if they could. But when she paused for a moment to lean on her shovel and look over her shoulder, she couldn't deny how wrong she'd been.

Oliver was sitting a stone's throw away, rubbing at eyes that had been closed in sleep the last time she looked. Libby stood a few feet beyond, spyglass raised and watchful, Telford at her elbow. Senara had remained on Tresco with the promise that she'd join them in the morning with some fresh-baked sustenance, but Emily still slumbered on her blanket, having refused to return to St. Mary's when they dropped the Howe sisters there yesterday afternoon.

They had business to attend to, they said. And since Sheridan had only nodded, his smile not dimming in the slightest, she hadn't questioned them on what this business could possibly be that was more important than finding the treasure before the Scofields and Vandermeer arrived.

To be perfectly honest, she still couldn't quite reconcile the idea of either of them at an excavation anyway. Obviously they were, and frequently. But until she saw them dressed in appropriate clothes for it and taking a shovel in hand, she just couldn't picture it.

It was challenging enough to accept that elegant, proper Ainsley was knee-deep in the trench they'd been digging, humming an old hymn as he dug.

Sheridan was sifting through each shovelful of dirt that came topside, humming right along, as if he hadn't been awake for twenty-four hours straight at this point.

Beth had stolen a few hours of sleep sometime in the hours of deepest night. Just a few. It hadn't been great sleep—not that she minded the hardness of the ground after making a bed of it for all that time earlier in the summer, but she'd been alert to every sound. Waiting, hoping to hear Sheridan shout, "Eureka!"

They could find nothing. She knew that. Their chances were especially slim of finding it in this sliver of a time window before the Scofields and their American arrived.

But then, they *could*. It was possible, given the precision of their location and the shallowness of the soil here. She drew in another breath and went back to shoveling.

Telford tromped their way, a bag in his hands. "Chocolate, any-one?"

Sheridan, his hands a mess with mud, simply opened his mouth. Telford took aim and lobbed a chocolate drop at him, letting out a whoop of victory when it went in.

She shook her head. "It's morning. Shouldn't you be mute again?"

Telford chuckled. "It's not morning until one has slept, Miss Tremayne. This is my favorite time of day. The last breath of night. The first brush of dawn."

She rather liked it herself—but preferably after a solid night's sleep. "You mean to tell me you always stay up all night?"

"Why do you think he can't be roused until nearly noon?" Sheridan grinned over at her. "Diggidy dig, darling. Or we can switch, if you like."

She duggidy-dug her shovel back in. He'd already taken many a turn with it—his back must be sore, even if he wouldn't admit it. "No sails on the horizon yet, I assume?"

"Not yet." Telford angled himself toward the incline. Probably looking at Scofield's site, naught but a hundred yards away. The granite slab that had nearly been her end. The campsite that had been taken down by the locals whom Nigel had hired when he was supposedly so distressed over her "accident."

Beth deliberately did *not* look that direction. She focused instead on her digging. And sighed when her shovel hit something hard, and with the distinctive sound of granite. "Bedrock again."

"To your right, then." Sheridan abandoned the dirt and came around to her. "We must be close now. Process of elimination and all that."

Half of her mouth smiled at his optimism. The other half at his obvious joy. "You want the shovel again, don't you?"

He clapped his hands together, eager as a pup. "If you're not ready for a respite, I can spell Ainsley. A-I-N—"

"Here." Ainsley tossed the shovel at him, though a smile peeked out. "Spell away."

"A-W—"

"All right, all right." Ainsley hauled himself out of his hole— they were shallower here than Scofield's up the hill—and stretched. "You should really rest for an hour or so, my lord. While you can."

"Bah." Sheridan jumped down the two feet to bedrock. "I can sleep after we've found our pirate hoard."

Or after the Scofields arrived and chased them away. Beth dug her shovel in once more, a bit of that negativity eclipsing the fun of it. Emily's family had no more right to dig here than the rest of them. And they were here first—today, anyway. Didn't that count for anything?

"Shall we join up?"

She eyed the narrow stretch of soil between her hole and his and nodded. "Seems reasonable. It has to be nearby."

"It most certainly is. Though off by an inch . . ."

She tossed a clod of dirt at him with a chuckle. "Not encouraging, dearovim."

"Of course it is!" He jerked his head up the hill. "Applies to them, too, after all."

He had a point. Scofield was off by quite a lot of inches, if their own calculations were right. And that had bought them weeks of time. "True enough. So then . . . let's pass the time. Tell me a story. Of when you last encountered Vandermeer, perhaps."

He hummed low in his throat. "Goodness. It was . . . I don't know, perhaps four or five years ago now. He'd beaten me to a site in Finland once already, and another on Iceland. It was becoming quite annoying, I have to say. Or rather, Millicent did. She was convinced someone was spying on her while she researched and passing her findings along to him." Sheridan chuckled and shook his head. "Abbie—always practical, you know—pointed out that he had access to the same books we did. Clearly it was just that we shared interests and resources and they led us to the same places."

"Clearly." It was certainly the disadvantage of relying on clues others had laid out in a text. To make altogether new discoveries, one needed original research. Like pirate maps and letters discovered in one's grandfather's foundation.

"Anyway. We were on the scent of a Viking tomb—figuratively, I mean. It wasn't literally smelly, though that would have made it easier to find. We were—where were we, Ains? Was that Holland or Norway?"

"Norway, my lord. You were working with Professor Larsen, if you recall."

"Ah, that's right. Lovely old gent, that one—I told you a bit about him already. I'd been studying a book he'd written, you see, and thought I saw something in the runes that he hadn't elucidated in the text." Sheridan cut free a section of grass with the side of his shovel. "We spent some time puzzling it out in Oslo together and then followed the clues toward what we thought might be an unexplored burial mound."

"But Vandermeer was already there?" She dug in again.

Sheridan sighed. "Quite the Viking aficionado. Understandable, I suppose, given his heritage. They were all over Holland back in the day, you know."

Which made her remember the question that had been niggling. "What do you suppose his interest is in Prince Rupert, though? Just a passing fancy, or something that sparked his interest? Not that it matters, I suppose, but I do wonder."

"The Caribbean." This from Telford, who was staring into his bag of chocolate drops again. "Dutch West Indies, didn't Abbie say?"

"Good point, Telly. Perhaps his family had some dealings with Mucknell or Rupert there." Sheridan lifted away the square of sod and they both started clearing away soil from opposite sides of the new earth he'd uncovered.

"That would make sense," she said. "But back to Norway."

"Ah, right. Well, it's as you guessed. He was already there and had been for at least a week. Had the whole mound sectioned off and had just broken through to the main chamber. The ship wasn't intact, though—that's what we were all hoping to find. The mound had collapsed on it at some point and broken it to pieces. Poor Larsen was beside himself with disappointment."

"But the runes his lordship helped him decipher turned up in another location a few months later." Ainsley reached for a canteen and unscrewed the cap. "And Mr. Vandermeer wasn't already at that one. Professor Larsen made his discovery."

"Indeed." Sheridan sounded quite chipper about it, despite the fact that this would have been the discovery he let the professor take all the credit for, asking only for a small artifact for his collection in return—the story he'd told her in the drawing room after the accident. "And that was about when I decided that the Druids were where I'd like to focus for a while, given that we're all but surrounded with evidence of them. So, really, I suppose I owe Vandermeer a thanks. I may not have turned my attention from the Vikings if not for him always crowding me."

Beth breathed a laugh and frowned when her shovel hit something harder than dirt, but not as hard as granite. Could just be a buried bit of driftwood—they'd found some of those already—or a harder than usual clump of soil. "Well, that might throw them all off their guards, if you rushed up to him when he arrives and thanked him."

"Sails!" Libby's shout shattered the lovely feel of the morning. "I see sails, coming from the east. They're still a long ways off, but . . . but it looks like three different boats."

And if it was the Scofields, then they were likely on a yacht, which meant they'd be coming fast. They may even be running on engines, not just wind power. She scraped away a bit of dirt from around whatever it was.

Something straight. Something even. "Theo. I may have found something. Wood . . ." She dragged her shovel over as much of it as she could, breath catching. "And a bit of metal, here."

He leaned over the spit of land they'd both been working to see, and then attacked his own side with renewed vigor. "It must stretch this way. Let me—yes! I think this is another corner of it."

She measured the distance between his shovel and her own with her eyes. "Looks the right size for a sea chest."

Their gazes met, held. They both smiled.

And got to work. Beth didn't need Sheridan's mutters to tell her that they had to proceed carefully. As the sun rose another degree higher, its light showed her that the wood was far from sound. Rot had crept in with time and rain, and the lid they'd soon uncovered looked as though it might collapse with a single tap.

The sides weren't much better. It was likely only the metal finishings holding the thing together at this point, and while they could certainly just pry the thing open and gather the contents separately, that would mean destroying the chest itself, and she wasn't willing to do that. What if it had some further clue on it? Something to prove it was Mucknell's?

"Hurry." Libby darted over to them, handing off the spyglass to Oliver, who hastened to take her place with it. "Perhaps we can get it on the *Adelle* before they arrive."

Emily joined them, too, her blanket in her arms. "Here. It looks like it might fall to pieces with a sturdy breeze. We may need to wrap it to carry it out."

"Good idea." Sheridan inserted his shovel carefully along one of the edges and scraped away from the chest.

"Lady Emily," Oliver said, "would you come and take a look? I can see a few figures on the decks of the yachts, but I don't know what your father looks like. I don't believe I see your brother."

Beth felt as though her brows would have to remain drawn together like this until they were safely home again. "Why three boats? If they're yachts, especially. They could easily fit on one."

Sheridan looked past her, to where Ainsley had taken up guard. "Well."

Ainsley sighed. "What his lordship doesn't want to say is that Mr. Vandermeer always travels with a considerable entourage. To aid in his excavation."

Good heavens. What, did they mean to crawl over every inch of Gugh? She couldn't fathom that the Lord Proprietor would even allow it. He'd been quite strict with Bonsor when he was excavating around the Old Man and . . . "Oh no. Or, perhaps, oh yes." She scraped soil from the side opposite Sheridan's. "The Lord Proprietor. We haven't thought to ask him for permission for this—but perhaps they didn't either. If we can get in touch with him, he's always been fond of our family. Perhaps he'll grant us leave to excavate instead of them."

Sheridan frowned now too. "Permission. Right. That's always Abbie's domain."

Oliver trotted over to them, Emily a step behind. "Lady Emily says the two yachts are most assuredly her father's party. She could make him out on one deck."

"Two?" They nearly had enough dirt removed to allow them to wriggle the chest. Perhaps they could free it from the rest of the dirt with a bit of muscle. "I thought Libby said three."

"Three vessels, but only two yachts. The third is a local sloop— and it must have been ahead of the yachts, though they've overtaken it. The Peppers', if I'm not mistaken. With your sisters aboard, Sheridan."

Sheridan must have had the same idea she had. He set his shovel aside and gripped the trunk corners on his side. "Oh good. Well, not that the yachts have overtaken them. That'll set Millicent off without question. Ready, darling? Let's wiggle it toward you first. If we can."

She nodded and set her own shovel down, gripping it as he was doing. "Go ahead."

The first push moved it an inch into her hole, which earned a cry of delight. The second push sent a creak into her ears, which turned her squeal into one of despair. "It's breaking."

"It's too heavy for its own bottom, I think. Telly, one of those boards, will you? Wedge it, maybe. Underneath, I mean."

Her hole got rather crowded over the next few minutes as they pushed and pulled and lifted and shoved a plank under the chest that they'd brought along in case they needed a ramp. But they hadn't quite finished when the sounds of far too many voices from the shore drifted up the hill.

One of them far too familiar. And decidedly furious. "Lord Sheridan, desist at once! I'll not have you interfering with my excavation!"

Nigel Scofield. Her own fury bubbling up with enough force to all but lift her from the hole, Beth turned her position over to Telford and jumped up to solid ground. Sheridan was only a step behind her.

But he'd be a few more behind her in a moment. "You!" The word was an accusation that tore from her throat and hopefully pierced the cad like an arrow. "You left me for dead, you arrogant prig!"

An arm caught her around the waist before she could fly at him. "Easy, darling. Don't give them anything to use against us."

Scofield stood there halfway between their site and his, all roguish confidence and hateful eyes. "I don't know what you're talking about, Miss Tremayne. I went as quickly as I could for help. And look! You're clearly *fine*."

Surely everyone else heard the disappointment in his tone as clearly as she did. Didn't they?

Sheridan certainly did, given the way his arm tightened around her. "No thanks to you." His voice wasn't calm so much as tight. A coil ready to snap. "You sent them to Annet. She could have been dead by the time they thought to check Gugh."

Scofield sneered. "And yet she isn't. No harm done. Father, up here! Mr. Vandermeer, I'm afraid it's as I feared. The local vermin have infested the place."

Vermin? Had he really just called them *vermin?* It was a good thing Sheridan was holding her back, or she would have flown at him again over that one.

Only, no one was holding *Sheridan* back. He swung her behind him and did a bit of flying himself.

29

One thought ricocheted through Sheridan's mind as he swung Beth safely behind him and moved toward Scofield: He had no desire at all to take another foot to the nose. But really, what choice did he have? For one thing, the prig had insulted Beth and her family. And for another, Sheridan had to do *something* to keep this swarm of interlopers from taking over absolutely everything before his sisters had a chance to catch them up.

Of course, even as he charged forward, he could see the odious Scofield—how was that for one of Beth's villain names?—settled into one of those deadly crouches of his that the boxing club had certainly never taught him how to counter.

He didn't mean to get close enough to taste his adversary's boot again. Though he would, if it was the only way to distract everyone from the Peppers' sloop that he saw was finally drawing near to the beach.

For now, he stopped just out of kicking range, and he didn't even spare Mr. Odious a glare. No, he directed it past the cad he'd never even met until he came here and to the two fellows hiking up the hill whom he'd come to expect better of. "Lord Scofield, I am absolutely appalled at the behavior of your son. How can you countenance such devious and even violent tactics as he has employed here? You're fortunate he hasn't been arrested—and think what a blemish it will be on the family name when he is, which he will be if you don't rein him in. And you, Vandermeer—you've always kept better company than *this*."

Young Scofield hissed a breath from between his teeth.

Lord Scofield scowled at him.

Vandermeer looked highly amused. "Sheridan," he said in that flat Yankee accent of his that always twisted the vowels of his name into something strange. "Ought to've known you'd be involved. But you can't mean to insinuate I'm making a mistake in trusting the British Museum, can you?"

He waved a hand behind him, which was when Sheridan bothered to look at the swarm of people crowding the shore around the two yachts, some of them starting up the hill. Blast and bother—a good dozen of them weren't in the khaki-colored garb typical of the field. They were in morning suits and bowler hats, and unquestioningly from the board of trustees of the museum.

He would know. He'd made it a point to ingratiate himself with each and every one, hoping someday he might be honored with a place among them. It was how he'd come to know Lord Scofield to begin with, and he'd thought—actually thought—he liked the family. But that was when the heir apparent to the Scofield holdings was off in Asia or wherever, probably leaving a trail of destruction that Sheridan hadn't realized the earl would simply help cover up.

Well, Sheridan may not yet be a trustee—but he was still a marquess, and that ought to earn him a bit of respect. "Gentlemen, I'm afraid I'm going to have to beg you to check your enthusiasm and reevaluate your alliance with Mr. Scofield. You wouldn't want to tarnish the good name of the museum, would you?"

It got their attention, anyway, though that meant all those feet were now aimed at him. And all those scowls too.

Young Scofield looked as though he might bring that violent foot of his to bear on him yet. "Ignore him, gentlemen," he called over his shoulder. "He's just sore that we beat him to a discovery."

356

"Again," Vandermeer added with a wink and a grin.

He'd deal with the American later. For now, he kept his gaze on Lord Scofield. "He didn't, actually. All the compromises your son is willing to make to morality, all the harm he has willfully done, despite the death of a local lad that can be laid at his feet—"

Nigel surged toward *him* now, though his father was near enough, praise the Lord, to catch him by the arm and halt him. "*You* are the one who hired Lorne!"

A technicality that was hardly to the point right now, given that that henchman of vile intent, as Beth called him, had taken up with *him*. "Your son's shameful and dare I say *illegal* ways have amounted to nothing, my lord. All your coddling and covering for him have still netted nothing but empty ground and a Druid cairn he hadn't even the sense to dig out properly."

Lord Scofield's face was turning decidedly red.

Vandermeer lifted his ebony walking stick and pointed behind them, toward where they'd been digging all night by lantern light. "That doesn't look like nothing. Looks a bit like a treasure chest."

Sheridan tried his best to smirk. "And *that* isn't at his dig site— it's at mine."

The Scofields both smirked right back, and he had a feeling they pulled it off far better than he did. But then, they had a lot more practice. And seeing the matching expression on their faces, he knew in his gut that father and son had more in common than he had wanted to believe. The earl didn't just cover up his son's bad behavior because of family pride. He approved it. And had just honed the skill of hiding his own depravity behind a layer of polish.

"That's where you're obviously laboring under misinformation, Lord Sheridan." The earl gave his son a little jerk backward, a silent *stay out of this* that clearly rankled. "We have written permission from Dorrien-Smith granting us excavation rights of all of Gugh. So whatever your friends are wrapping up in that blanket, the find is *ours*."

No. Sheridan sucked in a long breath, cursing himself for not thinking of those blasted permissions before. How could he have overlooked something so crucial?

A gentle hand landed on his arm, bringing an immediate measure of peace. He didn't want it to go down this way—for her more than anything. Beth had invested too much, lost too much in the search for this treasure. And now to have these reprobates swoop in and steal it from her? It wasn't right. Wasn't fair.

Wasn't going to happen. He knew that with certainty, not just hope, when he saw his sisters striding up the hillside, Abbie with a piece of yellow paper held high in the air. "Not so fast, Lord Scofield!"

It was their clothing that told him they'd won the battle he hadn't remembered to fight. No silly, frilly hats were on their heads today. No striped muslin or finest lawn artistically draping their figures. They were in what Millicent called their "safari chic" outfits—khaki cloth, lightweight, but still in a style befitting a lady.

The gentlemen all turned at their arrival, more than one grumble making its way up the heath to Sheridan's ears and giving him cause to grin.

His sisters *did* have a bit of a reputation for taking over every-thing. Absolutely everything. And they were so very good at it.

"Oh, heaven help us." Vandermeer planted his walking stick in the ground and let out a mighty sigh. "You're too late, Lady Millie— Lady Abigail. Dorrien-Smith—"

"Oh, Donald." Millicent sent Vandermeer a too-sweet smile and was probably planning how to deliver a ladylike kick to his shin for deliberately confusing which of them used a nickname and which didn't. "Who gives a fig about Dorrien-Smith and his permissions? This is the duchy of Cornwall. It's the duke who holds all salvage rights in and around the isles. Which means every single thing brought from the ground or the water here is *his*."

Sheridan blinked at his sister—was this supposed to be good news?—and then angled a look down and back at Beth.

She was wincing. "Right. I forgot about that. We tend to operate on the 'what they don't know' rule. . . ."

Abbie must have heard her. She chuckled and presented her telegram to Lord Scofield. "Well, he knows now, dearest. They both do. And I'm afraid my Duke of Cornwall trumps your Lord Proprietor, my lord."

Vandermeer pursed his lips. "The Duke of Cornwall."

Millicent batted her eyes at him. "Also known as the Prince of Wales, Donald darling. And dear George *did* owe us a bit of a favor."

Beth leaned close, her fingers digging into his arm. "Your sisters know Prince George?"

He grinned. "Of course they do. They know everyone."

Scofield was reading the telegram, his face getting redder by the second. "This is ridiculous. We already secured the permission from—"

"And the prince just countermanded it. But don't worry, dear." Millicent patted Vandermeer's arm. "We're not taking *all* of Gugh away from you. Only this portion here where my brother is digging. You all still have every right to excavate where Mr. Scofield began working."

"Which was really quite generous of George, considering that Nigel began his work without any permission whatsoever," Abbie put in.

"Whereas we had things in motion with the prince well before Theo's spade ever touched Gugh's soil." Millicent winked at him.

And Telford had questioned his instincts in bringing them here. Sheridan grinned back.

Nigel was sputtering. "Oh, so you leave us the worthless—"

"Worthless?" Sheridan didn't mean to interrupt, really. He just couldn't help it. He waved a hand at the site up the hill. "You found an undiscovered Druid cairn! Frankly, I'm quite put out that it's been left to you. You have no appreciation for it at all. My only comfort is that with the board of trustees involved, it will be treated with the respect it deserves."

"Druids." Vandermeer muttered the word as if it were the most boring two syllables in the world.

Nigel was snarling again, but his father restrained him. And crumpled the telegram in a fist. "I intend to appeal this. This is history you're treating so cavalierly, and no doubt you intend to make off with it all and put it in your private collection. Don't forget, my lord, that *I'm* the one you offered to pay for anything I found. I don't recall you mentioning Prince George and his salvage rights *then*, and you can be sure—"

"Listen to you, my lord." Abbie laughed, though there was nothing amused about it. "Acting as if the prince hasn't been fully aware of our brother's hunt all this time and doesn't trust him fully. Of *course* the majority of our discoveries will be turned over to the Crown, and no doubt much of it will eventually make it into the hallowed halls of the British Museum. It is *because* of the history of this site—"

"And Theo's proven respect for it." Millicent wrapped her arm around Vandermeer's, which made the American clench his jaw. No doubt as he bit back some rude retort.

"Just so." Abbie nodded. "He's contributed so much to the study of the Druids, you know, which has earned the prince's highest esteem. He agreed from the outset that Theo could keep a small token or two from whatever he discovered here."

"A mere finder's fee."

He had, had he? Sheridan reached for the hand Beth let slide down his arm. He could only imagine the thoughts that would be rampaging through *her* head—all the time, all the effort she'd put into this. All stripped away because of a bunch of technicalities and legalities and connections she couldn't have aspired to. "Beth?" he breathed, a bare whisper. He wove their fingers together. Would it look, to her, like his sisters were stealing her prize?

Beth shook her head, her words a whisper back. "They knew all along. Obviously. They were just using me. Probably meant to then swoop in with the permissions and take it all. Perhaps even threaten me with legal action." She sighed, her fingers tight around his. "How stupid I was to overlook this."

"An oversight." One he was just as guilty of.

Beth's lips turned up, though. She nodded to his sisters. "But they just beat them at their own game."

That was indeed what his sisters had done. What they could always be counted on for doing. He gave Beth's fingers a squeeze.

And besides, if it was the adventure she'd wanted from all this, they'd had it, and would continue having it. And if it was the promise of funds that would allow a Season or two in London—well, he'd give her all the Seasons she pleased. In London or Paris or New York or wherever else she fancied.

Young Scofield pulled free of his father. "This isn't over, Sheridan."

Millicent stepped away from Vandermeer, her chin coming up. "We did fear you'd take that stance, sir. Hence why a security team is on its way even now to safeguard *our* finds. And, in the meantime, our lovely band of local friends will help us transport what our brother has already found to somewhere safe."

At the wave of her hand, Mr. Pepper and a few other local chaps hurried forward from where they'd been clustered at the line where grass met sand, obviously happy to stay out of the cross fire until they were called upon. He pivoted to watch them join Telford and the others haul the now-wrapped chest away from the site.

He couldn't help but grin anew. Probably felt like a kick in the nose to the Scofields.

And it served them right. Turnabout, and all that.

In all the times Senara had come to St. Nicholas's and sat in the pew her family had occupied for generations, she'd never had cause to poke about in *this* part of the church. And it only took a few seconds for her sense of discomfort to outweigh her curiosity. This was the vicar's domain back here in this room, not a mere parishioner's.

Even if said parishioner was with said vicar's grandmother. "Mrs. Tremayne, are you quite certain—"

"No need to fret, Senara dear." Mrs. Tremayne chuckled and padded over to an enormous cupboard. It had scrollwork on its heavy wooden doors and a Latin inscription that she had no desire to try to translate just now. A cupboard so ornate and fine must hold something truly holy. The sacraments or vestments or illuminated manuscripts from the twelfth century or . . .

Nothing. The shelves within, she saw when her aged companion pulled open the doors, were completely bare. Senara frowned. "What goes in there?"

"It's where the parish records have always been kept. But I think it will do quite nicely for our new purpose. Quite nicely indeed. Have you the measuring tape, dearover?"

Senara reached into her pocket for the soft tape she'd pulled from her mending basket. She still wasn't certain what their "new purpose" was, but when Mrs. Tremayne took your hand from the porridge pot and asked you to come with her, you went. Even when she led you out into the morning street, up the road into the village, and through the back door of the island's single church.

She handed the tape to her companion, who immediately unrolled it and began measuring the interior dimensions of the cupboard. Her mutters of "Ah, good, good" did nothing to elucidate the situation.

"Mrs. Tremayne, what exactly are we doing?"

The lady turned to face her with an impish smile on her face but that troubling, clouded look to her eyes. "They'll need a place to stow it where no one will think to look for it. And I couldn't come up with a less likely place for pirate treasure than this. Can you?"

Pirate treasure? Senara sighed and tried to muster a small, placating smile. "But, madame, we don't even know that they'll find anything."

To be perfectly honest, she had her doubts they would. Though even so, she'd lain awake half the night regretting her decision to stay on Tresco rather than go with them to dig. At the time it had seemed wise—they didn't need one more set of hands, after all, but they *would* need food taken to them, given their unwillingness to wait yesterday for Mam to pack them enough, and she could easily help with that. But she rather regretted giving up the chance to see Ainsley with a shovel in his hands. Perhaps when she took them breakfast on the *Naiad*, she'd get a glimpse.

Or so had been her thought before Mamm-wynn apprehended her.

"They will. And I'm quite satisfied with the depth of this cupboard. We should be able to stack some records in front of it, even." Mrs. Tremayne held out a hand to Senara.

Senara assisted her to her feet. "But—"

"We'd better rouse Mark and Prue to help us cart the record books back up here. We're running a bit short on time. These old legs don't move quite as quickly as they once did."

Senara opened her mouth, ready to object to the idea of rousing Oliver's uncle, now retired, from the vicarage next door. But there was no point. Despite her claims of feebleness, Mrs. Tremayne was already striding out of the room and toward the back door again, and it was only a few steps after that to Mark and Prue's door. Senara had little choice but to keep up.

Mrs. Tremayne didn't bother herself with long explanations. She merely greeted Prue with "Come, then, both of you. Chop-chop."

Though Prue sent Senara a mystified look, she didn't argue. Just called out over her shoulder, "Mark! Mamm-wynn needs us."

And so, the four of them hurried back down the hill and into the Tremaynes' garden. Tas was tending the roses but looked up when he heard them.

Mrs. Tremayne smiled at him. "The cart please, dear. For the record books. Time to return them."

Senara's father nodded and set down his pruning shears.

Nobody, it seemed, questioned Adelle Tremayne when she began giving orders, which made Senara feel a bit less silly for not doing so herself. And Ollie and Beth wouldn't dare to sputter and spout any objections to them moving all their research materials back to the church, given that it was on the matriarch's command.

By the time they'd finished loading Tas's handcart with all the record books, Senara was perspiring from the constant hefting, hurrying, and stacking under the August sun. Then there was the hike back to the church, and the second round of hefting, hurrying, and stacking—though Mrs. Tremayne insisted on being the sole one to organize the books as she put them back in the cupboard.

Not like Ollie and Mark before him had kept them, no doubt. She started by instructing Tas to move the center shelf up a few inches, which required a few tools and a lovely fifteen-minute reprieve. Then she filled the space only around the edges and on the upper shelf, leaving a gaping hole in the middle.

"There," she pronounced at last, dusting her arthritic hands off on her dress. "That should fit it, I'd think. And just in the nick of time too."

Senara couldn't say what was so timely about it, but her stomach was reminding her that she hadn't taken time to eat any breakfast after helping Mam cook it. She was happy to follow Mrs. Tremayne back out of the room and into the sunshine.

"Mamm-wynn? Mrs. Dawe met us at the door of the house and said you told us to come here."

Senara was still blinking her vision back into focus in the bright sunlight when Beth's voice drew her face to the right.

Her friend stood there with the complete collection of people who had been with them on Gugh, and another handcart besides, this one laden with a blanket-wrapped something.

How in the world . . . ? Senara shot a questioning look at Ainsley, who had a look on his face that seemed an odd match to the uncharacteristic smudges of dirt—pride and satisfaction. He smiled at her, a slow-blooming smile that made her newly aware of the pearl in her pocket.

Mrs. Tremayne was chuckling. "Right on time, darlings. I have its hiding place ready for you. Have you opened it yet?"

Oliver stared at his grandmother for a moment but then shook himself, and his head too. "We didn't want to take the time. We spotted sails behind us, and I wouldn't put it past Nigel Scofield to tear through the whole island chain looking for the chest."

"Luckily, Beth can sail the straits with her eyes closed." Lord Sheridan picked up one corner of the blanket.

"And Mamm-wynn apparently has a hiding place ready for us." Oliver took another corner. "Which would be?"

"The record cupboard, dear. Where else? We'll have it hidden in minutes if you lads hurry."

The lads hurried. Senara trailed them by a few steps as Tas and Mark disappeared with the now-empty carts. In short order, the wrapped bundle, blanket and all, was slid carefully into the space left for it, and the record books still on the desk were piled in front of it.

Beth grabbed Senara's hand. "Come on. We'd better get back to the house before he shows up there. Think you can keep up?"

Senara laughed—and leaped into a run even before Beth did. She'd been chasing after little ones for the last decade, after all. She had no trouble flying through Old Grimsby. Though she would have liked to hear the story of how they ended up here with a mysterious chest in their church and an adversary on their heels.

"Through the back!" Beth darted to the back of their home even as she gave the advice, and Senara followed suit. They dashed through the door, shouted a quick greeting to Mam as they sped by the kitchen, and went straight to the front door.

A fist was pounding on it even now. Senara sucked in a long breath, willed her chest to quiet its heaving, and pulled Beth up short. "I'll answer." To prove it, she called out, "Just a moment," and then stepped toward the door.

One more deep breath. A polite smile affixed to her lips like she'd always put on whenever Lady Clifford came to the nursery for one of her obligatory visits with her children. And then she tugged open the door to an absolutely furious-looking young man who bore a marked resemblance to Lady Emily.

"Good day," she said, voice flat. "May I help you?"

He looked right through her, both figuratively and as literally as he could manage, craning to see around her. "Where are they? Where is it?"

She'd only opened the door about a foot, enough to fill the space herself. "I beg your pardon, sir? If you mean the Tremaynes, they're not at home."

It was society code for "they don't want to see you," but the man spun on his heel and snarled out, "Then I'll go and find them!"

The rest of the group *might* be back at the house by now . . . but they might also be on the road between here and there, which was a bit more likely. And since that was the last thing she wanted him to discover, she called out in her governess voice, "Sir."

It worked on him just as it had always done on the Clifford girls. He paused, turned back to face her.

He would have been handsome, had he bothered to control the cruel glint in his eyes and the sneer curling his lip. Senara narrowed her gaze in the way she imagined his own governess had, back in the day. The look that said, *"Don't slouch, chin up, where are your manners?"*

He straightened and schooled his features.

Which nearly made her give in to a victorious smile. But she had plenty of practice controlling such responses. "Kindly refrain from terrorizing our neighbors with that attitude of yours, as I can see you are set on doing. By 'not at home,' I obviously mean *indisposed.*" She made a show of checking over her shoulder. "They only just got back from a night out who-knows-where. My mother is feeding them, after which I imagine they will be retiring. But I am happy to take a card or even a message, and—"

"So they *are* here?" He surged toward the door.

She held it tightly, but she hadn't expected him to come barreling toward her, and she stumbled back with a shout when he shoved her aside and pushed his way in.

Wasn't this a lord? A gentleman? Why was he behaving like a ruffian in his cups? "Stop at once! What do you think you're doing? Father!" She'd never in her life called him *Father*, but she wanted this rude man to know she was calling for a man—and hopefully imagine a huge one—and didn't trust him to know what *Tas* meant.

She needn't have worried. When she regained her balance and turned, she found that Beth wasn't the only one standing in the entryway. She was surrounded by a veritable host of glowering friends.

30

Beth was aware of the reassuring crowd of friends and family behind her. She saw Ainsley slide his way along the wall toward Senara. She felt Sheridan at one elbow and Oliver at the other and knew that this time, they wouldn't leave injured from their encounter with Scofield. She didn't care what level of mastery he'd achieved in karate, he couldn't take all of them down in their own home. Especially not given the hunting rifle she heard being cocked. It would be in Mr. Dawe's hands, no doubt, and he would be serious as a hurricane over Scofield's rough handling of his daughter.

Beth folded her arms over her chest. "Really, Mr. Scofield, for an earl's son, your manners are atrocious."

He at least came to a halt upon spotting them. "You'll not get away with this. The site is mine, the whole island. Whatever you discovered today will be handed over to the museum by the week's end, so you might as well deliver it to me now."

"To you?" Beth laughed. "I think not. And, frankly, we'll be advising the authorities that they had better do a thorough investigation of each and every trustee before we will turn over anything."

Scofield's nostrils flared. He flicked a glance over the group, his attention snagging somewhere to the right and then returning to

Beth. Who had caught his eye? Mr. Dawe with his hunting piece? Or perhaps his sister?

Poor Em. She'd said nothing during the entire sail back to Tresco, but the way her fingers had twisted together spoke volumes.

Her father hadn't even looked her way, not once. Beth had to wonder if the ignoring struck even deeper than a reprimand would have.

"You seem to be laboring under the mistaken assumption, Miss Tremayne, that you have a choice here. Give me whatever you found!"

She opened her mouth to argue again, but Sheridan stepped forward, hand held out. "Will you please calm down, Scofield? Trust me, you don't even want what we have in the chest there." He motioned toward the drawing room.

She sent him a questioning scowl that he didn't even look down at her to see. What was he doing? He had to know that Scofield would charge into the room—which he did. But there was nothing in there to appease him, nothing at all except . . .

She sucked in a breath and grabbed Sheridan's arm. "Theo, *no*." Not all his collection! The drawing room was where Enyon had deposited his trunk the other day, the one his sisters had brought from the castle. Beth had laughed a bit when she'd seen it—had even joked that it looked like a bunch of rubbish someone had just dug up in the back garden. Rusted pieces of this and that, moldy books from the seventeenth century that Rupert had supposedly once owned, a few of his inventions.

Treasure, in Sheridan's eyes. And so in hers. Treasure that he couldn't mean to just hand over to Nigel Scofield.

He'd found it. She heard the trunk's lid crash against something, and his curses scalded the air as she hurried into the room.

A flying book nearly hit her in the head. Would have, had Sheridan not snatched it from the air two inches from her face with a growl. "Now see here! Gently! This stuff is destined for a museum, you know!"

"Not ours, it isn't. Rubbish, all of it." Something else went flying, though Beth couldn't even make out what it was. It landed with a loud clatter, though, and a sickening crack. "There should be silver. Gold. Jewels!"

All things easy enough to skim a bit off the top of. Was that what he'd been intending to do? Or was it the fame they'd bring that he sought?

"Are you mad? Those things are priceless!" Sheridan strode toward his chest.

They were, and he had to have known that Scofield would attack the contents. But he'd offered it up anyway, to protect the secret of the other find. *Their* find. Hers. That was the sort of man he was, though. He'd give up his own for theirs together.

Even though for all they knew, the chest was just a cruel joke on Mucknell's part, meant to lead people astray. It could be filled with lead shot. Rocks. Rubble. They didn't know—the lock had held tight, and they didn't want to break open the wood there on the deck of the *Adelle*. They'd resort to a pry bar only if Senara's key didn't do the trick.

Scofield growled and flung another book. "It's junk! Only you would care about this nonsense, Sheridan."

Sheridan had made a lunge for the book but missed. "Not true. Anyone would. Who had a bit of culture, I mean."

With a kick to the trunk that made Beth wince on Sheridan's behalf, Scofield pivoted back around and pointed a finger at Sheridan. "If you're keeping anything from me—"

"I beg your pardon." Oliver had come in without her even realizing it and stood now in that collected way of his, his face calm and intent. "But you are in *my* house, sir. Destroying *my* lord's property. After threatening *my* guests. And given that we in this room are all well aware of how you first threatened my fiancée a month ago, when you mistook her for my sister, pray do not think we have any patience left for your antics. Get out this instant, and be glad I'd rather be rid of you than call in the constable. Because while I may not be able to prove that you meant to harm my sister two weeks ago, I certainly *can* prove that you just trespassed into my home and began manhandling my employees and destroying priceless artifacts that are not yours."

Beth's lips parted in shock. Never in her life had she heard her brother scold *anyone* so harshly.

Scofield couldn't have known that, but he clearly heard the seriousness in Oliver's voice, or read it in his posture. He stilled, looked once more into the trunk, and then stomped over to Sheridan. "Don't think I believe for a minute that this is all there was in there. I don't know what you've done with the rest, but I'll find it."

"Will you?" Beth let her mouth quirk up. "Funny, sir—thus far you've not found a blessed thing without someone else doing the work for you. And I'm afraid we won't be helping you anymore."

For a moment, she thought he meant to strike her or give her a taste of that high kick he'd knocked Sheridan flat with back in July. But instead he spat out a few words that singed her ears and stormed back out. The door slammed a moment later, though whether he pulled it shut or Senara sent it home after him, she didn't know.

Her shoulders sagged the moment he was gone. "Theo. Your collection!"

"It's all right," his lips said, while his eyes looked mournfully on the book splayed open on the floor, its binding looking a good deal worse for the wear. "Necessary. Only a few things—blast it all." He scooped up the book and caressed its now-detached spine. "What sort of monster treats a book that way?"

"An odious one." She wasn't sure why that earned her so quick a smile, but she wasn't about to question it. She moved to his side, covered his hand with her own, and rested her cheek against his shoulder. "I know what will cheer you up, though. Just as soon as we know he's left Tresco."

Sheridan chuckled. "You know, Beth. You do know how to sweet-talk a fellow."

—————○—————

Sheridan stepped back out of St. Nicholas's without adequate words to put to the wonder in his heart. It was . . . they'd . . . and then there was . . . He settled for a sigh, one that he first gathered in slowly and then let out long and patiently.

He'd searched for many treasures in his life. Found plenty, though the world, much like Nigel Scofield, didn't always agree with him on that. But never one like this.

Senara's key had worked the lock, and the decrepit chest had opened under Oliver's hand with a creak of rusted hinges. The next bit had been like a scene from some adventure novel, or one of Gibson's tales. Gold coins gleaming. Silver winking. A few jewels even sparkling their hello.

They'd all looked at it for a moment, silence filling the church. And then Sheridan had closed the lid again and tugged Beth outside with him.

They'd actually found pirate treasure. Honest-to-goodness, indisputable treasure that would earn the gasps of appreciation from anyone, layman or expert. They'd followed a mad set of clues to the exact location and dug up a veritable hoard.

So, why was part of him disappointed that it hadn't just been lead shot or rocks or other rubbish?

Ah, right. Because it meant they weren't finished with Scofield. They'd have to report it all to Dorrien-Smith and Prince George— which Abbie would probably do before the day was out, knowing her—and the Scofields would get wind of it. Perhaps legally and publicly there was nothing they could do. But he had a feeling neither the earl nor his son would let it end at that.

Beth squeezed his hand and led him out onto the street, past the national school with its now-quiet yard, given that it was summer holidays, and down the hill, in the direction away from her house. "Are you all right?"

"Perfectly." He looked down at her. Smiled. Because there she

372

was, at his side. Her fingers in his. Looking up at him with what he hadn't dared hope he'd get from her for a decade or two. *Love.* "How couldn't I be? I have you."

She smiled and shook her head. "And silver and gold worth a fortune."

"Mm. Your eyes. Your hair. A whole future ahead of us."

Bumping their arms together, she laughed. "Right. I'm so worth spending a lifetime trying to acquire."

"Well, yes. I thought it would require a decade, at least, if you recall. To win you, I mean. Or to convince you to try to win me. And I would have spent it in that pursuit most gladly." He still couldn't quite believe it hadn't been necessary. "Not that I'm arguing, mind you. With the quicker time frame."

"I should hope not." She lifted her chin and gave him that adorably haughty look she'd slapped him with regularly back at the start. And then drifted to a halt and looked down at the scene rolling out before them.

A village road, weaving its way down the hill until it tumbled into the sea. Village houses here and there, ending in gardens and flower fields and sheep pastures. A village she'd always called home. Likely always would, in her heart of hearts. Because a rosefinch always knew to come home to nest in the place where it had been born.

Which was fine by him. He lifted her hand and kissed it. And tried to tell his heart to calm itself down. Though that was a losing battle. He knew as he watched her go toe to toe with Scofield that he didn't want to let another day pass without speaking up. They never knew, after all, what tomorrow held. What dangers and discoveries awaited.

He wanted to face them all with her by his side.

And he had a full arsenal of arguments, now, to convince her. But he knew without a doubt which one was the best. "You know, I've been thinking. About the trinket box."

She lifted her brows and started them down the hill. "Have you? I imagine you're thinking up a way to steal it from me again, since you have to turn everything else over to the Crown. Even the silverware."

George would let them keep some of it, like Abbie had said. But that wasn't the point. "Only if you force me to it. I was thinking that, instead—well, sharing it is clearly the best option. I mean, I know it comes from your family. And it means a great deal to you. But I *did* become rather attached to it, and I like to think it enjoyed its tenure in my collection, among other items it probably once knew well."

Her laugh was a dance of elements, fire and wind and rain and the earth they both still carried the scent of. "Did it tell you so?"

He nodded as somberly as he could manage. "Whispered it straight into my ear. So, for its sake, Elizabeth Tremayne, you simply must marry me. You've no other choice."

Her smile was sunshine and crashing waves. "For the sake of the trinket box."

Well, it sounded silly when she said it like that. So, he quickly added, "And for your grandmother. Because she adores me."

She tilted her head. "She *is* a woman of wisdom and taste."

"And my sisters too. Because they adore *you*."

"Marks of their own discernment." Her eyes twinkled like the moon and stars and the whole heavenly host. "You're forgetting one very important thing, though, Theo." She touched a fingertip to his chest. "I think if I'm going to marry you, it had better be for *you*."

Was it any wonder he loved her so? "Would you? Because I can't imagine ever living through a day again without you by my side."

"That's good." She pulled him off the road, onto the bluff overlooking the sea, and wrapped her arms around him. "Because as I've said before, dearovim—I don't intend to ever let you sail away without me."

There was nothing to do but seal the bargain with a kiss.

Author's Note

This book may be the most comedic one I've ever written, thanks to Sheridan's wit and delightful manner. But the writing itself endured quite a bit of hardship.

I put the first half of the book down in one lovely week spent on retreat with my best friend and critique partner, Stephanie. And then, a mere four days after returning home, my plans to pick the story back up were put on hold by a medical emergency in my family, when my twelve-year-old son ended up in the PICU with the sudden onset of type 1 diabetes. My next two months were spent not mentally gallivanting around the Isles of Scilly but learning how to manage a disease that Rowyn will have to live with for the rest of his life. A disease that has ruined my sleep and made this non-worrier a paranoid basket case some days. A disease that, had we lived in these days about which I'm writing, would have killed my son. Praise God for the discovery of insulin in the 1920s and its lifesaving abilities for diabetics!

But as we writers always claim to do, I eventually got to the point where I could funnel the fears and the joys and the new lessons learned into my writing. Certainly I now understand better than ever what the Tremaynes would have experienced with Morgan, who in my mind suffered from what we now know as mitochondrial disease, making him prone to every illness that hit the area. I took another week for another retreat (this one at home) and hammered out the second half of the book. And though I would have preferred a more leisurely exploration of Beth and Sheridan's romance, they were nevertheless a bright spot in my world during those trying couple of months.

And I knew from the moment I saw Prince Rupert of the Rhine's name appear in *The Pirate John Mucknell and the Hunt for the Wreck of the John* by Todd Stevens—one of my resources for the series—that I *had* to include him in this book. I mean, a pirate prince! Who could pass that up?

I obviously fabricated his romance on Tresco and that secret marriage—the accepted history that Sheridan shares about him is in fact the *real* history of the prince. His father was very briefly a king, he was a nephew of England's ousted monarch, and he went to war as a mere child of fourteen. He prowled the waters along with Mucknell, from whom he learned the fine art of piracy, and eventually settled in England when his family was back on the throne. There, he kept a few mistresses but never married, though he did recognize his illegitimate daughter, Ruperta—who did indeed marry a Howe. He was known not only for taking over the pirate fleet—royalty trumped Mucknell's vice admiral title—but for his development of weapons, skill with ciphers, and scientific advancements later in life.

The newly discovered Druid cairn on Gugh—and its pirate treasure—are completely fictional. But what's true is that similar cairns were still being discovered at that time on the islands, and the excavation of Obadiah's Barrow by Bonsor is completely factual . . . other than Beth's story about planting chicken bones and beads in it, of course. The islands are littered with Druid sites as well as ruins of priories and hermitages and other evidence of life on now-uninhabited islands from the early days of Christianity there and before.

What I found utterly fascinating as I researched the history of the island chain is that the Scillies were, in the Roman era, a single island with a nearly tropical climate. Orange trees did indeed grow there in that day and age, and the water level was a great deal lower. Sometime around the year 1090, in the days when records weren't really kept, the islands "sank into the sea," drowning the straits between the higher portions that are now all that's left.

There's also much speculation as to whether said single island, before sinking, is in fact the island of Lyonesse from the tragic tale of Tristan and Isolde. Such things can't be proven . . . but they make for a lot of fictional fun, which I'll be exploring more deeply in the next book!

My husband found it amazing that I managed to write a book about two characters with a heavy dose of wanderlust when I myself am a homebody through and through. He, on the other hand, would have us flitting all over the world like a rosefinch if circumstances permitted, so it was fun to tip my hat to his adventurer's soul in this story. I have to thank him, as always, for his support and encouragement, and for laughing his way through his early read. It made those hours of staring at my screen worthwhile!

Thanks to my amazing kids, who have really stepped up during this trying period in our lives; to our awesome parents, who are always there for us; to my sister with her goodie baskets and giving heart; to Rachel for keeping my world running; to Stephanie for always, always listening and encouraging; and to Elizabeth, who always reads my books to make sure Americanisms don't slip into my Englishmen's speech. And, of course, the awe-inspiring team at Bethany House, from my brilliant editors to the amazing cover designer to the best publicity and marketing team on the planet. Whatever my books end up being is because of their help!

I hope you're enjoying the continued adventure in this beautiful island setting as my characters search for pirate treasure. There's still plenty more to discover! I don't know about you, but I'm looking forward to exploring the finish of the tale through Lady Emily's eyes . . . if I can manage to write it without sneaking my own chocolate every time Telford reaches for a sweet.

As always, you can find more information about the book and series, along with resources for continuing the conversations on topics that arise in the books, on my website, along with recommended further reading and more on the history I draw on. Find that at RoseannaMWhite.com.

And, much like Beth, I've also discovered a passion for collecting the stories of those around me, because preserving those stories is what connects us to our past, helps us understand one another, and broadens our hearts and minds. I've created a website called SeeingtheStory.com to be a gathering place for storytellers and story collectors, where their tales can be recorded and shared. I invite you to come and read others' histories and to tell your own stories—either in written, audio, or video format.

Finally, never forget this most important truth: Adventure can be found wherever you seek it. Until next time, keep chasing it in your own life!

Discussion Questions

1. Beth and Sheridan both have a heavy dose of wanderlust and adventure-seeking personalities. Did you like that about them? Do you dream more about traveling the world and exploring new places, or are you a homebody?

2. Beth and her brothers have always loved one another, but don't always understand one another, especially when it comes to Beth's spreading her wings. Whose viewpoint do you understand better, hers or Oliver's? How do you play out your beliefs on the subject with your own family, especially where dreams and views are different?

3. Sheridan has a pronounced and often self-deprecating sense of humor but also some vulnerabilities that are easy to see. What did you think of how this played out in his changing relationship with Beth? Do you know anyone who hides behind jokes? Or who uses them to share truth?

4. Senara nearly makes a second bad choice because she thinks it will redeem an earlier one. Do you understand this mindset? Have you ever struggled with how to "undo" a failing?

5. Who is your favorite character? Your least favorite? Why?

6. Was there a part of the story that completely surprised you? What was your favorite moment?

7. In this story and series, we see many different sorts of sibling relationships—Libby and Bram, Oliver and Beth (and Morgan), Sheridan with his sisters, and then Emily with Nigel. Which relationships struck a chord with you? Did you find any of them amusing? Relatable? Baffling? Do any of them explain a bit about the characters in your mind?

8. Were Lady Abbie and Lady Millicent what you expected Sheridan's sisters to be like? Did you like them? Did they bring anything unexpected into the story for you?

9. Did the treasure hunt turn out how you envisioned it? What did you expect them to find or not find? What about the role of Senara's necklace?

10. The islands are now bursting at the seams with archaeologists, treasure hunters, and museum trustees. What do you think is coming in book 3 for Emily and Bram? How do you think the argument with her family will play out?

About the Author

Roseanna M. White is a bestselling, Christy Award–nominated author who has long claimed that words are the air she breathes. When not writing fiction, she's homeschooling her two kids, editing, designing book covers, and pretending her house will clean itself. Roseanna is the author of a slew of historical novels that span several continents and thousands of years. Spies and war and mayhem always seem to find their way into her books . . . to offset her real life, which is blessedly ordinary. You can learn more about her and her stories at www.roseannamwhite.com.